MICHAEL CONNELLY

RESURRECTION WALK

ORION

First published in Great Britain in 2023 by Orion Fiction,
an imprint of The Orion Publishing Group Ltd.,
Carmelite House, 50 Victoria Embankment
London EC4Y 0DZ

An Hachette UK Company

1 3 5 7 9 10 8 6 4 2

A CIP catalogue record for this book is
available from the British Library.

ISBN (Hardback) 978 1 3987 1896 8
ISBN (Export Trade Paperback) 978 1 3987 1897 5
ISBN (eBook) 978 1 3987 1899 9

Printed in Great Britain by Clays Ltd, Elcograf, S.p.A.

www.orionbooks.co.uk

This one is in memory of Sam Wells.

RESURRECTION WALK

THE FAMILY GATHERED in the visitor lot. Jorge Ochoa's mother and brother and me. Mrs. Ochoa looked as if she were going to church in a pale yellow dress with white cuffs and collar, her hands wrapped in rosary beads. Oscar Ochoa was in full cholo regalia: baggy low-slung jeans cuffed over black Doc Martens, wallet chain, white T-shirt, and black Ray-Bans. His neck was wrapped in blue ink, complete with his Vineland Boyz moniker "Double O" prominently on display.

And me, I was in my Italian three-piece, looking good for the cameras, wrapped in the majesty of the law.

The sun was dropping in the sky and coming at a nearly flat angle through the prison's twenty-foot exterior fence line, casting us all in the chiaroscuro light of a Caravaggio painting. I looked up at the guard tower and through the smoked glass thought I could see the silhouettes of men with long guns.

This was a rare moment. Corcoran State wasn't a prison where men often left on their own two feet. It was an LWOP facility, for men serving life without parole. You checked in but you never checked out. This was where Charlie Manson died of old age. But many inmates didn't make it to old age. Homicides in the cells were common. Jorge Ochoa was just two steel doors down from an inmate who had been beheaded and dismembered in his cell a few years back. His avowed

3

Satanist cellmate had strung together his ears and fingers to make a necklace. That was Corcoran State.

But somehow Jorge Ochoa had survived fourteen years here for a murder he did not commit. And now this was his day. His life sentence had been vacated after a court finding of actual innocence. He was rising up, coming back to the land of the living. We had driven up from Los Angeles in my Lincoln, two media vans trailing us, to be at the gate to welcome him.

Promptly at 5 p.m. a series of horn blasts echoed across the prison and drew our attention. The cameramen from the two L.A. news stations hoisted their equipment to their shoulders while the reporters readied their microphones and checked their hair.

A door opened at the guardhouse at the bottom of the tower and a uniformed guard stepped out. He was followed by Jorge Ochoa.

"*Dios mío,*" Mrs. Ochoa exclaimed when she saw her son. "*Dios mío.*"

It was a moment she'd never seen coming. That nobody had seen coming. Until I took the case.

The guard unlocked a gate in the fence and Jorge was allowed to walk through. I noted that the clothes I had bought him for his release were a perfect fit. A black polo and tan chinos, white Nikes. I didn't want him looking anything like his younger brother for the cameras. There was a wrongful-conviction lawsuit coming and it was never too early to engage in messaging the Los Angeles County jury pool.

Jorge walked toward us and at the last moment started to run. He bent down and grabbed his diminutive mother, lifted her off the ground at first and then gently put her down. They held each other for a solid three minutes while the cameras captured from all angles the tears they shed. Then it was Double O's moment for hugging and manly back-pounding.

And then it was my turn. I put out my hand but Jorge pulled me into an embrace.

"Mr. Haller, I don't know what to say," he said. "But thank you."

"It's Mickey," I said.

"You saved me, Mickey."

"Welcome back to the world."

Over his shoulder I saw the cameras recording our embrace. But in that moment I suddenly didn't care about any of that. I felt the hollow I had carried inside for a long time start to close. I had resurrected this man from the dead. And with that came a fulfillment I had never known in the practice of law or in life.

PART ONE

MARCH — THE HAYSTACK

1

BOSCH HAD THE letter propped on the steering wheel. He noted that the printing was legible and the margins were clean. It was in English but not perfect English. There were misspellings and some words were misused. *Homonyms,* he thought. *I din't do this and want to higher you to clear me.*

It was the last line of that paragraph that held his attention: *The attorny said I had to plea guilty or I would get life for killing a law enforcement officer.*

Bosch turned the page over to see if there was anything written on the back. There was a number stamped at the top, which meant someone in the intel unit at Chino had at least scanned the letter before it was approved and sent out.

Bosch carefully cleared his throat. It was raw from the latest treatment and he didn't want to make things worse. He read the letter again. *I didn't like him but he was the father of my child. I would not kill him. Thats a lie.*

He hesitated, unsure whether to put the letter in the possibles stack or the rejects stack. Before he could decide, the passenger door opened and Haller climbed in, grabbing the stack of unread letters off the seat and tossing them up on the dashboard.

"You didn't get my text?" he asked.

"Sorry, I didn't hear it," Bosch said.

He put the letter on the dashboard and immediately started the Lincoln.

"Where to?" he asked.

"Airport courthouse," Haller said. "And I'm late. I was hoping you would pick me up out front."

"Sorry about that."

"Yeah, well, tell that to the judge if I'm late for this hearing."

Bosch dropped the transmission into drive and pulled away from the curb. He drove up to Broadway and turned into the entrance to the northbound 101. The rotary was lined with tents and cardboard shanties. The recent mayoral election had hinged on which candidate would do a better job with the city's teeming homeless problem. So far, Bosch hadn't noticed any changes.

Bosch immediately transitioned to the southbound 110, which would eventually get him to the Century Freeway and a straight shot to the airport.

"Any good ones?" Haller asked.

Bosch handed him the letter from Lucinda Sanz. Haller started reading it, then checked out the name of the inmate.

"A woman," he said. "Interesting. What's her story?"

"She killed her ex," Bosch said. "Sounds like he was a cop. She pleaded nolo to manslaughter because they were holding life without over her head."

"Man's laughter..."

Haller continued to read and then tossed the letter on top of the stack of letters he had thrown onto the dashboard.

"That's the best you got?" he asked.

"So far," Bosch said. "Still have more to go."

"Says she didn't do it but doesn't say who did. What can we do with that?"

"She doesn't know. That's why she wants your help."

Bosch drove in silence while Haller checked his phone and then called his case manager, Lorna, to go over his calendar. When he was finished, Bosch asked how long they would be at the next stop.

"Depends on my client and his mitigation witness," Haller said. "He wants to ignore my advice and tell the judge why he's not really all that guilty. I'd rather have his son beg for mercy for him, but I'm not sure he'll show, whether he'll talk, or how that will go."

"What's the case?" Bosch asked.

"Fraud. Guy's looking at eight to twelve. You want to come in and watch?"

"No, I'm thinking that while we're over there, I might drop by and see Ballard — if she's around. It's not far from the courthouse. Text when you're finished in court and I'll swing back."

"If you even hear the text."

"Then call me. I'll hear that."

Ten minutes later he pulled to a stop in front of the courthouse on La Cienega.

"Later, gator," Haller said as he got out. "Turn your phone up."

After he shut the door, Bosch adjusted his phone as instructed. He had not been completely open with Haller about his hearing loss. The cancer treatments at UCLA had affected his hearing. So far, he had no issue with voices and conversation, but some electronic noises were at the limits of his range. He had been experimenting with various ringtones and text alerts but was still searching for the right setting. In the meantime, rather than listening for incoming messages or calls, he relied more on the accompanying vibration. But he had put his phone in the car's cup holder earlier and therefore missed both the sound and vibration that came when Haller wanted to be picked up outside the downtown courthouse.

As he pulled away, Bosch called Renée Ballard's cell. She picked up quickly.

"Harry?"

"Hey."

"You all right?"

"Of course. You at Ahmanson?"

"I am. What's up?"

"I'm in the neighborhood. Okay if I swing by in a few minutes?"

"I'll be here."

"On my way."

2

THE AHMANSON CENTER was on Manchester ten minutes away. It was the Los Angeles Police Department's main recruitment and training facility. But it also housed the department's cold-case archive—six thousand unsolved murders going back to 1960. The Open-Unsolved Unit was located in an eight-person pod at the end of all the rows of shelving holding the murder books. Bosch had been there before and considered it sacred ground. Every row, every binder, was haunted by justice on hold.

At the reception desk Bosch was given a visitor's tag to clip to his pocket and sent back to see Ballard. He declined an escort and said he knew the way. Once he went through the archive door, he walked along the row of shelves, noting the case years on index cards taped on the endcaps.

Ballard was at her desk at the back of the pod in the open area beyond the shelves. Only one of the other cubicles was occupied. In it sat Colleen Hatteras, the unit's Investigative Genetic Genealogy expert and closet psychic. Colleen looked happy to see Bosch when she noticed his approach. The feeling wasn't mutual. Bosch had served a short stint on the all-volunteer cold-case team the year before, and he had clashed with Hatteras over her supposed hyper-empathic abilities.

"Harry Bosch!" she exclaimed. "What a nice surprise."

"Colleen," Bosch said. "I didn't think you could be surprised."

Hatteras kept her smile as she registered Bosch's crack.

"Still the same old Harry," she said.

Ballard turned in her swivel chair and broke into the conversation before it could go from cordial to contentious.

"Harry," she said. "What brings you by?"

Bosch approached Ballard and turned slightly to lean on the cubicle's separation wall. This put his back to Hatteras. He lowered his voice so he could speak as privately to Ballard as possible.

"I just dropped Haller off at the airport courthouse," he said. "Thought I might just come by to see how things are going over here."

"Things are going well," Ballard said. "We've closed nine cases so far this year. A lot of them through IGG and Colleen's good work."

"Great. Did you put some people in jail or were they cleared others?"

What occurred often in cold-case investigations was a DNA hit leading to a suspect who was long dead or already incarcerated for other crimes with a life sentence. This, of course, solved the case, but it was carried on the books as "cleared other" because no prosecution resulted.

"No, we've put some bodies in lockup," Ballard said. "About half, I'd say. The main thing is the families, though. Just letting them know that it's cleared whether the suspect's alive or dead."

"Right," Bosch said. "Yeah."

But telling members of a victim's family that the case had been solved but the identified suspect was dead had always bothered Bosch when he'd worked cold cases. To Bosch, it was admitting that the killer had gotten away with it. And there was no justice in that.

"So that's it?" Ballard asked. "You're just dropping by to say hi and bust Colleen's chops?"

"No, that wasn't what..." Bosch mumbled. "I wanted to ask you something."

"Then ask."

"I've got a couple names. People in prison. I wanted to get case numbers, maybe pull cases."

"Well, if they're in lockup, then you're not talking about cold cases."

"Right. I know."

"Then, what...you want me to — Harry, are you kidding?"

"Uh, no, what do you mean?"

Ballard turned and sat up straight so she could glance over her privacy wall at Hatteras. Hatteras had her eyes on her computer screen, which meant she was probably trying to hear their conversation.

Ballard stood up and started walking toward the main aisle that ran in front of the archives.

"Let's go up and get a coffee," she said.

She didn't wait for Bosch to answer. She kept going and he followed. When he glanced back at Hatteras, she was watching them go.

As soon as they got to the break room, Ballard turned and confronted him.

"Harry, are you kidding me?"

"What are you talking about?"

"You're working for a defense attorney. You want me to run names for a defense attorney?"

Bosch paused. He hadn't seen it that way until this moment.

"No, I didn't think that—"

"Yeah, you didn't think. I can't run names for you if you're working for the Lincoln Lawyer. They could fire my ass without even a board of rights. And don't think there aren't people over at the PAB gunning for me. There are."

"I know, I know. Sorry, I didn't think it through. Forget I was even here. I'll leave you alone."

He turned toward the door, but Ballard stopped him.

"No, you're here, we're here. Let's have that cup of coffee."

"Uh, well, okay. You sure?"

"Just sit down. I'll get it."

There was one table in the break room. It was pushed up against the wall, with chairs on the three open sides. Bosch sat down and watched as Ballard filled to-go cups with coffee and brought them over. Like Ballard, Bosch took his coffee black, and she knew this.

"So," she said after sitting down. "How are you, Harry?"

"Uh, good," Bosch said. "No complaints."

"I was over at Hollywood Division about a week ago and ran into your daughter."

"Yeah, Maddie told me, said you had a guy in a holding cell."

"A case from '89. A rape-murder. We got the DNA hit but couldn't find him. Put out a warrant and he got picked up over there on a traffic violation. He didn't know we were even looking for him. Anyway, Maddie said you got into some kind of test program at UCLA?"

"Yeah, a clinical trial. Supposedly running a seventy percent extension rate for what I've got."

"'Extension'?"

"Extension of life. Remission if you're lucky."

"Oh. Well, that's great. Is it getting results with you?"

"Too early to tell. And they don't tell you if you're getting the real shot or the placebo. So who knows."

"That kinda sucks."

"Yeah. But…I've had a few side effects, so I think I'm getting the real stuff."

"Like what?"

"My throat is pretty rough and I'm getting tinnitus and hearing loss, which is kind of driving me crazy."

"Well, are they doing something about it?"

"Trying to. But that's what being in the test group is about. They monitor this stuff, try to deal with side effects."

"Right. When Maddie told me, I was kind of surprised. Last time we talked, you said you were just going to let nature take its course."

"I sort of changed my mind."

"Maddie?"

"Yeah, pretty much. Anyway…"

Bosch leaned forward and picked up his cup. The coffee was still too hot to drink, especially with his ravaged throat, but he wanted to stop talking about his medical situation. Ballard was one of the few people he had told about it, so he felt she deserved an update, but his practice had been not to dwell on the situation and the various possibilities for his future.

"So tell me about Haller," Ballard said. "How's that going?"

"Uh, it's going," Bosch said. "Staying pretty busy with the stuff coming in."

"And now you're driving him?"

"Not always, but it gives us time to talk through the requests. They keep coming, you know?"

The year before, when Bosch worked as a volunteer with Ballard in the Open-Unsolved Unit, they broke open a case that identified a serial killer who had operated unknown in the city for several years. During the investigation, they'd also determined that the killer was responsible for a murder for which an innocent man named Jorge Ochoa had been imprisoned. When politics in the district attorney's office prevented immediate action to free Ochoa, Ballard tipped Haller to the case. Haller went to work and in a highly publicized habeas hearing was granted a court order freeing Ochoa and declaring him innocent. The media attention garnered by the case resulted in a flood of letters and collect phone calls to Haller from inmates in prisons across California, Arizona, and Nevada. All of them professed their innocence and pleaded for his help. Haller set up what amounted to an in-house innocence project and installed Bosch to do the initial review of the claims. Haller wanted a gatekeeper with an experienced detective's eye.

"These two names you wanted me to run—you think they're innocent?" Ballard asked.

"It's too early for that," Bosch said. "All I have are their letters from prison. But since I started this, I've rejected everything except these two. Something about them tells me I should at least take a further look."

"So based on a hunch, you're going to run with them."

"More than a hunch, I think. Their letters seem...desperate in a certain way. Hard to explain. I don't mean like desperate to get out of prison but desperate...to be believed, if that makes sense. I just need to take a look at the cases. Maybe then I find their bullshit."

Ballard pulled her phone out of her back pocket.

"What are the names?" she asked.

"No, I don't want you to do anything," Bosch said. "I shouldn't have asked."

"Just give me the names. I'm not going to do anything right now with Colleen in the pod. I'm just going to send myself an email with the names. It'll remind me to get back to you if I get something."

"Colleen. She's still sticking her nose into everything?"

"Not so much, but I don't want her to know anything about this."

"You sure? Maybe she can just get a feeling or a vibe and tell me whether they're guilty or not. Save both of us a lot of time."

"Harry, give it a rest, would you?"

"Sorry. Had to."

"She does good work on the IGG stuff. That's all I care about. It makes it worth putting up with her 'vibes' in the long run."

"I'm sure."

"I have to get back to the pod. Are you going to give me the names?"

"Lucinda Sanz. She's in Chino. And Edward Dale Coldwell. He's at Corcoran."

"Caldwell?"

"No, *Cold*—Coldwell."

She was typing with her thumbs on her phone. "DOBs?"

"They didn't think to add those in their letters. I have inmate numbers if that helps."

"Not really."

She slid her phone back into her pocket.

"Okay, if I get anything, I'll call you."

"Thanks."

"But let's not make it a habit, okay?"

"It won't be."

Ballard took her coffee and headed toward the door. Bosch stopped her with a question.

"So who's gunning for you?"

"What do you mean?"

"Downstairs you said there are people gunning for you."

"Oh, just the usual shit. People hoping I'll fail. Your everyday woman-in-charge stuff."

"Well, fuck them."

"Yeah, fuck them. I'll see you, Harry."

"See you."

3

BOSCH WAS ALREADY back on La Cienega by the courthouse when Haller texted that he was finished with the sentencing hearing. Bosch texted that he'd be out front. He pulled the Navigator up to the glass exit doors just as Haller was coming through. Bosch hit the button to unlock the doors, and Haller opened the back and jumped into the seat. He closed the door but Bosch didn't move the SUV, just stared at him in the rearview.

Haller settled in and then realized they weren't moving.

"Okay, Harry, we can—"

He realized his mistake, opened the door, and got out. The front door opened and he climbed into the passenger seat.

"Sorry," he said. "Force of habit."

They had a deal. On the occasions that Bosch drove the Lincoln, he insisted that Haller ride in the front seat so that they could converse side by side. Bosch had been adamant: he would not play chauffeur to a defense lawyer, even if that attorney happened to be his half brother who had hired him so that he could get private health insurance and be in the clinical trial at UCLA.

Satisfied he had made a proper stand, Bosch pulled away from the curb and said, "Where to?"

"West Hollywood," Haller said. "Lorna's apartment."

Bosch moved into the left lane so he could make a U-turn and head north. He had already driven Haller to many meetings with Lorna, either at her place or at Hugo's up the street if food was involved. Since the so-called Lincoln Lawyer worked out of his car instead of an office, Lorna managed things from her condo on Kings Road. It was the center of the practice.

"How'd things go back there?" Bosch asked.

"Uh, let's just say that my client received the full measure of the law," Haller said.

"Sorry to hear it."

"The judge was an asshole. I don't think he even read the PSR."

It had been Bosch's experience when he was a sworn officer that presentencing reports weren't usually favorable to the offender, so he wasn't sure why Haller thought a careful reading of the PSR by the judge in this case could have resulted in a lesser sentence. Before he could ask about it, Haller reached forward to the center screen on the dashboard, pulled up the favorites list from his contacts, and placed a call to Jennifer Aronson, the associate in the firm of Michael Haller and Associates. The Bluetooth system brought the call up on the vehicle's speakers and Bosch heard both sides of it.

"Mickey?"

"Where you at, Jen?"

"My house. Just got back from the city attorney's office."

"How'd that go?"

"Just round one, really. Bit of a game of chicken. Nobody wants to say a number first."

Bosch knew that Haller had trusted Aronson with the Jorge Ochoa negotiation. Haller and Associates had filed a lawsuit against the city and the LAPD for his wrongful conviction and incarceration. Though the city and police department were protected by state-mandated limits to financial settlements in such matters, there were aspects of the poor and possibly corrupt handling of the case that allowed Ochoa to seek other financial penalties. The city hoped to head that off with a negotiated settlement.

"Hold the line," Haller said. "They'll pay."

"Hope so," Aronson said. "How'd it go at the airport?"

"He got the full Monty. The judge probably never even looked at the childhood-trauma stuff. I tried to bring it up but he shut it down. And it didn't help that my guy pleaded for mercy by telling the judge he hadn't really meant to defraud all those people. So off he goes. He'll probably do seven years if he doesn't act out."

"Anybody there for him except you?"

"Only me."

"What about the guy's kid? I thought you had him queued up."

"Didn't show. Anyway, moving on, I'm going to sit down with Lorna in about thirty to look at the calendar. You want to sit in?"

"I can't. I just came home to grab something to eat. I promised my sister I'd go up to Sylmar to see Anthony today."

"Right. Well, good luck with that. Let me know if I can help."

"Thanks. Are you with Harry Bosch?"

"Sittin' right next to him."

Haller looked at Bosch and nodded as if he were making up for jumping in the back seat earlier.

"Are we on speaker?" Aronson said. "Can I talk to him?"

"Sure can," Haller said. "Go."

He pointed to Bosch.

"You're on," he said.

"Harry, I know you've drawn a line about not doing defense work per se," Aronson said.

Bosch nodded his head but then realized she couldn't see this.

"Right," he said.

"Well, I could really use you to just look at a case," Aronson said. "No investigatory work. Just look at what I've got so far from the DA."

Bosch knew that the main juvenile detention center for the north county was in Sylmar in the San Fernando Valley.

"It's a juvie case?" he asked.

"Yes, my sister's son," Aronson said. "Anthony Marcus. He's sixteen but they're going to move to try him as an adult. There's a hearing next week and I'm desperate, Harry. I need to help him."

"What's the charge?"

"They say he shot a cop but there's just nothing in this boy's character that says he would do something like this."

"Where? What agency?"

"LAPD. It's a West Valley case. It happened in Woodland Hills."

"Is he alive or dead? The cop."

"He's alive. He only got shot in the leg or something. But Anthony wouldn't have done this and he told me he didn't. He said there had to be another shooter because it wasn't him."

Bosch reached up to the dashboard screen and punched the mute button. He looked over at Haller.

"Are you kidding?" Bosch said. "You want me to work for a kid who shot an LAPD cop? I'm already looking at this case from Chino where the woman shot a LEO. You know what this could do to me out there?"

"Hello?" Aronson said. "Did I lose you?"

"I'm not asking you to work the case," Haller said. "She is, and all she wants is for you to look at the file she has. That's it. Just read the reports and tell her what you think. Then you're done with it. You won't be attached to it and nobody will ever know."

"But I'll know," Bosch said.

"Hello?" Aronson repeated.

Bosch shook his head and unmuted the call.

"Sorry," he said. "Lost you for a few seconds there. What kind of documents do you have?"

"Well, there's an investigator's chronology," Aronson said. "And there's an incident report and the medical report on the officer. There's an evidence report but there's really nothing on it. I was going to call the assigned prosecutor today and see when the next discovery drop will be. But bottom line is I just think there's something wrong here. I've known this kid all his life and he is not violent. He's gentle. He's —"

"Are there any witness reports?" Bosch asked.

"Uh, no, no witnesses," Aronson said. "It's basically his word against what the police say."

Bosch was silent. It sounded like a case he wouldn't want to be anywhere near. Haller broke into the silence.

"Tell you what, Jennifer," he said. "Email what you've got to Lorna and tell her to print it. Harry will have eyes on it in thirty minutes. We are headed to her place now."

Haller looked at Bosch.

"Unless you're saying no," he said.

Bosch slowly shook his head. This was not what he had signed up for. He didn't want the last act of his professional life to be helping criminals. The haystack work, as Haller called it, was one thing. Finding innocence among the many convicted felt to Bosch like a check on a system he knew firsthand was imperfect. But assisting in the defense of someone accused was something else in his mind.

"I'll take a look," he said grudgingly. "But if there's any follow-up work needed, you have to go to Cisco for that."

Dennis "Cisco" Wojciechowski was Haller and Associates' long-time investigator — and Lorna Taylor's husband.

"Thank you, Harry," Aronson said. "Please call me as soon as you've had a chance to look it over."

"Sure," Bosch said. "Why does your sister want you to go up there to see the kid?"

"Because she says he's not doing well," Aronson said. "He's getting bullied by other kids there. I figure if I can sit with him for an hour, that's an hour he doesn't have to be afraid."

"Okay, well, I'll look at the stuff from the file as soon as I get it," Bosch said.

"Thank you, Harry," Aronson said again. "I really, really appreciate it."

"Anything else on your end, Jennifer?" Haller asked.

"No, just what I said," she said.

"When's the next meet with the city attorney's office?" Haller asked.

"Tomorrow afternoon," Aronson said.

"Good," Haller said. "Keep the pressure on. Let's talk after that."

Haller disconnected and they drove in silence for a bit. Bosch was not happy and wasn't trying to hide it.

"Harry, just look at the file and tell her you got nothing," Haller said. "She's too emotionally invested in the case. She's got to learn to—"

"I know she's invested," Bosch said. "I don't blame her. But what is happening now is exactly what I told you I didn't want to happen. One more time and I'm out. You understand?"

"I understand," Haller said.

They made good time to West Hollywood, which was a relief to Bosch since there was a steely silence in the car after the phone call with Aronson. Bosch turned off Santa Monica Boulevard onto Kings Road and cruised two blocks south. Haller had texted Lorna about their imminent arrival and she was standing at a red curb waiting, file in hand. The windows on the Navigator were smoked. When Bosch pulled to a stop, Lorna stepped off the curb, walked around the back of the SUV, and got in the passenger seat behind Bosch.

"Oh," she said to Haller. "I thought you'd be in your usual spot."

"Not when Harry's driving," Haller said. "Did you print out the stuff from Jennifer?"

"Got it right here."

"Pass that up to Harry so he can take a look while I jump in the back with you."

Bosch was handed a file. He opened it and tried to tune out the conversation from the back as Haller started going over his court calendar and other case-related matters with Lorna. Bosch's starting point was the incident report.

The kid's name was Anthony Marcus. He was about to spend his seventeenth birthday in the juvenile detention center in Sylmar. He was accused of shooting a patrol cop named Kyle Dexter with the officer's own gun. According to the report, Dexter and his partner Yvonne Garrity had responded to a burglary-in-progress call at a home on Califa Street in Woodland Hills. Upon arrival they searched the exterior of the house and found a sliding door on a rear pool deck open. They called for backup, but before other officers arrived, Dexter saw a figure in dark clothing run from the house, climb over a wall behind the pool, and drop down to Valley Circle Boulevard, which ran parallel to Califa. He told Garrity to get the patrol car while he chased the fleeing figure. Dexter climbed the wall and pursued. The chase lasted several blocks and ended when Dexter followed the suspect around a corner at Valerie Avenue. The suspect had stopped, apparently thinking he had lost his pursuer, and Dexter turned the corner and came upon him. He drew his weapon and ordered the suspect to kneel and lace his fingers behind his head. The suspect complied and Dexter radioed his location to his partner and backup officers. When he moved in to handcuff the suspect, a struggle ensued and Dexter was shot. The suspect then ran off but was quickly apprehended by the other officers who were now responding to Dexter's officer-down call.

The suspect was arrested and identified as Anthony Marcus. He denied burglarizing the house or running from the police. He claimed he had snuck out of his nearby home and was walking to his girlfriend's house for a secret rendezvous when he was suddenly confronted by Dexter. He also denied shooting Dexter but admitted that he ran from the scene after the shot was fired and Dexter went down because he didn't know what was happening and who was shooting at them.

Bosch read the report twice and pulled up Google Maps on his phone. He looked at a map and then street photos of the chase route and compared them to the details contained in the report. This gave him a better understanding of the direction, terrain, and distance of the chase. He then moved on to the medical report filed by the Force Investigation Division. FID handled all officer-involved shootings, even those where an officer was the victim. The medical report stated that Dexter was wounded twice by the same bullet, which grazed the outside of his right calf at a downward angle and then passed through his shoe and foot. He was treated in the ER at the Warner Medical Center and discharged.

Bosch heard Haller in the back seat telling Lorna to turn down a prospective client charged with distributing Chinese fentanyl, even though the client was willing to pay a $100,000 retainer for the Lincoln Lawyer's services.

"Fentanyl's on my no-fly list," Haller said. "Tell him no."

"I know," Lorna said. "I just thought you'd want to know what he was offering on the retainer."

"Worse than blood money. Next."

Lorna told him about another case: The potential client was charged with fraud for selling a guitar he claimed had been signed by John Lennon; the buyer found out after the deal went down that the guitar had been manufactured after Lennon died, so clearly he could not have signed it. The defendant was a dealer of online rock and roll memorabilia and the DA was reviewing other past sales of guitars allegedly signed by now-dead rock stars like Jimi Hendrix and Kurt Cobain. The case could get more serious.

Haller told Lorna he'd take that case but would need a $25,000 retainer up front.

"Think that will be a problem?" Haller asked.

"I'll find out and let you know," Lorna said.

Bosch went back to reading the reports for the Marcus case. There was an investigative chronology with brief entries covering the steps the FID investigators had taken. One of the last entries noted that investigators met with a fingerprint technician at the house on Califa Street. Bosch knew from experience that this meant they were trying to tie Marcus to the break-in that had spawned the whole event. If they could put him in the house, it would block a possible defense claim that Marcus was not the burglar whom Dexter and Garrity saw fleeing. The chrono did not say what, if anything, the fingerprint tech had found.

Among the reports was an inventory of property taken from Marcus after his arrest and a description of his clothes. He had been wearing blue jeans, black Nikes, and what was described as a USC hoodie. In his pockets were a house key, a condom packet, and a roll of breath mints. There was also a lab report for a gunshot-residue test conducted on the suspect, which was positive for GSR on his hands and the right arm of his hoodie.

The last document in the package was a transcript of the radio calls Dexter and Garrity had made during the event. The first was

Garrity's initial call for backup, followed by her call saying there was a fleeing suspect and giving a description of someone in dark pants and a dark hoodie. Bosch paid close attention to the calls for help that came from Dexter moments later and noted that the transcript showed that only eight seconds elapsed between Dexter calling in his location and stating that he had the suspect in custody and his officer-down call:

> 01:43:23 — Officer Dexter: Suspect code four Valerie west of Valley Circle.
> 01:43:31 — Officer Dexter: Officer down, officer down...
> 01:43:36 — Officer Dexter: He shot me. He shot me...
> 01:43:42 — Officer Dexter: Suspect is GOA, going west on Valerie. Maroon USC hoodie.

After Bosch reviewed everything in the file, he had some definite thoughts about what had gone down in the shooting. He checked the rearview mirror. Haller and Lorna were now talking about clients who had not yet paid for legal services rendered. It was too close a space to carry on two separate conversations.

"I'm going to step out and call Jennifer," Bosch said.

"Thank you, Harry," Haller said.

4

BOSCH PUT THE file containing the Marcus case reports on the hood of the Navigator and called Aronson. She answered right away.

"Harry, I'm waiting to see Anthony at the detention center. They're going to take me back anytime now."

"Okay, you can call me later. I looked at the records you sent on his case."

"Thank you so much. Did you see anything?"

"Listen, I don't want my name mixed up in this. Are we clear on that? Whatever you do with what I tell you, it doesn't include me. Okay?"

"Of course. I already agreed to that. It goes no further than this call."

Bosch was silent for a long moment as he decided whether to trust her.

"Are you still there?" Aronson said.

"Yes, I'm here," Bosch said. "So, you said you were going to call the prosecutor to see if there was any update on discovery. Did you do that?"

"Uh, no, not yet."

"Well, the chrono says they brought a print tech to the house your client supposedly broke into."

"Which he says he didn't do."

"Right. But the chrono doesn't say what the tech found. They were obviously looking for a print from your client in the house because that would tie him to the burglary and catch him in a direct lie in his initial statement. So you've got to get a report on what the print guy found, if anything."

"Okay, I'll get on that. What else?"

"I looked at the Google Maps of the area where this went down, and the house at the corner of Valley Circle and Valerie Avenue has a hedge that runs the lot lines."

"Okay. What does that mean?"

"Well, Dexter chased the burglary suspect up Valley Circle and then he followed when the guy turned left onto Valerie. Because of the hedge, he would have lost sight of the suspect."

"Which supports Anthony's claim that he's not the burglar Dexter was chasing."

"Possibly, yeah."

"That's good, but the burglary is the least of our problems. It's the shooting they want to burn him for. What else did you see?"

"The property report. Anthony had a condom in his pocket along with breath mints and a house key."

"Which of course supports his story, not theirs."

"But what he didn't have is important. No burglary tools, no gloves. There are no gloves in the evidence report. This is why they sent the fingerprint tech into the house. If he wasn't wearing gloves then they should have found his prints in there. And if they didn't, then..."

"Good, Harry. That's the first thing I'll ask about when I get to the DA."

"The radio transcript you have here is also important. When the chase starts, Dexter's partner Garrity calls out a description. She says the suspect is a white male in dark clothes. Then after Dexter gets shot, he gets on the radio and says the suspect is GOA and wearing a USC hoodie."

"'GOA'?"

"Cop code for 'gone on arrival.' It means he ran. But the important thing is the hoodie. USC hoodies are usually maroon with gold letters. How come Garrity didn't get the USC part when they first saw the guy?"

"Maybe his back was to them and they couldn't see."

"Possibly, but it's a discrepancy. Another is if there are no prints putting him in the house."

"Right. That's a good start, Harry. I think I can work with that. Anything else?"

Bosch hesitated. He believed there were more significant inconsistencies in the police reports and possibly even something more wrong with what had gone down that night on Valerie Avenue. But somehow he felt guilty about giving this information to a defense attorney. And then Aronson asked the question he was most reticent about answering.

"So then who shot Dexter?" she said. "You think the real burglar came up from behind or something? Anthony said he didn't see anybody else."

"No, I don't think that's what happened," Bosch said. "I think the real burglar probably cut between a couple of the houses and hid out in a backyard until it was clear."

"Then what happened? The reports say there's gunshot residue on Anthony's hands."

"The GSR can be explained. I think there is a possibility that Dexter shot himself and blamed Anthony so he wouldn't lose his job."

"Harry, you're a fucking genius."

"I'm not telling you this as some kind of defense strategy. Based on these reports, I think it could have happened."

"Okay," Aronson said. Her tone was deadly serious. "Walk me through it."

"Look, again, I'm not saying this is what happened, okay?" Bosch said. "I don't know what happened. But it wouldn't be the first time that some dumbass cop shot himself and tried to blame somebody else for it. If you admit you shot yourself by accident, you're pretty much done in the department. It's time to find a new job."

"I understand. Just walk me through what *could* have happened and I'll take it from there."

"Well, we know from Anthony that Dexter had his weapon out and drew down on him. It was an adrenaline-fueled chase and then arrest. Before approaching him, he made Anthony get on his knees and lace his fingers behind his head. The procedure would then be to grab and hold the suspect's wrists with one hand and holster your weapon with the other. Then you cuff the suspect. According to the transcript of the radio calls, Dexter said the suspect was code four, which means in custody. And then eight seconds later he makes the officer-down call."

"Oh my God, Dexter shot himself!"

Aronson was almost gleeful in her response as she saw an open route to successfully defending her sister's kid.

"I don't know what happened," Bosch said. "And neither do you. But a couple things. The first is that Anthony did not have Dexter's handcuffs on his wrists when he was caught later. So whatever happened, it happened before Dexter was able to handcuff him. Then you have the trajectory of the bullet that was fired."

"Down through his foot," Aronson said.

"After wounding the outside of his right calf. Definite downward trajectory. What you need to find out is if Dexter is right-handed and holstered his weapon on his right side. It could mean he unintentionally fired the gun while attempting to holster it. Remember, it was a high-tension, adrenalized moment. It's happened before."

"And he's willing to send a sixteen-year-old boy to prison to cover his own fuckup."

"Maybe. There was nothing in what you got that said how long he's been with the LAPD. I'm guessing not long. Accidental discharge is usually a rookie mistake. This could also explain the GSR on Anthony. He was in a kneeling position, hands behind his head, Dexter right behind him. Depending on how tall Dexter is, this position puts Anthony's hands and right arm close to a right-handed discharge of the weapon."

"Oh my God...I'll be getting all that information before the end of the day."

"Well, keep in mind that if you're looking at it this way, FID probably is too. That fingerprint report is important."

"Harry, I can't thank you enough for this."

"You can thank me by keeping me out of it."

"You don't have to worry. You are completely out. But I have to go. They just signaled me that they've put Anthony in the attorney-client room."

"Okay, good luck."

Aronson disconnected. Bosch took the file off the hood and got back into the driver's seat of the Navigator. Haller and Lorna were apparently finished with the casework and engaged in small talk about Haller's daughter, Hayley, who was studying for the bar exam after having finished law school at USC.

"You'll have to change the firm's name to Haller, Haller, and Associates," Lorna said.

"I don't think she wants to pursue criminal law," Haller said. "She wants to go into environmental law and help save the planet."

"Good intentions, but boring as hell."

"She'll find her way."

"All right, boys, I'm out of here. Mickey, I'll let you know about the guitar fraud. Hopefully he can pay the retainer."

"Hopefully."

Bosch heard Lorna pull up the door handle to get out.

"Hold it," he said.

He checked the side-view mirror to make sure she wasn't about to swing the door out into traffic.

"Okay, you're clear," he said.

"Thanks, Harry," Lorna said.

She got out and closed the door.

"Would it have killed you to get out and open the door for her?" Haller asked.

"Probably not," Bosch said. "My bad. Where to now?"

"That's it," Haller said. "I'm done for the day and you can take me home."

Bosch checked the dash clock. It wasn't yet two, and this would be an early work stop. He didn't put the car in gear. He waited and soon Haller realized why.

"Oh, right," he said.

He got out and then got back in, this time in the front seat, moving the Anthony Marcus file to the dashboard.

"You come up with anything on this case?" he asked. "Looked like you did most of the talking on that call."

"I think so," Bosch said. "Gave her a pathway, you could say."

"Well, good. I hope it didn't darken your soul, having to do that."

"A bit. But I'll deal with it. Just remember, that was a one-off, Mick, and it was easy. But I'm going back to the haystack now."

"Which is exactly where I need you. Find me the needle."

Bosch checked the side-view, pulled away from the curb, and

headed toward Haller's home. After a few minutes of silence, Bosch spoke.

"On that Ochoa negotiation with the city attorney, what do you stand to make from that?"

"Well, we have a sliding rate for all such cases. We get a standard twenty-five percent of the first million, goes up to thirty-three on a prorated scale. Most lawyers have a flat rate of a third or higher all the way through. Me, my cut gets bigger only if the check gets bigger."

"Not bad when it's a slam dunk like that one looks to be."

"It's never as easy as it looks."

"But with the haystack, you're not doing it for that second-level payout, right?"

"It's strictly pro bono on all the work we do up front. Now, if we get somebody out, I'm happy to represent them in a suit for damages and compensation at my usual rate. But that's pie-in-the-sky money. In most cases compensation is limited by state caps. So could there be money down the line, yes. But this is not a moneymaking operation. Why do you think I was going over cases with Lorna? I need to put gas in the tank. I need paying cases so you can work the haystack."

"I just wanted to be sure, that's all."

"Well, you can be. The deal I made with Ochoa was made before all the letters started coming in, and it was Hayley who suggested I create my own little innocence project. The only difference is the real Innocence Project takes donations to the cause. I don't."

"Got it."

They dropped back into silence until Bosch started up the hill on Fareholm. He passed Haller's house and turned around at the top, then came back down and parked at the curb by the stairs to Haller's front door.

They both got out.

"Thank you, Harry," Haller said.

"What are you going to do?" Bosch asked.

"Well, I haven't had a half day off like this in months. I don't want to waste it. I might go over to Wilshire and hit the range."

"You play golf?"

"Taking lessons."

"And you're a member at Wilshire?"

"Joined a few months ago."

"Good for you."

"What's that mean, that tone?"

"Nothing. Just means good for you that you're in a club. You deserve it."

"I got a friend in the public defender's office who's a member. He sponsored me."

"Nice."

"What are you going to do this afternoon?"

"I don't know. Probably take a nap."

"You should."

Bosch handed him the keys to the Lincoln and started walking down the street to where he had parked his Cherokee. Haller called after him.

"How's the new car?" he said.

"Like it," Bosch said. "Still miss the old one."

"That's so Bosch."

Bosch wasn't sure what that meant. He had found and bought a 1994 Jeep Cherokee to replace the one he had lost in a crash during the investigation he'd been on with Ballard the year before. The "new" old car had fewer miles on it and a better suspension. It had come with new tires and a recent paint job. It didn't have all the bells and whistles that the Navigator had, but it was good enough to get him home.

5

AFTER WAKING FROM a lengthy afternoon nap, Bosch checked his phone and saw he'd slept through a series of texts; he read the messages from his daughter, Ballard, Aronson, and a bartender at the Catalina Bar and Grill. He got up, washed his face, and went out to the dining room, where the table had long ago become a desk. He stopped at the shelves by the turntable, flipped through his record collection, and pulled out an old one that had been one of his mother's favorites. Released in 1960—a year before her death—the album had been kept in pristine condition. Bosch's care over the years had been motivated by respect for the recording artist as well as for his mother.

He carefully dropped the needle on the second track of *Introducing Wayne Shorter*. Stepping out from Art Blakey's Jazz Messengers to record his first effort as a leader, Shorter soon after was playing the tenor saxophone alongside Miles Davis and Herbie Hancock. Theo at the Catalina had left Bosch the message that Shorter had just passed on.

Bosch stood there in front of his speakers and listened to the moves made by Shorter on track two. His breath, his finger work, it was all there. It had been more than six decades since Bosch had first heard these notes, but the news of Shorter's death had triggered the memory of this song that still meant so much to him. The track ended and Bosch carefully lifted the arm, drew it back, and started "Harry's Last Stand" once more. He then moved to the table to go back to work.

Maddie's message was short, her daily check on him. He would respond with a call to her later. Ballard had texted to say she'd sent him an email. He logged in and saw she'd forwarded links to two *Los Angeles Times* stories from five years earlier. Bosch started to read them in chronological order.

Ex-Wife Charged in Slaying of Hero Deputy
By Scott Anderson, *Times* Staff Writer

The former wife of a Los Angeles County sheriff's deputy once lauded for his bravery in the face of fire has been charged with his death after a domestic confrontation in Quartz Hill.

Lucinda Sanz, 33, was charged Monday with first-degree murder for shooting her ex-husband, Roberto Sanz, in the back as he walked across the front lawn of the home the two once shared with their young son. Sheriff's investigators said the former couple had been in a heated argument just moments before. Lucinda Sanz is being held on $5 million bail in the county jail.

Homicide investigators said the killing occurred around 8 p.m. Sunday in the 4500 block of Quartz Hill Road shortly after Roberto Sanz had returned his son to his ex-wife's home after a weekend visitation that was part of the couple's custody agreement. Sgt. Dallas Quinto said the two adults had argued in the house and Roberto Sanz left through the front door. Moments later he was shot twice in the back while he crossed the lawn to his pickup truck parked on the street. The couple's young son did not witness the shooting, Quinto said.

Roberto Sanz was not wearing a bulletproof vest at the time of the shooting because he was not on duty.

"It's just so sad that it came to this," Quinto said. "Roberto was under constant threat when he worked on the streets, protecting the community. To have the ultimate threat come from inside his family is heartbreaking. He was much loved by his fellow deputies."

Roberto Sanz, 35, was part of a gang-suppression team assigned to the sheriff's Antelope Valley substation. Prior to that he was assigned to the jail division. A year ago, he was praised by Sheriff Tim Ashland and awarded the department's medal of valor after a shoot-out with members of a Lancaster gang who ambushed Sanz when he stopped at the Flip's hamburger stand. Sanz was unhurt in the shooting but one gang member was shot and killed and another was wounded. Two other gunmen got away and have never been identified.

Bosch read the story again. Quartz Hill was a suburb of a suburb called Palmdale, located in the vast northeastern expanse of the county. Once a small desert town, it had, like the nearby equally small town of Lancaster, experienced tremendous population growth since the turn of the century when housing prices in Los Angeles exploded, sending thousands of people into the far-flung areas of the county to find affordable homes. Palmdale and Lancaster grew into a single mini–desert metropolis with all the problems that came with urban life. That included gangs and drugs. The sheriff's department had its hands full out there.

Quartz Hill was nestled next to Palmdale and Lancaster. Bosch had been out there on cases in the past and he remembered tumbleweeds and sand-swept streets. He expected all of that might be different now.

Bosch admired what Ballard had done. Rather than sending him a case extracted from a law enforcement computer and risk losing her job, she had looked up the case and found links to newspaper stories that were available to anyone. In fact, he was annoyed with himself for not thinking to run Lucinda Sanz's name through an *L.A. Times* search before going to Ballard.

He clicked on the second link, and another story on the Sanz case downloaded. It had been published nine months after the first story.

Slain Hero Deputy's Ex-Wife Convicted
By Scott Anderson, *Times* Staff Writer

The former wife of a Los Angeles County sheriff's deputy once lauded for his bravery was sentenced to prison Thursday for killing him after a dispute over the custody arrangements of their young son.

Lucinda Sanz, 34, pleaded no contest to a single count of manslaughter in Los Angeles Superior Court. Under a plea agreement, she was sentenced by Judge Adam Castle to a term of 11 years in prison.

Sanz had maintained her innocence in the killing of Deputy Roberto Sanz. He was leaving the Quartz Hill home where his ex-wife and son lived when he was shot twice in the back. He died on the front lawn of the house. The son did not witness his father's killing.

The defendant's attorney, Frank Silver, explained that his client had no choice but to take the deal offered by prosecutors.

"I know she has been steadfast in claiming she's innocent," Silver said. "But the evidence was stacked against her. At some point the reality was that she could throw the dice and go to trial and likely end up spending the rest of her life behind bars, or she could be assured of some daylight. She's a young woman. If she does well, she'll get out and still have a life and her son waiting for her."

The couple had a long history of domestic issues, including restraining orders, court-appointed child-visitation monitors, and a past assault charge against Lucinda Sanz that was later dismissed. On the day of the killing, she sent her ex-husband several threatening text messages. No weapon was recovered at the scene, but sheriff's investigators said that the defendant had enough time to hide the gun and that her hands and clothing tested positive for gunshot residue after the shooting.

"Where was the gun?" Silver said. "That's always going to bother me. I think I could have done something with that at trial, but I had to go with my client's wishes. She wanted to take the deal."

It was Lucinda Sanz who initially called 911, and investigators said there was a nine-minute response time, giving her ample opportunity to hide the gun. Multiple searches of the house and the surrounding area did not produce the gun, and investigators have not ruled out the possibility that there was an accomplice to the crime who secreted the weapon.

Roberto Sanz, 35, was an 11-year veteran of the sheriff's department. He was assigned to the Antelope Valley substation, where he was part of a gang-suppression team. A year before his death he received the sheriff's medal of valor after being engaged in a gun battle with four gang members who ambushed him at a hamburger restaurant. Sanz shot and killed one of the assailants and wounded another; the two others were never identified or apprehended.

By pleading no contest—technically, nolo contendere—Lucinda Sanz did not have to acknowledge in court killing her ex-husband. Her mother and brother watched as she was led off to prison. Part of the plea agreement included her placement at the California Institution for Women in Chino so that she could be close to family, including her son, who will be raised by his grandmother.

"This isn't how it should be," Muriel Lopez, Lucinda Sanz's mother, said outside court. "She should be raising her son. Roberto always threatened to take him away from her. In his death he finally did."

Bosch reread this story too. It carried many more details of the crime. The new details in the second story bothered him. The murder weapon was never found despite what must have been intensive and repeated searches. That suggested that it had somehow been taken far away from the scene. Since Sanz was a deputy, Bosch suspected that there would have been a full-court press on the investigation and that the first search would have been followed by at least two more with different teams and different sets of eyes. He was satisfied that the gun was not there, and that suggested preplanning and premeditation.

But shooting Sanz in the back as he walked across the front yard to his car suggested a spur-of-the-moment act of anger. It contradicted any idea that the murder was planned. That and the missing murder weapon were most likely the reasons the prosecution floated a deal to Silver for a reduced charge.

Bosch knew of Frank Silver and had once faced him on a case. He wasn't one of the elite lawyers in town. He was no Lincoln Lawyer. He was a solid B-level defense attorney who had likely known he couldn't win the case if it went to trial. Despite what he had told the newspaper, he probably welcomed the offer of a disposition, and that would have entered into his selling it to his client.

Bosch picked up his phone and sent a text to Ballard thanking her without mentioning what he was thanking her for. He then pushed his luck by cryptically asking if she had found anything on the other thing—meaning the other name he had given her.

While he waited for a response, he ran *Edward Dale Coldwell* through the *Times* search engine but drew a blank. He tried it without the middle name and drew another blank.

He checked his phone. Nothing from Ballard.

Bosch didn't like waiting for information. It made him restless, agitated. All his years as an investigator had taught him that momentum was key and losing it could permanently stall a case. This applied even to cold cases, where the momentum was most often carried inside the investigator's own head. Bosch felt as though he had little momentum now, but the contradiction he had seen in the newspaper stories about the Sanz case coupled with the letter from Lucinda had lit a fire in him. He wanted to keep moving on it if there was no progress yet on Coldwell.

He picked up his phone but hesitated before calling Ballard. He didn't want to lose her as a friend and source, and he knew he would if he kept pestering her with calls asking her to break the rules.

He put the phone down but checked the time on its screen. He silently cursed himself for taking the nap that had sucked up the afternoon. Even if he could make it downtown to the courthouse, there would be little time for him to review what might still be in Lucinda Sanz's case file in the basement archives. That trip would need to wait till the morning.

He picked up the phone again and called his daughter, knowing that hearing her voice and learning what was happening in her world would pull him away from Lucinda Sanz and the frustration of the momentum block. But the call went to voice mail. Disappointed, Bosch left a perfunctory update, telling her that he was doing fine and was busy with a couple of investigations for Mickey Haller.

After disconnecting, he remembered the text from Jennifer Aronson. She had asked him to call her. He did and could tell she was driving as she took the call.

"Harry, I talked to the prosecutor and she admitted that Anthony's prints were not found in the house on Califa."

"Did she say if there were any other prints not belonging to the occupants?"

"I asked but she said I have to wait for the next discovery drop. It was hard enough to get her to admit Anthony's prints weren't there."

"So then when's the next discovery drop?"

"She said she's waiting until the judge decides whether Anthony will be tried as an adult."

"Okay, what else? Did you tell her about your theory that Dexter shot himself?"

"I did. I thought maybe it would scare her away from trying him as an adult. If they move this to superior court, it will be open court and this will all come out publicly. Juvenile court is closed to the public and press."

"And what did she say?"

"She sort of laughed it off and said 'Good try.' She thought I was bluffing."

"Who's the prosecutor?"

"Shay Larkin. She's younger than me."

"Well, she'll find out it's no bluff. How's Anthony?"

"He's scared shitless. I need to get him out but there's nothing I can do — legally, at least."

"What's that mean?"

"I want to hold a press conference. Put this stuff out there about Dexter and put pressure on them to look at him and know that this is no bluff."

"Won't that give them a heads-up on your case?"

"Yes, but if it gets Anthony out...I also think it would be better if Mickey does it. The media follows him around like dogs. He would draw attention to this."

"That's an idea."

"And someone like you, with your experience, standing with him would certainly lend credibility to it."

Bosch closed his eyes and told himself that he should have known better.

"Jennifer, that's not going to happen," he said. "We had a deal. I look at the file but then I'm out."

"I know, I know," Aronson said. "But it's my sister's kid, Harry. I can't stand seeing him in there when I know he's innocent."

"If he's innocent, you'll get him out."

"Eventually, Harry. But what happens in between? He could get hurt in there. Or worse."

"Then hold your press conference and see what that does. Get Mickey up there, but don't ask me. I have relationships and a reputation in this town that I'm not about to destroy because of what amounted to less than an hour's work on this case. You have to find some other way."

There was silence and when Aronson finally responded, her tone was as cold as winter rain.

"I understand," she said. "Goodbye."

She disconnected but Bosch held his phone to his ear for a long time, wondering why he felt like a coward.

He thought about Anthony Marcus up there alone in Sylmar juvie. When Bosch was a kid he had been held in juvenile detention a few times as a runaway from foster homes. He was so slightly built as a teenager that a few years later he was put on an army tunnel crew in Vietnam. His size was an advantage while moving through the dark and narrow tunnels used by the Vietcong. But it had made him an easy target in juvenile detention. Things were done to him, taken from him, and he didn't like to dwell on the memories. But thinking about Anthony Marcus in Sylmar brought them back now. Despite the position he had taken with Haller and Aronson, Bosch was struck by what Aronson had said about Anthony being bullied. He knew firsthand that it was a dog-eat-dog world inside the children's jail. He secretly hoped Aronson would be able to rescue her nephew with the help he had just given her.

6

BOSCH WAS BACK on the Lucinda Sanz case by 9 a.m. the next day, standing at the service window at the archives division of the Los Angeles Superior Court in downtown. The archives were in the basement of the Civic Center, located three floors below the vast green lawns and pink chairs of Grand Park. Few people knew that beneath the park was a windowless concrete bunker where case files and court exhibits from decades of criminal prosecutions were available for public viewing.

But Bosch knew and he was the first person at the counter when the clerk slid back the plexiglass window and opened for business. He had already filled out the request form for all materials in the archives related to *California v. Lucinda Sanz,* having pulled the case number off the county court system's public database the night before.

The clerk studied the request form, told Bosch to take a seat, and disappeared into the vast archives.

Bosch wasn't expecting much because the case had never gone to trial. That meant that there would be no exhibits—photos and documents—that would have been shown to a jury. But what he was hoping for was the presentencing report submitted by the Department of Probation and Parole. It would have been required by the judge before he accepted the plea from Lucinda Sanz and passed sentence. The PSRs Bosch had seen before were usually stocked with case reports and other documents filed in support of the sentencing recommendation. Those reports were what he wanted, and he hoped there would be enough to give him a baseline knowledge of the case.

While he waited, Bosch took out his phone so he could call the cancer center at UCLA to push back his appointment to the afternoon. But being as he was three levels underground and surrounded by reinforced-concrete walls, he had no cell service. He thought about going up topside to make the call but he didn't want to miss the return of the clerk.

Ten minutes later the clerk emerged from the archives carrying a single manila folder no thicker than a slice of bread. He read Bosch's reaction.

"All I could find," he said. "But it was a nolo case. No trial, no exhibits, no transcripts. Lucky there was even a file."

Bosch took the file and walked it over to a side room where there were individual desk pods for viewing documents and exhibits. He opened the file and found a handwritten list on an index card on the inside cover noting only six documents, ordered by date filed with the court. The top sheet was the most recent. It was the order from Judge Castle sentencing Lucinda Sanz to prison. Behind this were three letters that had been sent to the judge asking for leniency for the defendant. They had come from her mother, her brother, and a man who stated in his opening paragraph that he had been Lucinda's employer at an onion farm in Lancaster where she had worked for many years in the packing-and-shipping warehouse.

Bosch quickly skimmed these before moving to the next

document, which was the agreement signed by Lucinda Sanz pleading nolo contendere to a charge of voluntary manslaughter. The document, also signed by Andrea Fontaine, the deputy district attorney who had handled the case, additionally set out the term range from medium to high, with an enhancement for use of a firearm. It all added up to Sanz going before the judge and receiving a sentence that could be anywhere between seven and thirteen years. It seemed to Bosch to be a good deal for someone who had supposedly killed a law enforcement officer.

The last document was the presentencing report. Bosch fanned it open and saw that it was lengthy and at least half the pages were police and autopsy reports. This was what he had hoped for. Summaries of the investigation that would allow him to understand how the case had been worked.

The report was authored by a state probation officer named Robert Kohut. It was written in narrative form and was essentially a deep dive into Lucinda Sanz's life with specific sections regarding her childhood, family structure, adolescent legal troubles, education, employment history, residency history, adult law enforcement interactions, and any documented psychological treatment.

Kohut's report was largely favorable. He described Sanz as a single mother who worked sixty-hour weeks at Desert Pearl Farms in Lancaster in order to provide for herself and her young son. She had no criminal record prior to the homicide charge, though there were two incidents listed in which deputies were called to the house in Quartz Hill to quell domestic disputes. In one case, Lucinda was arrested, but the district attorney did not file a charge against her and the case was dropped. In the second incident, neither Lucinda nor her husband was arrested. Both incidents were pre-divorce and Bosch assumed that Roberto Sanz and his wife had been cut a break because he was a deputy.

The report also said there was no record of mental-health or drug issues, and Lucinda was deemed by Kohut to be a good candidate for rehabilitation and eventual probation. However, Kohut's recommendation was to sentence Sanz on the high end of the manslaughter term range because of the circumstances of the crime. Those centered on the fact that Roberto Sanz was shot twice in the back, once when he was apparently already on the ground.

Bosch planned to request a copy of the PSR, so he moved on to the official records that had been included in the support material. This was where Bosch lived as an investigator. He had a facility for digesting reports and being able to view the case from all angles. He could see the logic jumps as well as the discrepancies and conflicts between reports. He understood that this was where he would come to a decision about Lucinda Sanz's claim of innocence.

He first reviewed the initial crime report on the killing. The summary stated that Lucinda Sanz told responding officers that she had argued with her ex-husband because he had been two hours late returning their son home from a weekend visit, a violation of their custody agreement. The argument continued until Roberto Sanz turned and walked out of the house in an apparent effort to leave the dispute behind. Lucinda Sanz said she slammed and locked the front door after he left but then heard what sounded like gunshots from the front exterior of the house. Unsure whether her ex-husband had fired at the house, she hid with her son in the boy's bedroom and did not reopen the door. From her son's room she called 911 on her cell phone and reported the gunfire. Arriving officers found Roberto Sanz lying facedown in the front yard. Paramedics were called but he was declared dead at the scene.

The medical examiner's report on the autopsy of Roberto Sanz was part of the support package. Bosch flipped to it now so he could look at the diagram of exactly where the wounds were located.

The single-page diagram contained two side-by-side generic line drawings of a male human body, front and back. There were markings, measurements, and annotations hand-printed by the deputy medical examiner who had conducted the autopsy. Bosch's eyes were immediately drawn to the two Xs on the upper back of the rear profile. A note indicated that the distance between the wounds was 5.7 inches.

There were also notations on the diagram about the angle of entry of the wounds, and from these it was determined that the two shots had distinctly different trajectories. One shot, presumed to be the first, was from a relatively flat angle, indicating the victim was likely standing when struck by the bullet from behind. The second shot entered the body at an acute angle, indicating that the victim was already down when fired on a second time. The trajectory was upward through the body from back to front, breaking the right collarbone before lodging in the upper pectoral muscle.

To Bosch the second shot was key because it undercut arguments of accidental discharge, self-defense, and heat of passion. The shooter took aim a second time at a victim who had been knocked down by the first shot. It was a coup de grâce.

Bosch took out his phone and photographed the diagram. He planned to get copies made of the entire file but he wasn't sure how long that would take and he wanted to have the diagram with him when he talked to Haller about the case.

After putting the phone down on the table, he flipped through the other pages of the autopsy report. He noted that two 9-millimeter slugs were recovered from the body. Also included in the report were black-and-white copies of the photos of the body taken before the autopsy. The body was naked and lying on a stainless-steel autopsy table. The photos showed both front and rear views of the body as well as close-ups of the entry wounds.

Bosch was quickly flipping through these when something caught his eye, and he held on the page. There was a tattoo running below the beltline of the left hip. It was in script and Bosch could easily read it.

Que Viene el Cuco

Bosch picked up his phone again and took another photo, this time enlarging the field to clearly show the tattoo without revealing the rest of the body. He knew what the tattoo meant. Not just in terms of literal translation, but in a larger and more telling sense:

The Bogeyman's Coming

7

TOPSIDE IN GRAND Park, Bosch sat in one of the pink chairs scattered randomly on the lawn in front of the Criminal Courts Building and overshadowed by "Old Faithful," the familiar tower of City Hall. He texted Haller. He knew his docket and remembered that he had an arraignment on the schedule.

> *You in the CCB? Can you talk?*

After sending the message, he switched to the phone's internet browser and typed in *L.A. County sheriff's gangs.* Before any results appeared, a call came in from Haller.

"Yes, I'm in the CCB," he said. "And you should be at UCLA, correct?"

"I should be but I'm not," Bosch said. "I gotta call them, push it till later."

"Don't fuck around with that program. Took me a lot of wheeling and dealing to get you in there."

"And I appreciate that. But something came up. Your arraignment on the guitar fraud happen yet?"

"Just did. But this driving-myself thing is a pain in the ass. Gotta go all the way over to the garage where jurors park to get the Lincoln."

"I'm in the park outside. In the pink chairs. It'll be on your way. I need to talk to you about the Sanz case."

"Okay, then. I'm heading out now. No telling how long the elevator is going to take, though."

"I'll be here."

Bosch disconnected and went back to the phone's browser. He eventually pulled up an *L.A. Times* story from seven years earlier that reported on the FBI's wide-ranging investigation into corruption in the sheriff's department. The department had an entrenched culture of deputies joining cliques that were formed in jail units as well as in certain substations and patrol areas.

Bosch scrolled down and found a list of known cliques with names like the Executioners, the Regulators, the Jump Out Boys, the Banditos, and the Bogeymen. The story noted that the far-reaching FBI investigation had started small, with an inquiry into alleged improprieties within the county's massive jail system, which was operated by the sheriff's department. The Bureau found that deputies assigned to the jail division had created cliques within each detention facility. Members engaged in illegal activities that ranged from betting on fights between inmates to passing messages to inmates from outside gang leaders to facilitating and looking the other way when gang beatdowns and even assassinations occurred.

The Bureau further found that when deputies rotated out of jail assignments to substations serving the public, they formed new cliques, leading to a variety of corrupt behaviors there as well.

When either the Bureau or the sheriff's department referred to these groups publicly, they called them cliques. But to Bosch, they were no different from street gangs. These were gangsters with badges. And he now believed Roberto Sanz had been one of them.

"You check that chair for bird shit?"

Bosch looked up from his phone. Haller was approaching, carrying one of the pink chairs.

"I did," Bosch said.

Haller put his chair down beside Bosch's so they could sit next to each other with a view of City Hall across the park. He put his slim briefcase down on the grass between his feet.

"I had an interesting call with Jen Aronson last night," he said.

Bosch nodded. He'd thought this might come up. "She told you about wanting to do a press conference on her nephew's case?" he asked.

"She did," Haller said. "And she also said you want no part of it."

"I don't."

"Harry, you planted the seed but want no part of the tree that grows from it."

"I don't know what that means. Can we talk about Lucinda Sanz? That's what I'm working on."

"We can, but I want to make sure you get to UCLA."

"I'm going this afternoon."

"Good. What've you got?"

It took Bosch a moment to switch tracks and get back to thinking about Lucinda Sanz. When Haller brought Bosch on to review and cull the requests that came in from the prisons, one of the rules of the road he'd set was that Bosch was not to reach out to any sender of a request without his approval. These were long shots and Haller wasn't in the business of offering false hope to incarcerated individuals. He didn't want Bosch making that move until he had been apprised of Bosch's thinking and agreed on next steps.

"It's the court file," Bosch said. "It's pretty thin but there's enough there to make me want to go out to Chino and talk to Lucinda Sanz."

"The one who killed her husband, the deputy?" Haller said.

"Her ex-husband."

"Well, tell me what you got. But she pleaded nolo, right? That makes it a steep mountain to climb. You know what El Capitan is?"

"At Yosemite? Yeah."

"Reversing a nolo is like climbing El Cap."

"Yeah, but she didn't have the Lincoln Lawyer on her side back then. She had some second-stringer works out of that lawyer commune in Chinatown."

While still with the LAPD, Bosch had been to the office of Frank Silver, the attorney who had represented Lucinda Sanz. It was in a brick building on Ord Street that was nicknamed "the commune" because several solo-practice attorneys worked there out of cubbyhole offices in a cut-rate space that allowed them to share the overhead expenses of reception, internet, copying, coffee, and paralegal and other support services. And it was walking distance to the CCB.

"I'd rather work out of my car," Haller said. "Who was the lawyer? Maybe I know him."

"Frank Silver," Bosch said. "I had a case with him once. When I was with Hollywood Homicide. He was a water-seeks-its-own-level kind of guy. Not too impressive, you ask me."

"Silver — don't know him. They give you the silver medal for second place. And in trial, second place is a guilty verdict."

"Never thought of it that way."

"At least over there they're close to Little Jewel and Howlin' Ray's."

After COVID, those were two of the best restaurants left, not only in Chinatown but in all of downtown.

"True, but I miss Chinese Friends," Bosch said.

"It's closed?" Haller asked. "You mean permanently?"

There was surprise and disappointment in Haller's tone. There weren't many quick and reliable lunch places near the CCB, especially since the pandemic.

"Last year," Bosch said. "After fifty years."

He realized that he had probably been going to Chinese Friends all fifty of those years. Until he went one day in August and there was a sign on the locked glass door that said ALL GOOD THINGS COME TO AN END—like a message from a fortune cookie. He had never spoken to the man who ran the restaurant and was always posted at the cash register. Bosch had always just nodded to him when he paid, assuming there was a language barrier.

"Anyway," Haller said. "What did you find in the basement?"

Bosch pushed himself back on track with the case.

"Okay, a few things bother me on this one," he said, "to the point that I want to take it further. First off, Silver. I think he talked Sanz into accepting a plea. He probably knew they would get the full-court press if he took it to trial. The victim was a deputy, after all. So he pushed for a deal and then he pushed her into taking it."

"I get that," Haller said. "What else?"

"The PSR was in the basement file. It contained the autopsy report and some crime reports and there's some stuff that just doesn't add up for me."

"Like what?"

"Well, first of all, the weapon. Never found. This was painted as a crime of passion, like an argument that went too far, but they never found the gun. And then they let her plea nolo without turning it in."

"Maybe she didn't have it. She got rid of it and it was destroyed or otherwise irretrievable."

"Maybe. But I read the plea agreement everybody signed, and it was not mentioned as lost or acknowledged at all. She was not required to reveal what she'd done with it."

"Okay, noted. What else?"

"The choreography of it."

"What's that mean?"

"Lucinda Sanz was not the registered owner of a firearm. So the gun had to be hot. That would indicate she bought this gun illegally, and the only reason to do that was—"

"Premeditation—she got it to kill him."

"Yeah. Like she had a plan. But the way it goes down doesn't jibe with that. He goes storming out of the house, she grabs the gun, and, in a fit of anger, shoots him when he's outside the house and walking to his car. Right on the front lawn. Then she shoots him again when he's down."

Haller leaned back in his pink plastic chair and gazed at the top of City Hall.

"Vultures," he said. "There are always vultures up there."

Bosch looked up and could see birds flying around the top of the spire.

"How can you tell they're vultures?" he asked. "They're so far up."

"Because they're circling," Haller said. "Vultures always circle."

"I've got one more thing, if you're interested. On the case."

"Go ahead."

"The autopsy. Roberto Sanz was hit twice in the back. Now look at this."

Bosch pulled out his phone and opened the photo of the body diagram from the autopsy. He handed the phone to Haller.

"What am I looking at?" Haller said.

"That's the diagram that shows the impacts," Bosch said. "Two shots in the upper back, perfectly placed. Small grouping, only five point seven inches apart."

"Okay. And?"

"And that was some good shooting. Moving target, dark out, but she hits him in the back, then when he's down, she pops him again. Two entry wounds, less than six inches apart."

"And she didn't even own a gun."

"Right, no gun."

"Did he teach her to shoot? When they were together?"

"Yeah, the PSR says there were photos in evidence of them at a range when they were still married. The photos weren't in the file. Silver may have them."

Bosch could tell Haller was intrigued. He continued to stare at the image on the phone. He had his trial face on and was most likely running through what he could do in court with what Bosch was telling him.

"Kind of looks more like a hit than a crime of passion," Haller said, mostly to himself.

"Yeah, and one last thing," Bosch said. "When this went down, all the news stories talked about how Roberto Sanz was a hero, got the medal of valor after a gang shooting and all of that. Now slide to the next photo."

Haller swiped his finger across the screen. Bosch leaned over and saw a photo of his daughter, Maddie, with a black eye.

"Wrong way," Bosch said.

"What the hell is this?" Haller exclaimed.

"She's working undercover. The other night she took down a purse snatcher on Melrose and because she's a woman, the guy thought he could throw a punch and get away. He was wrong."

"That's kind of cool. Except for the black eye."

"Yeah. I told her to send me a selfie before she covered it with makeup. I wanted to see how bad it was. Swipe the other way."

Haller did so and the image of Roberto Sanz's tattoo came up on the screen. He hesitantly read the words out loud.

"'*Que Viene . . . el Cuco.*' What's this?"

"You know what it means?"

"Not really."

"You're half Mexican."

"I grew up in Beverly Hills."

"It says *se habla español* on your billboards and bus benches all over town."

"*Hablo español,* but it doesn't mean I'm fluent in tattoo or every colloquial phrase out there. Are you going to tell me what or who El Cuco is?"

"It's Mexican folklore. El Cuco is the bogeyman—the monster that lives under the bed or hides in the closet. He comes out to grab children who are bad. There's a whole song about it. The bogeyman's coming, he's going to eat you, and so on. I remember the older kids singing it when I was in juvie hall. I guess you probably didn't hear it in Beverly Hills."

"With good reason. So adults sing that to their kids?"

"I guess it keeps them in line."

"No doubt. So he had this tattoo? Sanz?"

"On his hip below the beltline, where most people wouldn't see it unless they were in the locker room at the substation. Sanz was in a clique. A sheriff's gang."

Haller went silent again as he thought about this, his lawyer face firmly back in place. Bosch imagined that he had gone off to a courtroom in his mind and was seeing himself holding up the photo in front of a jury. Roberto Sanz's obvious affiliation with the Cucos—the Bogeymen—changed things about the case.

Bosch finally interrupted his reverie.

"So, what do you think?"

"It raises a lot of possibilities, that's what I think. We need to go out to Chino."

"We?"

"Yeah. Tomorrow. I want to talk to her. I'll clear the schedule. Today, you get your bony ass over to UCLA."

"Okay. What about Silver?"

"I'll deal with him. We'll need his files."

Bosch nodded. They were finished. For now. Both men stood up. Haller leaned in close to Bosch.

"You know, this could get . . . " Haller said.

His voice trailed off.

"I know," Bosch said.

"We need to be careful," Haller said. "No footprints till we're ready."

Haller bent down to grab his briefcase. Bosch looked up at the top of City Hall.

The vultures were still circling.

PART TWO

THE NEEDLE

8

THE COMMUNE CONSISTED of a long row of side-by-side attorney offices on the right and an open space with work pods on the left for support staff. Only I didn't see any support staff.

Each of the individual offices had a small frame mounted to the right of the door where an attorney could slot in or slide out his or her business card. It was a commune for legal transients, lawyers who came and went on the whims of cases and clients.

I looked at the cards as I walked down the row. All of them featured the standard scales-of-justice symbol with little variation. Some had a tiny photo of a smiling or seriously staring attorney. No embossing. The quality of all the cards suggested that the lawyers were attempting to keep costs down while also trying to project some semblance of success and dignity in the shared office space.

Six offices down, I saw the first card embossed in silver. It belonged to Frank Silver, of course, and the embossed card was either left over from better times or an effort to stand out from the others in the legal row. The office door was open but I reached in and knocked on it anyway. A man at a faux-wood-veneer desk looked up from a laptop screen.

"Frank Silver?"

"That's me."

I saw a flash of recognition in his eyes. He was fifteen years my junior with a thin build and dark curly hair. I guessed that the walk from here to the courthouse kept him in fighting form.

"You. You're the Lincoln Lawyer."

I entered the room and extended my hand. We shook.

"Mickey Haller. Were we on a case previously?"

"Frank Silver. No, I recognize you from the billboards. 'Reasonable doubt for a reasonable fee'—surprised the bar lets you get away with that one. Have a seat."

I looked down at the one chair available for a visitor in the cramped office and saw a foot-high stack of files on it.

"Oh, sorry, wait a second," Silver said. "Let me get that stuff out of the way."

He came around the desk. I stepped back in the small space so he could get to the chair. He lifted the stack, took it back with him around the desk, and put it down next to his computer.

"Okay, now have a seat. What can I do for you? Need a tune-up?"

Silver laughed.

"What?" I asked as I sat down.

"You know, Lincoln Lawyer," Silver said. "Need a tune-up."

He laughed at his joke again. I didn't. I was distracted by the wall behind him. It was lined with shelves containing lawbooks and penal codes, all beautifully leather bound with embossed titles on the spines. But it was all fake—a fake law library on wallpaper. He noticed my stare and glanced back at it.

"Oh, yeah," he said. "Looks real on Zoom."

I nodded.

"Got it," I said. "That's good."

I pointed to the jumbled stack of files he had just moved to the desk.

"I'm here to help you declutter," I said.

He cocked his head, unamused and worried that I was serious.

"How so?" he said.

"I need to pick up a file from you. A closed case your former client has asked me to take a look at."

"Really? What case is that?"

"Lucinda Sanz. You remember her?"

Surprise played across Silver's face. It wasn't a name he was expecting.

"Lucinda — of course I remember her. But..."

"Yeah, she pled nolo. But now she wants me to take a look at it. If I could get the files on the case, I'll get out of your hair and be on my — "

"Whoa, wait a second. What are you talking about? You can't just come in here and take my case like that."

"No, what are *you* talking about? It's a closed case. She pleaded and has been in Chino for almost five years."

"But she's still my client."

"She was your client. But she reached out to me. She wants me to take a look at her case. If you remember the case, then you remember she never said she did it. And she still doesn't."

"Yeah, but I got her that sweet deal. She would be doing life without if it weren't for the dispo I got her. Manslaughter with a midrange sentence."

I knew what this was about. Or I thought I did.

"Look, Frank," I said, "if you're worried about a five-oh-four, fear not. That's not what this is about. I'm looking for actual innocence and whether I can prove it. That's it. This is a habeas case to me or it's nothing. If it's a pass, I'll send the files right back to you."

One of the more disappointing and frustrating parts of being a criminal defense lawyer is being named in a 504 motion to vacate a conviction based on ineffective assistance of counsel—bad lawyering. No matter how well you think you represented your client or how good you think the result was, if your client sits in prison long enough, you'll be named in a Hail Mary effort to overturn the conviction. And no lawyer wants that. Not only can it damage a professional reputation, but it takes time to review and defend one's steps in a case.

"Then why did she go to you?" Silver asked. "If she's not going to claim ineffective assistance, she should have come to me."

"I had a case last year," I said. "It blew up in the news pretty big. I got a guy out of prison on a habeas. I proved actual innocence. She saw the story somehow in Chino and wrote me a letter. A lot of inmates wrote me letters. My investigator did some preliminary checking on the Sanz case and recommended I take it to the next step. To do that, I need the files. Whatever you've got. I need to know everything there is to know about the case."

Silver was quiet for a long moment.

"So?" I said. "Can I get the files? I can have them copied and the originals back to you by the end of the day. I don't see the big deal here."

"That won't be necessary," Silver said. "Since we're partnering on it."

"Excuse me?"

"Partners. You and me. Whatever happens, wherever you take it, we're partners."

"Uh, no, we're not. Lucinda Sanz has engaged me on this. Not you. Not us. And there's no money. I'm not charging her a dime. It's a pro bono case."

"It's pro bono *now*. But if you get her out, the sky's the limit on a false-imprisonment claim."

"Look, if you want me to, I'll have my investigator email a copy of her letter asking me to take her case. She's entitled to her file and if you refuse to give it up, that's an ethics violation. You'll have to deal with a bar complaint that'll stick on your record for five years."

Silver smiled and shook his head dismissively.

"I'm not worried about a bar grievance," he said. "Last I heard, they're still working off a COVID backlog over there at the California Bar. So you go ahead and file your complaint and I'm sure they'll jump right on it—in maybe three years."

He had me. I was silent, trying to work out a countermove. I was unprepared for an unethical lawyer trying to extort me and his former client.

"Look, I'm not trying to be an asshole, okay?" Silver said. "But I know what this is. I know what you're doing."

"Really?" I said. "What am I doing?"

"You're paying for all those billboards out there, right? The bus wraps, the benches, all of it. That case you had last year where you sprung the guy on the murder rap? How much you get on the wrongful-conviction lawsuit that followed? The city must have cut you a nice juicy check on that one. I'm guessing high six figures."

"Wrong. There's been no settlement in that case."

"Doesn't matter. The case is a rainmaker and you and I know it. And there's nothing wrong with that. But now you come here and want to make the money rain with *my* case and *my* work, and fair is fair."

"Your work? You walked her into prison. How much work was that?"

"I got her manslaughter for killing a deputy. That was a fucking miracle."

"Sure."

"I want my piece."

"What you're talking about is a long shot in a dark night. She pleaded nolo—you remember that, right? You can't do a whole lot on a wrongful-conviction suit when the client went nolo. The State's defense will be that she *consented* to go to prison and that was on *your* advice."

"But you're the Lincoln Lawyer. They see you coming, they get out the checkbook. They run scared from you."

His sincerity was as real as the lawbooks on the wall behind him.

"I don't want you anywhere near this case," I said. "So what's it going to take to get you to go away?"

Silver nodded, pleased that he had won. I immediately regretted that I had faltered and given him the opening.

"Partners, right?" he asked. "I want half."

"No way," I said. "I'd rather walk away from it. I'll give you ten points, that's it."

I stood up, ready to go.

"Twenty-five," he said.

I headed toward the doorway.

"Come on," Silver said. "A twenty-five/seventy-five split is a major payday for you. I invested a lot in that case and got nothing out of it. I deserve this."

I stopped at the door and looked back at him.

"You don't *deserve* shit," I said. "You missed things and you put your client in prison. It was only a good deal if she was guilty. But she's not. I could file an action for replevin, which might then blow up into a matter before the California Bar."

He stared at me and I could tell he wasn't clear on the definition of *replevin*.

"I could go ask a judge to order you to turn over the files," I said. "But, you know what, it doesn't help her cause to make you an adversary."

If I ever got the Sanz case into a habeas hearing, I might need Silver to explain his moves to a judge.

"I'll tell you what," I said. "I'll give you twenty-five percent of my fee after costs. Take it or leave it."

"I'll take it," Silver said. "As long as I get to audit the costs."

He had no idea how creative Lorna Taylor could be in building a case-cost summary.

"Not a problem," I said. "Now, where are the files?" I didn't expect the file on a case closed five years ago to be in the office.

"It'll take me a few minutes," Silver said. "I have a storage locker in the garage here."

"Nice," I said. "I'll wait."

Silver got up and came around the desk.

"I want one other thing," he said.

"No, we have a deal," I said.

He was getting something out of his pocket.

"Relax, it won't cost you a dime. I just want a selfie with the Lincoln Lawyer."

He pulled out a cell phone. He quickly and expertly opened the camera app, held the phone up at an angle, came in close, and wrapped his free arm around my back. He took the photo before I could push him away.

"I'll text you a copy," he said.

"No, thanks," I said. "Just go get the files."

He headed toward the exit. I reached over to the frame on the outside wall and slid the silver-embossed business card out of the slot. I put it in my pocket. I thought I might have a use for it somewhere down the line.

9

BOSCH AND THE Lincoln were out front at the curb. I opened the back passenger door, not by mistake, and saw a white bag on the seat. I moved it over and got in, caught the stink-eye from Bosch in the rearview.

"I got the files and I have to spread them out back here," I said. "So, no disrespect, but I need to know what there is to know by the time we get to Chino."

"So we're going?" Bosch asked.

"If you're up for it. You're usually . . . you know, dragging the day after UCLA."

"Maybe they gave me the placebo. I feel fine."

I doubted that. I thought he might be hiding the exhaustion he usually exhibited. Or maybe it was the adrenaline from the case that had him running in high gear.

"If you're sure, then we're going. If I get through this before we get there, you can pull over and we'll trade places and you can look through it. Cool?"

"Cool."

Bosch pulled away from the curb and headed south toward Alameda.

"You know the way, right?" I asked.

"Been there many times," Bosch responded. "If you get hungry, I got po' boys from Little Jewel in that bag back there."

"Almost sat on them. Oyster or shrimp?"

"Shrimp. You want me to go back for oysters?"

"No, I don't like oysters. Just wanted to make sure."

"I don't like them either."

The women's prison in Chino was about an hour out from downtown. While Bosch worked his way toward the 10 freeway to go east, I took the band off the pocket file and opened it up to see what I had gotten from Silver. Immediately I realized I'd been sandbagged. The first three pockets contained documents, but the four pockets behind them contained completely unused legal pads. Silver had put them in the pocket folder to give it some heft when he handed it to me. An abundance of documents was an indicator of time and effort spent on a case. It seemed obvious that Silver was attempting during the handoff to disguise how little he'd done for Lucinda Sanz. Before I left the office, he'd made me sign a receipt acknowledging that he had given me Sanz's entire file. Score one for Silver. I should have seen that coming and gone through the file before signing.

"Fucking weasel."

Bosch looked at me in the rearview again.

"Who?"

"Second-Place Silver."

"What do you mean?"

"He stuffed the case file with blank legal pads so I'd think he was giving me a lot of work product."

"Why? Did you make some kind of deal with him?"

"I had to give him twenty-five points after costs in trade for the file. Tell you what, though, I'm going to take every dime I can think of off the top. Including what I pay you."

From my angle on Bosch, I thought I saw him smile.

"You think it's funny?"

"I think it's ironic. One defense lawyer calling another a weasel. Welcome to my world for forty years."

"Yeah, well, don't forget who's signing your paychecks and who put you on the health plan."

"Don't worry, I won't."

"Speaking of which, how'd it go at UCLA yesterday?"

"Got the infusion, they took some blood, and then I was out of there."

"Glad you made it. The stuff in the infusion is what they're testing?"

"Yeah, that's the isotope. They hang a bag, plug a line into my arm, and pump it in. Twenty to thirty minutes and I'm done, depending on how much of a dose they're giving. That changes week to week."

"And they draw blood to see if it's working?"

"Not really. They're making sure my platelets aren't too low— whatever that means. And checking for kidney and liver damage. In about thirty days, they'll go into the bone for a biopsy. That'll be the real test."

"Keep me informed, please."

"I will. Back to Sanz, now. You gave Silver twenty-five points. That mean you think there's money to be made on the case?"

"Not really. If her conviction is vacated, she ought to be able to recover statutory compensation for an erroneous conviction, but there's not much a lawyer gets from that. And I don't see much chance of success for a civil action for wrongful incarceration because she entered a plea accepting imprisonment. Second-Place Silver doesn't have much experience keeping people out of prison and none whatsoever getting them out. He's just hoping for an undeserved windfall that will never come."

I turned my attention back to what in the pocket file was useful.

The first of the three inside files was a client-information form — a standard document filled out with a new client that contained addresses, names of relatives, and credit card information. It was largely used so a lawyer could know where his client was at any time and as a means, hopefully, of ensuring payment for work done. In this case, Lucinda Sanz never made bail so her whereabouts were never in question. And since Silver had told me that he had made very little off the case, I assumed that the two credit cards listed on the form had low limits and were tapped out early on.

I wondered why Sanz hadn't asked for a public defender instead of paying for a midlevel lawyer, but that was water under the bridge. I moved on to the next pocket and here I found a transcript of the interview Lucinda had given the sheriff's investigators assigned to the Roberto Sanz case.

I read it from the top, the moment Lucinda foolishly waived her rights and agreed to talk to investigators, identified as Gabriella Samuels and Gary Barnett. The investigators had asked general, open-ended questions and let Lucinda run with them in her answers. It was a familiar ploy. The prisons were filled with people who had literally talked themselves through the gates. That is, instead of keeping their mouths shut, they decided to explain their actions or reasons. But once they waived their rights, they were done for.

During the interview, Lucinda told the same story Bosch had pulled from the presentencing report. At least that was a good thing. Her story of what happened that night in Quartz Hill had been consistent over time.

Samuels: He left through the front door?
Sanz: Yes, the front.
Samuels: And what did you do then?
Sanz: I slammed the door and locked the dead bolt. I didn't

want him coming back in and I knew he had kept a key even though he wasn't supposed to.

Samuels: Then what?

Sanz: I was standing there and I heard a shot. And then there was another shot. I was scared. I thought he was shooting at the house. I ran back to my boy's room and we hid there. I called 911 and waited.

Samuels: How did you know they were gunshots?

Sanz: I don't know. I guess I didn't know for sure but I've heard gunshots before. Growing up. And when we first got married, Robbie and I went to the gun range a few times.

Samuels: Did you hear anything else besides the two shots? Any voices? Anything like that?

Sanz: No, I didn't hear anything. Just the shots.

Samuels: I saw that the front door has a peephole. Did you look out after the shots?

Sanz: No, I thought maybe he was shooting at the door. I backed away.

Samuels: Are you sure?

Sanz: Yes, I know what I did.

Barnett: Do you own a gun, Mrs. Sanz?

Sanz: No, I don't like guns. When we divorced, I told Robbie to take all the guns. I don't want them.

Barnett: So you're saying there were no guns in the house?

Sanz: Yes. No guns.

Samuels: What did you do after you called 911?

Sanz: I waited in the bedroom with my son. And then when I heard the sirens coming, I told him to stay in the room and I went to look out the front window. That's when I saw the deputies, and Robbie was on the ground.

Barnett: Did you shoot him?

Sanz: No. Never. I wouldn't do that. He's the father of my son.

Barnett: But you see what we're looking at here, right? You two argue, he leaves the house and gets shot in the back twelve feet from the front door. What are we supposed to think?

Sanz: I did not do this.

Barnett: Well, who did it if it wasn't you?

Sanz: I don't know. We've been divorced three years. I don't know who he was with or what he was doing.

Barnett: Where's the gun?

Sanz: I told you, I don't have a gun.

Barnett: We're going to find it, but it would be better for you if you just told us and cleared this up right now.

Sanz: I didn't do it.

Samuels: Were you afraid that he was going to the car to get his gun?

Sanz: No. I thought he already had his gun and shot at the house.

Samuels: But you said before that you were afraid. What were you afraid of in that moment?

Sanz: I keep telling you. I was afraid he was shooting at the house. We'd just had a big argument. I could not take Eric to my mother's because we had missed dinner because he was so late.

Samuels: Did he tell you why he was late?

Sanz: He said he had a work meeting and I know he lied. The gang team never works on Sunday.

Samuels: So you yelled at him?

Sanz: A little bit. I was mad at him, yes.

Samuels: Did he yell at you?

Sanz: Yes. He said I was a bitch.

Samuels: Is that why you got mad?

Sanz: No, no, don't put words ... I was mad at him because he was so late. That's it.

Samuels: Lucinda, if this was about you feeling threatened, we can work with you on that. You're scared. He has guns. Did he tell you he was going to his car to get a gun?

Sanz: I told you, no. He was leaving. I told him to leave and he was leaving. I locked the door and that was it.

Barnett: It doesn't add up, Lucinda. You have to help us here. He's in your house. He walks out and he is shot from behind. Was somebody else in your house?

Sanz: No, nobody. Just me and Eric.

Barnett: Do you know what gunshot residue is?

Sanz: No.

Barnett: Well, when you fire a gun, microscopic particles explode out of the gun. You can't see them but they get on your hands and your arms and your clothes. Remember a deputy took samples from you at the house? He wiped your hands with those little round pads?

Sanz: It was a she. The deputy who did that.

Barnett: Well, the test came back positive. You had gunshot residue on your hands and that means you fired a weapon, Lucinda. So stop all the lies and talk to us. Work with us here. What happened?

Sanz: I told you, it wasn't me. I wouldn't shoot him.

Barnett: How do you explain the gunshot residue?

Sanz: I don't know. I can't. I think I want to have a lawyer now.

Barnett: Are you sure about that? We could clear all of this up right now so you can get back home with your boy.

Sanz: I didn't do this.

Samuels: Last chance, Lucinda. You call a lawyer and we can't help you anymore.

Sanz: I want to call a lawyer.

Barnett: Okay, this is over. You're under arrest for the murder of Roberto Sanz. Please —

Sanz: No, I didn't.

Barnett: Stand up now. We're going to book you. And your lawyer will come see you.

I put the transcript aside and looked out the window. The freeway was elevated out here and I could see the tops of businesses and signs on poles high enough to be seen by the people in cars speeding by. I was angry. I had yet to meet Lucinda Sanz but I could tell she was unsophisticated in the ways of the police, despite having been married to a law officer. She'd tried to hold her own during the interview. She'd denied killing her ex. But she'd also given them many of the things they needed to make a case against her. She had talked herself through the gates.

"These guys..." I said. "Not very original."

"Who?" Bosch asked.

"The interviewers, Samuels and Barnett."

"How so?"

"Just leading her down the garden path with lies and false empathy. The old we-can-work-this-out routine. Just makes me mad."

"You'd be surprised how often that works. Most killers...they want to be understood."

"And they talk themselves right into jail."

"What did they lie to her about?"

"More like what didn't they lie to her about. But for starters they ran the GSR game on her. She didn't bite."

"Not sure that was a game if they told her she tested positive."

"It better be or we have a problem with this whole innocence thing. Why don't you think they were gaming her?"

"It was in one of the newspaper stories I read. Back when I was... well, we usually didn't put our lies in the press releases. So I figure that part is true. She tested positive for GSR."

"Get off at the next exit."

"Why?"

"We're turning around. I've wasted enough time on this."

"Because of GSR?"

"I'm looking for habeas cases. I told you that, Harry. If she had gunshot residue on her hands, then we're fucked."

"GSR is not an exact science. I had cases... the lawyers brought in experts with whole lists of household products they claimed would pull the same result on the swipe pad."

"Yeah, that was the inexact-science defense. A desperate move to sow doubt with a jury that won't get us through the courtroom door on a habeas petition."

"Look, we're only ten minutes away from Chino. Let's just go talk to her."

I looked down at the transcript again and shook my head. I was changing my opinion of Second-Place Silver. Maybe he had gotten Lucinda Sanz the best outcome possible.

"Look," I said, "just so we're clear. Her appellate window would have closed at least two years ago. The only way back into this case is through a habeas petition offering new evidence that supports actual innocence. Then, by the way, we have to put up or shut up. We have to prove her innocent, like we did with Ochoa. So, fine, we can eat our po' boys and then go in and talk to her. But if it's not there, we're done with this one and we'll move on to the next."

Bosch said nothing. I waited for his eyes to show in the rearview.

"So we're cool?" I said.

"Totally," Bosch said. "We're cool."

10

WE SAT AT a table in an attorney-client room at the prison in Chino and waited for the guards to bring in Lucinda Sanz. I could hear the muffled sounds of steel doors banging and loudspeaker commands from guards. The sounds of a prison, even a prison for women, were never pleasant, even when muffled by concrete walls and steel.

"How are you going to start with her?" Bosch asked.

"The usual," I said. "Begin with open-enders and then narrow the focus if we hear something good. But first she's got to sign the papers or we're out of here."

Before Bosch could ask any further questions, the door opened and a female guard walked Lucinda Sanz into the room. I stood up, gave her my best smile, and nodded; Bosch stayed seated. She was placed in a chair across the table from us, then one wrist was locked to a bar that was bolted to the side of the table.

"Thank you, Officer," I said.

The guard said nothing and left the room. I lowered my eyes

to Lucinda and started to sit down. She was a small woman in a short-sleeved blue jumpsuit. She had light brown skin complemented by dark brown eyes and hair tied back in a short tail. She wore a long-sleeved T-shirt beneath the jumpsuit, probably for warmth. She didn't smile back at me and I thought that was because she thought we were detectives. Bosch gave off that air, even at his age. It was a non-court day, so I wore no tie.

"Lucinda, you sent me a letter. I'm Michael Haller, the attorney."

Now she smiled and nodded.

"Yes, yes, yes," she said. "The Lincoln Lawyer. Will you take my case?"

"Well, that's what we're here to talk about," I said. "Before we start, I want you to understand a little bit about this situation. First off, this is Harry Bosch, my investigator and the one who thinks there could be merit to your claim of innocence."

"Oh, thank you," Sanz said. "I am innocent."

Bosch just nodded. I noticed that she spoke with a slight accent.

"I also need to tell you something up front," I said. "I am not promising you anything. If you agree to take me on as your attorney, we will diligently investigate your case, and if we find a cause of action that we can take into court, then we will do that. But again, no promises. As you probably know, being innocent is not enough in court. In your situation, you must prove your innocence. In fact, at this point, you are guilty until proven innocent."

She was nodding before I finished.

"I understand," she said. "But I did not kill my husband."

"Your ex-husband, you mean," I corrected. "But let me finish. If you want me to represent you in this matter, I will need you to sign an engagement form that gives me your power of attorney and allows me to represent you in all criminal and civil matters that may arise from this case. That means if this criminal case happens to lead to a civil case, I am your attorney all the way on that. You understand?"

"Yes. I will sign."

I opened the file I had placed on the table upon our arrival and removed the engagement letter and agreement.

"There is a fee schedule attached to this that you may want to look at before you sign," I said.

"I don't have money," Sanz said.

"I understand. You don't need money. I collect only if you collect. I get a portion for my good work in getting you money. But we don't have to think about that. That is far off in never-never land at the moment. What is important now is seeing if we have a shot at getting you out of here."

I slid the document across the table to her.

"Before you sign, one more thing," I said. "The document is in English. Are you comfortable with that and with speaking English with us today?"

"Yes," Lucinda said. "I was born here. I've been speaking English my whole life."

"Okay, good. I just needed to check because I noticed a slight accent."

"My parents came from Guadalajara. When I grew up, we spoke Spanish at home."

I took out a pen and put it down on the document. Because one of her hands was manacled to the pipe at the side of the table, I anchored the document with my hand so it wouldn't slide when she signed it.

"Do you want to read it first?" I asked.

"No," Sanz said. "I trust you. I know what you did for Jorge Ochoa."

She signed the document and I slid it back across the table and into the file. She handed me the pen and I put it away.

"Thank you," I said. "We now have an attorney-client relationship. This includes Mr. Bosch as my investigator. You can tell me anything right now and it will never be revealed outside of these four walls."

"I understand," Sanz said.

"And I also need to make you aware of what's at stake here so that you can decide what the risks are and whether you want us to proceed."

"I'm already in prison."

"Yes, but you have a sentence that you are serving and will eventually be released from. If we move forward with a motion to reexamine your case in what is called a habeas petition, there is a risk involved. There can be three outcomes. One is that the petition is denied and you serve out your sentence. Another is that your conviction is vacated and you are set free. But there is also a third possibility: that a judge vacates your conviction but you are held to stand trial. And if that happens, you could be convicted by a jury and face a much harsher sentence — up to life without parole."

"I don't care. I am innocent."

I paused for a moment to consider how quickly she had responded. No hesitation about the risks. She had said it without blinking or taking her eyes off mine. It reassured me that if this case eventually did land in a trial, Lucinda would be able to look at the jury — whether from the defense table or the witness stand — with the same indomitable stare.

"Okay," I said. "I just want you to be aware of the risks of moving forward."

"Thank you," she said.

"Okay, then, like I said, we have attorney-client privilege now. Anything you say remains confidential. So I need to start by asking: Is there anything you need to tell me and that I need to know about this case?"

"I did not kill him. That's what you need to know."

I held her eyes for a long moment before continuing. Again, she didn't look away as liars often do. It was another good sign.

"Then, hopefully, there is something we can do for you," I said. "I have a few questions and then Mr. Bosch will have more. We have about forty minutes left and I want to make the best of them. Is that okay, Lucinda?"

"Yes, okay. But people call me Cindi."

"Cindi. Okay. Cindi, why don't we start with you telling me how you came to hire Mr. Silver as your attorney back when you were arrested?"

Sanz had to think for a moment before responding.

"I didn't have money for a lawyer," she finally said.

"So he was appointed?" I asked.

"No, I had the public defender. But then Mr. Silver, he went to them and he volunteered. He said he would take my case."

"But you said you had no money. I saw that you signed a document with credit card information."

"He told me he could get the credit cards for me and I could pay that way."

I nodded and knew that my early assessment of Silver as a weasel had been spot-on. Lucinda Sanz was in trouble from the start.

"Okay," I said. "Now, looking over your sentence, you got mid-range plus the gun enhancement and that totaled eleven years. With good behavior, you'd do about nine years max. So here you are, more than halfway through your sentence, and your letter to me indicates a desperation to get out. Is there something going on in this place? Are you in danger? Do we need to get you moved?"

"No, this place is good. Very close to my family. But my son, he needs me now."

"Your son. That's Eric, right? What's going on with him?"

"He's with my mother in the old neighborhood."

"How old is Eric?"

"He's going to be fourteen."

"Where's the old neighborhood?"

"Boyle Heights."

East L.A. I knew that the White Fence gang was deeply entrenched in Boyle Heights and membership recruitment started as young as twelve years old. I turned and gave Bosch a slight nod. We both understood that Lucinda Sanz wanted to get out of prison to save her son from going down that path.

"You grew up in Boyle Heights?" I asked. "How did you end up in Palmdale?"

"Quartz Hill," Sanz said. "When my husband got out of jail division, they put him there at Antelope Valley. So we moved."

"Was he from Boyle Heights too?" Bosch asked.

"Yes," Sanz said. "We grew up together."

"Was he White Fence?" Bosch asked.

"No," Sanz said. "But his brother and his father . . . yes."

"What about when he started at the sheriff's department?" Bosch asked. "Did he join any of the deputy gangs?"

Sanz was silent for a long moment. I wished Bosch had eased into that question with a little more finesse.

"He had friends," she said. "He told me they had cliques, you know."

"Did Roberto join a clique?" Bosch asked.

"Not when we were married," Sanz said. "I don't know what happened after. But he changed."

"How long before his death did you divorce?" I asked.

"It was three years," Sanz said.

"What happened?" I asked. "To the marriage, I mean."

I read the look on Sanz's face. She wondered what this had to do with whether or not she was innocent. I wished I had used a little more finesse myself.

"Cindi, we need to know as much as we can about your relationship with the victim," I said. "I know that it's painful to recount all of this, but we need to hear it from you."

She nodded.

"We just...he had girlfriends," Sanz said. "Deputy dollies. When he started doing that, he changed. We changed, and I said that's it. I don't like to talk about it."

"I'm sorry," I said. "We can drop it for now. But we may need to come back to it. Do you know the names of any of these women?"

"No, I didn't want to know them," Sanz said.

"How did you know about them?" I asked.

"I just knew," Sanz said. "He was different."

"Was it a source of argument after the divorce?"

"After? No. I didn't care what he did after we divorced."

"So the argument that night was about him being late with Eric."

"He was always late. On purpose."

I nodded and looked at Bosch.

"Harry, you have more questions?" I asked.

"I have a few," Bosch said. "Who were some of his friends in the department and at the substation?"

"He was on the gang team," Sanz said. "They were his friends. I don't know their names."

"He had a tattoo on his hip," Bosch said. "Below the beltline. Do you know when he got it?"

Sanz shook her head.

"I didn't know about that," she said. "He didn't have tattoos when we were together."

Since we had not choreographed the interview before getting there, I wasn't sure why Bosch was trying to determine when Roberto

Sanz had gotten the tattoo. I decided I'd wait and ask about it on the drive back to the city.

Bosch then asked another question I hadn't seen coming.

"Would it be possible for me to talk to Eric?"

"Why?" Sanz responded.

"To see what he remembers about his father," Bosch said. "And about that night."

"No," Sanz said emphatically. "I don't want that. I don't want him to be part of this."

"But he already is, Cindi," I said. "He was there that night. More important, he was with his father all day before coming home to you. As far as we know, no one ever talked to him about what happened that day. I want to know why his father was two hours late getting him home."

"He's thirteen now," Bosch said. "Maybe he remembers something about that day that will help us. That will help you."

Sanz pursed her lips as if she were getting ready to dig in her heels on her refusal to give permission. But then she changed course.

"I will ask him," she said. "If he says yes, then yes, you can talk to him."

"Good," I said. "We'll do our best not to upset him."

"That will be impossible if you are asking about his father's death," Sanz said. "Eric loved his father. My greatest pain is for him to have his mother in prison for killing his father when I know I didn't do it."

"I understand," I said and nodded. I tried to move on. "How often do you and Eric talk?"

"Once or twice each week," Sanz said. "More if I get phone access."

"Does he come to visit you?"

"Once a month. He comes with my mother."

There was a momentary pause as I considered how much this woman had lost whether she was innocent or not. Bosch barged into the silent space, once again without any finesse.

"The gun is not going to show up, is it?" he asked.

Lucinda seemed baffled by the sudden change in direction. I knew that this was a police tactic — ask questions out of sequence or out of context to generate reactions and keep interview subjects from getting too comfortable.

When Lucinda didn't answer, Bosch pressed.

"The gun used to kill your ex has never turned up," Bosch said. "It won't now, will it?"

"I have no idea!" Sanz yelled. "How would I know?"

"I don't know," Bosch said. "That's why I asked. I'm worried that the gun could turn up while we're in the middle of this and that could cause us and you a lot of problems."

"I did not kill my husband and I don't know who did," Sanz said with a sharp edge to her voice. "And I don't have the gun."

She looked fixedly at Bosch until he looked away. One more time I saw the unblinking stare. I was starting to believe her. And that, I knew from experience, was a dangerous place to be.

11

I DROVE BACK. Bosch took the front passenger seat and went through the pocket file from Frank Silver, apparently to show me that a review of the case could be done without spreading it out on the rear seat. I acted like I didn't notice and kept my eyes on the road, thinking about Lucinda Sanz and how I might be able to save her.

Going to the prison had been the right call. Seeing her in person, hearing her voice and watching her eyes, made all the difference. She became more than a person at the center of a legal case to me. She became real, and in the sincerity of her words I sensed the truth. I sensed that she might be that rarest of all creatures: an innocent client.

But that belief only left me feeling hollow as I drove back to the city. What my gut was telling me meant nothing in a court of law. I had to find a way. And though it was early in the case, I also knew that in front of me was a daunting task that would leave deep scars on me if I failed.

Bosch and I had stayed with Lucinda and questioned her until the moment when the humorless guard who had brought her into the interview room returned to take her out. Lucinda left with a piece of paper with our phone numbers on it and a promise from us to do our best in evaluating the case and quickly coming to a decision on how to proceed. That, too, would be hollow if the ultimate decision was to do nothing because there was nothing I could do.

I glanced over at Bosch. We had not spoken about Lucinda since we'd left the prison. I'd offered to drive and Bosch had taken me up on it. He got right into the pocket file once we were on the road. He barely looked up the whole way, even when I hit the brakes and the horn a few times.

"What are you thinking, Harry?" I finally asked.

"Well," Bosch said. "I've sat across the table from a lot of killers over the years. Most of them can't look you right in the eye and deny it. She scored points with me for that."

I nodded.

"Me too. I had the craziest idea in that room when she was telling us she didn't do it."

"What was that?"

"I had this idea of putting her on the stand and letting her win the judge over."

"I thought you always preached the opposite. Clients should stay out of the witness chair. Wasn't it you who said people talk themselves into prison?"

"I did say that, and I do normally preach it. I like to say that the only way my client is going to testify is if I miss the tackle, but something about her makes me think she could win. Judges are different from juries. They see so many liars. They hope someday to hear the truth. I think Silver should have talked her out of the deal and taken it to court. She could win a jury too. That failure alone was five-oh-four material, if you ask me."

"Five-oh-four?"

"Ineffective assistance of counsel. I told Silver I wouldn't take it that way, but now I'm not so sure. It would buy us some time, at least."

"How so?"

"I file a habeas motion based on ineffective assistance, and that becomes our placeholder with the court. Gives us time to come up with something better before we go in front of the judge."

"If there is something better."

"Well, that's actually what I meant when I asked what you were thinking. I wasn't really asking about Lucinda. I meant the files. Anything helpful to our cause?"

"Well, there's not a lot here, but the chrono is revealing."

"How so?"

"I think you could make an argument for tunnel vision. Once the GSR came back positive on Lucinda, they ignored everyone else."

"They focused solely on her?"

"Pretty much. The chrono says they initially called out the sergeant who oversaw the gang-suppression unit Roberto Sanz was assigned to. A guy named Stockton. They wanted to talk about the possibility that Roberto was killed in revenge for his taking out that gangbanger in the shooting the year before. But it looks like that line of inquiry stopped as soon as the GSR came back and pointed at Lucinda."

"Good. That might be something I could use down the road. Anything else?"

"Just that. They dropped all other possible avenues of investigation once they had the GSR test."

I nodded approvingly. Tunnel vision was a defense lawyer's best friend. You show that the cops were not looking at other possibilities and it can make a jury suspicious. When you've got them suspicious, you've got them losing respect for the integrity of the investigators and you've sown the seeds of doubt. Reasonable doubt. Of course, a habeas petition would be decided not by a jury but by a judge who would be wise to the tricks of the trade and much harder to convince. But Bosch's observation was still a good thing to have in my back pocket.

"I could look into that angle," Bosch said. "The revenge aspect."

"No," I said. "That's not our job. Our job is to prove our client innocent. Pointing out that the original investigators were lazy or had tunnel vision helps our cause. But we're not going to chase alternative theories. We don't have time for that."

"Got it."

"This is different, Harry. You're not a homicide investigator. We're not solving the crime. We're proving Lucinda didn't do it. There's a difference."

"I said I got it."

Bosch went back to the file and started reading again. A few minutes later, he stopped. "Her story hasn't changed," he said. "I'm reading the transcript from the police interview. Her story back then was exactly what it was today. That's gotta count for something."

"Yes, but not enough. It's an indicator of truthfulness, like the eye contact, but we need more. A lot more. By the way, why did you ask her back there about when Roberto got the tattoo?"

"I think it's important to know. You get a tattoo and it's sort of a life statement."

"Says the man with a rat tat on his arm."

"That's another story. But to get a tattoo that most people won't see, that says something. I just thought it would be good to know, but it came after they split."

"Got it."

Bosch continued reading the file. We were halfway back to Los Angeles. I started thinking about next steps with the case and whether to take it federal or state. There were arguments for and against both. Federal judges weren't beholden to the electorate and would not hesitate to set a convicted murderer free if the evidence of innocence was there. But with lighter caseloads, federal jurists were generally more scrupulous in their consideration of motions and evidence.

My phone rang over the car's Bluetooth connection. It was Lucinda Sanz calling collect from the prison. I accepted the call and told her that Bosch and I were still driving back to the city and we were both listening.

"I called my mother and she put Eric on so I could talk to him," she said. "He said he would talk to you."

"When?" I asked.

"Whenever you want," she said. "He's at the house now."

I looked over at Bosch and he nodded. It had been his idea to talk to the boy.

"And your mother would be all right with it?" I asked.

"She said yes," Lucinda said.

"All right, give me her number and I'll call and tell her we're heading there now."

"Today? Are you sure?"

"Might as well, Cindi. We've got the time today. I don't know about tomorrow."

She gave the number and I saw Bosch write it down. I hit the mute button on the dashboard screen. "You got anything you want to ask while we have her?" I asked.

He hesitated but then nodded. I took the mute off.

"Cindi?" I asked.

"Yes," she said.

"Harry has something he wants to ask," I said. "Go ahead, Harry."

Bosch leaned toward the center of the dashboard as if he thought he could be heard more clearly that way.

"Cindi," he said. "Do you remember being told by the detectives that your arms and hands tested positive for gunshot residue?"

"They said that but it was a lie," Lucinda said. "I didn't shoot the gun."

"I know, and that's what you told them. My question is about the test. In the interview with the detectives, they said a man tested you but you told them it was a woman. Do you remember that?"

"The deputy just came up to me and said she had to test me for a gun. And she wiped my hands and my arms and the front of my jacket."

"So it was definitely a female?"

"Yes."

"Did you know her or get her name?"

Before she could answer, an electronic voice interrupted the call and announced the connection would be terminated in one minute. Bosch prompted Lucinda once the interruption was over.

"Cindi, who was the deputy who tested you?"

"I don't know. I don't think she told me her name. She said she worked with Robbie. I remember that."

"Was she a detective?"

"I don't know."

"Well, was she in a sheriff's uniform or plain clothes?"

"No, she was in regular clothes. She had her badge on a chain."

"Around her neck?"

"Yes."

"Would you know her if you saw her again?"

"Uh, I'm not so sure . . . I think yes, I —"

The call ended.

"Shit, she's gone," Bosch said.

"What was that about?" I asked.

"I'm reading the interview transcript right here. The detectives confront her with the GSR and explain that a deputy, who they don't name but refer to as he, swiped her for GSR. Then she says it was a she."

"Okay. So what's the issue?"

"Well, the whole thing reads as off to me. I don't know what the sheriff's department crime scene protocols are but they can't be that different from the LAPD's. And I can tell you, at the LAPD, gunshot-residue testing is done by the detectives. Or at the very least, a criminalist. Definitely not somebody who works with the victim."

I now remembered reading the exchange in the transcript. It hadn't raised a flag for me in the way it did for Bosch. But that was Bosch. I had seen it before. He had this facility for seeing the details and evidence of a case and how it all matched up, or didn't. He was playing chess while most people were playing checkers.

"Interesting," I finally said. "So it was a female detective?"

"Not necessarily," Bosch said. "It could have been somebody called in from home, no time to put on a uniform. But it sounds like somebody from Roberto's unit. Detectives usually carry the badge on the belt. A badge on a chain indicates a plainclothes unit, like gangs or drugs. They use the chain so they can hide it and pull it out when shit goes down, like a raid or at a crime scene."

"Got it."

Bosch began looking through the pockets in the file on his lap. I glanced over and saw him pull out a document.

"This is the first crime report. It has the names of the two deputies who first responded: Gutierrez and Spain."

"Well, we need to talk to them."

"Maybe not right away. Remember, you said no footprints till we're ready?"

I nodded. "Right."

Bosch pulled out another document.

"What's that?" I asked.

"The evidence log," Bosch said. "Tracks chain of custody."

He scanned it for a few moments before continuing.

"It says the GSR-swab disks were collected by a deputy named Keith Mitchell."

"We need to follow up on that."

"It might mean nothing. But I will."

"So how do you want to play talking to the boy?"

"I don't know yet. Let me finish the file first, then we can talk about it. Why don't you call Cindi's mother and tell her we're on the way?"

"Sounds like a plan."

12

THE HOUSE WHERE Lucinda Sanz grew up was on Mott Street in Boyle Heights. It was a neighborhood ravaged by gang graffiti and neglect. Many of the homes had white picket fences around the front lawns, a sign of allegiance and protection from the generationally entrenched street gang that ruled the neighborhood. Sanz's mother was named Muriel Lopez. Her home had the fence and a couple of gangbangers to go with it. Two men in chinos and wifebeaters that showed off their tattoo sleeves were hanging on the front porch as we pulled up to the curb.

"Oh, boy," I said. "Looks like we have a welcome committee."

Bosch glanced up from the report he was reading and looked at the two men, who were staring back at us.

"We have the right address?" he asked.

"Yep," I said. "This is the place."

"Just so you know, I'm not armed."

"I don't think it's going to be a problem."

We got out and I pushed through the gate in the picket fence ahead of Bosch.

"Fellas, we're here to see Ms. Lopez," I said. "She around?"

Both men were in their early thirties. One was tall, the other squat.

"You the lawyer?" the tall one asked.

"That's right," I said.

"And what about him?" he said. "Looks like po-po to me. Old-ass po-po."

"He's my investigator," I said. "That's why he's with me."

Before things could get any tenser, the front door opened and a woman with silver hair looked out and spoke in Spanish too fast for me to follow. It was as though I were looking at Lucinda in twenty years. Muriel had the same dark eyes and complexion, the same set of the jaw. Her hair, though silver-gray, was pulled back in a ponytail, revealing the same widow's peak as her daughter had.

The two men didn't respond to her but I could see them back down a few notches on the testosterone scale.

"Mr. Haller," the woman said. "I am Muriel. Please come in."

We stepped up onto the porch and moved toward the door. The two men parted and stood on either side of the house's entrance. It was the tall one who spoke again.

"You going to get Lucinda out?" he asked.

"We're sure going to try," I said.

"How much she have to pay you?"

"Nothing."

I held his eyes for a moment and then entered the house. Bosch passed by them next.

"You still look like police," the tall one said.

Bosch didn't reply. He just walked into the house, and Muriel closed the door.

"I will get Eric," she said.

"*Un momento,* Muriel," I said. "Who are those guys and how did they know we were coming?"

99

"The one who spoke to you is my son Carlos—Lucinda's little brother. Cesar is her cousin."

"You told them we were coming to talk to Eric?"

"They were here when you called to say you were coming."

"They live here?"

"No, they live down the street. But they come by."

I nodded and now had a firsthand understanding of Lucinda's urgency: she had to win her freedom so she could rescue her son from a future in a gang.

Muriel led us to the living room and said she would go get Eric from his room. We heard muffled words while we waited and then finally Muriel returned holding Eric Sanz's hand. He wore green shorts and a white polo shirt and red-and-black gym shoes. I immediately saw the unmistakable continuance of genetic heritage. The dark eyes, light brown skin, and hairline were all there. In a matter of a few hours I had seen three generations of this family. But the boy seemed smaller and more delicate than I'd imagined he would be at thirteen. His shirt was at least two sizes too big and hung off his bony shoulders.

I started to regret asking Lucinda to allow me to talk to this small boy about the death of his father and the conviction of his mother because he looked so fragile. Bosch and I had worked things out on our final approach to Boyle Heights and decided that he would handle the questioning after an introduction from me. I hoped that Harry would get the same vibe I'd gotten and go gently with the interview.

The living room was overcrowded with furniture and family pictures on the walls and tables. There were many of Lucinda and of Eric as a younger child. It seemed to me that the photos would not be on display if Eric had grown up believing in his mother's guilt.

Bosch and I sat on a chocolate-brown couch with worn and out-of-shape cushions, while Eric and his grandmother sat across from us on a matching chair wide enough for them both. Muriel had not offered us coffee, water, or anything besides an audience with our client's son.

"Eric, my name is Mickey Haller," I began. "I am your mother's lawyer. And this is Harry Bosch, an investigator. We are trying to get your mother home to you. We want to take her case into court and prove to the judge that she did not do the thing they say she did. You understand, Eric?"

"Yes," he said. The boy's voice was small and tentative.

"We know this is difficult for you," I said. "So if at any point you feel like you want a break or want to stop, just say so and we'll stop. Is that okay with you?"

"Okay."

"Good, Eric. Because we really want to try to help your mother if we can. I'm sure you wish she could be home with you."

"Yes."

"Good. So now I'll let Harry take over. Thank you for talking to us, Eric. Harry?"

I looked over and saw that Bosch had a pen and notepad out and ready.

"Harry, no notes," I said. "Let's just talk."

Bosch nodded, probably thinking my instruction came from a desire to be less formal with the boy. I would explain to him later that written notes could end up in the opposition's hands through discovery requests. It was one of the rules I operated by — no notes, no discovery. Bosch would need to adjust his methods if he stuck with defense work.

"Okay, Eric," Bosch said, "I want to start with a few basic questions. You are thirteen years old?"

"Yes."

"And which school do you go to?"

"Home school."

I looked over to Muriel for confirmation.

"Yes, I teach Eric," she said. "The children at the school were cruel."

I took that to mean that Eric had been bullied or taunted about his size or maybe, if the other children knew, about having his mother in prison for killing his father. Bosch rolled with it and kept going.

"Do you like any sports, Eric?" he asked.

"I like football," Eric said.

"Which football? Soccer or, like, the Rams?"

"I like the Chargers."

Bosch nodded and smiled.

"Me too. But that was a bad exit last year. Have you been to a game yet?"

"No, not yet."

Bosch nodded.

"So, like Mr. Haller said, we want to try to help your mother," he said. "And I know it was an awful day when you lost your father and your mother was taken away, but I was wondering if we could talk about that. Do you remember that day, Eric?"

The boy looked down at his hands clasped between his knees.

"Yes," he said.

"Good," Bosch said. "Do you remember, did the sheriff's deputies ever talk to you about what you may have seen or heard that day?"

"There was a lady. She talked to me."

"Did she have on a uniform? With a badge?"

"No uniform. She had a badge on a chain. She put me in the car in the back seat where they put the bad people."

"You mean when people are arrested?"

"Yes, but we didn't do anything wrong."

"Of course not. I bet she said she was putting you there so you'd be safe."

Eric shrugged. "I don't know."

"Did she interview you in the car?"

"She asked me questions about my mom and dad."

"Do you remember what you told her?"

"Just that they were yelling at each other and my mom said I had to go to my room."

"Did you see or hear anything else?"

"Not really. They said my mom shot my dad, but I didn't see that."

Muriel put her arm around the boy and squeezed him against her body.

"No, *mijo,* no," she said. "Your mother is *inocente.*"

The boy nodded and looked like he was about to cry. I wondered if I should step in and end the interview. It did not appear that Eric would be giving us any information that deviated from what was already known. I was left curious about who had interviewed him, because there was no transcript of an interview in the admittedly incomplete records we had amassed from Silver and the court file from archives. My guess was that Eric had not been viewed as a key witness because of his age—eight at the time—and the fact that he had been in his room and did not witness the shooting.

Bosch continued, moving off the actual killing and in a new direction.

"You spent that weekend with your father, didn't you?" he asked.

"Yes," Eric said.

"Do you remember what you did with him?"

"We stayed at his apartment and Matty made us dinner one night and then—"

"Let me back you up for a second, Eric. Who is Matty?"

"That was my dad's girlfriend."

"Okay, got it. So she made dinner. Was that on the Saturday?"

"Yes."

"And what about Sunday?"

"We went to Chuck E. Cheese."

"Was that near where your dad lived?"

"I think so. I don't know."

"And it was just you and your dad or did Matty go too?"

"Matty came. She watched me when my dad had to leave."

"How come he had to leave?"

"He got called on the phone and then he said he had a work meeting he had to go to. And I got to stay and play until he came back."

"Is that why you got back late to your mother's house?"

"I don't remember."

"That's okay, Eric. You're doing great. Do you remember anything else about that day besides going to Chuck E. Cheese with your dad and Matty?"

"Not really. Sorry."

"No, don't be sorry. You've given us a lot of information. One last question. Did Matty go with you and your dad when you were dropped off at home?"

"No, my dad took her back to the apartment first because he thought my mom would be mad if she came."

"I see. So she just got out at the apartment."

"They went inside while I stayed in the car. Then he came out and we went. It was dark."

"When you two were heading back to your home, did your dad say anything else about why he had to go to work?"

"No. I don't remember."

"Did you tell the lady who talked to you in the car about his meeting that day?"

"I can't remember."

"Okay, Eric. Thanks. Is there anything you want to ask me or Mr. Haller?"

The boy shrugged his shoulders and looked from Bosch to me and then back.

"Will you get my mom out of prison?" he asked.

"We can't promise anything. But like Mr. Haller said, we're sure going to try."

"Do you think she did it?"

There it was. The question the boy lived with every day of his life.

"Tell you what, Eric," Bosch said, "I will never lie to you. So I'll say this: I don't know yet. But there are enough things about the case that don't work for me, that don't add up, you know what I mean? So I think there is a chance they made a mistake about her and she didn't do it. I'm going to investigate it more and then I'll come back here and tell you what I know. And I won't lie. Is that okay with you?"

"Okay," Eric said.

The interview was over. We all stood up, and Muriel told Eric he could go back to his room to play on his computer. After he was gone, I looked at Muriel.

"Do you know who Matty is?" I asked.

"Matilda Landas," she said. "Roberto's whore."

She almost spit the words out. She had a deeper accent than her daughter and the words came out sharp and bitter. I recalled what Lucinda had said about deputy dollies being a cause for the destruction of her marriage.

"Was Roberto involved with her before the marriage broke up?" I asked.

"He denied it," Muriel said. "But he was a liar."

"Have you heard from her or seen her since then?" Bosch asked.

"I don't know where she is," Muriel said. "I don't want to know. *Puta!*"

"Well, I think we'll leave it at that, then," I said. "Thank you for your time, Muriel, and for allowing us to talk to Eric. He seems like a bright kid. You must be a good teacher."

"It's my job to make him a good man," she said. "But it is hard. The gangs want him."

"I understand," I said.

I considered suggesting that she limit his exposure to Uncle Carlos and Cousin Cesar but decided against it.

"You must get her out so she can take him away from here," Muriel said.

"We're going to try."

"Thank you."

Muriel's eyes revealed her hope that her daughter would come home soon. Bosch and I thanked her again and headed to the door.

After Muriel closed the front door behind us, I saw one of the men from the welcoming committee sitting in a blanket-covered chair on the porch. He stood up. He was the talker from before, Lucinda's little brother, Carlos.

"Lincoln Lawyer," he said. "I seen you on the billboard. You look like a clown up there in your *pinche pendejo* car."

"Probably not my best shot," I said. "But I guess it's a matter of opinion."

He walked up close to me, holding his hands together to better flex his heavily inked biceps. In my peripheral vision I could tell Bosch had tensed. I smiled, hoping to defuse the situation.

"I take it you're Eric's uncle Carlos?" I said.

"Don't fuck this up, Lincoln Lawyer," he said.

"I don't intend to."

"Promise it."

"I don't make promises. Too many vari—"

"There will be consequences if you fuck up."

"Then how 'bout I quit right now and you explain that to your sister."

"You can't quit now, Lincoln Lawyer. You are in."

He stepped aside to let me go down the steps.

"Remember: consequences," he said to my back. "Make it right, or I'm gonna make it right."

I waved without looking back.

13

BOSCH TOOK THE reins of the Navigator and we pulled out of Mott Street. He said something about being prepared to take evasive action should any other White Fence gangsters want an audience with the Lincoln Lawyer. I told him to take Cesar Chavez Avenue over to Eastern, where we made an unscheduled stop at Home of Peace Memorial Park. I directed him to the main chapel and told him to pull off to the side of the access road.

"I won't be long."

I got out and walked into the chapel and down one of the hallways lined with the names of the dead. I had not been here in almost a year and it took me a few minutes to locate the etched brass plaque I had paid for. But there it was, between someone named Neufeld and someone else named Katz.

DAVID "LEGAL" SIEGEL

ATTORNEY-AT-LAW

1932–2022

"ALL GOOD THINGS COME TO AN END"

It was as he had wanted it, as he had written it out in his last requests. I just stood there for a quiet moment, the light coming through the colored glass on the wall behind me.

I missed him a lot. In and out of the courtroom, I had learned more from Legal Siegel than from any parent, professor, judge, or attorney I'd ever known. He was the one who'd taken me under his wing and showed me how to be a lawyer and a man. I wished he'd been with me to see Jorge Ochoa walk out of prison a free man, no legal strings attached. There were not-guilty verdicts to cherish, cross-examinations to savor, and the adrenaline-charged moments when you just know the jury's eating out of the palm of your hand. I'd had all of those over the years. In spades. But nothing could ever beat the resurrection walk — when the manacles come off and the last metal doors slide open like the gates of heaven, and a man or woman declared innocent walks into the waiting arms of family, resurrected in life and the law. There is no better feeling in the world than being with that family and knowing you were the one who made it so.

Frank Silver was wrong about what he thought I was doing. Sure, there was long-shot money at the end of the rainbow. But that wasn't what I was looking for. With Jorge Ochoa, I had felt the adrenaline charge of the resurrection walk and I was now addicted to it. It might happen only once or twice in a lawyer's career, but I didn't care. I wanted that moment again and I'd do anything to get it. I wanted to stand outside the prison gates and welcome my client back to the land of the living. I didn't know if Lucinda Sanz would be that client. But the Lincoln Lawyer had a full tank and was ready to drive down Resurrection Road again.

I heard the chapel door open and soon Bosch was standing next to me. He followed my sightline to the plaque on the wall.

"Legal Siegel," he said. "What's he doing out here in Boyle Heights?"

"He was born here," I said.

"I had him as a Westside guy."

"Back in the thirties and forties, there were more Jews than Latinos in Boyle Heights. Did you know that? Instead of East Los it was called the Lower East Side. And Cesar Chavez Avenue? That was Brooklyn Avenue."

"You know your history."

"Legal Siegel knew it. He passed it on to me. A hundred fifty years ago, this cemetery was in Chavez Ravine. Then they dug everybody up and moved them over here."

"And now Chavez Ravine isn't even Chavez Ravine. It's a baseball field."

"Nothing in this city stays the same for very long."

"You got that right."

We stood in respectful silence for a few moments. Then Bosch spoke.

"How was he at the end?" he asked. "You know, with the dementia."

"Full on," I said. "He'd moved from knowing he had it and being scared shitless to being completely gone."

"Did he know you?"

"He thought I was my father. Same name but I could tell he thought I was him, his law partner for thirty years. He'd tell stories that at first I'd think were true but then I'd remember they were scenes from a movie. Like payoffs stuffed in shirt boxes from the laundry."

"Not true?"

"*Goodfellas*—you ever see it?"

"Missed it."

"Good movie."

We went silent again. I wished Bosch would go back to the car so I could have a private moment. I thought about the last time I had seen Legal Siegel. I had snuck a corned-beef sandwich from Canter's into his room at the hospice. But he didn't remember the place or the sandwich and didn't have the strength to eat it anyway. Two weeks later he was gone.

"You know, Canter's was over here too," I said. "The deli. Like a hundred years ago. Then they eventually moved out to Fairfax. *Shelley versus Kraemer* changed a lot of things."

"*Shelley versus Kraemer*?" Bosch asked.

"A case decided by the Supreme Court seventy-five years ago. It knocked down racial and ethnic covenants and restrictions on the sale of property. Jews, Blacks, Chinese—after that ruling, they could buy anywhere, live anywhere they liked. Of course, it still took a lot of courage. That same year Nat King Cole bought a house in Hancock Park and the bigots burned a cross on his lawn."

Bosch just nodded. I stayed up on the soapbox.

"Anyway, back then the Court was moving us forward. Toward the Great Society and all that. Now it seems to want to move us back."

After another moment of silence, Bosch pointed to the plaque.

"That saying about good things coming to an end," he said. "That was on the locked door at Chinese Friends the last time I tried to eat there."

I stepped up and put my hand on the wall, covering Legal's name, and held it there for a moment. I bowed my head.

"They got that right," I said.

We didn't talk about the threat from Carlos Lopez until we were back in the Navigator.

"So what do you think he meant about making it right if you don't make it right?" Bosch asked.

"No earthly idea," I said. "Guy's a gangster caught up in the macho-gangster ethos. Even he probably doesn't know what he meant by that."

"You don't take it as a threat?"

"Not a serious one. It's not the first time somebody thought they could make me work the law better by trying to scare me. Won't be the last. Let's get out of here, Harry. Take me back to my place."

"You got it."

PART THREE

SIDE EFFECTS

14

BOSCH COULD FEEL the isotope moving in him, coursing coldly through his veins, over the shoulder and across his chest like a broken-dam flood. He tried to concentrate on the open file in front of him. Edward Coldwell, fifty-seven, convicted of killing a business partner four years before, fresh out of appeals and asking the Lincoln Lawyer to work a miracle in his name.

Bosch was only halfway through the file he'd put together with case documents from the court archives. Coldwell had gone to trial and the jury had believed the evidence against him over his denials. Now it was up to Bosch to determine if the case was worthy of the Lincoln Lawyer's time and efforts.

Bosch had decided to do the deep dive into Coldwell's case solely on the basis of the letter the convicted murderer had sent to Haller. The majority of requests for Haller's legal expertise came with repeated claims of innocence and allegations of prosecutorial abuse and evidence missed or improperly dismissed. Coldwell's letter had its fair share of that but it also contained what seemed to be a sincere plea to reveal the real killer and stop him from killing someone else. Bosch had not seen that in the other requests he'd reviewed and it struck a chord. In his forty-plus-year career of working murder cases, he had been motivated in part by the same sentiment — that if he could catch the killer, he would save another victim and another family from destruction down the line.

The case had been handled by the Los Angeles Police Department. The lead detective had been a solid investigator named Gusto Garcia, whom Bosch knew and respected. He was one of the old bulls in the Homicide Special Unit who had been there before Bosch joined the unit and was still there when he left. When Bosch saw Garcia's name on the author line of the first case summary, he almost stopped his review there. He didn't think Garcia would have blown the case — that is, sent an innocent man to prison for a murder he didn't commit. But the file was all he had brought with him to read and he probably had a half hour or more before he'd be released by the research team.

So he kept reading. Garcia had kept a neat and lengthy chronological record of the investigation and that made it an enjoyable read for someone of Bosch's experience. But page after page, he saw nothing amiss. No lead unfollowed, no step not taken, no interview skipped. In Coldwell's initial letter to Mickey Haller, he'd claimed he'd been set up to take the fall for the murder of Spiro Apodaca, the man whose Silver Lake restaurant Coldwell had invested in. According to the reports and evidence Bosch had already gotten through, the two had a falling-out over what Apodaca had done with that investment and it had led to murder. Coldwell had been convicted largely on the strength of testimony from the hit man he had allegedly contracted to kill Apodaca. The killer for hire, John Mullin, had been identified and arrested thanks to Garcia's good work and he'd elected to make a deal with prosecutors to testify against the man who'd hired him for the hit in exchange for leniency on his sentence.

As far as Bosch could see, the only possible way that Coldwell could be innocent was if Mullin had lied about who hired him to kill Apodaca. The file Bosch had had copied in the archives contained a transcript of Mullin's trial testimony. Bosch had yet to do a deep dive on it, but he'd skimmed it and seen that Mullin was battered during questioning by Coldwell's defense attorney but did not change his story: Coldwell had reached out to him through an intermediary and hired him to kill Apodaca for $25,000 in cash up front and an equal amount upon completion of the job. In testimony, Mullin said Coldwell stiffed him on the second payment, which explained his readiness to testify against him.

Bosch was engrossed in a lengthy entry in the chrono about Garcia and his partner running down how Coldwell accumulated the cash he'd allegedly paid to Mullin. It involved cashing checks and making ATM withdrawals in small amounts over several weeks until it finally added up to $25,000. The amounts were listed in a column in the chrono entry. Bosch was going over the math, so he didn't look up when the door to his room was opened. He assumed it was the NMT coming to check his IV bag.

"Hi, Dad."

Bosch looked up and saw his daughter. She was in tight-fitting workout clothes and Nikes.

"Mads, how'd you get in here?" he said. "I don't think it's safe."

"They told me it was fine," Maddie said. "Said I could just walk back."

"You sure? The NMT said that?"

"The nurse up front. What is an NMT?"

"Nuclear medicine technician. She's the one who sticks the needle in, hangs the bag, starts the process. But I think she wears a lead vest when she comes in here," Bosch said.

"Probably because she's exposed all the time," Maddie said. "Or she wants to have babies."

"She's at least sixty years old."

"Oh. Well, I'm not going to stay that long. I just wanted to come at least one time to see what they're doing to you. And to drive you home."

"I can take an Uber. That's what I usually do. I still don't think you should be in here. And we shouldn't share a car. You might want to have babies someday."

"Dad, let me do this, okay?"

"Okay, okay. Thank you for coming. We'll ask the doctor if it's all right."

"Fine. Whatever."

She pointed to the IV bag.

"So that's the stuff," she said. "What exactly is in it?"

"That's just saline," Bosch said. "It goes from there to the radio-active isotope, which then goes into me. Supposedly they put enough in to kill the cancer but not enough to kill the patient—me. That's the trick."

Maddie seemed hesitant in her response, but then she blurted out the key question.

"Do they know if it's working?" she asked.

"Not yet," Bosch said. "This is my last dose and then in a couple months they'll run some tests and see what's going on."

"I'm sorry, Dad, to make you go through this. I know you didn't...really want to."

"No, it was my call. And look, if I can stick around a little longer, I get to watch you become the cop you will be, and I may even get some good work done too."

He gestured to the side table and the file he had been reading.

"Is that one of the innocence-project cases?" she asked.

"Yes," Bosch said. "But you can't call it that or the real Innocence Project may take offense."

"Got it. So what do you call it, then?"

"Good question. I don't know if Mickey has a name for it yet."

"What's the case you have there?"

"Guy convicted of hiring a hit man to take out his business partner. Only he says he didn't hire him. Somebody else did. Problem is, the hit man testified against him at trial."

"So why are you looking at it?"

"I don't know, really. Something about his letter to Mickey struck me as worth a look. But maybe I was fooled. I got the whole file out of court archives and I'll read it through and then decide if it's worth pursuing further. I mean, what else am I going to do sitting here? Play video games on my phone?"

"That'll be the day. What about the other case? The one with the woman in..."

"Chino? Mickey's going to file for a habeas hearing and we're getting our ducks in a row for that. There are still a lot of holes to fill. Mickey's investigator Cisco just located a key witness I'll need to go talk to."

Maddie pointed to the IV bag again.

"But this will knock you down for a few days, won't it?"

"Maybe a day. I'm not sure. They've been increasing the dose each time, so, yeah, it'll put me on my back for a bit. At least the rest of the day."

"You have to quit working for Mickey and concentrate on your health. Be all in on this."

"Look, I'll be fine in —"

"I'm serious, Dad. Your health has to come first."

"But I think doing this work and being engaged is part of the whole picture, you know? I feel good when I'm doing this stuff. Otherwise I feel useless and I get depressed."

"I'm just saying you need to take it easy. If this treatment works, then you can go back to these cases. I mean, these people aren't going any—"

She cut herself off when the door opened and a man wearing a light blue lab coat entered. He had a trim build, eyeglasses, and thinning hair, but he looked to be no older than thirty. He didn't appear to be wearing a lead vest under his lab coat.

"Oh, didn't know you had a visitor, Harry," he said.

"My daughter, Maddie," Bosch said. "She's going to drive me home if you say she's safe doing that."

The man held his hand out to Maddie.

"Austin Ferras," he said. "Your dad's doctor."

"Oh," Maddie said.

"Is something wrong?" Ferras said. "I can come back."

"No, nothing's wrong," Maddie said. "I just...well, I guess I was expecting someone a bit older."

"I get that all the time," Ferras said. "But don't worry, your dad is in good hands. He's got me and a lot of people watching over him. And you're safe to drive him. Harry may be ornery but he's not particularly radioactive."

Ferras turned to Bosch.

"How do you feel today, Harry?"

"Bored," Bosch said.

Ferras stepped over to the IV pole and inspected the bag. He reached up and flicked it with a finger.

"Just about done here," he said. "I'll get Gloria in to disconnect and then you'll be on your way in a bit."

There was a clipboard in a pocket attached to the pole. Ferras pulled it out and checked the notations made by the NMT. He spoke while reading.

"So, side effects?" he asked.

"Uh, the usual," Bosch said. "Mild nausea. Feels like I'm going to throw up but I never do. Haven't tried to stand since I got here, but I'm sure that will be an adventure."

"Vertigo—yes, a fairly common side effect. It shouldn't last long but we'll want you to stay until we're sure you're okay to go. How's the tinnitus?"

"Still there when I think about it or when it gets mentioned."

"Sorry, Harry, but I have to ask."

"If it's all right with you, I want to go as soon as I get detached. I'm not driving, and Maddie will get me home."

Ferras looked to Maddie for confirmation.

"I'll get him home," she said.

"All right, then," Ferras said.

Ferras wrote something on the clipboard and returned it to its pocket. He turned to go.

"Nice to meet you, Maddie," he said. "Take care of him."

"I will," Maddie said. "But before you go...I'm sure you have learned over the past weeks that my dad is not A-plus on communication skills. Can you tell me in layman's terms what you're doing to him and what this clinical trial is all about? He hasn't really told me anything—"

"I didn't want you to worry," Bosch interjected.

"Happy to," Ferras said. "As you probably know, your father's cancer is in his bone marrow. What we're doing here in the trial is taking a medium that has proved to be beneficial in the treatment of other cancers and trying it on his specific cancer."

"Medium?" Maddie asked. "What does that mean?"

"It's the isotope," Ferras said. "Technically, it's called lutetium one-seventy-seven. It's been used successfully in recent years to treat prostate and other cancers. So our study and clinical trial seeks to determine if Lu one-seventy-seven therapy can achieve the same positive results with Harry's cancer. We'll know the results soon."

"And how do you measure results?" Maddie asked.

"Well, in four to six weeks, we'll bring Harry back to do a biopsy," Ferras said. "He will definitely need a ride home from that, and the results will tell us where we stand."

"What kind of biopsy?" Maddie asked.

"We'll go into the bone and draw marrow to get the truest measure," Ferras said. "But it's invasive, and I have to say there will be discomfort. We need to go into one of the bigger bones for this, so we'll go into the hip."

"Can we stop talking about this?" Bosch said. "It's not what I want to think about right now."

"Sorry, Harry," Ferras said again.

"One last question," Maddie said. "After you do the biopsy, how long until you know the result?"

"Uh, not too long," Ferras said. "Depending on what we see, we might do a second biopsy three months later."

Maddie turned and looked pointedly at Bosch.

"You need to include me," she said. "I want to know."

Bosch held up his hands in surrender.

"I promise," he said.

"I've heard that before," she said.

On the ride home Bosch's daughter again pressed the point about communications.

"Dad, really, you have to let me know what you know," she said. "You're not in this alone. I don't want you to feel that you are."

"I get it, I get it," Bosch said. "I'll—"

He felt his phone vibrating in his pocket. He pulled it out and saw it was a call from Jennifer Aronson. He guessed it was going to be another plea for his involvement in her nephew's case. He didn't want to take the call but knew that he should. He also knew he had just stopped talking to his daughter in the middle of a sentence.

"When I know something, you'll know something," he said. "Do you mind if I take this call? It'll be quick."

"Might as well," Maddie said. "You clearly don't want to talk about your health with me."

Rather than argue, Bosch put his finger on the phone screen and accepted the call.

"Jennifer," he said. "I'm kind of in the middle of something, can I —"

"That's all right," she cut in. "I just wanted to say a big thank-you. The DA nol-prossed Anthony's case. I'm waiting for him now at Sylmar."

It meant the district attorney's office had declined to prosecute the case.

"Wow, that's good," Bosch said.

"And all because of you, Harry," Aronson said. "I brought up the whole scenario that you spun — and don't worry, I never used your name. I asked if the officer was checked for gunshot residue and they understood how I was going to play it if it went to trial, especially if they bumped Anthony to adult status and the case was in open court. They folded like a paper napkin, Harry, and Anthony has you to thank."

"Uh, well, I'm glad it worked out. But he should thank you. You made his case to the prosecutor."

"Following your interpretation of the evidence."

"Well..."

Bosch didn't know what to say and wasn't sure he wanted his daughter the cop overhearing this discussion.

"I know you're busy," Aronson said. "I'll let you go. I just wanted you to know what had happened and to say thanks from both Anthony and me."

"Okay, well, glad it worked out," Bosch said.

"See you soon, Harry."

"Yes."

He clicked off and put the phone back in his pocket.

"Sorry about that," he said.

"Who was that?" Maddie said. "Sounded like a woman."

"Mickey's associate Jennifer. It was about one of her cases."

"Sounded like it was one of your cases."

"I looked at a couple reports. No big deal."

Bosch was worried that Maddie would keep asking questions about the case and eventually realize he had worked on the defense of someone accused of shooting an LAPD officer. But luckily, Maddie changed the subject.

"Do you know why Mickey isn't bringing Hayley into the firm once she passes the bar?" she asked, referring to her cousin, Haller's daughter.

"Supposedly she doesn't want to do criminal work," Bosch said. "I think he said she wants to specialize in environmental law. You're closer to her than me. Did you two talk about it?"

"We haven't talked in a while. I always thought that with me following in your footsteps, she might end up following in his."

Bosch thought for a moment before responding. Maddie turned off Cahuenga onto Woodrow Wilson and started the steep ascent to his house.

"You're not following in my footsteps, Mads. You'll be your own cop. You'll make your own path."

"I know that, but it's about the badge. We both put on the badge, you know. I'm proud of that, Dad."

"I'm glad. Me too. And by the way, Mickey saw the picture I have of you with the shiner. He had my phone and pulled it up by mistake. Thought you should know in case you hear from him about it."

"Well, I hope you told him he should have seen the other guy."

"I should have. Probably one of his clients."

They both laughed but his sarcasm about Haller was apparently not lost on Maddie.

"Dad, I know Mickey got you into the program at UCLA, but it doesn't mean you have to spend the rest of your life working cases for him."

"I know. I won't. But there's something..."

"What?"

"I don't know. But like this case we're looking at...if this woman has spent five years in prison for something she didn't do, then getting her out...it's like that saying about it being better for a hundred guilty people to go free than for one innocent person to suffer in prison. I guess I'm saying that this could make it all worth it."

"If she's innocent."

"Yeah, the big if."

Maddie pulled to a stop at the curb in front of Bosch's house.

"You want to come in?" Bosch asked. "I got a Miles Davis triple album from the Third Man Vault. *Live at the Fillmore East* in 1970. The late great Wayne Shorter's on the sax. I'm going to give it a listen."

At Christmas, she had gifted Bosch with a subscription to the distributor of rare vinyl out of Nashville.

"No, but thanks," Maddie said. "I think I'm going over to the reservoir for a run. Will you be okay?"

"Of course. I'll talk to you tomorrow. Thanks for the ride and for being there today. It means a lot."

"Anytime, Dad. Love you."

"Love you."

Bosch got out and decided to enter his house through the carport. As he unlocked the side door to the kitchen, he thought about how empty his life would feel without the connection to his daughter. It was more than the shared experience of police work. It was sacred. She was his legacy. He knew that she was what made everything he did seem worth it.

15

IT WAS MONDAY before Bosch felt steady enough on his feet and mentally focused enough to return to the Lucinda Sanz case. Early on he had put together a lengthy to-do list but there had been no bigger priority than finding and interviewing the victim's girlfriend, Matilda "Matty" Landas. Bosch had exhausted all the means of locating her that were available to a man without a badge and the access that came with it. Having learned his lesson in asking Renée Ballard to do something that could get her disciplined or even fired, he refrained from calling on her or his daughter for help. When he reported his failure, Haller said he would put his other investigator on the quest for Matilda.

And Dennis "Cisco" Wojciechowski came through, locating the woman who had previously been known as Matilda Landas in less than a day. He didn't pay off a cop to make a computer run and he didn't have to use his size and muscles to intimidate anyone. Because she had not been found through voter registration, property records, or utility records, Cisco had a hunch that she had changed her name, possibly through marriage but also possibly out of fear resulting from the Sanz case. When he found no records substantiating this in Los Angeles County, he hopped on his Harley and headed to San Bernardino County, where public birth records showed that Landas had been born in the town of Hesperia. Legally changing a name in California required petitioning a court and publishing the petition in a local newspaper. If Landas was operating out of fear, it was unlikely that she would advertise her plan to change her identity in the L.A. area. Cisco thought she would go to her hometown, where she might even know a lawyer who could help with her legal task. *The Hesperian* was a weekly newspaper that didn't offer access to online archives. So he went to the *Hesperian* offices, and after less than an hour combing through hard copies of old editions, he found the public notice of Matilda Landas's intent to change her legal name to Madison Landon. He then went to the courthouse in Victorville and confirmed that a court order had been issued three weeks later. It appeared that Matty had become Maddy.

The name change had been made seven months after Roberto Sanz was murdered.

Once Cisco had the name Madison Landon, he returned to L.A. and ran it through the usual means of tracing an individual. He was able to learn that Landon was a Democrat, had a mortgage on a home in South Pasadena, and had a matching address on her driver's license.

Cisco passed this information to Bosch and now it was time to talk to her. He called Cisco, who'd kept a loose surveillance on Landon while Bosch was on the mend.

"I'm heading out," he said. "Where is she?"

"She's in a bookstore," Cisco said. "Vroman's. You know it?"

"Yes, on Colorado Boulevard."

"She's parked in the back lot. She's only been in there a few minutes."

"I'm probably a half hour out. Call me back if she leaves."

"Will do. But I'm happy to take the interview if you're not feeling up to it."

"I'm fine. Mickey wants me to do it. In case I have to testify at the hearing."

"Got it. Well, I'm here."

"On the bike?"

"No, I don't do surveillance on the bike. Too conspicuous. I'm in Lorna's Tesla."

"Where do I meet you?"

"You're in that old Cherokee, right?"

"Yeah, old, but new to me."

"Just pull in and park at Vroman's. I'll see you."

"On my way."

A half hour later Bosch was in the bookstore's back lot. He parked, and by the time he killed the engine and got out, Cisco was waiting for him behind the Cherokee.

"You know what she looks like?" Cisco asked.

"Just from the driver's license you came up with," Bosch said.

"She looks different now. Dyed her hair, wears glasses."

"Huh."

Cisco held up his phone and showed Bosch a photo of a woman with blond hair and black-framed glasses walking across the parking lot they were standing in. He had obviously gotten the shot earlier.

"That's her?" Bosch asked.

"No, I just took this for laughs," Cisco said.

"Right, sorry. Look, if you want to come in with me, we can do this together. I know Mickey said he—"

"No, you do it. I might scare her off."

Bosch nodded. It was a reasonable concern. He knew that Haller used Cisco when he wanted an element of intimidation or needed protection himself. Finessing a reluctant witness into talking, one who might have gone so far as to change her name and looks as a protective measure, was not in his wheelhouse.

"Okay, then," Bosch said. "Here goes. Text me that photo, would you?"

"Will do," Cisco said. "Good luck."

Bosch headed to the bookstore, going down a set of steps to a sidewalk where the handprints of various authors had been immortalized in concrete. He entered and nodded to a woman at the checkout counter to his left. The place was huge and on two levels. It also had an exit on the Colorado Boulevard side of the building. Bosch quickly realized he might have an issue finding Landon. It was possible that she was not even in the store and had simply used its parking lot, passed through like a customer, and gone on to any of the nearby shops and restaurants that lined Colorado. It had been almost an hour since Cisco watched her enter. That seemed to Bosch like a long time to spend browsing in a bookstore.

He decided to start on the second floor and quickly search the store before raising an alarm with Cisco. He went up a wide set of stairs in the center and realized that he would not be able to scan the second level from one position. The bookshelves were too high. He moved along the main aisle, looking right and left down each row of shelving. It took him five minutes to cover the entire second level and another five to do the search again. There was no sign of Madison Landon.

He went down the steps to search the first level but spotted the woman from Cisco's photograph in line at the register, holding a stack of books. Bosch indiscriminately grabbed a book off a bestsellers' table and got into the checkout line behind Madison Landon.

When he got there, he read the spines of the books she was holding in both hands. They were all books about raising a child. Landon did not appear to be pregnant but judging from the titles, it looked like she was getting ready for motherhood. One of the books was *Raising Your Child Alone*.

"I raised a child alone," Bosch said.

Landon turned to look at him. She smiled but not in a way that invited further comment on her reading choices.

"When she was a teenager," Bosch said. "It's a tough job."

She looked at him again.

"And how did she turn out?" she asked.

"Pretty great," Bosch said. "She went into law enforcement."

"Then you must worry about her."

"All the time."

Landon's eyes dropped to the book Bosch was holding.

"I loved that book," she said.

Bosch looked down to see what he had grabbed. It was *Tomorrow, and Tomorrow, and Tomorrow*. He had never heard of it. He had not been in a bookstore since before the pandemic.

"I heard it was good," he said. "I'll give it a try and then give it to my daughter."

"She'll like it," Landon said. "I'm not so sure about you."

"Why's that?"

"It's about three people but it's also about developing video games and the creativity it involves."

"Hmm. Well, sounds like something at least Maddie will like."

He noticed that Landon smiled at the mention of the name but did not reveal that it was also her own name.

"Why don't you go ahead of me," she said. "I have a lot here and you just have the one."

"You sure?" Bosch said. "I don't mind —"

"No, go ahead, because I'm also going to ask them to order a book for me."

"Thank you. That's very nice of you."

She stepped back and he moved up in the queue just as the customer ahead finished her purchase and left. Bosch put the book down on the counter, and the cashier scanned it. He paid with cash. He turned back to Landon, held up the book, and said, "Thanks."

"I hope she likes it," Landon said.

Bosch exited and then took a position leaning against a wall by the stairs up to the parking lot. He opened the book he had just bought and started reading. A few minutes later, Landon came out of the store with a bag containing all her purchases. Bosch looked up from his book and Landon quickly turned away, probably thinking he was going to make an awkward attempt at some sort of pickup.

"You're Maddy, right?" he said.

Landon stopped in her tracks at the foot of the stairs.

"What?" she said.

"Or is it Madison?" Bosch asked.

He pushed off the wall and closed the book.

"Who are you?" Landon said. "What do you want?"

"I'm a guy trying to get an innocent woman out of prison," Bosch said. "So she can raise her child."

"I don't know what you're talking about. Please leave me alone." She turned back to the stairway.

"You know what and who I'm talking about," Bosch said. "And why I can't leave you alone."

She stopped. Bosch watched her eyes dart around, looking for an escape route.

"Roberto Sanz," he said. "You changed your name, moved away. I want to know why."

"I don't want to talk to you," Landon said coldly.

"I understand that. But if you don't talk to me, there will be a subpoena, and a judge will make you talk to me. Then it could go public.

If you talk to me now, I can try to keep you out of it down the line. Your name, where you live — none of it should have to come out."

She brought her free hand up and held it across her eyes.

"You're putting me in danger," she said. "Don't you see that?"

"Danger from who?" Bosch asked.

"Them."

Bosch was flying in the dark without instrumentation. He was simply following his instincts in what he had said so far. But Landon's reactions here told him that he was clearly on the right path.

"The Cucos?" he asked. "Is that who you mean? We can protect you from them."

The mere mention of the sheriff's clique seemed to send a shudder through her body.

Bosch had been careful to keep his distance. But now he casually stepped closer.

"I can see to it that you have no part in what's about to go down," he said. "No one will ever know your new name or where you are. But you have to help me."

"You found me," Landon said. "They can find me."

"They, whoever they are, won't even know. This is just you and me. But you need to talk to me about the day Roberto got shot — what was going on, what he was into."

"Have you talked to Agent MacIsaac?"

"Not yet. But I will. When I know more from you."

Bosch didn't recognize the name but he didn't want to let Landon know that. It might undercut her confidence in the promise he had just made. But her calling MacIsaac an agent raised an immediate flag. It indicated that MacIsaac was a fed, which meant that any number of agencies in the federal sandbox could have been involved with Roberto Sanz. Even if Landon refused to cooperate, he now had a new lead to pursue.

"I have to think about this," Landon said.

"Why?" Bosch said. "For how long?"

"Just give me today," she said. "Give me a number and I'll call you in the morning."

Bosch knew better than to let a potential witness go off to think about things. Fears could multiply, legal advisers could be pulled into the decision. You never let a fish off the hook.

"Can we just talk now, off the record?" Bosch said. "I won't record it. I won't even take notes. I need to know about that day. A woman who may be innocent—a mother—is in prison. For her, every single day, every hour, is a nightmare. You knew Eric, her son. She needs to be with him to raise him right."

"But I followed the case and she pleaded guilty," Landon said. "Now she says she's innocent?"

"She pleaded no contest to a reduced charge of manslaughter. Because she had to risk life imprisonment in a trial."

Landon nodded as though she understood Lucinda Sanz's plight.

"Okay," she said. "Let's get this over with. Where?"

"We can sit in my car," Bosch said. "Or yours. Or find a coffee shop to sit in."

"My car. I don't want to do this in public."

"Then your car it is."

16

HALLER DIDN'T RETURN the call until Bosch was driving up Woodrow Wilson to his house, where he planned to rest. The flow of adrenaline that had kicked in once Madison Landon started talking about the day Roberto Sanz was murdered had tapered off and left him exhausted. Before leaving the parking lot at Vroman's, he had texted Cisco to thank him once again for finding Landon and then he'd put in the call to Haller. Forty minutes later, Bosch was almost home and ready to go horizontal for an hour or so when Haller called back.

"Sorry, was in court. What's up?"

"Sanz was late bringing his son home to Lucinda because he was with the FBI."

There was a long moment of silence.

"You there, Mick?"

"Yes, just digesting this. Who told you this, the girlfriend?"

"Yes. Off the record. She wants no part of this. She's scared."

"Of who?"

"The Cucos."

135

"Who were the agents? Did you get any names?"

"One partial. Agent MacIsaac. It won't be hard to get a full name and assignment. I'm going to start making calls once I get home."

"This changes everything, you know."

"How so?"

"MacIsaac won't talk to you. I can pretty much guarantee that. And the feds routinely swat state court subpoenas away like Mookie Betts swats fastballs over the plate. Did the girlfriend—what's her new name again?"

"Madison Landon."

"Did Madison Landon know what the meeting with Agent MacIsaac was about?"

"No, she just knew it was serious. Sanz told her he was 'jammed up' on something—his words—and had to talk to the FBI. The only reason she knew the name MacIsaac was that she heard Sanz say it on a call when they were setting up the meeting that day."

Haller went silent again. Bosch knew he was thinking of the possible legal scenarios this new information presented. He pulled the Cherokee into the carport of his house. He killed the engine but stayed seated, phone to his ear.

"So, what are you thinking?" he finally prompted.

"The FBI changes things," Haller said. "I'm thinking I may need to find a way to get this into federal court without first showing our hand in state court."

"I don't know what that means."

"Well, like I said, we'll never get MacIsaac into superior court. But we have a good shot at getting him into federal court. The thing is, you're supposed to exhaust all state appeals before you file in a U.S. district court. But if we go that route, they'll see us coming a mile away. They'll be locked and loaded, prepared for us. We don't want MacIsaac knowing what's coming when I say, 'Agent MacIsaac, tell us about this conversation you had with Roberto Sanz a couple hours before his murder.'"

Now Bosch was silent as he considered the path they were on with Lucinda Sanz.

"I think we need to hold up on reaching out to MacIsaac," Haller said.

"But we need to know why he was with Sanz the day he was killed," Bosch countered.

"We do. But let's circle around him a little bit and see what else we can find before we knock on the FBI's door."

"Not sure where else to circle."

"That's because you're thinking like a cop and not a defense investigator."

"What's the difference?"

"The difference is that it's a stacked deck. When you're a cop or a prosecutor, you have the almighty power of the state behind you every step of the way. All the state's resources and reach. On the defense side, it's just you. It's David and Goliath, and you're David, baby. It's why getting a win is so special. And so very rare."

"I think that's a little simplistic—especially with all the red tape and rules slanted in favor of the defendant—but I get the point. So if I'm laying low on the FBI, what do you want me doing instead?"

"I'm sure you'll think of something. Just give me a few days to figure how we deal with the feds. I need to talk to some people to see if we can make this jump to federal court."

Still parked in the carport, Bosch stared straight ahead, thinking of possible next moves. He assumed that the FBI had something on Sanz and that was the reason for the clandestine meeting on a Sunday afternoon. Sanz was jammed up and MacIsaac was applying pressure for him to turn informant. Based on recent and very public history, the Bureau had been heavily focused at the time on corruption in the sheriff's department, with a particular interest in the flourishing of deputy cliques there. Bosch didn't need to talk to MacIsaac to know this.

The question was, what did the FBI have on Sanz that was more serious and actionable than him being in a clique, and had it led to his murder? Bosch knew that Haller didn't need to have all the facts to carry out his duties. Most defense attorneys operated by the "Where there's smoke, there's fire" creed. They needed to sow the seeds of doubt but didn't necessarily have to believe in the doubts sown. But Bosch could not operate that way, even if he was working for a defense lawyer. He needed to get through the smoke to the fire. If there was a fire.

As his mind pushed through the smoke he came to realize what his next move would be. If he could not go directly to MacIsaac, he knew who he could take a run at.

As he pulled back his thousand-yard stare he realized he had been looking through the windshield at the door to the kitchen and hadn't even noticed something.

It was three inches ajar.

"Are you there, Bosch?" Haller said. "Or did I lose you in the hills?"

"I'm here," Bosch said. "But hold on a second."

Bosch removed the key from the ignition and used it to unlock the glove compartment. He grabbed his gun and got out of the car, weapon in one hand, phone in the other. In a low voice he spoke to Haller.

"I just got home and my door's open. Pretty sure I didn't leave it that way."

"Then hang up and call the cops."

"I'm going to check it out first."

"Harry, you're not a cop. Let the cops check it out."

"Just hold on."

Bosch dropped the phone into his pocket without disconnecting. He approached the door with the gun in a two-handed grip and used the muzzle to push it all the way open. Standing still, he listened for a moment before entering, but heard nothing. From his vantage, he saw nothing amiss in the galley kitchen. He tried to recall how he had left that morning after getting the call from Cisco. He had been in a hurry, but he could conceive of no circumstance where he would have left the door open. He had lived in the house more than thirty years. Pulling the door closed until the lock clicked was automatic, pure muscle memory.

He took a step back into the carport to check whether he had missed seeing his daughter's car parked on the street when he had pulled up to the house.

Maddie's car was not there and there were no other vehicles that drew Bosch's suspicion. He turned back to the kitchen door and quietly entered the house again, holding the gun up at the ready. His most valuable tool now was his hearing but his left ear was afflicted with low-level tinnitus. He strained to hear any sound. He made the turn out of the kitchen and into the entry area by the front door. This gave him a view of the living room and dining area. He moved forward but noticed nothing unusual until he got into the living room and saw a record spinning on the turntable.

The tonearm was up; no music was playing. Bosch switched the player off and stared at the record until it stopped turning. It was the Miles Davis *Live at the Fillmore East* album he had last played days before. He knew he had left it on the platter, but he was sure he had turned off the player.

"Harry, what's happening?"

Bosch heard Haller's tinny voice coming from his pocket. He pulled out his phone and responded.

"So far nothing seems wrong. But somebody was here. And they wanted me to know it."

"You sure?"

Bosch realized that someone had been smoking in the house. He hadn't smoked in twenty years but he knew the smell that hung in the air in a closed space when someone recently had.

"I'm sure," he said.

"Who?" Haller asked.

"I don't know. Yet."

"You need to call the cops. Get it on the record."

"I'm not finished checking the house. Let me call you back."

"Fine, but you need to call the—"

Bosch disconnected, dropped the phone in his pocket, and continued the sweep of the house. He checked the bedrooms and bathrooms but saw no further evidence of intrusion. He sat down on his bed. He thought about things and wondered again if it was possible that he had left the door open and the turntable spinning. Maybe the smell of a cigarette was a ghost memory of his own former addiction or a side effect of his medical treatment. He knew that short-term memory loss and a heightened or diminished sense of smell or taste were possible side effects of the therapy he was receiving.

Dr. Ferras had given Bosch his personal cell number, and Bosch thought about calling now. But he quickly dismissed the idea. What was Ferras going to say beyond what was already in the small print of the materials Bosch had signed? Forgetfulness was a possible side effect.

Bosch felt tired and old. And defeated. He put the gun on the side table. The pillow looked so inviting. He thought about calling his daughter to see if she had come by and left the door open. She didn't smoke, as far as Bosch knew, but the man she was dating did. He decided he would do it later. He would also decide whether to call the police later. Right now he needed to rest.

He lay down and soon his dark thoughts about mortality slipped away and he was dreaming of himself as a younger man, moving through a tunnel with a dying flashlight.

17

IT WAS A five-hour drive and Bosch left home in predawn darkness to get ahead of traffic and make it to the prison by 10 a.m., the start of visiting hours. He knew he was risking a ten-hour round trip and the waste of a whole day if Angel Acosta refused to see him. But he was riding on a hunch based on decades of experience in law enforcement and banking that a twenty-nine-year-old lifer would welcome any interruption or change of pace in a schedule that offered little of it for the next forty or fifty years. The trick would be getting him to open up and talk once they were face-to-face.

Along the way he burned through his whole playlist of favorite jazz recordings, from Cannonball Adderley to Joe Zawinul, finishing with Weather Report's "Birdland," Zawinul's signature fusion composition, as he pulled into the visitors' parking lot at Corcoran State Prison. The music had cleared his mind of the concerns he'd been carrying since arriving home to see his kitchen door open three days earlier. He had found himself in the strange position of hoping it had been an intruder and not the other option: the first indication of a slide into dementia. He had filed a police report but knew that it was the kind of crime that would receive little attention from the LAPD's North Hollywood Division burglary unit. The officer who took the report was not convinced there had been a break-in, since Bosch could not say whether anything was taken. The officer did not bother to call a fingerprint technician to the house either. Bosch could not fault him for this, given his own uncertainty.

Bosch had been to the state prison at Corcoran many times as a badge-carrying detective, but this was his first time as a civilian. Finding Angel Acosta had not been as difficult as locating Madison Landon. Bosch had gone back to the digital archives of the *L.A. Times* and combed through all the follow-up stories on the shoot-out between Roberto Sanz and gang members at a Lancaster hamburger stand. One gangster was killed, one was wounded and arrested, and two got away. The one that was arrested was identified in subsequent stories as Angel Acosta. He had been shot once in the abdomen but recovered in the hospital ward at the county jail and a year after the shoot-out pleaded guilty to assaulting a law enforcement officer. To Bosch it looked like a sweetheart deal — three to five years for shooting at a sheriff's deputy. On top of that Acosta wasn't tagged with responsibility for his fellow gangbanger's death. That was usually an add-on in gang cases when someone was killed in the commission of a crime. California prosecutors no longer followed this practice because of adverse appellate rulings, but six years ago it was still a routine enhancement slapped on the defendant. Why Acosta hadn't faced it from his initial arrest was unclear.

The light sentence didn't matter in the long run because Acosta was later convicted of murdering a fellow inmate. His new conviction carried a life sentence without parole. He had been moved to Corcoran, where it was likely he would be for the rest of his life.

Bosch wanted to talk to Acosta for a few reasons. He was suspicious about that first sentence and how Acosta got it. The newspaper accounts were short and didn't mention his attorney or the prosecutor who'd handled the case. Added to this was the new information that Roberto Sanz had been talking to an Agent MacIsaac. Bosch knew that the Bureau investigation likely had to do with the wide-ranging probe of the cliques and corruption that had proliferated inside the sheriff's department. Any focus on Sanz and his affiliation with the Cucos would have included a look at the shoot-out that had made Sanz a hero in the department. If Bosch could get Acosta talking, that was what he would ask about.

People making unscheduled visits had to fill out a form and then stand by in a waiting room while the inmate was asked if he would agree to the visit. There was no timetable. The corrections officer who Bosch gave the completed form to did not run back into the prison dorms with it to find Acosta. He simply put the form on top of a stack and told Bosch to make himself comfortable in the waiting room and listen for his name to be called.

Bosch waited almost two hours and then heard his name. Acosta had agreed to the visit. Bosch knew that was the easy part. The next — getting Acosta to talk to him — was the hard part.

He was led to a room where twenty stools and interview booths lined one side and a catwalk ran along the opposite one. A corrections officer walked a back-and-forth circuit watching over the booths.

Bosch was instructed to take booth seven. He sat down on a steel stool in front of a thick piece of scratched plexiglass with a telephone receiver on a side hook. He waited another ten minutes before a thin, wiry man in prison blues showed up on the other side of the glass. The man hesitated, then picked up the phone but didn't sit down. Bosch picked up his phone. The next thirty seconds would determine if he'd wasted the day.

"You a cop?" Acosta said. "You look like a cop."

"Used to be," Bosch said. "Now I work for people like you."

Acosta's entire neck was collared in prison-ink tattoos that showed his allegiance to La Eme — the Mexican Mafia that controlled all Latino gangs in California prisons. He had one teardrop tattoo at the corner of his left eye, and his head and face were shaven. He stared at Bosch, curious about his answer. He slowly slid onto his stool.

"Who are you?" he asked.

"It was on the paper the guard showed you," Bosch said. "My name's Bosch. I'm a private investigator."

"Okay, private investigator, no bullshit, what do you want?"

"I'm trying to get a woman named Lucinda Sanz out of prison. You know that name?"

"Can't say I do and I don't care."

"She was married to the deputy who shot you six years ago. You remember now?"

"I remember she did a righteous thing, that lady, putting his ass in the ground. I heard about that. But what's it got to do with me? I got a perfect alibi. When that shit went down, I was already in prison, thanks to him and his lying ass."

"He was lying? Then how come you pled?"

"Let's just say I had no choice, *cabrón*. I got nothing else to say."

He took the phone away from his ear and reached out to hang it up. Bosch held up a finger as if to say *One last question*. Acosta brought the phone back to his ear.

"I don't talk to cops or ex-cops, *pendejo*," he said.

"That's not what I heard," Bosch said.

"Yeah, what did you hear?"

"That you talked to the FBI."

Acosta's eyes widened slightly for a moment.

"That's bullshit," he said. "I didn't tell them shit."

Acosta's answer confirmed that the Bureau had come to him whether he had talked or not. Bosch's hunch was looking good.

"Agent MacIsaac's report says different," he said. "It says you told him what really went down at Flip's hamburger stand that day."

Bosch was still working without a net. But he was staying with his hunch that the shoot-out at Flip's had not happened the way the sheriff's department publicly reported it. Based on what he knew so far about Roberto Sanz, he doubted there'd been any heroes that day at Flip's.

"It was no ambush, was it?" he said.

Acosta shook his head. "I don't talk to cops, I don't talk to FBI, I don't talk to *pendejo* private eyes."

"You talked to MacIsaac and told him that the ambush wasn't an ambush. It was really a meeting with a corrupt cop that went sideways. That's how you got your sweetheart deal."

Acosta took the phone away from his ear again, hesitated, and brought it back.

"Sweetheart deal?" he said. "I'm in here for the rest of my fucking life."

"But it wasn't supposed to be like that," Bosch said. "You were supposed to go away for a little while and get out after cooperating with the Bureau. But then Sanz got killed and that was the end of that. And then, of course, you did a prison hit for La Eme and that got you a teardrop and life without parole."

"You don't know what the fuck you're talking about."

"Maybe I don't have the whole picture yet, but I will. I know you talked to MacIsaac and I know you got a deal from the feds."

"You're wrong. My lawyer got me that deal. Silver said I didn't have to cooperate, and I didn't. I just had to keep my mouth shut like I'm doing right fucking now."

Bosch stared at Acosta for a long moment before responding. His hunch was paying off but not in any way he had expected.

"Your lawyer was Frank Silver?" he finally asked.

"Yeah, that's right," Acosta said. "So go talk to him and you'll find out I'm no fucking snitch. I didn't talk to MacIsaac or any of them."

"But you talked to Silver, right? Your attorney. Everything you told him was confidential. You told him about Flip's? That's how he got the deal."

"This is over, man. I didn't talk to any of them and I'm not talking to you."

Acosta abruptly hung up the phone, slamming it down on its hook so hard that the report in Bosch's ear sounded like a gunshot. Acosta backed off his stool and was gone.

Bosch held steady for a long moment, reviewing in his mind what he had just heard. Attorney Frank Silver had represented Angel Acosta the same year he'd represented Lucinda Sanz. He tried to remember what Lucinda had said about how Silver had come to represent her. He had pushed his way onto the case, volunteering to take it off the public defender's hands.

Bosch put the phone back on the hook and got up off the stool. He knew there were real coincidences on cases. He didn't believe this was one of them.

PART FOUR

LADY X

18

I FOUND SILVER where I had last seen him, behind his desk in his tiny office in the legal commune on Ord Street. I noticed that he had replaced the business card I had taken from the slot on the wall. The door was open like it had been before, but this time I walked in without knocking. Silver didn't look up from what he was writing on a legal pad. The room smelled of Chinese takeout.

"How can I help you?" he said.

I didn't answer. I put the stapled document down in front of him. He glanced up and did a double take when he saw who stood in front of his desk.

"Da Lincoln Lawyer," he said. "What's up, partner?"

"You ever go to court, Frank?" I asked.

"I always thought a good lawyer tries to avoid court. Bad shit happens in court, right?"

"Not always."

He picked up the document and leaned back in his chair to read it. "So what do we have here?" he asked.

"That's a copy of my habeas petition," I said. "I'll file it tomorrow. I thought you should have it in case the media gets wind of it. Lately they seem to be following my cases and my moves pretty closely."

"That's because you're a winner. And winners get the ink."

"It's mostly digital now. But I get the point."

Silver started to read.

"Let's see what we've got here," he said.

I noticed an open takeout container filled with what looked like fried rice. It was giving the claustrophobic room a sharp odor of fried pork.

As soon as Silver read the case styling—*Sanz v. the State of California*—he leaned forward and looked up at me.

"You're going federal with this?" he asked. "I thought you said—"

"I know what I said," I interrupted. "That was before we took a deep dive into the case and found out a few things."

"I've never worked in federal."

"I try to avoid it, but there are reasons this time."

"Such as?"

"Just keep reading. You'll see."

Silver nodded and went back to the document. The top sheet was boilerplate, listing the reasons why the U.S. district court should hear the motion. The second page was more case-specific and outlined how my efforts to secure cooperation from the FBI for a habeas motion in state court had been thwarted by a blanket denial of requests from the district's U.S. Attorney's Office. Silver nodded as he read as though agreeing to the facts outlined on page two. When he saw the notation about the attached exhibit he flipped to the back of the document and read the short, terse letter from the Central District of California U.S. Attorney's Office denying my request to speak to FBI agent Tom MacIsaac and warning that any effort to serve him with a state court subpoena would be blocked.

"Perrrrfect," Silver said, drawing the word out.

He went back to the second page and then moved on to page three. This was what I was waiting for. Page three was the meat of the document. It contained the reasons why the petition should be granted and a habeas hearing scheduled. I watched closely as Silver continued reading and nodding, acting like he was checking off boxes and approving as he went.

But a few seconds later he stopped nodding.

"What the fuck, Haller?" he said. "This says ineffective assistance of counsel and you said you weren't going that way."

"I told you, things have changed," I said.

"How the fuck have they changed? You think you're going to file this and then leak it to the press? That's a big nonstarter, buddy boy. That isn't happening."

I was still standing. I didn't want to sit down for this. I didn't want to be in this room and in front of this guy any longer than I had to. I put my hands down on his desk after shoving some of the clutter out of the way. I leaned down but was still above Silver's level.

"Things changed when I found out about you," I said.

"Me?" Silver exclaimed. "What are you talking about? Found out what?"

"That you sold Lucinda Sanz down the river. That you took a dive."

"Bullshit."

"No bullshit. You could've beaten this case easy. But you folded, and that woman's been sitting in Chino for five years."

"Are you nuts? None of that is true. I got her a great fucking deal. But even if it was a bad deal, I didn't take it. She did. It was her call."

"You talked her into it."

"I didn't have to. She knew they had her. And she knew it was a good deal. I just had to lay it out for her and she did the rest. You ask her, she'll say the same."

"I did ask her. She did say it was her call, but she didn't know at the time that a few months earlier, you'd represented a client named Angel Acosta."

Silver failed to keep the surprise out of his eyes.

"That's right," I said. "Angel Acosta, the guy your new client's ex-husband shot during a firefight at a hamburger stand."

"It's not a conflict of interest," Silver said. "It's a coincidence. Definitely not ineffect—"

"Acosta told you that was no ambush. It was some kind of meeting between the gang and a corrupt cop. I don't know the details yet, but you do. Whatever it was, it went bad fast and the shooting started. Sanz was no hero and you knew it. That was the ace up your sleeve with Acosta. Your leverage. That's how you got him the sweet deal. You threatened to put it all out there, put the sheriff's department on trial."

"You really don't know what you're talking about, Haller."

"I think I do. You then saw the opportunity to double dip with Lucinda. Get the case from the public defender, then use the same intel from Acosta to get a deal. But the reality was you had an innocent client. And you had everything you needed to go to trial and win. But, no, you're Second-Place Silver. You took a dive."

Silver shoved the food container to the side of his desk but he pushed too hard and it fell off and showered the floor and wall with fried rice.

"Goddamn it!" he said.

He started to bend down to clean it up but then sat back up straight and looked at me.

"It was a judgment call," he said. "We make them every single day and no judge will grant you a habeas on a judgment call. You file this and you'll be laughed out of federal court."

The document I had prepared that morning was simply a prop. Silver was right about one thing: Going for a habeas in federal court with just ineffective assistance of counsel was a nonstarter. It would go nowhere and I wasn't planning to file it. It was just a tool to help me get to Silver and get him talking.

"I might be laughed out of court," I said. "Or the public might learn that you took a dive on an innocent client's case."

"As I said, you don't know what the fuck you're talking about," Silver said.

"Then here's your chance to school me, Frank. Tell me what I don't know."

"I was fucking threatened, you dumbass. I had no choice."

There. I had broken through. Now I pulled out the chair in front of his desk and sat down.

"Threatened by who?" I said.

"I can't get into it," he said. "The threat is still out there and it's real. You need to be careful or it will be your ass in a sling next."

"Wrong answer. You need to get into it right now or I'll file that in the morning and put a press release out to every newsroom in the city."

"You can't do this to me."

I pointed to the document on the desk in front of him.

"It's already done. You want to stop it, tell me what went down with Sanz. Who threatened you and why?"

"Jesus Christ."

Silver shook his head like a man who sees no way out of a trap.

"There's only one choice here, Frank," I said. "You're working with me or you're working against me. And I will burn the ground you walk on to get my client out of that prison."

"All right, all right," Silver said. "I'll tell you what happened, okay? But you need to treat it as intel. You can't reveal who you got it from."

"I can't make that promise. Not until I know what you know."

"Fuck…"

He was stalling. I pushed my chair back.

"Okay, I'm out of here. Good luck tomorrow."

"No, no, no, wait. Okay, I'll tell you, I'll tell you. You were right, Angel told me everything. Sanz was a collector for this sheriff's gang who call themselves the Cucos. Acosta and his gang were paying for protection, and Sanz was the bagman. That day was supposed to be a regular cash pickup but then Sanz upped the ante. The Cucos wanted more. There was an argument and it turned into a shoot-out. After Angel told me that, a friend of Sanz's called me and said that if I went into court with what I knew, it would be the last case I ever tried."

"A friend? Who are we talking about?"

"I don't know. One of the Cucos."

"That doesn't help me. I need a name."

"I don't have a name. I didn't want a name."

"I'll protect you."

"Are you fucking kidding me? You can't protect me from them. They're cops!"

"How did you know they were cops?"

"I just did. It was obvious, wasn't it? With what Acosta had told me."

"I still need a name, Frank, or we're done here. Who called you?"

"He didn't say his name and I didn't ask for it."

"What exactly did he say?"

"He told me to tell Acosta that if he kept his mouth shut, he'd get a deal from the DA. I said fine. I knew getting him a deal would be a big victory. And so did Acosta. I didn't have to sell it. He was happy to take it."

"Who was the prosecutor who offered the deal?"

"Same one who handled all the heavy cases out there. Andrea Fontaine. But she's downtown now."

I considered everything just said and then moved on.

"Okay," I said. "Lucinda Sanz. You went to the PD and took the case."

"Because I was told to," Silver said.

"By who? The same one who called you on Acosta?"

"No, this time it was a woman. She knew about the whole Acosta deal and she said there would be an offer from Fontaine. She told me to make Lucinda take the deal and plead her out. And that if I used what I knew about Roberto Sanz and the shoot-out from before, I was a dead man, plain and simple."

I thought about this. Lucinda had said a woman had conducted the GSR test on her, a woman who said she worked with Roberto Sanz.

"The second caller, do you know who it was?" I asked.

"No, man, I told you," Silver said. "No names were mentioned. They weren't that stupid."

"Did Lucinda know about any of this?"

Silver lowered his eyes.

"I never told her," he said. "I just told her to take the deal. That it was the only way."

I thought I could see shame and regret in Silver's eyes. Maybe he had believed at the time that Lucinda was guilty as charged and that the callers were putting a cap on what could blow up into another scandal for the sheriff's department. But either way Silver knew deep inside that he'd never be more than a hack lawyer from the Ord Street commune.

"You did all this based on phone calls from nameless people who claimed they were cops," I said. "But how did you know the threats were legit?"

"Because they knew things," Silver said. "Things that had never gotten out, that had to have come from the inside."

"Like what?"

"Like they knew what Acosta could spill if I put him on the stand. That Roberto Sanz was no fucking hero that day at the shoot-out."

I changed direction with Silver, using Bosch's tactic of keeping a witness off balance with unexpected questions.

"Tell me about Agent MacIsaac," I said.

"Who?" Silver asked.

Through a few phone calls Bosch had been able to learn MacIsaac's full name and posting in the Bureau's L.A. field office. That part of the document was fact and I was hopeful it would draw a response from Silver.

"FBI Special Agent Tom MacIsaac," I said. "He's the guy the U.S. attorney won't allow me to talk to or subpoena. Did he ever show up around here to talk to you?"

"No, I never heard of him till now. What's his—"

"He had a lengthy meeting with Roberto Sanz on the day he was killed. If you were any kind of an attorney, you would have found that out and not talked your client into a plea deal."

Silver shook his head.

"Look, man, I keep telling you, I was threatened," he said. "I had no choice."

"So you turned around and gave your client no choice," I said. "You talked her into the plea. You talked her into prison."

"You weren't there, man. You have no idea what kind of pressure was on me and what evidence they had on her. She was going down either way."

"Sure, Frank. Whatever lets you sleep at night."

I had an almost overwhelming desire to get away from Frank Silver and his office, which stank of failure and pork fried rice. But I stayed to hear him finish his confession.

"All right," I said. "Go back to Angel Acosta and tell me

everything you know. I need every detail you can remember. You do that and this motion never gets filed."

I pointed to the prop doc on his desk.

"How do I know you won't fuck me over in the end?" Silver asked.

"Well, buddy boy," I said, "I guess you don't."

19

THE LINCOLN WAS at the curb, Bosch behind the wheel, when I came out. I had completely broken the habit of jumping in the back and I got in the front seat without a second thought.

"Did it work?" Bosch asked.

"Yes and no," I said. "He pretty much confirmed what we had already put together. But he said he didn't know anything about MacIsaac or the FBI."

"Do you believe him?"

"I do. For now."

"Well, what did he know?"

"He said that on both the Acosta and Sanz cases he was threatened by deputies. First he had to get Acosta to take a deal, then later the same thing all over again with Lucinda. He didn't have names. It was all on his phone. One call from a male, the second from a female. Each time he was told that the DA would come across with an offer and his client had to take it or there would be consequences. For him."

"Just that? Anonymous phone calls?"

"Each time the caller had inside information. Knew details about the shoot-out with Sanz. He believed the threat."

"One caller male, the other female. Lucinda says it was a woman who did the GSR."

"What I was thinking. For now we call her Lady X. But we need to identify everybody who was in Sanz's unit at the time, especially any women. Between you and Cisco, run them down, full bios, and we'll start building a witness list."

"Got it. Where to now?"

"Hall of Justice. Time to rattle a cage over there."

Bosch checked the mirrors and then pulled the Lincoln away from the curb on Ord Street.

"Whose cage?" Bosch asked.

"The deputy DA who handled both the Acosta and Sanz cases is Andrea Fontaine. Back then she was assigned to the Antelope Valley courthouse. Now she's downtown in Major Crimes. I was thinking we'd pay her a visit and see what she has to say about those cases and the deals she made on them. Looks to me like she might've made a deal for herself."

"You're talking major conspiracy here. The sheriff's department *and* the DA's office."

"Hey, man, conspiracy theories are a defense lawyer's bread and butter."

"Great. What about the truth?"

"You don't find that too often in the courtrooms I've been in."

Bosch had no comeback for that. It took us five minutes to get to the Hall of Justice and another ten to find a parking spot. Before we got out, Bosch finally spoke.

"What you said about building a witness list. What do you expect to get from Sanz's teammates?"

"I expect them to get on the stand and lie their asses off about this. They do and we take out the biggest piece of evidence against Lucinda."

"The GSR."

"Now you're thinking like a defense attorney."

"Never."

"Look, do you believe that Lucinda killed her ex and is where she should be right now?"

Bosch thought a moment before answering.

"Come on," I said. "You're not under oath."

"I don't think she did it," he finally said.

"Well, neither do I. So what we gotta do is knock down the evidence against her like dominoes. And if we can't do that, then we have to own it and explain it. They come up with photos of her shooting at targets, then we own it and say yes, that's her, but she was doing that because she couldn't shoot for shit and certainly not well enough to put two bullets in her ex-husband's back nearly six inches apart. Like that. You get it?"

"I get it."

"Good. Now, let's go see what this prosecutor has to say."

"You're going to ask about this? The GSR?"

"Yeah, without giving anything away."

Bosch nodded and we opened our doors and got out.

The Hall of Justice was across from the Criminal Courts Building. It had at one time housed the sheriff's department, and its top three floors were the county jail. But then the sheriff's department moved most of its operations out to the STARS Center in Whittier and a county jail was built. The building was repurposed and the jail floors were turned into offices for prosecutors who worked cases in the courtrooms across the street.

Andrea Fontaine was not welcoming of our unscheduled visit.

She met us in a waiting area after being notified by the reception-
ist of our request for an audience. We introduced ourselves and she
walked us back to her office, explaining that she had only a few minutes before she needed to leave for a hearing in a courtroom across the
street.

"That's okay," I said. "We only need a few minutes."

She walked us into an office that was smaller than Frank Silver's
and clearly had once been a cell: three walls of concrete block and a
fourth behind her desk that was a latticework of iron bars and glass
with no opening bigger than six inches square.

The office was neat and not as cramped as Silver's. There was
room for two chairs in front of her desk and we all sat down.

"I don't think we have a case together, do we?" Fontaine asked.

"Uh, not yet," I said.

"That sounds mysterious. What's this about?"

"Two cases you handled during your Antelope Valley days."

"I was moved down here four years ago. Which cases?"

"Angel Acosta and Lucinda Sanz. I'm sure they're on your
greatest-hits list."

Fontaine tried to keep a poker face but I could see the flare of fear
enter her eyes.

"I remember Sanz, of course," she said. "She killed a deputy I
actually knew. It's rare you get a case where you know the victim. And
Acosta . . . help me with that one. It rings a bell but I can't place it."

"The ambush at the Flip's burger stand the year before Sanz was
killed," I said. "The shoot-out?"

"Oh, yes, of course. Thank you. Why are you asking about those
cases? They were both closed with dispositions. Guilty people pleading guilty."

"Well, we're not so sure about that. The guilty part."

"On which one?"

"Lucinda Sanz."

"You're going to challenge that conviction? She got a great deal. You want to risk getting a redo? If we go to trial she could end up with a life sentence. With what she's got now, she'll be out in, what, four or five more years? Maybe even sooner."

"Four and a half, actually. But she says she didn't do it. And she wants out now."

"And you believe her?"

"Yeah, I do."

Fontaine turned her eyes to Bosch.

"What about you, Bosch?" she asked. "You worked homicide."

"Doesn't matter what I believe," Bosch said. "The evidence isn't there for conviction."

"Then why did she plead guilty?" Fontaine asked.

"Because she had no choice," I said. "And actually, she pled nolo. There's a difference."

Fontaine just stared at us for a few moments.

"Gentlemen, we're done here," she finally said. "I have nothing more to say about those cases. They're closed. Justice was done. And I'm going to be late for court."

She started stacking files on her desk and getting ready to go.

"I'd rather talk now than have to subpoena you," I said.

"Well, good luck with that," Fontaine said.

"The most damning piece of evidence you had on her was the GSR. I'll tell you right now, we can blow that up."

"You're a defense lawyer. You can find a so-called expert to say whatever you want. But over here we deal in facts, and the fact is she shot her ex-husband and is where she deserves to be."

She stood up and dumped her gathered files into a leather bag with initials in gold near the handle. Bosch started to stand up. But I didn't.

"I'd hate to see you dragged through the shit that's about to come out," I said. "When this gets to court."

"Is that a threat?" Fontaine asked.

"It's more like a choice. Work with us to find the truth. Or work against us and hide it."

"That'll be the day, when I find a defense attorney really interested in the truth. Now, you need to go or I'm going to call security to escort you out."

I took my time standing up, holding her angry stare as I did.

"Just remember," I said. "We gave you the choice."

"Just go," she said loudly. "Now!"

Bosch and I didn't speak until we were on the elevator going down.

"I'd say you succeeded in rattling her cage," Bosch said.

"Hers and a few others down the line, I'm sure," I said.

"Are we ready for that? What happened to 'no footprints'?"

"Changing course. Besides, somebody out there already knows what we're doing."

"How do you know that?"

"Easy. Somebody broke into your house because they wanted us to know."

Bosch nodded and we were silent while the old elevator made its way down.

When we stepped out into the lobby, Bosch brought up what I had been mulling over myself.

"So," he said. "Fontaine. Think she's bent or is she a victim?"

"Good question," I said. "They threatened the defense attorney into doing what they wanted. Maybe they did it with the prosecutor too. Or maybe she's just as corrupt as the Cucos."

"Maybe it's somewhere in the middle. She was pressured into

protecting the sheriff's department from scandal. It is, after all, the sister agency to the DA's office."

"I think you're being too kind, Harry. You gotta remember, two years after this shit went down, she gets a transfer from Antelope fucking Valley to Major Crimes downtown. That feels like a payoff to me."

"True, I guess."

"We can't guess. We have to have it down solid before we get into court."

"You'll subpoena her as a witness?"

"Not with what we know now. Too many things that aren't clear. It would be too dangerous to bring her in. No telling what she'd say on the stand."

We pushed through the heavy doors onto Temple Street and headed back to the Lincoln.

20

I WANTED TO get home so I could start writing the real petition that I would file on behalf of Lucinda Sanz. No more props, no more games. It was time to put together the narrative that would make the case for my client's actual innocence. As I had told Lucinda, the world was turned upside down. She was now considered guilty until proven innocent. The initial document I would write in the next few days needed to make clear, without giving away the store, what I would present and what I would prove. It needed to do more than shake cages in the sheriff's department. It had to be compelling enough to make a U.S. district court judge sit up in his or her comfortable chambers and say, "I want to hear more." I had at least two solid things going for me at this point that were not hearsay or otherwise dismissible. One was the revelation that Roberto Sanz was in a sheriff's clique, which brought a clear implication of organized corruption. The other was the meeting between Sanz and an FBI agent just an hour before his murder. That was new evidence that pointed to a wide range of suspects other than Lucinda Sanz. I believed that these could get me through the habeas door. But I knew I would need more — much more — once I got through.

I told Bosch to take me home. He had his own assignment: Identify the other members of Roberto Sanz's unit, especially any female deputies. He needed to put a name to Lady X.

Bosch pulled to the curb on Fareholm by the stairs to my front door.

"So, I'm around if you need me," he said. "I'll let you know when I have the crew names put together."

"You know where to find me," I said. "I cleared my schedule to write —"

I stopped mid-sentence when I looked up the stairs to the front door.

"What is it?" Bosch asked.

"My front door's open," I said. "Those bastards..."

We both got out and proceeded cautiously up the steps to the deck.

"I don't have a weapon," Bosch announced.

"Good," I said. "I don't want another shooting in here."

More than fifteen years earlier, I had exchanged fire in my home with a woman intent on killing me. It was the one and only gunfight I'd ever been in. I had won it and I wasn't interested in risking a perfect record.

"Besides, I doubt there's anyone inside," I added. "Like at your place, they're just sending a message: 'We know about you, we're watching you.'"

"Whoever 'they' are," Bosch said.

I entered first and found the front room empty and undisturbed. It was a small house with a big view, on the other side of the hills from Bosch's place. Living room, dining room, and kitchen were in the front, and two bedrooms and an office were in the back. The back-yard was barely big enough for a deck and the hot tub I never used.

As we moved through, I saw no signs of a break-in. We saw nothing out of place until we moved down the hallway and reached the office.

The intruders had left the room in shambles: Drawers pulled out of the desk and overturned on the floor, couch upholstery slashed with a blade, lawbooks knocked off shelves. The coup de grâce came from a bottle of maple syrup I'd brought back from a trip to Montreal with my daughter the year before. I had left it on a shelf as a reminder of the fun we'd had. Now it was shattered on the floor, its contents having been poured onto the keyboard of the laptop lying open next to the shards of glass.

"With you, they only made you think there was a break-in, right?" I asked.

"That or made me think I was losing my mind," Bosch said.

"Well, I would rather have had that than this."

"Yeah. Did you call it in?"

"Did you?"

"I made a report. You told me to. But nothing's going to come of it."

"I get the feeling that's what they want me to do."

"How so?"

"I don't know. It's their plan, not mine. But I don't have time to deal with a police investigation that won't lead to anything. They want to distract me."

"Who is 'they'?"

"I don't know. The Cucos? The FBI? It could be anybody at this point. We've obviously poked the hornets' nest."

I scanned the entire room, surveying the damage.

"I need to figure out what they took," I said. "And go to the Apple Store."

With a foot, I shoved the laptop a few feet across the floor. It left a trail of maple syrup.

"This one is done," I said. "But I've got everything on the cloud. I'll be back in business as soon as I pick up a new one."

"What makes you think they took something?" Bosch asked.

I spread my hands to take in the whole ransacked room.

"They were covering something up by trashing the place," I said. "Something they found."

Bosch didn't respond.

"You don't think so?" I asked.

"Not sure," he said. "Could've been a lot of things. First of all, we don't know this has anything to do with the Sanz case. I'm sure you've made your fair share of enemies over the years. It could be unrelated to Sanz."

"Don't kid yourself, Bosch. We've both had break-ins just days apart. What's the connection? Sanz. This is them. Believe me. And it's not going to stop us. Fuck them. This will just make it taste all the better when we take them down and Lucinda does the resurrection walk."

"Resurrection walk?"

"When she is raised from the dead."

"Okay."

He looked a little baffled by the term.

"You gotta make sure you're there for that, Harry," I said. "That will be something."

"You get her out, I'll be there," he said.

PART FIVE

OCTOBER — FINAL PREP

21

BOSCH WAS LYING chest down, his left cheek on the dry scrub grass that had sprouted in the yard after the torrential rains of last winter. It was now October and the grass had dried to a yellow-brown over the summer months. Each blade was crisp and felt like a knife's edge against his skin. He heard the woman's voice from behind him.

"Okay, both hands at your sides, palms up," she said. "There was no effort to break his fall. He was essentially dead before he hit the ground."

Bosch adjusted his hands accordingly.

"Like that?" he asked.

"Uh, move your right about four inches farther out from your body," she said. "No, left. Sorry, I meant your left hand four inches farther out."

Bosch adjusted.

"Perfect," she said.

She was Shami Arslanian, a forensics expert Mickey Haller had brought out from New York. The hearing on the Lucinda Sanz habeas petition was a week away and Arslanian had come out to prep for her presentation and testimony. Bosch had brought her to the scene of the crime, the front lawn where Roberto Sanz had been fatally shot twice in the back. She had determined that Bosch was within an inch of Sanz's height and twenty pounds of his weight, so Bosch would be Sanz's stand-in — actually, his lie-in. She set up a camera with a laser focus on a tripod.

"Okay," she said. "Almost done."

"No worries," Bosch said. "Just glad we aren't doing this in the summer."

His breath kicked up a puff of desert dust.

"Okay, got it," she said. "We're good."

Bosch rolled to his side and started to get up.

"You sure?" he asked.

"Actually, stay like that, on your knees," she said. "Let me capture that while we're here. Just turn to your left about forty-five degrees."

Moving on his knees, Bosch turned. Arslanian tweaked his position slightly and then told him to drop his hands limply to his sides. He did so and she told him to hold still.

"Okay," she said. "Do you need help getting all the way up?"

"No, I'm good," he said.

He got to one knee and pushed himself up. He started brushing the dust and loose scrub grass off his clothes. He was wearing jeans and a patterned shirt with the tails out.

"Sorry about your clothes," Arslanian said.

"Don't be," Bosch said. "Part of the job. I had a feeling I would get dirty out here."

"But I'm sure your job description doesn't include playing dead."

"You'd be surprised. Driver, investigator, subpoena service. I've worked for Haller for nine months or so and there's always a new job within the job, you know?"

"I do. This is my third case with him. I never know what to expect when he calls me."

Bosch walked over to where she was taking the camera and laser mount off the tripod. She, too, was wearing blue jeans and a work shirt with several pens in a breast pocket. She was short and compact, her body shape largely hidden beneath the baggy shirt she wore untucked. And she was newly blond, which Bosch had learned when he picked her up at the airport the day before. Initially he'd looked around baggage claim for a woman whom Haller had described as a redhead.

"So, with all of this, you're going to make a re-creation of the shooting?" he asked.

"Exactly," Arslanian said. "We'll be able to show the murder as close to the way it happened as possible."

"Amazing."

"It's a program that I was involved in developing. It can be tweaked according to height, distance, all physical parameters. What I call the forensic physics of a case."

Bosch wasn't sure what all of that meant, though he did know artificial intelligence was a controversial subject, depending on the application. It reminded him of when people first started talking about DNA in law enforcement. It took a while for the technology to be accepted, but now it was considered, wrongly or rightly, to be the easy solve for violent crimes.

"I like what I do," Arslanian said. "It's fun to figure out exactly how something happened and why."

"I get that," Bosch said.

"How long were you a cop?"

"About forty years."

"Wow. And military before that? Do you know what the high-ready gun stance is?"

"Sure."

"That's what we're going to show. When Lucinda was married to Roberto, he taught her to shoot. He took her to the range and there are photos of her in high-ready stance. That's what I'll base this on."

"Okay."

Bosch had seen the photos in the discovery material Haller got after filing the habeas petition, and he knew that at first glance they weren't helpful to the case for Lucinda Sanz's innocence. He wasn't sure how Arslanian's re-creation would work, but he knew that Haller had full trust in her. And he remembered Haller talking about taking adverse evidence and finding ways to own it, make it work for you rather than against you. The photos of Lucinda at the range had seemed damning. But maybe now, not so much.

"I'm going out to Chino tomorrow to show Lucinda some photos," Bosch said. "Do you need me to ask her anything?"

"I don't think so," Arslanian said. "I think we're covered. And I've got what I need here. We can head back to the city and I'll get to work on it."

"Sounds like a plan," Bosch said. "I'm just going to tell the owners we're done."

Bosch walked up the stoop to the front door and knocked. A woman quickly answered, and Bosch got the idea that she had been watching them through a window.

"Mrs. Perez, we're all done here," Bosch said. "Thanks for letting us use the front yard."

"Is okay," Perez said. "Uh, you said you work for the lawyer?"

"Yes, we both do."

"Do you think the woman is innocent?"

"I do. But we have to prove it."

"Okay, I see."

"Do you know her?"

"Oh, no, I don't. I just...I just wondered what would happen."

"Okay."

Bosch waited to see if she would say more, but she didn't.

"Well, thank you," he said.

He went down the two steps and joined Arslanian in the yard. She had collapsed her tripod and was stowing it in a carrying bag.

"When she bought the house, did she know what happened here?" she asked.

"She's just renting," Bosch said. "Her landlord didn't tell her."

"Was she freaked out when you told her?"

"Not so much. It's L.A., you know. There's probably a history of violence wherever you go."

"That's sad."

"That's L.A."

22

ON THE DRIVE back from the desert, Arslanian didn't have to be told to sit up front. She took the seat next to Bosch but focused her attention on her notes and a laptop she opened once they were on the smooth surface of the Antelope Valley Freeway. She spoke without taking her eyes off the screen or interrupting the input of data into her computer program.

"Funny that they call it the Antelope Valley," she said.

"Why is that?" Bosch asked.

"I did my research on the plane. There haven't been any antelope here in over a century. The species was hunted out by the Indigenous people before it was ever called the Antelope Valley."

"Didn't know that."

"I was thinking I might see antelope roaming free. But then I looked it up."

Bosch nodded and tried to draw her attention away from the computer screen.

"Do you see that?" he said. "The rock outcropping."

Arslanian looked up at the jagged formation they were passing to the north of the freeway.

"Wow, beautiful," she said. "And immense!"

"Vasquez Rocks," Bosch said. "They call it that because about a hundred and fifty years ago a bandido named Tiburcio Vasquez hid out in there, and the sheriff's posse never found him."

Arslanian studied the formation for a long moment before responding.

"Not many places are named after bad guys," she said.

"How about Trump Tower?" Bosch responded.

"Self-named. And I guess it depends on who you talk to about that."

"I guess so."

She lapsed into silence and Bosch wondered if he had offended her. He had just been trying for some kind of reaction. He was intrigued by her and the way she did her work and looked at things. He wanted to know her better but knew her time in L.A. would be short. After the hearing she would return to New York.

When, after a few minutes, they had connected to the Golden State Freeway, she spoke again.

"Mickey told me you two are brothers."

"Half brothers, actually."

"Ah. Which was the common parent?"

"Father."

"But you two didn't know about each other until you were grown up?"

"Yeah. Our father was a lawyer like Mickey. Mickey's mother was his wife. My mother was a client."

"I think I see why you were kept apart. Was it consensual — your mother and father?"

It was a surprising question. Bosch didn't answer at first because he realized he had never asked himself that. It was now too late to ever know for sure.

"I'm sorry, you don't have to talk about it," Arslanian said. "Sometimes I'm too blunt with people I feel comfortable with."

"No, it's not that," Bosch said. "I just never thought about it that way before. I assumed it was consensual. Started as a business arrangement — payment for services rendered. My mother was gone by the time I figured out who he was. And I met him only once, and very briefly at that. He was dying at the time, and soon afterward he was gone too."

"I'm sorry."

"Nothing really to be sorry about. I didn't know the guy."

"I mean sorry you had to grow up . . . like that."

Bosch just nodded. She moved on.

"So, how'd you and Mickey meet? One of those DNA services?"

"No, it was a case. We met on a case and sort of figured it out."

"Harry, can I ask you something? Something personal?"

"Seems like all you ask are personal questions."

"True. I guess that's just me."

"So, go ahead. Ask away."

"Are you ill?"

The question caught Bosch off guard. His vanity had led him to believe she was going to ask whether he was married. It took a few moments for him to form a response.

"Mickey told you that?"

"Uh, no. I just could tell. Your aura. It feels weakened, you could say."

"My aura . . . well, I was sick but I'm getting better."

"Sick how?"

"Cancer. But like I said, it's under control."

"No, you said you were getting better. That could mean something different from 'under control.' I assume you are under care. What kind of cancer is it — or was it?"

"It's called CML for short."

"Chronic myeloid leukemia. That's not a hereditary cancer. It comes from chromosomal changes. Any idea how — I'm sorry, I shouldn't be asking you this."

The freeway traffic became clogged and slowed down as they dropped back into Los Angeles at the top of the Valley.

"It's okay," Bosch said. "I worked a case where I got exposed to radioactive material. I didn't know it until it was too late. Anyway, it could have been that, but it could have been a lot of things. I used to smoke. Diagnosing origin is not an exact science. I'm sure as a person of science, you know that."

Arslanian nodded.

"You said both that the cancer is under control and that you're getting better," she said. "Which is it?"

"You'd have to ask my doctor," Bosch said. "Mickey got me into a clinical trial. That's why I've been working for him — health insurance and the access he has to the upper levels of medical care. Anyway, the doctor in charge of the trial said the treatment they'd tested on me worked. To an extent. It was not full remission but close. They want to do it again and hopefully knock the rest of it out."

"I hope so too. Where did you go for this trial?"

"UCLA Med."

Arslanian nodded her approval.

"That's a good facility," she said. "Would you allow me to take a DNA sample from you?"

"Why?" Bosch asked.

"It could give us further insight into what's going on with you biologically. Did they run genetic tests on you at UCLA?"

"Not that I know of. I don't ask them about everything they're doing. It's kind of above my pay grade. But they sure took a lot of blood."

"Of course. But you might ask them. It could be part of the clinical trial. If not, I'd like to do it."

"Why? Is this something Mickey wants from me?"

"You are such a detective, Harry Bosch. No, Mickey knows nothing about this. But I would also go to him for a DNA sample. Since you're half brothers, you have very similar genomes. A comparison might be beneficial to you both. Have you heard of precision medicine?"

"Uh . . . no, not really."

"It's got a lot to do with genetic makeup and targeting care and treatment. Do you have children?"

"A daughter."

"Same as Mickey. This could be beneficial to them as well."

Bosch had always been suspicious of science and technology. Not that he didn't believe that the advances made were good for the world, but he had a detective's suspicion about early adopters and didn't buy into the cult-like belief that all scientific discoveries were beneficial. He knew this put him on the outside looking in, an analog man in a digital world, but his instincts had always served him well. For every great technological advancement, there were always people out there looking to misuse it.

"I'll think about it," he said. "Thanks for the offer."

"Anytime," Arslanian said.

They rode in silence most of the way downtown. It became awkward and Bosch tried to come up with something to say.

"So," he finally managed. "What have you been doing with the computer there?"

"Just plugging the data into the re-creation program," Arslanian said. "It will do the work and then in court it will be my job to show and tell. Like it is for you, this is new stuff for juries."

"We'll just have a judge making the call on a habeas. No jury."

"Same thing. Judges need to be schooled too."

"I'm sure you'll be a good teacher."

"Thanks. I'm in the process of patenting the program."

"I'm sure prosecutors and defense attorneys all over the country will be jumping on this."

"That's why I need to protect it. Not to keep them from using it but to protect the investment of time, money, and research my partner at MIT and I put into it."

Bosch pulled into the entrance tunnel of the Conrad hotel and lowered his window to tell the valet who rushed up that he was just dropping off his passenger.

"Thank you, Harry," Arslanian said. "I enjoyed our conversation and I hope you think about precision medicine."

Her door was opened by the helpful valet and she got out.

"I guess I'll see you in court," Bosch said.

"I'll be there," Arslanian said.

The valet unloaded Arslanian's equipment from the back seat and Bosch pulled out into traffic. He wished he had said more to her, maybe asked if she wanted to get dinner. He felt embarrassed. As old as he was, he still hesitated to pull the trigger on matters of the heart.

23

THE SHIFT BOSS at the prison denied Bosch's request for an attorney-client meeting room because Bosch was not an attorney. He had to make a regular visitation request and then wait two hours before he heard his name called over a loudspeaker. He was ushered to a stool in front of a thick plexiglass window in a long line of stools and visitation booths very similar to the setup at Corcoran. The wait for Lucinda Sanz wasn't long after that. They both took their phones off the hooks and spoke.

"Hello, Mr. Bosch."

"Hello, Cindi. Call me Harry."

"Okay, Harry. Is it over?"

"Is what over?"

"Did the judge turn Mr. Haller down?"

"Oh. No, nothing's over. The hearing is happening. It's this coming Monday. They'll be transporting you to the city for it."

Bosch saw a little bit of life return to her eyes. She had been prepared for the worst.

"I'm here because I want to show you some photos," he said. "Remember you told us that it was a female deputy who wiped your hands and arms for gunshot residue?"

"Yes, a woman," Lucinda said.

"I have some photos. I want to see if you recognize any of them as the woman who swabbed you."

"Okay."

"They wouldn't let us meet in an attorney room with a table where I could spread them out like a lineup, so I'm going to hold up the photos one at a time. I want you to study all of them before you respond. Even if you're sure about a photo, wait till I show you all six. Take your time. And then if you recognize one, you tell me by number one through six. Okay?"

"Okay."

"All right, here goes."

Bosch hung up the phone to make sure he would not hear Lucinda if she blurted out a number or other exclamation before he had shown her all the photos. He opened a manila file on the shelf in front of the window. The six photos were facedown in a stack. Each had a number written on the back. He held them up to the glass one at a time, did a silent five-second count, then lowered the photo and went on to the next. Lucinda leaned toward the glass to look closely at them. Bosch watched her eyes and saw recognition when he held up the fourth photo. It was immediate and clear. But Lucinda, who had let her phone hang loose on its cord, did not make any exclamation.

The photos were not face shots. They were surveillance shots taken surreptitiously with a long-lens camera handled by Cisco Wojciechowski. It had taken him nearly a week outside the Antelope Valley sheriff's station with the camera and a radio scanner to identify and photograph the members of the anti-gang task force that at one time included Roberto Sanz. There were only two women currently on the team and only one of them had been in the unit when Roberto Sanz was assigned to it. Her photo was among the six Bosch was now showing Lucinda. The other women in the photos were of similar age and shown in similar candid situations but none of them were sheriff's deputies. None were in uniform.

When he was finished showing them, he put the photos back in the file and closed it. He picked up the phone.

"Do you want me to show them again?" he asked.

"Number four," Lucinda said. "That's her. Four."

"Are you sure?" Bosch said. "Do you want to look again?"

He kept his voice as deadpan as possible.

"No, it's her," Lucinda said. "She's the one. I remember."

"She's the deputy who wiped your hands and your clothes with the GSR pads?" Bosch asked.

"Yes."

"And you're sure?"

"Yes. Four."

"Percentage-wise, how sure are you?"

"One hundred percent. It's her. Who is she?"

Bosch leaned toward the glass to take in as much of Lucinda's side of the booth as possible. He looked past her shoulder and up. He saw the camera mounted on the upper wall that ran behind the booths where the convicts talked to their visitors. Lucinda's identification of Stephanie Sanger would be on video, if needed.

Lucinda turned around, following Bosch's sightline to the camera. She looked back at him.

"What?" she asked.

"Nothing, really," Bosch said. "Just wanted to see if there was a camera."

"Why?"

"In case the identification you've made is challenged in court."

"You mean like if I'm not there? Do you think I'm in danger because I identified her?"

Lucinda suddenly looked scared.

"No, I don't think that," he said quickly to reassure her. "I'm just covering all the bases. Normally these are done in a room without glass between us and you sign your name to the photo you pick. We can't do that here. That's all. Nothing's going to happen to you, Cindi."

"Are you sure?" she asked.

"I'm sure. I just want everything to be bulletproof for when we get to court."

"Okay, I trust you and Mr. Haller."

"Thank you."

"The one I picked, who is she?"

"Her name is Stephanie Sanger. She worked with your ex-husband."

"Yes, she told me that."

"Do you remember what else she said?"

"She just said they had to do the test so they could rule me out."

"That was a trick to get you to do it."

Bosch picked up the file containing the photos and held it up.

"When we go to court next week, you may be asked about this, okay?"

"Why?"

"What I mean is you may have to make the identification again. By photo or if she's there."

"She'll be there?"

"She may be, yes. We're going to subpoena her as a witness. But I don't know for sure whether she'll be in court if you testify."

"When will they move me to L.A.?"

"I'm not sure about that either. I'll get Mr. Haller to check on it."

"I don't want to be held in the county jail. The sheriffs run that."

"You won't be. It's a federal case. You'll be transferred from here to federal custody — the U.S. Marshals Service — so they can bring you to court on Monday."

"You're sure?"

A loud buzz sounded in the phone's earpiece, followed by an electronic voice stating that the interview had one minute left.

"I'm sure, Cindi," Bosch said. "Don't worry about that."

A look of desperation came over her face as she realized the final seconds of the interview were ticking away.

"Mr. Bosch, are we going to win?" she said.

"We're going to do our best," Bosch said, immediately knowing his words were inadequate. "The truth will come out and we're going to get you home to your son."

"Do you promise me?"

Bosch hesitated, but before he could answer, the connection went dead. He just looked at Lucinda Sanz and nodded. He knew as he did so that it was a promise that would haunt him if things didn't turn out the way he hoped.

He got up from the stool and gave Lucinda a half-hearted wave goodbye. She did the same and her face showed the uncertainty of what lay ahead. Promises or no promises, nothing was for sure in court.

He followed the arrows on the floor to the prison's exit gate. He felt bad about how the interview had ended but tried to concentrate on what had been accomplished. She had identified Stephanie Sanger as the one who started the chain reaction that resulted in Lucinda Sanz being charged with her ex-husband's murder. That was a big get and as soon as he got to the prison's parking lot, he turned his phone back on and called Haller.

The call rang through to voice mail. Bosch guessed that Haller was in court. He started to leave a message but heard a beep and saw that Haller was calling him back. He ended the message and took the call.

"So, what's happening in Chino?" Haller said.

"Cindi identified Sanger as the one who conducted the GSR test," Bosch said.

Haller whistled. Bosch could hear traffic noises and guessed that he was in the Lincoln.

"This is good," Haller said. "It's what we thought but nice to have it on the record."

"Sort of," Bosch said. "They wouldn't give me the lawyer room. I had to show her the photos through the glass. She couldn't sign the photo, but there was a camera behind her. It's on video if we ever need it."

"Good. Anything else?"

"She's nervous, especially about Sanger. Afraid."

"Well, we're six days out. I'd say it's time to initiate our plan."

"Subpoena Sanger?"

"And her pal Mitchell."

"Yeah, they're not going to like it."

"That's an understatement. I also want you to pick up the thumb drive AT and T has been holding for us."

"Doesn't it become discovery the minute I do?"

"Technically it's not discoverable until I decide I'm going to present it in court. But if I wait and sandbag 'em with it the day before, they'll scream bloody murder and get a continuance from the judge."

"So what do we do?"

"You pick it up, download the data, then print out the entire file. Should be a couple thousand pages, I'm guessing. Then we give them the hard copy while you keep the searchable electronic file. My guess is they'll look at that haystack and think we're scamming them into wasting time on it. And they'll have no valid complaint when we put it into evidence."

"*If* we put it into evidence."

"That's a big if. We have our hunches about what you'll find, but it's all got to pan out or we've wasted our time and our client's chance at freedom."

"Well, I'll get to work on the cell data as soon as I have it."

"Let me know what you get."

"Wait—what about the FBI?"

"I'm not going to play that card until I have to."

Bosch wasn't exactly sure what that meant, but he knew not to ask further questions about it. Haller was trying to play hide the ball with the attorney general's office—handing over what he had to but only when he had to and disguising his court strategy as best he could. It was a high-wire act with no net that could ultimately come down to an angry federal judge wanting to know what he knew and when he'd known it. It was the kind of defense ploy that would have made Bosch's blood boil when he carried a badge. Now he almost admired Haller for the moves he was making. He saw the Lincoln Lawyer as a master at staying just inside the ethical boundary lines when it came to dealings with those sitting across the aisle. Haller called it dancing between the raindrops.

In the seven months they had worked the Sanz case together, Bosch had come to realize that working on the defense side made Haller the long-shot underdog. He was like a man on the beach holding a surfboard and looking up at a hundred-foot wave coming in. The power and might of the state was limitless. Haller was just one man making a stand for his client. He was willing to paddle out to that crushing wave. Bosch was beginning to see that there was something noble in that.

"You heard anything from Morris yet?" Bosch asked. "We're still good to go Monday?"

Hayden Morris was the assistant attorney general for California who would defend the conviction of Lucinda Sanz at the federal habeas hearing. He had made little contact with Haller other than sending him a note every Monday morning demanding full discovery.

"Not a word," Haller said. "So, as far as I'm concerned, all systems are go for Monday. Be there or be square."

"Got it," Bosch said. "I'll pick up the AT and T stuff on my way in. I'll dive in tonight and then go paper Sanger and Mitchell tomorrow."

"If you find what we hope is in there, you call me right away. But remember, no emails, no texts."

"Right. Nothing you'll have to turn over to the AG."

"There you go. You're thinking like a defense lawyer again."

"I hope not."

"Embrace it. It's the new you, Harry."

Bosch disconnected without further comment. Or denial.

PART SIX

THE TRUTH TRAP

24

THE EAGLE HAD angry, righteous eyes. It looked as if, given the opportunity, it would drop the arrows and olive branch it grasped in its sharp talons, swoop down from the wall, and tear your throat open for having even thought of coming here for justice. I studied it as I grew accustomed to my new surroundings. I had spent most of my decades-long practice trying to avoid being in federal courtrooms. The U.S. District Court for the Central District of California was where defense cases went to die. The feds operated with a near 100 percent conviction rate. Defense cases here were managed, not often tried, and almost never won.

But *Lucinda Sanz v. the State of California* was different. A habeas petition was a civil motion. My opponent wasn't the federal government. I was in a battle against the state, with a federal judge presiding as referee, and that opened the door of hope. After I took in the seal with the angry eagle affixed to the wall above the judge's bench, my eyes moved about the august room with its deep, rich woods, flags in the front corners, and textured oil portraits of former jurists on the side walls. This room had stood the test of time better than any lawyer who had ever stepped in here with a prayer for justice. This was what Legal Siegel had taught me so long ago. *Breathe it in. This is your moment. This is your stage. Want it. Own it. Take it.*

I closed my eyes and repeated the words in my head, ignoring the sounds around me: people shuffling into the benches of the gallery behind me, whispers from the AG's table to my left, the court clerk in his corral muttering into his phone to the right. And then came an intrusion I could not ignore.

"Mickey! Mickey!"

An urgent whisper. I opened my eyes and looked at Lucinda. She nodded toward the back of the room. I turned and saw the reporters in the first row and the courtroom artist working for one of the TV stations, since cameras were not allowed in federal court. And beyond them I saw Deputy Stephanie Sanger sitting in the last row. It was the first time I had seen her in person. Since the habeas was a civil motion, I could have deposed her but that would have given her, and the AG, a heads-up on my case strategy. I didn't want that. So I'd gambled and skipped the depo, and I would question her for the first time when I called her as a witness.

I locked eyes for a moment with Sanger. She had sandy-blond hair and pale eyes; her stare was as cold and angry as the eagle's up on the wall. She was in full uniform, badge and commendation pins on display. This was the oldest trick in the book when it came to reminding a jury of the authority of a testifying law enforcement officer. But this wasn't a jury trial and the uniform most likely would not impress the judge.

"Can she do that?" Lucinda asked. "Sit behind us like that?"

I looked from Sanger to my client. She was scared.

"Don't worry about her," I said. "When court starts, she'll leave. She's a witness and they're not allowed to be in court until they testify. That's why Harry Bosch isn't here."

Before Lucinda could respond, the courtroom marshal stood at his desk next to the door to the courtside holding cell and announced the arrival of Judge Ellen Coelho. The timing was perfect. As people in the courtroom stood, the door behind the bench opened and the black-robed judge took the three steps up to the black leather chair from which she would preside.

"Be seated," she said, her voice amplified by the coffered ceiling and the other acoustics of the courtroom.

As I sat down, I leaned toward Lucinda and whispered, "There will be some discussions with the judge and then it will be your turn. Like we talked about, be calm, be direct, look at me or the judge when you answer. Don't look at the other attorneys."

Lucinda nodded hesitantly. She still looked scared, her light brown complexion turning pale.

"It's going to be okay," I said. "You're ready for this. You'll do fine."

"But what if I don't?" she said.

"Don't think like that. These people at the other table want to take the rest of your life away. They want to take your son away. Be angry at them, not scared. You need to get back to your son, Lucinda. They are trying to stop you from doing that. Think about that."

I noticed motion behind her and looked up from our huddle to see Frank Silver pull out the chair on her other side and sit down.

"Sorry I'm late," he whispered. "Hi, Lucinda, do you remember me?"

Before she could answer I put my hand on Lucinda's arm to stop her and leaned across her to address Silver as quietly as my anger would allow.

"What are you doing here?" I whispered.

"I'm co-counsel," he said. "That was our deal. I'm here to help."

"What deal?" Lucinda asked.

"There is no deal," I said. "You need to leave, Frank. Now."

"I'm not going anywhere," Silver said.

"Listen to me carefully," I said. "You can't be here. It will throw—"

I was cut off by the judge.

"In the matter of *Sanz versus the State of California* we have a habeas corpus petition. Is counsel ready to proceed?"

Hayden Morris and I stood at the same time at our separate tables and affirmed that we were ready to proceed.

"Mr. Haller," the judge said, "I have no record of you having a co-counsel. Who is seated next to your client?"

Silver stood up to answer the question himself, but I beat him to it.

"Mr. Silver is the plaintiff's original defense attorney in this case," I said. "He just came by to show his support for her. He is *not* co-counsel."

Coelho looked down at the paperwork in front of her on the bench.

"He is on your witness list, is he not?" she asked. "I recall that name, I believe."

"Yes, Your Honor," I said. "He is. And he just wanted to be here at the start, as I said, to show his support. He will step out now. In fact, Your Honor, plaintiff requests that all witnesses be excused from the courtroom until they are called upon to testify."

Morris, who had already sat down, shot back up to his feet and told the judge that the witness I was referring to was Sergeant Stephanie Sanger, who was in the courtroom for a state motion to quash her subpoena for improper service.

"All right, we'll get into that," Coelho said. "But first, Mr. Silver, you are excused from the courtroom."

I was still standing, readying for the argument about Sanger, and I'd already dismissed Silver from my thoughts. I had to keep my eyes on the prize and not be distracted. Morris obviously wanted to keep

Sanger off the stand and as far away from the case and my question-ing as possible. I could not allow that.

In my peripheral vision I saw Silver slowly stand and push back his chair. I turned and gave a quick nod so it looked like we were close colleagues and of one mind on this miscarriage of justice. He played along, giving Lucinda a pat on the shoulder before moving by me to the gate. He smiled and nodded in a supportive way while he whis-pered, "Fuck you. And I'm not testifying. Good luck hitting me with a subpoena."

I nodded as though he had just whispered words of great inspiration.

And then he was gone. I remained standing for the argument to come while opening a file on the table with a copy of the subpoena Bosch had dropped on Sanger. I had no idea how Morris was going to challenge this.

Judge Coelho waited until Silver was almost to the courtroom door before continuing.

"Mr. Morris, you may proceed," she said.

For the next five minutes Morris argued that the subpoena served on Sergeant Sanger should be quashed because opposing counsel — me — was on a fishing expedition with no evidentiary basis for put-ting Sanger on the stand.

"Sergeant Sanger is involved in ongoing investigations that could be compromised if counsel strays willy-nilly in his questioning. He is trying to grandstand with this witness, Your Honor, and it could come at the expense of justice in other cases. Additionally, counsel's application for the subpoena is based on an identification made by the plaintiff that was highly suspect and did not conform to standard pro-cedures for photographic identification. That alone makes the sub-poena invalid."

"Tell me about the photo identification," Coelho said.

"Yes, Your Honor. Plaintiff's investigator showed her a series of photos in the visiting room at the prison where she was housed. This allowed him to steer her identification to Sergeant Sanger. This then became the basis for the subpoena you signed. As the court knows, a proper photographic display to a witness would be what is commonly known as a six-pack, where the individual is shown six photos at once and without any outside influence as to which photo, if any, to choose. But now it is too late; the identification is tainted, and the People ask that the subpoena be quashed." Morris sat down.

I was relieved. The assistant AG's argument was complete bullshit. Morris was clearly grasping at straws, which told me how concerned he was about Sanger testifying. I now just had to make sure I could get her on the stand.

"Mr. Haller?" the judge said. "Your response?"

"Thank you, Judge," I said. "I would love to respond. First of all, I've practiced law in this town for decades and this is the first time I've ever heard the term *willy-nilly* put forth as the basis of an objection. I must have missed that in law school, but to use my colleague's word, his argument is willy-nilly and, I'll add, absurd. My investigator Harry Bosch spent more than forty years as a police officer and detective with the Los Angeles Police Department. He knows how to conduct a proper photo lineup. He first asked the supervisors at the prison for a private attorney room to meet with Ms. Sanz but he was denied that. So he met with Ms. Sanz in a booth in the visitation room and proceeded as outlined in my request for a subpoena. He showed Ms. Sanz one photo at a time and did not pick the phone up until after she had seen all six photos. That was when she made the identification. There was nothing untoward, nothing sneaky, nothing even willy-nilly — whatever that means. And, Your Honor, a prison camera recorded every moment of it. If there were any truth to the accusation of a tainted identification, then Mr. Morris would have shown us the video from that camera. If we want to delay this hearing and further the illegal incarceration of Lucinda Sanz, we can halt everything while the court orders that the video be brought forward for review."

"Your Honor?" Morris said.

"Not yet, Mr. Morris," Coelho said. "Mr. Haller, a response to the first part of the objection?"

"Mr. Morris makes reference to other investigations of a confidential nature," I said. "He's clearly desperate. I have no intention of bringing up any investigation other than the flawed and corrupt investigation into the killing of Roberto Sanz. The witness he is trying to keep from testifying was knee-deep in that investigation and Mr. Morris wants to prevent the court from finding out the truth about this matter. No other investigation will be mentioned. I stipulate to that right now. If I stray from it, the court can shut me down."

There was a pause and then Morris tried for a second bite of the apple.

"Your Honor, if I could respond briefly," he said.

"That won't be necessary," Coelho said. "Do you have a video recording of the investigator showing the plaintiff the photos?"

"No, Your Honor, I don't," Morris said.

"Have you seen it?" Coelho pressed. "Was it the basis of your motion?"

"No, Your Honor," Morris said meekly. "Our basis was the subpoena request from the plaintiff."

"Then you are unprepared to support your argument," Coelho said. "The motion to quash is denied. Sergeant Sanger is excused from the courtroom until such time as she is called to testify. Anything else, gentlemen, before we start hearing from witnesses in this matter?"

Morris stood up at his table again.

"Yes, Your Honor," he said.

"Very well," Coelho said. "What have you got?"

"As the court knows, this motion was sealed by the court at the request of the State," Morris said. "This was to prevent it from being played out in the media, as opposing counsel has shown a propensity to do in past cases."

I stood up.

"Objection," I said. "Your Honor, the assistant attorney general is doing anything and everything in his power to distract the court from the fact—"

"Mr. Haller," Coelho said forcefully. "I don't like counsel interrupting each other. If I deem that Mr. Morris's argument has merit, you will get your chance to respond. Now, sit down, please, and let him finish."

I did as I was told, hoping my objection would at least throw Morris off his game.

"Thank you, Your Honor," Morris said. "As I was saying, this motion was sealed by the court until such time as a hearing on the matter began."

"Which is right now, Mr. Morris," Coelho said. "I know where you are going with this. I see representatives of the media in the gallery and have approved a request for a courtroom artist. This matter is no longer sealed. We are in open court. What is your objection?"

"The court received the request for a courtroom artist on Friday," Morris said. "We were all copied. At that time this matter was still under seal and yet the media was somehow alerted to it. The State asks for sanctions against plaintiff's counsel for violating the court order sealing the petition."

I stood once again but did not interrupt. I just wanted the judge to know I was ready to respond. But she held out a hand and patted the air, a signal for me to sit down again. I did.

"Mr. Morris, you are doing what two minutes ago you accused Mr. Haller of," Coelho said. "Playing to the media. I am sure that if I asked Mr. Haller whether he alerted the media to this hearing before the seal was lifted, he would say he did not and that there is no evidence to the contrary. Frankly, I think he is too smart to have done such a thing himself. So, Mr. Morris, unless you can provide such evidence, then all you are doing here is grandstanding. I would rather you did not. I would rather get to what we are actually here to do. There will be no sanctions. Now, Mr. Haller, are you ready to proceed?"

I stood up, this time buttoning my jacket as though it were a shield and I was going into battle.

"We are ready," I said.

"Very well," the judge said. "Call your first witness."

25

I HAD TURNED down an offer from Judge Coelho to allow Lucinda Sanz to dress in street clothes supplied by her mother. I didn't want to agree to anything that would distract from the fact that this woman had been in prison for five years for a crime she did not commit. I wanted her appearance to be a constant reminder to the judge of how a wrongful prosecution had taken everything away from her — her son, her family, her freedom, and her livelihood — and left her with a blue jumpsuit with CDC INMATE stenciled on it, front and back.

Sitting in the witness chair, Lucinda seemed small, her face barely rising above the ornate wooden railing in front of her. Her hair was pulled back in a short ponytail; the line of her jaw was sharp. She looked scared but resolute. I would question her first. That would be the easy part. Morris's cross-examination was where the danger lay. He had the transcripts from the first interview she'd given investigators almost six years ago and the deposition taken at Chino two months ago. While I had avoided using the deposition option that came with a civil action, Morris had elected to depose Lucinda, a clear sign of his strategy. If he could catch her in a single lie, he could discredit her and the whole claim that she was innocent.

"Is it all right if I call you Cindi?" I asked.

"Uh, yes," she said.

"Cindi, please tell the court where you live and how long you have lived there."

Before Lucinda could speak, Morris cut in.

"Your Honor, the aspects of Ms. Sanz's incarceration for a crime she confessed to are well known to all parties and the court," he said. "Can we just move to matters germane to the petition?"

"Is that an objection, Mr. Morris?" Coelho asked.

"Yes, Your Honor, it is."

"Very well. Sustained. Mr. Haller, move on and get to the reason we are here today."

I nodded. So it was going to be like that.

"Yes, Your Honor," I said. "Cindi, did you kill your ex-husband, Roberto Sanz?"

"I did not," Lucinda said.

"But you pleaded no contest to manslaughter in the case. Why would you plead to something you now say you didn't do?"

"I'm not saying it just now. I have said it all along. I told the sheriffs. I told my family. I told my lawyer. I did not shoot Roberto. But Mr. Silver told me the evidence was too much, that a jury would find me guilty if we had a trial. I have a son. I wanted to see my son again. I wanted to hug him and be part of his life. I didn't think I would get so many years."

It was said in such a heartfelt manner that I paused and looked at the legal pad in front of me on the lectern so I could let Lucinda's words hang in the courtroom like a ghost. But the judge, who had been appointed for life more than a quarter of a century ago, had witnessed every trick in the book and wasn't having it.

"No further questions, Mr. Haller?" she said.

"No, Your Honor, I have more," I said. "Cindi, why don't you tell the court what happened that night nearly six years ago."

This was the dangerous part. Lucinda could not stray from what was already repeatedly on the record. We could add to it, which I intended to do, but we could not deviate from what was there. To do so would give Morris all he needed to send her back to Chino to finish her sentence.

"Roberto had our son for the weekend," Lucinda began. "He was supposed to bring him home at six so we could go to my mother's house for dinner. But he didn't bring him till almost eight o'clock and he'd had dinner already at Chuck E. Cheese."

"Did that upset you?" I asked.

"Yes, I was very upset and we had an argument. Me and Robbie. And he—"

"Before we get to that, did Roberto tell you why he was late?"

"He just said he had a work meeting, and I knew that was a lie because it was Sunday and his unit didn't work on Sundays."

"Okay, so you didn't believe him and you argued. Is that what happened?"

"Yes, and then he left. I slammed the door because he had ruined my plans for that night."

"And what happened next?"

"I heard the gunshots. Two."

"How did you know they were gunshots?"

"Because I grew up hearing guns in Boyle Heights, and Roberto, when we were married, took me to a gun range to teach me how to shoot. I know what a gunshot sounds like."

"So you hear two gunshots and what do you do?"

"I thought it was him—Roberto—shooting at the house because

he was mad, you know? I ran back to my son's room and we got on the floor. But that was it, no more shots."

"Did you make a 911 call?"

"I called, yes. I told them my ex-husband is out there shooting at my house."

"What did they tell you to do?"

"To stay with my son and hide until they checked it out."

"Did they tell you to stay on the line?"

"Yes."

"Then what happened?"

"I don't know how much time went by but then they said it was safe outside and that I should go to the door because a deputy was there."

"Did you do that?"

"Yes, and that's when I saw him. Roberto was lying on the ground and they said he was dead."

I paused and asked the judge to allow me to play the recording of the 911 call Lucinda had just described. Morris did not object and the recording was played on the courtroom's AV equipment. It did not deviate from the description Lucinda had just given, but her voice on tape had an urgency and fear in it that was absent in her recounting of the event all these years later. I felt that it was good for the judge to hear it and was surprised that Morris had not tried some sort of objection to block.

After the call was played I pivoted to a new line of questioning.

"Now, Cindi, a few minutes ago you mentioned that when you and Roberto were married, he took you to a range to learn how to shoot. Can you tell the court more about that?"

"Like what?"

"Like how many times you went to the range."

"It was two or three times. It was before our son was born. Once he was born I didn't want to have guns or shoot."

"But at that time, before your son was born, did you own a gun?"

"No, they were Robbie's guns. All of them."

"How many guns did he have?"

"I'm not sure. Like five."

"And he had bought all of these?"

"No, he told me he took some of them away from people. Bad people. If they found them with guns they would take them away. Sometimes they kept them."

"Who is 'they,' Cindi?"

"His unit. It was—"

Morris objected, but not fast enough. Mention of the unit was out there. Morris argued that the answer should be stricken from the record and that the story and whatever else Lucinda was about to say would be hearsay based on the alleged statement of a man who was now dead. The judge sustained the objection without giving me a chance to argue it. But that was okay because everyone in the courtroom, including, and most important, the judge, knew who "they" were—the other members of Roberto Sanz's anti-gang unit.

"Okay," I said. "Cindi, tell us about the training at the range you did with your then-husband."

"Well," Lucinda began, "he taught me about the different parts of the gun and how to stand and point when firing. We shot at targets."

"Do you remember what stance you were taught to take?"

"Yes."

"And what was it called?"

"Oh, I thought you meant if I remembered the stance. I don't remember if it was called anything."

"Are you saying you could demonstrate it if the court allowed it?"

"Uh, yes."

I asked the court's permission to have Lucinda step down from the witness stand and demonstrate the shooting stance her husband had taught her. Morris objected, arguing that such an exercise would waste the court's time because the demonstration could not be connected in any way to the shooting of Roberto Sanz.

"Your Honor," I countered, "I plan to prove that Lucinda Sanz did not fire the shots that killed her ex-husband. This demonstration is one of the dots that will be connected along the way."

"I'll allow it," Coelho said. "But I will hold you to your promise to connect those dots. Proceed."

"Thank you, Judge. Cindi, would you show us what you were taught by your husband?"

Lucinda stepped down into the well, the open space in front of the judge's bench. She spread her feet at least two feet apart for stability and brought her arms up straight and extended at shoulder height. She used her left hand to steady her right, the index finger pointing like the barrel of a gun.

"Like this," she said.

"Okay, thank you," I said. "You can return to the witness stand."

As Lucinda returned, I went to the plaintiff's table to get a file. I opened it and asked permission to show two photographs to the witness. I gave copies to Morris, even though he had already received these in discovery and they had been part of the so-called evidence against Lucinda five years before. I also gave copies to the judge. They showed Lucinda at the range, holding a gun in the same stance she had just demonstrated in the courtroom.

"Mr. Haller, I'm concerned," the judge said after reviewing the photos. "You are asking to place into exhibit two photos that would tend to show that your client had access to a firearm and knew how to use it. Are you sure this is wise?"

"It's one of the dots, Your Honor," I said. "And the court will soon understand that the photos are exculpatory, not damning to my client's cause."

"Very well," Coelho said. "It's your show."

I walked a third set of photos to the witness stand and put them down in front of Lucinda.

"Lucinda, can you identify when and where those two photos were taken?" I asked.

"I don't know the exact date," Lucinda said. "But it was when Robbie taught me how to shoot. This was the range we would go to in Sand Canyon."

"Sand Canyon — is that in the Antelope Valley?"

"I think it's Santa Clarita Valley."

"But nearby?"

"Yes, not too far."

"Okay, in that second photo, who is that man next to you?"

"That's Robbie."

"Your husband at the time."

"Yes."

"Who took that photo?"

"It was one of his friends from the unit. He was teaching his wife how to shoot there too."

"Do you remember his name?"

"Keith Mitchell."

"Okay, and in the pictures, the gun you are holding, where is that now?"

"I don't know."

"When you and your husband divorced, did he leave you any of the guns he possessed?"

"No, none. I didn't want them in my house. Not with my son there."

I nodded as if her answer were important and looked at my legal pad, where I had outlined my examination. I used a pen to check off the different avenues of questioning I had covered.

"Okay," I said. "Let's go back to the night of your ex-husband's death. What happened after you opened the door for the deputy and saw Roberto's body on the lawn? Was he facedown or face up?"

"Facedown," Lucinda replied.

"And what happened next with you?"

"They took me and my son and made us sit in the back of a patrol car."

"And how long were you there?"

"Um, it seemed like a long time. But then they took me and put me in a different car from my son. An unmarked car."

"You were eventually driven to the Antelope Valley substation and questioned?"

"Yes."

"Before that, were you asked to allow your hands and clothes to be tested for gunshot residue?"

"Yes. I was asked to step out of the car and they tested me."

"You were swabbed with a foam disk?"

"Yes."

"And who conducted this test?"

"A deputy. A woman."

"Now, there came a time when my investigator Harry Bosch visited with you at the prison in Chino and asked if you would look at some photographs."

"Yes."

"He wanted to see if you could identify the female deputy who swabbed you, correct?"

"Yes."

"He showed you six different photographs?"

"Yes."

"And did you pick one of those photographs and identify the person who swabbed you?"

"Yes."

I gave copies of the photo of Stephanie Sanger from Bosch's photo lineup to Morris and the judge. Permission was quickly granted to enter the photo as plaintiff's exhibit 2 and show it to the witness.

"Is that the woman you identified as the deputy who tested you for gunshot residue?"

"Yes, that's her," Lucinda said.

"Did you know her?"

"No."

"You didn't know she was in your husband's unit with the sheriff's department?"

"No, I didn't know her but she told me she worked with Robbie."

"Did she seem upset that Robbie was dead?"

"She was calm. Professional."

I nodded. I had gotten everything I needed on the record. Most of it would pay dividends at later points in the hearing. I was pleased. I now had to hope that Lucinda would stand up to a cross-examination from Morris. If she survived that, I knew we had a solid chance.

"I have no further questions," I said. "But I reserve the right to call the witness back to the stand."

"Very well, Mr. Haller," the judge said. "Mr. Morris, would you like to take a break before you begin your cross-examination?"

Morris stood.

"The State would welcome a short break, Your Honor," he said. "But I have only two questions for this witness, and they require only yes-or-no answers. Perhaps the break could come after the witness is excused."

"Very well, Mr. Morris," the judge said. "Proceed."

To say I was surprised would be an understatement. Morris was either a lot smarter than I'd given him credit for or a lot dumber. It was hard to tell because I had never seen him in court before this day. The AG usually hired the best and brightest, and for most of them, habeas hearings were a walk in the park. But based on his previous motions and his habit of contesting what he called my "lack of good-faith discovery," he hadn't seemed to be mailing it in. So his letting the petitioner off the stand with just two questions gave me pause. Maybe he sensed that he could not shake Lucinda's story because she was telling the truth.

I watched attentively as Morris went to the lectern to ask his two questions.

"Ms. Sanz, you reside at the state prison for women in Chino, correct?" Morris asked.

"Uh, yes," Lucinda said. "Correct."

"Do you know another inmate there named Isabella Moder?"

Lucinda looked over at me, a momentary flash of *What do I do?* panic entering her eyes. I hoped the judge didn't see it. I simply nodded. There was nothing else I could do.

Lucinda looked back at Morris.

"Yes," she said. "She was in my cell. Then she got transferred to another prison."

With that answer, I knew exactly what the State's strategy was and how Morris planned to play it.

26

I TALKED TO Lucinda and then came out of the courtroom like an escaped prisoner. Moving fast, looking up and down the hall, I saw Stephanie Sanger sitting on a bench against the wall opposite the courtroom entrance. She smirked when she saw me, as if she knew what Morris had just done.

I didn't have time to throw a smirk back at her. I kept scanning the hall until I saw Bosch standing by the elevator. He looked like he was chatting with the marshal who ran the metal detector. The courtrooms on this floor were used primarily for criminal cases, thus the security scan in addition to the metal detector on the first floor of the building.

Bosch glanced over, saw me, and held up an *I'll be right back* finger to the marshal. I stopped and waited for him to join me halfway down the hall so we would be out of earshot of both Sanger and the deputy Bosch had been conversing with.

"How'd she do?" Bosch whispered.

"Fine on the direct," I said. "But it took only two questions from the assistant AG to undo everything."

"What? What happened?"

"He's going to sandbag us with a prison informant. I need you to find out everything you can by tomorrow morning about an inmate named Isabella Moder—I think it's M-o-d-e-r."

"What about handling the witnesses?"

"I'll have to do it. I need you on Moder. Now."

"Okay. Is she at Chino? Who is she?"

"She was Lucinda's old cellmate. But they moved her about six months ago—about the time I filed the habeas."

"And her name didn't come up in discovery? Isn't that a vi—"

"Morris didn't need to put her in if she was going to be used for rebuttal. So no violation. A good, clean sandbagging. I should have seen it coming."

"So what's the hurry if Morris isn't going to call her until after your case?"

"Because the best defense is a good offense. I need to know if we're going to be able to neutralize her whenever they put her on the stand."

"Got it. Did Cindi tell you what she'd told Moder?"

"She didn't tell her anything. Moder's a jailhouse snitch. She's going to lie. She's going to say Lucinda admitted to killing her husband."

"That's bullshit."

"It doesn't matter. That's why I want you to get out of here and find out everything you can about her. Find me something I can burn her to the ground with."

"I'm on it."

"Call Cisco if you need help. No stone left unturned, but you're working against the clock. I should be finished with my witnesses tomorrow. That's when Morris will bring Moder in."

"If I'm on this, I won't be able to get Dr. Arslanian to court tomorrow morning."

"I'll deal with her. You go. Call me as soon as you have something. Court is dark this afternoon because Coelho has a judges' conference. I'm going to put Sanger on the stand now, Arslanian and the rest tomorrow. That includes you, so get going on Moder."

"I'll call you. Good luck with Sanger."

"Luck won't have anything to do with it."

Bosch walked off toward the elevator. I checked my watch. There were still a few minutes left in the break. I went into the restroom, cupped my hands under the cold water at a sink, then held my hands to my face. There was a heaviness growing in the center of my chest. It was the feeling of being unprepared. I hated that feeling more than anything in the world.

On my way back to the courtroom I saw Sanger still posted on the bench.

"Not going so good, is it?" she said.

I stopped and looked at her. She had that smirk again.

"It's going great," I said. "And you're next."

With that, I opened the courtroom door and went in.

The marshals were returning Lucinda from the courtroom lockup to the plaintiff's table, a sign that the judge was ready. I took my seat next to my client as the shackles came off her wrists and ankles, and one wrist was locked to the steel ring on the underside of the table.

"What will happen now?" she whispered.

"I'm going to call Sanger, put her on the record, then tomorrow we prove she's a liar."

"No, I mean what happens now with Isabella?"

"Harry is working on it, trying to find something we can impeach her with."

"'Impeach'?"

"Prove she's lying. You sure you never talked about your case with her?"

"Never. We never talked about her case either."

"All right. I need you to think, Lucinda. Is there anything you know about her that will help us? I can almost guarantee she's going to come in here and testify that you told her you killed Roberto. I need to come back at her with something. Is there—"

The marshal interrupted us with his call to rise. We stood and the judge entered the courtroom and bounded up the steps to the bench. Ellen Coelho had been on the federal bench for nearly thirty years. She was a Clinton appointee, which tended to put her on the liberal side, which was good for us. But when push came to shove, I had no idea what her view of jailhouse snitches would be.

"Continuing in the matter of *Sanz versus the State of California,*" she said. "Mr. Haller, call your next witness."

I called Stephanie Sanger. Since Bosch was no longer in the hall to wrangle witnesses, I asked the judge to send one of the courtroom marshals to get her. The judge seemed annoyed but complied, and while we waited I turned back to my client.

"I need something to go at Isabella with," I whispered. "Try to remember what you talked about. When they put the lights out at night, did you two talk?"

"Yes. It's hard to fall asleep."

"I can imagine. Did she ever—"

The rear door of the courtroom opened and the marshal entered, followed by Sanger, who walked down the center aisle and through the gate. She stopped by the witness chair and took the oath from the clerk before sitting. I moved to the lectern with my files and notes.

"Your Honor," I said, "before I begin, I ask the court to declare Deputy Sanger a hostile witness."

"She's your witness, Counselor," Coelho said. "On what grounds should I declare her to be hostile to the petitioner?"

I wanted Sanger declared hostile because it gave me more freedom during direct examination. I could pose leading questions to which only a yes or no was required. This would allow me to stock those questions with facts I wanted the judge to hear, even if Sanger denied them. The information would still get through.

"As you saw this morning, she has already attempted to avoid testifying, Your Honor," I said. "Add to that a short conversation I just had with her during the break. She clearly doesn't like me, my client, or being here."

Morris stood to respond, but Coelho held her hand up like a stop sign.

"Let's just see how it goes, Mr. Haller," she said. "Proceed with your examination."

Morris sat down and Sanger seemed pleased with my failure to persuade the judge.

"Thank you, Judge," I said. "Deputy Sanger, you are employed by the Los Angeles County Sheriff's Department, correct?"

"I am," Sanger said. "And it's Sergeant."

"When did you get that promotion?"

"Two years ago."

"What is your current assignment with the department?"

"I'm assigned to the Antelope Valley substation, where I'm in charge of the gang-intervention unit."

"You have been with that unit for several years, yes?"

"Yes."

"And now you are in charge of it."

"I just said that."

"Yes, thank you. You were assigned to that unit at the time of Deputy Roberto Sanz's death, correct?"

"I was."

"Were the two of you partners?"

"No, we don't have partners per se on the unit. There are six deputies and a sergeant. We work as a team and on any given day, depending on vacations and sick-outs, you could be partnered with any of the five other deputies. It changes all the time."

"Thank you, Deputy, for that clarif—"

"Sergeant."

"I'm sorry. Sergeant. Thank you for the clarification. So, based on that sort of round-robin of interactions and partnerships, is it correct to say you knew Deputy Sanz well?"

"Yes. We worked together for three years before he was murdered by his ex-wife."

I looked up at the judge.

"Your Honor," I said, "I'd say that's pretty hostile. The witness is revealing a belief that is counter to my client's cause."

"Just proceed, Mr. Haller," Coelho said.

I looked at my notes and quickly regrouped. I had to move carefully now and walk Sanger into a truth trap. If I got her under oath and on the record saying something I could later prove false, it would go a long way toward making the case that Lucinda was corruptly or at least wrongfully convicted.

"Let's talk about the murder of Deputy Sanz," I said. "It happened on a Sunday. Do you recall how you found out that he had been killed?"

"I got a SORS text," Sanger said. "Like everybody in the department."

"Can you tell the judge what a SORS text is?"

"The Special Operations Reporting System is a texting service that allows the department to get messages to all sworn personnel. A text went out that said there had been a deputy-involved shooting in the AV division and that we had lost one of our own."

"AV as in Antelope Valley?"

"Correct. I then made a call and found out that the deputy killed was Roberto Sanz from my unit."

"And what did you do?"

"I called another deputy in the unit and we proceeded to the scene to see if we could be of any help."

"Which deputy was that?"

"Keith Mitchell."

"Why did you only call him when you say the unit consisted of six deputies and a sergeant?"

"Because Keith was the closest to Robbie Sanz."

I opened the file I had brought to the lectern and took out three copies of a document. I distributed them to Morris, the witness, and the judge and asked Coelho for permission to enter the document as the next plaintiff's exhibit and to question the witness about it. Permission was granted.

"What is that, Sergeant?"

"It's a copy of the SORS text that went out," Sanger said.

"And what time does it say it went out?"

"Twenty-eighteen hours."

"Or eight eighteen p.m. in nonmilitary time, correct?"

"Correct."

"How soon after that went out did you arrive at the crime scene?"

"Probably no more than fifteen minutes later."

"The AV, as you call it, is a big place. How was it that you were so close you could be there within fifteen minutes?"

"I happened to be eating dinner at a restaurant nearby."

"What restaurant was that?"

"Brandy's Café."

"Were you with anyone?"

"I was alone at the counter. I got the text, put down some money, and immediately left. I called Keith Mitchell on my way."

She said it in a tired tone, as if I were asking irrelevant questions with no bearing on the case. The judge must have felt like this as well; she interrupted me.

"Mr. Haller," she said. "Is this line of questioning really necessary?"

"It is, Judge," I said. "That will become clear when other witnesses testify."

"Well, please hurry through this so we can get to those witnesses sooner rather than later."

"We would get there sooner if my examination were not interrupted."

"If that remark is intended as a rebuke to the court, we have a problem, sir."

"I'm sorry, Your Honor, it was not intended as a rebuke in any way. May I continue?"

"Please, but hurry."

I nodded and checked my notes to make sure I picked up where I had left off.

"Sergeant Sanger, were homicide investigators on the scene when you arrived?" I asked.

"No, not yet," Sanger said.

"Who from the sheriff's department was there?"

"A lot of deputies had arrived to secure the scene for the homicide unit rolling from the STARS Center in Whittier."

"That would put them as much as an hour out, correct?"

"Yes, most likely."

"So, during that time of waiting for the homicide team, you decided to do their job for them, didn't you?"

"No, that's not correct."

"Well, didn't you take Lucinda Sanz from the car she had been placed in and conduct a test for gunshot residue on her body and clothes?"

"Yes, I did that. It's best to conduct such a test as soon as possible after a shooting crime has been committed."

"Was it procedure for a deputy who worked with the victim to swab the arms and hands of a suspect for a gunshot-residue test?"

"She was not a suspect at that time. It —"

"Not a suspect? Why was she put in the back of a patrol car and swabbed for GSR if she was not a suspect?"

Morris stood up and objected.

"Your Honor," he said. "Counsel is badgering the witness and not allowing her to finish her answers."

"Mr. Haller," Coelho said. "Let her complete her answers and dial back the tone. There is no jury here to impress."

I nodded contritely.

"Yes, Your Honor," I said. "Sergeant Sanger, by all means, please continue and finish your answer."

"As I said, it is important to test for gunshot residue early in an investigation," Sanger said. "Otherwise, the evidence can dissipate or be removed or transferred. I knew in this case that it might be an hour or more before homicide investigators were on scene, so I swabbed the defendant and secured the swab disks in an evidence bag."

"She's the petitioner, not the defendant, Sergeant. Once you completed this test you say was required so urgently, what did you do with that evidence bag containing the swab disks?"

"I turned it over to Deputy Mitchell, who later gave it to the homicide team. It should be noted in the evidence chain-of-custody report, which I'm sure you've seen."

"What if I told you it is not in the chain-of-custody report?"

"Then that would be a slight oversight on Deputy Mitchell's part."

"Nice of you to throw Deputy Mitchell under the bus, but why didn't you just turn it over to the homicide team yourself? You conducted the test. Were you trying to hide that, Sergeant?"

"I wasn't hiding anything. I was going to leave the crime scene. I went to tell Deputy Sanz's girlfriend at the time what had happened. I thought she should hear it from one of Robbie's friends before she saw it on the news."

"That was very noble of you, Sergeant Sanger."

"Thank you."

She said it with a solid tone of sarcasm. I was near the end of my questioning. I decided it was time to rock her boat with a big-time wave.

"Sergeant Sanger, were you aware that at the time of his murder, Roberto Sanz was in a sheriff's gang?"

Sanger actually did rock back in her seat a few inches. Morris quickly stood and objected.

"Assumes facts not in evidence," he said. "Your Honor, counsel is on a fishing expedition, hoping the witness will misspeak and give him something he can blow out of proportion."

I shook my head. I walked to the petitioner's table and opened a file containing several copies of the photos from the Roberto Sanz autopsy. I made sure Lucinda did not see them.

"Your Honor, this is no fishing expedition and I think counsel knows it," I said. "I am prepared, if the court will indulge me, to show this witness proof that her colleague was a member of a sheriff's clique. If the court needs it, I can also bring in an expert on the internal investigation by the sheriff's department and the external investigation by the FBI into these clusters of gangsters with badges, probes that resulted in a former sheriff going to prison and wholesale changes in personnel and training within the department."

It was a bluff. The expert was the FBI agent MacIsaac, and so far

I hadn't been able to get to him. If pressed by the court, I would bring in the *Los Angeles Times* reporter who exposed the scandal and covered its multiple investigations.

Luckily, I needed neither.

"I don't think we need an expert to tell us about the well-known problems in the sheriff's department at the time of this murder," Coelho said. "The witness will answer the question."

All eyes in the courtroom returned to Sanger. I asked if she needed me to repeat the question.

"No," she said. "I was not aware of Roberto being in a clique or a gang or whatever you want to call it."

"If the court allows, I am going to show you two photos," I said. "They were taken during the autopsy of Roberto Sanz."

I approached the bench and handed the judge a set of photos showing Sanz's body on the autopsy table and the close-up of the tattoo on the body's hip. I turned and gave Morris a set. He immediately stood and objected to the inflammatory nature of the photos.

"This man was a hero, Your Honor," he said. "Counsel wants to flaunt these photos that purport to show gang affiliation when they show and prove nothing."

"Your Honor," I countered, "the petitioner can bring in an expert on this subject who will identify the tattoo on Roberto Sanz's body — incidentally located in a place that would not be seen by the public — if necessary. But just a casual Google search by the court or anyone else would confirm that Sanz's secret tattoo directly connects him with a so-called clique that operated in the Antelope Valley."

The judge did not take long to render a decision.

"You may show the witness," she said.

I approached the witness stand and handed Sanger a set of photos.

"Do you recognize that tattoo, Sergeant Sanger?" I asked.

"I do not," Sanger said.

"You did not know of your unit member's association with the Cucos, a known sheriff's clique?"

"I did not and I don't think a tattoo is proof of that."

"Do you have such a tattoo, Sergeant?"

"I do not."

I paused there and in my peripheral vision saw Morris stand, anticipating that my next move would be to ask the court to have Sanger's body inspected for tattoos. But I didn't. I wanted that possibility to hang over the judge's eventual decision on the petition.

"I have one more question for now," I said. "Sergeant, what was your phone number that was linked to the Special Operations Reporting System?"

Morris, who was in the act of sitting down, suddenly bolted to his feet. He spread his arms wide and displayed an exaggerated look of shock and horror on his face.

"Objection, Your Honor," he said. "What could the plaintiff possibly want with the revelation of this law enforcement officer's private number other than to expose it to the media and the public?"

"Can you answer that, Mr. Haller?" the judge asked.

"Your Honor, I am not trying to expose her private number to the public," I said. "But she testified to having received notice of the Sanz killing on her cell phone, and the petitioner is entitled to that phone number as part of the evidence in this case. If the court would order the witness to privately disclose the number to me through Mr. Morris or the clerk of the court, that would be fine."

"But why would he need the number other than to harass the witness with phone calls?" Morris said.

"Judge, I will never distribute or call the number," I said. "And you can hold me in contempt if I do."

"Then why do you need the number, Mr. Haller?" the judge asked.

I spread my arms in surprise in the same way Morris had just moments earlier.

"Your Honor, please," I said. "Are you asking me to stand here and outline my case strategy for Mr. Morris?"

"Let's just calm things down here," the judge said.

She seemed to understand her misstep. She considered her ruling for a long moment before responding.

"Very well," she finally said. "The court orders the witness to provide the clerk with the phone number requested, and it will be turned over to the plaintiff's counsel."

"Your Honor," Morris said, "the State asks that the number be sealed."

"Is that necessary, Mr. Morris?" Coelho asked.

"Yes, Your Honor," Morris said. "To protect Deputy Sanger from harassment."

"It's Sergeant Sanger," I said.

"Sergeant Sanger," Morris corrected himself.

"Very well," Coelho said. "There is to be no distribution or use of the number by the plaintiff. It is under court seal. To violate the seal, Mr. Haller, will be to incur the wrath of this court."

"Thank you, Your Honor," Morris said, his tone suggesting that he had just attained some sort of victory.

"Thank you, Your Honor," I echoed, because I knew that the victory was mine.

27

IT WAS LATE when I got the text from Bosch. I was working at the kitchen table because my home office was still a shambles. I had been writing out questions for Shami Arslanian on a legal pad when my phone buzzed with the message. It was an address in Burbank. A third-floor apartment. Bosch told me to come quickly and provided the combo for the building security gate.

I left the legal pad on the table, took the Navigator down the hill, and cut through Laurel Canyon to get to the Valley. I reached the destination near the Burbank Airport in forty minutes. The gate combo Bosch had sent worked and I was knocking on the door of apartment 317 two minutes later. Cisco answered the door and brought me in. Bosch was in the tiny apartment's living room, sitting on a garish green couch next to a man with unkempt red hair and pale white skin. He looked to be in his late twenties, but that was just a guess because the scabs on his face disguised his true age. He was an obvious tweaker and that meant he could have been fifty or twenty. I almost turned around and walked. Tweakers were bad witnesses.

"Mick, this is Max Moder," Cisco said. "His sister is Isabella."

Moder pointed at me with recognition in his eyes.

"Hey, you, you're the guy on the billboards, right?" Moder said. "I seen you up there."

"Yeah, that's me," I said. "What've you got for me?"

Moder turned to Bosch as if to get his approval. Bosch nodded, giving him the go-ahead.

"Well, about three or four months ago my sister called me from the prison where she is," he said. "She asked me to go to the library where they keep the old newspaper archives. She told me to try to find stories about a murder case. A sheriff's deputy that got killed up in Quartz Hill."

"So did you do it?" I asked.

"Yeah, I went," Moder said. "Had to go to the big library downtown."

"And what did you find there?"

"I found the stories she wanted."

"Okay. What did you do then?"

Moder glanced at Bosch and then up at Cisco.

"Is this guy going to take care of me?" he asked them.

Cisco and Bosch stayed silent. I answered the question.

"I need to know what you know first," I said. "We can talk about what I can do for you after. What did you do when you found the newspaper stories?"

"I had to pay them to print them out for me," Moder said. "Then when she called me back, I read them to her. Each one."

"She called you collect from the prison? Or did she have a cell phone in there?"

"She borrowed a cell. I don't know how she got it."

"But she called you on your cell, right?"

"Yeah, my cell."

"Where is that phone?"

"Uh, I don't have it anymore. I sold it. I needed the money."

"When?"

"When did I sell it, you mean?"

"Yes, when did you sell it?"

"A couple months ago. Thereabouts."

"Where did you sell it?"

"Uh, actually I traded it to a guy."

For drugs. He didn't need to add that part. Everyone in the room knew it.

"Do you have any bills from the carrier?" I asked. "From the phone company?"

"Not really," Moder said. "I wasn't that good at paying the bill, to tell you the truth. They cut me off and then I traded it."

"What about the number? Do you remember it?"

"I don't really remember the number."

"Then what about the printouts from the library? Where are they?"

"I think I left them at my last place. They're gone."

I nodded. Of course he didn't have them — that would have been too easy. I thought about whether to pursue this further. Drug addicts were extremely unreliable witnesses who could hurt you more than help you on the stand. There appeared to be nothing I could use to back up his story.

"Are you going to pay me?" Moder asked. "I need to get well, man."

"I don't pay for testimony," I said. "All I can give you is a get-out-of-jail-free card."

"What's that mean?"

"It's my business card. You call the number on it the next time you're arrested and I'll get you out and take your case."

Moder looked up at Cisco with a scowl.

"What the fuck, man?" he said. "You said he'd pay me."

"I never said that," Cisco said. "I said if he likes what you say, he'll take care of you. That's it."

"Fuck!" Moder said.

"Calm down," I said. "You —"

"No, you calm the fuck down!" Moder yelled. "I need real money, man. I'm hurtin', man!"

"The only witnesses I pay are expert witnesses," I said. "And I don't think you're an expert in anything but getting high on crystal meth."

"Then get the fuck out of here. All a' you. Just get the fuck out. I ain't fucking over my sister for a fucking business card. Get out!"

Bosch got up from the couch and started for the door. Cisco didn't move. He was waiting for me so he could be the last man out in case Moder foolishly decided to get physical. I pulled out my wallet and retrieved a business card.

"You already fucked her over," I said.

I tossed the card onto the coffee table and followed Bosch out the door.

The three of us didn't speak until we got back to the street and stood around the Navigator.

"What do you think?" Cisco asked.

"It'd be nice if I had something solid to back up his story," I said. "But I think I can make do if push comes to shove with the sister."

"Subpoena him?" Bosch asked.

"No," I said. "I don't want the AG to know we found him. How *did* we find him?"

Bosch lifted his chin in Cisco's direction.

"Cisco's the man," he said.

"I found out where she used to live in Glendale and asked around the neighborhood," Cisco said. "People didn't like her or her brother. It got easy from there."

I nodded approvingly.

"So what is she inside for?" I asked.

"DUI manslaughter," Cisco said. "Ran through a light in Sun Valley and T-boned a nurse coming home from work at St. Joseph's. She blew a point-three. Got fifteen years for it. The nurse had a family."

"What do you think, Harry?" I asked. "What could she get in exchange for snitching on Lucinda? I mean, going back to the sentencing judge is a nonstarter. No judge is going to chip time off the sentence on a case like that. That doesn't win you any votes."

"Don't know," Bosch said. "Maybe just a promise from the AG to try. She's already been in eight years. She'll start getting parole hearings in a year. Maybe Morris will put in the word there."

"Yeah, gotta be it," I said. "Good job, fellas. I've got something I can work with if need be."

Neither investigator responded to the compliment.

"So, anybody hungry?" I said. "I'm starved. Musso's is still open and I'm buying."

"I could eat," Cisco said.

"You can always eat," I said. "Harry?"

"Sure," he said.

"Okay, then," I said. "I'll call Sonny at the bar and see if he can get us a good table. Meet you both there."

28

EATING LATE AT Musso and Frank had been a mistake. I consumed no alcohol but couldn't say no to a New York strip with all the trimmings. In the morning I felt heavy and sluggish. Luckily, Bosch was waiting on the front deck when I stumbled out. He drove while I pulled out the legal pad and got reacquainted with my case as we headed downtown.

"Who you calling first this morning?" Bosch asked.

"Well, first we see what comes up when Morris crosses Sanger," I said. "I might need to take another go at her. I'm hoping she wears her uniform again today."

"Why is that?"

"Oh, just a little groundwork I forgot to lay yesterday."

"Okay, then who? Keith Mitchell?"

"Yeah, we'll go with Mitchell. Get him on the record with his story, and then we bring in Shami. I need you to get her after you drop me at the courthouse. Just in case Sanger and Mitchell go down in a hurry."

"You got it."

My strategy was twofold. First and foremost, I had to show that the investigation of the case was off the rails from the beginning. There was either tunnel vision that led solely to Lucinda Sanz or, worse, a cover-up in which Lucinda was set up and sold down the river. The second part of the strategy was to somehow hand the judge a villain. I needed to point the finger at someone convincingly enough to show that Lucinda Sanz should be declared innocent or, at the very least, allowed to pull back her plea and go to trial. Exactly who that villain would be was yet to be determined, but thanks to Shami Arslanian's computer modeling, I had an idea.

Bosch made good time. My eyes were on the paperwork and I didn't notice the turns he made, but I got to the courthouse and through the two security screens early enough to ask Nate, the main courtroom marshal, to allow me back into the holding area so I could visit with my client.

Lucinda was in the same short-sleeved blue jumpsuit, but on this day she wore a heavy white long-sleeved T-shirt underneath. It didn't matter what time of year it was—federal lockup was always a cold place to be.

"Cindi," I said. "You doing all right?"

"I guess so," she said. "When does court start?"

"They'll get us in a few minutes. I just wanted to come back and tell you, so far so good. I think we're right on track with how we want to present our case. Also, I don't think you need to worry about Isabella Moder. We have that covered."

"What do you mean, you have it covered?"

"If the AG puts her on the stand and she testifies about you, we should be able to show her to be the lying jailhouse snitch that she is."

"Okay. Then what happens today?"

"Well, we put on our main case, and we hope it's enough to force the judge to allow me to bring Agent MacIsaac in to testify. He's the key, but we haven't been able to get him into court. The feds are playing hide the ball with him."

"Why won't he come?"

"Well, because what the feds did is embarrassing to the Bureau. They looked the other way when you got charged, Cindi, and that wasn't right."

"And you can prove this?"

"I think so. If I can get him on the stand."

The door behind me opened and Marshal Nate came in.

"Time to go," he said.

I turned back to Lucinda and told her to stay strong.

A few minutes later we were seated at the table in the courtroom, and Judge Coelho took the bench. Sergeant Sanger was called back to the stand for cross-examination. I was pleased to see that she was once again in uniform.

Morris's cross was pedantic. He painstakingly walked Sanger through her seventeen-year career with the sheriff's department, detailing her different postings, promotions, and commendations. He went so far as to present as an exhibit the plaque she had received the year before from the Antelope Valley Rotary Club as Law Enforcement Officer of the Year. In doing so, Morris was revealing his strategy — the case would come down to the believability and character of the deputies involved. That's why he was laying it on thick.

He finished strongly with questions that went to the heart of Lucinda Sanz's claim of malfeasance in her conviction.

"Sergeant Sanger, are you aware of any sort of corruption or wrongdoing in the investigation of Roberto Sanz's death?" he asked. "And I remind you that you are under oath."

"No, sir," Sanger responded.

The reminder that the witness was under oath was grandstanding, but Morris's message to the judge was clear: *This is a professional and highly decorated law enforcement officer and it is her word against that of the petitioner, who previously pleaded no contest to this crime.*

When Morris was finished, it was my turn again. I moved quickly to the lectern.

"Brief redirect, Your Honor," I said.

"Proceed, Mr. Haller," the judge intoned.

"Sergeant Sanger, when Mr. Morris went over your career and commendations, he seemed to leave one item out," I said. "Isn't that correct?"

"I don't know what you're talking about," Sanger said.

"Well, I'm talking about that pin you're wearing on your uniform above the breast pocket. What is that for, Sergeant Sanger?"

I had seen the pin the day before, but it was only after reviewing Sanger's testimony that I realized what I could do with it.

"That's a badge for qualifying at the sheriff's range," Sanger answered.

"The shooting range, you mean?" I asked.

"Yes, the range."

"To get a pin like that for your uniform, you have to do more than qualify, don't you?"

"It's given to the top percentage of shooters."

"What percentage is that?"

"Top ten percent."

"I see. And what is a pin like that called?"

"I don't know."

"It means you are an expert marksman, does it not?"

"I don't use gendered words."

"Okay, how about the word *shooter* instead of *marksman*? That pin you proudly wear on your uniform means you qualified as an expert shooter, does it not?"

"I've never used those words."

In a show of frustration, I raised my hand and then dropped it down on the lectern with a thud. I asked the judge if I could approach the witness to show her an exhibit previously accepted by the court. After permission was granted, I carried over the photos of Lucinda at the shooting range.

"Can you identify the people in that photo?" I asked.

"Yes," Sanger said. "It's Robbie Sanz and his then-wife, the defendant, Lucinda Sanz."

"You mean the petitioner?"

"Yes, the petitioner."

She said it in a sarcastic tone.

"Thank you," I said. "Now, in the second photo in your possession, you have the man you identified as Robbie Sanz using his hands to improve the posture and stance of his then-wife. Is that correct?"

"Yes," Sanger said.

"As you are a law officer and a shooting expert, with the commendation to go with it, can you tell me what stance the petitioner is learning in that photo?"

"It's the high-ready stance."

"Thank you, Sergeant Sanger. I have no further questions, Your Honor, but the petitioner reserves the right to recall the witness at a later stage of the hearing."

"Okay," Coelho said. "Mr. Morris, do you wish to re-cross?"

"No, Your Honor," Morris said. "The State is ready to move on."

"Sergeant Sanger, you are excused," Coelho said. "Mr. Haller, call your next witness."

Keeping to my plan, I called Deputy Keith Mitchell. He was brought in from the hallway, placed under oath, and seated in the witness stand. He was a large Black man with a shaved head. His biceps stretched the sleeves of his uniform shirt to their limit. I moved back to the lectern with my legal pad. I didn't bother asking the judge to rule that Mitchell was a hostile witness.

After a few preliminary questions that established that Mitchell was a member of the same anti-gang unit as both Roberto Sanz and Sanger, I got down to the meat of his testimony.

"You are a big man, sir," I began. "How tall are you?"

Mitchell looked confused by the question.

"Uh, six four," he said.

Morris stood up.

"Your Honor, can we keep the examination to things pertinent to the case?" he asked.

"Sorry, Your Honor," I said. "I'll move on."

Coelho frowned.

"Don't meander, Mr. Haller," she said.

"I won't, Your Honor," I said. "Deputy Mitchell, you were at the crime scene on the night of Roberto Sanz's murder, correct?"

"That is correct," Mitchell said.

"But you were off duty, were you not?"

"I was."

"How did you come to be there?"

"The department sent out a text alert that there had been an officer-involved shooting in the AV, and then like maybe ten minutes later another member of our unit called me and said it was Robbie who got shot. We were close, Robbie and me, so I went to the house."

"And that was Stephanie Sanger who called, correct?"

"Correct. Sergeant Sanger."

"Was she a sergeant at that time?"

"Uh, no. Not then."

"And where were you when Deputy Sanger called you?"

"I was at my home in Lancaster."

"What is your home address?"

Mitchell hesitated and Morris jumped up to object to revealing the witness's home address to the public.

"Your Honor," Morris said. "This could put this witness and his family in danger."

"I withdraw the question," I said before the judge had to rule.

"Very well," the judge said. "Proceed."

Morris nodded his approval like he had once again scored some kind of point over me.

"Deputy Mitchell, let's go back to that night," I said. "Were you part of the investigation of Deputy Sanz's death?"

"No, I was not," Mitchell said.

"But on the evidence report, it says you had possession of the gunshot-residue pads taken during the examination of Lucinda Sanz. Is that true?"

"Yes. That evidence was handed to me by another deputy to safeguard until investigators were on the scene. When the homicide investigators arrived, I handed the evidence over."

"What exactly was the evidence?"

"As I recall, it was two GSR pads in an evidence bag."

"And which deputy gave that bag to you to, as you say, safeguard?"

"Sergeant Sanger. I mean, Deputy Sanger at the time."

I paused and looked down at my pad and braced myself for more pushback on my next line of questioning.

"Deputy Mitchell," I finally said, "were you aware that Deputy Roberto Sanz was a member of a sheriff's clique that had become the focus of an FBI invest —"

"Objection!" Morris practically shrieked before I could finish my question. He jumped to his feet.

"Assumes facts not in evidence," he said. "Counsel for the petitioner is again trying to cloud these proceedings with innuendo he has absolutely zero evidence to support."

"Mr. Haller, response?" the judge said.

"Thank you, Your Honor," I said. "If allowed to continue with the petition, these facts will come to light."

The judge considered this for a long moment before responding.

"Once again, I'm going to hold you to that, Mr. Haller," she said. "The witness may answer."

"Your Honor," Morris said. "This is highly — "

"Mr. Morris, did you not hear the court's ruling?" Coelho said.

"Yes, Your Honor," Morris said. "Thank you, Your Honor."

Morris sat down and all eyes returned to Mitchell. For dramatic effect, I asked the question again.

"Deputy Mitchell, were you aware that Deputy Roberto Sanz was a member of a sheriff's clique that had become the focus of an FBI investigation?"

Mitchell hesitated in case Morris wanted to try a new objection, but the assistant AG remained quiet.

"No, I was not aware of that," Mitchell said.

"At the time of Sanz's death, were you a member of a sheriff's clique called the Cucos?" I asked.

"No, I was not."

"Were you ever questioned by the FBI in regard to being a member of a sheriff's clique?"

"No, I was not."

"Do you have a tattoo anywhere on your body that indicates that you are a member of a sheriff's clique called the Cucos?"

Morris stood up again. "Your Honor, the State adamantly objects," he said. "Counsel has a habit of trying to smear his own witness. What comes next? Will he ask the witness to take off his clothes so he can look for tattoos?"

Coelho held a hand up to stop me from responding.

"I want to see counsel in chambers before we proceed further down this path," she said.

With that, she adjourned court and left the bench for her chambers. Morris and I soon followed.

29

JUDGE COELHO DIDN'T bother removing her black robe as she took a seat behind a massive desk that dwarfed any I had ever seen in the Criminal Courts Building, where state jurists presided.

"Well, gentlemen," she said, "the gloves have certainly come off. And before things get too combative out there, I thought we'd have a little sit-down to discuss where we're going in this hearing. Mr. Haller, you went down this road with Sergeant Sanger and here we are back again with Deputy Mitchell."

I nodded as I collected my thoughts. I knew that my response would determine how the rest of the hearing would go.

"Your Honor, thank you for this opportunity to explain," I said. "If we're given the chance to present our full case, the court will see that Roberto Sanz was killed because he had become an FBI informant. He was, in fact, talking to an FBI agent an hour before he was killed. Lucinda Sanz was set up to take the fall for his murder and coerced into taking a plea."

"Your Honor, this is crazy," Morris said. "He can't prove any of this, so he's going to use open court to make outrageous and slander-ous claims against law enforcement officers who were just doing their jobs."

"Thank you, Mr. Morris," the judge said. "But don't speak until I ask you to. Now, Mr. Haller, how do you plan to show this? There is nothing in your moving papers that supports it."

"Your Honor, the petition does state that we have evidence of a conspiracy to frame Lucinda Sanz," I said. "This is that conspiracy. I could not outline it in detail because that would give the conspira-tors a heads-up and they would cover their tracks. I need the court's latitude now so I can bring it out. My next two witnesses will make it abundantly clear, and I believe the court will then order the appear-ance of Roberto Sanz's FBI handler — Agent MacIsaac — so he can be questioned under oath about what really happened on the day Sanz was murdered."

"Your Honor," Morris said, "if I could be heard."

"No," Coelho said. "That won't be necessary, because I know what you're going to say, Mr. Morris. But I am the trier of fact in this hearing. As such, I am obligated to seek the facts before rendering a decision. Mr. Haller, I am going to let you go forward but I warn you to move carefully. If you stray from the provable facts, I will shut you down hard and you won't want that. Neither will your client. Am I making myself clear?"

"Yes, Judge," I said. "You're clear."

"Very well," Coelho said. "You can return to the courtroom and I will be there presently to continue the hearing."

Morris and I got up and headed out the door. I followed him into the hall that ran behind the courtroom. As we approached the door that led to the court clerk's corral, Morris suddenly turned and con-fronted me.

"You fucking asshole," he said. "You don't care who you drag through the mud as long as you can make a play in front of the media. How do you sleep at night, Haller?"

"I don't know what you're talking about, Morris," I said. "Lucinda Sanz is innocent and if you had given the case a full workup, you'd see that. The people I drag through the mud belong there. And you're going to get splashed with it too."

He turned and grabbed the handle on the door but then looked back at me.

"The Lincoln Lawyer, my ass," he said. "More like the Lying Lawyer. No wonder your wife left you and your kid moved away."

I grabbed Morris by the jacket collar, turned him, and drove him into the wall next to the door.

"How do you know about my wife and daughter?" I demanded.

Morris held his hands up against the wall, maybe hoping that somebody would come into the hall and see he was being attacked.

"Get your hands off me, Haller, or I'll have you arrested for assault," he said. "It's common knowledge how you blew up your marriage."

I released my grip and reached for the door handle. I swung the door open and looked back at him. He still had his hands up.

"Fuck you," I said.

I walked back into the courtroom. The marshals had kept Lucinda in place, anticipating that the meeting in chambers would be quick. I sat down next to her and filled her in as best I could. I tried to be reassuring.

"As soon as we get through with Mitchell, we go to our forensics expert and then I think things will start turning our way. So let's see where we are by the end of the day. We should know a lot by then."

The judge returned to the courtroom and we were back on record. Morris initially helped move things along by passing on cross-examining Mitchell. The big deputy was excused from the courtroom, and that left me down to my last two witnesses and the recall of Stephanie Sanger. That is, unless I was able to convince the judge to order Agent MacIsaac to testify. I also had Frank Silver on my witness list, though I had done that largely to keep him out of the courtroom. I now had to consider calling him to the stand. It would be a risky move and he most assuredly would be a hostile witness. If I could find him.

I called Shami Arslanian to the stand, and Morris immediately stood up to object.

"On what grounds, Mr. Morris?" the judge asked.

"Well, Your Honor, as you know, plaintiff's counsel filed a request with the court yesterday afternoon," Morris said. "The request was to use the courtroom audiovisual equipment. As of this moment, Your Honor, the State has received nothing in discovery that would require AV equipment. Counsel is clearly planning to spring something on us that we are not prepared for, and the State objects."

The judge turned to me.

"Mr. Haller, I did receive and grant your request yesterday afternoon," she said. "What do you plan to do with my AV equipment that has Mr. Morris so bothered?"

"Thank you, Your Honor," I said. "May I first state that there has been no violation of the rules of discovery, as Mr. Morris suggests. Today I plan to call Dr. Shami Arslanian as a witness. She is a world-renowned forensics expert who has testified at more than two hundred trials, including several times in Los Angeles in both state and federal court. She has examined this case and the circumstances of Roberto Sanz's murder and will use the AV equipment to project her findings. If Mr. Morris had paid attention, he would have seen her name on the plaintiff's witness list from the start. He could have deposed her at his leisure anytime during the past six weeks to find out what she was going to do in court, but he chose not to and now complains that I've sandbagged him before I've even called Dr. Arslanian to the stand."

"'Project,' Mr. Haller?" Coelho said. "What does that mean exactly?"

"She has produced a re-creation of the crime," I said. "It is based on forensics, witness statements, and photographic evidence from the crime scene. All of which, I might add, Mr. Morris has had access to for longer than the petitioner."

The judge's attention swung back to Morris.

"Your Honor, counsel is leaving out a few facts," he said. "My office did reach out to Dr. Arslanian on three different occasions to set up a deposition, but each time she said she was still reviewing the case and was not ready to be deposed. Now, on the eve of her testimony, we find out that there is going to be some sort of smoke-and-mirrors re-creation that we are not prepared for and that may not conform to rule seven-oh-two."

I didn't wait for the judge to turn her attention back to me. I jumped in.

"Smoke and mirrors, Your Honor?" I said. "Dr. Arslanian has testified as an expert forensics witness for the prosecution more often than for the defense. According to counsel's statement, all those times she helped convict a defendant were smoke and mirrors too."

"Okay, counsel, let's leave the semantic bickering for another day," Coelho said. "What the court will do is hold a Daubert hearing in which we will hear Dr. Arslanian's testimony and see this demonstration. At that point, as the trier of fact in the proceeding, as I said before, I will make a decision under seven-oh-two as to whether it helps the court understand the evidence or determine a fact at issue. Mr. Haller, we are losing the morning. Please bring in your witness so we may proceed."

For a moment I stood still and tried to digest the judge's ruling.

"Mr. Haller, is your witness here?" the judge said sternly.

"Uh, yes, Your Honor," I said. "The petitioner calls Dr. Shami Arslanian."

I sat down and waited while one of the courtroom marshals went out to the hall to retrieve Arslanian. Almost immediately Lucinda grabbed my arm.

"What is going on?" she whispered. "What is Daubert?"

"It's a hearing within the hearing," I said. "Dr. Arslanian will testify and show her video re-creation so the judge can determine if it is...valid and useful to her in making a decision in the case. That's where rule seven-oh-two comes in. It requires expert witnesses to prove their expertise. I'm not worried about it, Lucinda. I mean, if this were in front of a jury I would be unhappy, but the judge will make the call on this, so one way or the other she's going to know what Dr. Arslanian came up with."

"But she can kick the whole thing out if she wants?"

"Yes, but remember, you can't unring a bell. Have you heard that saying before?"

"No."

"It means that even if the judge kicks out everything, she is still going to know what Dr. A found. So let's just see what happens, okay?"

"Okay. I trust you, Mickey."

Now I had to make sure her trust wasn't misplaced.

30

DR. ARSLANIAN ENTERED the courtroom carrying a slim computer case. She put it down on the witness chair while she raised her hand and swore to tell the truth. I was already at the lectern and had with me a copy of the Federal Rules of Evidence, the tome open to a page that listed the parameters of rule 702 governing the admissibility of expert testimony. I wanted to be ready for any objections from Morris.

Once Arslanian was seated I began my direct examination.

"Dr. Arslanian, let's start with your educational background," I said. "Can you tell the judge what degrees you have earned and from where?"

"Sure," Arslanian said. "I have a bunch. I got my master's in chemical engineering at the Massachusetts Institute of Technology. I then went down to New York and got a PhD in criminology at John Jay College, where I am currently an associate professor."

"What about your undergraduate degree?"

"I have two of them too. I graduated from Harvard with a bachelor of science in engineering, and then I went down the road a bit and got a bachelor of music from Berklee College. I like to sing."

I smiled. I wished at that moment that she were testifying in front of a jury. I knew from experience that they'd be eating out of her hand at this point. But Judge Coelho, almost thirty years on the bench, seemed less enamored. I moved on.

"And what about honorary degrees?" I asked. "Do you have any of those?"

"Oh, sure," Arslanian said. "I have three of those so far. Let's see…from the University of Florida—Go, Gators!—and from its cross-state rival Florida State in forensic sciences, and then another degree in forensic sciences from Fordham in New York."

I flipped a page on my legal pad and asked the judge to approve Arslanian under rule 702 as an expert witness. She did so. Surprisingly, there was no objection from Morris.

"Okay, Dr. Arslanian," I said. "For the record, you are being paid as an expert witness in this case, correct?"

"Yes, I charge a flat fee of three thousand dollars to review a case," she said. "More if it requires any travel. And more if it requires giving testimony about my findings in court."

"How did you come to review the evidence in this case?"

"Well, you hired me, plain and simple, to review the known evidence in the case."

"Have I hired you in the past?"

"Yes, this was the sixth time you hired me over a span of sixteen years."

"And what is the ethical standard that you hold yourself to when you review a case?"

"It's simple: I call 'em like I see 'em. I review a case and let the chips fall where they may. If I think the evidence points to the guilt of your client, I won't testify to anything but that."

"You said that I hired you six times. Did you testify for the defense in all six of those cases?"

"I did not. In three of them my review led me to believe that the evidence pointed to your client as culpable. I reported this and my involvement in the case ended there."

I flipped a page and checked on the judge to be sure she was listening to the witness. Many times — in state court, at least — I had noted that the judges appeared distracted during a witness's testimony. Many judges thought that once they ascended to the bench, whether by appointment or election, they had the power and ability to multitask while hearing a case. They were up there writing opinions or reviewing submissions in other cases while presiding over my cases. One time a judge started snoring into his microphone while I was questioning a witness. The clerk had to wake him.

But none of this was true of Judge Coelho. She had turned in her seat and was looking directly at Arslanian as she testified. I continued.

"But here you are, Dr. Arslanian," I said. "Can we take it by your testifying today that you believe that Lucinda Sanz is possibly innocent in the killing of her ex-husband?"

"It is not about guilt or innocence for me," Arslanian said. "It's about the forensics. Do they add up and point in the direction of the accused? That is the question. When I reviewed this case, the answer I came to was no."

"Can you walk us through what made you arrive at that answer?"

"I can show you."

I asked the judge's permission for the doctor to project images from her digital re-creation of the crime onto the large screen on the wall opposite the jury box. Morris objected under rule 702(c), which requires expert testimony to be the product of "reliable principles and methods" of forensic investigation. This would apply to any sort of re-creation of a crime.

"Thank you, Mr. Morris," Coelho said. "I am going to allow the witness to proceed with the demonstration and then I will make a ruling under seven-oh-two."

Morris sat down and I saw him make an angry slash with a pen across the top page of his legal pad.

Arslanian connected her laptop to the courtroom AV equipment, and soon there was a table of contents for various versions of her presentation.

"So, from the investigative file, we know the State's version of what happened," she said. "What I've done here is produce a re-creation of the crime based on known parameters, such as body location, projectile trajectory, and witness statements. Take a look."

On her laptop she ran the program. I watched the judge and saw that her eyes were sharply focused on the wall screen. The re-creation began with a front view of Lucinda Sanz's house from a photograph Arslanian had taken on the field trip with Bosch. The door opened and a male avatar—a generic digital creation—exited. The door was slammed by an unseen hand behind him. The man went down the three steps of the stoop, left the stone path, and started slowly crossing the lawn on a diagonal. The front door opened again and a female avatar emerged carrying a handgun in her left hand. As the man crossed the lawn away from her, she raised the weapon to a high-ready position, aimed, and fired. The man was hit; he dropped immediately to his knees and then pitched forward to the ground. The woman fired again and this bullet struck the man while he was down. The bullets left red tracer lines from gun to target.

"This is what the investigators and prosecutors originally said happened," Arslanian said.

"And is what they said happened possible?" I asked.

"Not in the world of physics that I know," Arslanian said.

"Please tell the court why."

"Because, Your Honor, there are variables, such as the victim's speed in crossing the lawn. As you saw from the re-creation, after the door was slammed shut, he had to walk very slowly across the lawn in order to be at the spot where he was shot and fell to the ground."

Morris stood and objected.

"Your Honor, this is pure conjecture and speculation, not fact," he complained.

Before I could even begin to reply, Coelho responded to the prosecutor.

"She called it a variable, Mr. Morris," the judge said. "I would like to hear the variables and hope they are supported by facts before rendering a decision on this demonstration. Continue, Dr. Arslanian."

I took it as a good sign that the judge addressed Arslanian as "Doctor."

Arslanian continued. "In every interview Lucinda Sanz has given, from the night of the murder to the most recent interviews with her attorney and investigator, she has maintained that she slammed the front door after her ex-husband left the house. She then would have had to reopen the door to step out to shoot. That is a variable of time, which includes the question of where and how she retrieved the gun, and it makes it highly unlikely that Roberto Sanz was only fourteen feet from the stoop when he was shot. Let's look at it again with re-creation number two, which has Roberto Sanz walking at an average speed of two-point-eight miles per hour."

Arslanian went back to her keyboard and chose the second re-creation from the table of contents. This time the male avatar stepped off the stoop more quickly and was well past the fourteen-foot mark when he was shot.

"So, as you can see, that doesn't work," Arslanian said. "And Mr. Morris, you are right that this is speculation, but it is based on known facts. Now, let's add in more facts, shall we?"

"Please, more facts," Morris said sarcastically.

He shook his head in a show of disbelief.

"Mr. Morris, I can do without the tone and the theatrical performance," the judge said.

"Yes, Your Honor," Morris responded.

"Dr. Arslanian," I said. "What are you showing us next?"

"Well, the coroner's people did a good job with the body. They probably took extra care because the victim was a law enforcement officer. They checked the wound tracks and bullet trajectories and were able to determine that the bullets that struck Deputy Sanz hit him at very different angles. The first, which struck him while he was walking, hit him at almost no angle. It severed his spine, and we know from abrasions on the legs that he immediately dropped to his knees and fell forward. He was then hit with the second shot, which came at a very sharp angle. What I will show you next is a re-creation that illustrates that the physics of this shooting do not match the official story. This re-creation doesn't show the shooter. It shows the angle of the bullets and where the weapon would have had to be located to make those shots."

Arslanian played a third re-creation on the big screen. Once again the male avatar came out of the house and the door was slammed and then reopened. This time no female emerged but the trajectories of the bullets were traced in red across the screen. They clearly showed that both shots had to have been fired from a low angle if they came from the stoop.

"These shots incorporate the trajectories arrived at by the coroner's report," Arslanian said.

"And what did you conclude from this re-creation?" I asked.

"That it is highly unlikely that the shots came from the stoop," Arslanian said. "The shooter, whoever it was, would have had to be crouching like a baseball catcher on the stoop to make the shots."

"Did you measure the height of the stoop when you were conducting your research, Doctor?"

"Yes, I did. Each of the three steps is ten inches high, putting the stoop at thirty inches high."

"So what you are saying, Dr. Arslanian, is that the shots that killed Roberto Sanz did not come from the stoop, correct?"

"That is correct, yes."

I glanced at the judge before moving on. She was staring at the screen. Another good sign.

"Doctor, did you form an opinion as to where the shots did come from?" I asked.

"I did, yes."

"Can you share that with the court?"

"Yes, I have a final re-creation that I believe, based on the known facts regarding trajectory and victim location, shows where the shots were fired from."

As Arslanian started the final re-creation on the big screen, I watched Morris. There was a look of dread on his face.

On the screen, the male avatar emerged from the house and the door was slammed behind him. This time as the figure crossed the lawn, red tracer lines started from the front wall of the house, to the left of the stoop. The male figure was struck, went down, and was struck again. Arslanian stopped the playback.

"What other facts were you able to determine from this re-creation, Doctor?" I asked.

"Well," Arslanian said, "if you place the shooter against the front wall of the house, you can create a triangle — with the sides being the ground, the wall, and the bullet trajectory — that gives us an approximate height from which the shots were fired."

"And what height was that?"

"Between five foot two and five foot six would be a liberal range."

"And if you had a woman who was five foot two, like Ms. Sanz, could she make those shots from a high-ready stance?"

"No, she would not be tall enough. For a woman that height to make that shot at that angle, she would have to be holding the weapon above eye level. Over her head, in fact. When you take into account the proximity of the impacts in the victim's center mass, I believe that it would be impossible for her to make one of those shots, let alone two in a short space of time."

Morris stood and weakly objected, again citing unfounded speculation by the witness.

And again, I didn't need to respond.

"Mr. Morris, you did not object when I accepted Dr. Arslanian as an expert witness," the judge said. "Now that her expertise runs counter to your case, you object. I find the factual basis behind her opinions and testimony sufficient, and the objection is overruled."

I waited to see if Morris would make a different challenge but he remained quiet.

"Proceed, Mr. Haller," the judge said.

"Thank you, Judge," I said. "At this time I have no further questions for Dr. Arslanian, but I reserve the right to recall her if needed."

"Mr. Morris, do you care to question the witness?" Coelho said.

"Your Honor, it is approaching noon," Morris said. "The State asks for a recess now so that we have the lunch hour to digest the witness's presentation and opinions and decide whether to conduct a cross-examination."

"Very well, we will break," Coelho said. "All parties will return at one o'clock to continue with the witness. And Mr. Morris, please check your sarcasm at the door. We are adjourned."

The judge left the bench. Morris was left chin to chest at his table.

I didn't know if it was the judge's final rebuke or the weight of Arslanian's testimony, but he looked like a man on a sinking ship that hadn't come with a life raft.

I turned to Lucinda and saw that she had been crying. Her eyes were rimmed in red and there were smear marks on her cheeks from wiped-away tears. I realized that I had forgotten to warn her about the re-creations, which showed the man she had once loved and had started a family with being shot down in her front yard.

"I'm sorry you had to see that, Lucinda," I said. "I should have prepared you for it."

"No, it's okay," she said. "I just got emotional."

"But you have to know Dr. Arslanian did us a lot of good with it. I don't know if you were watching the judge, but she was all in. I think she's convinced."

"Then it's good."

The marshal came to take her back into holding. He paused to let us finish our conversation, a nicety he had not shown previously. I took it as an indicator that he too had been swayed by what he had seen on the big screen.

"I'll see you in a little while," I said. "And we're going to go from this to another strong witness in Harry Bosch."

"Thank you," she said.

Marshal Nate released her from the ring under the table and then cuffed her wrists together for the short walk to the courtroom lockup, where she would spend the lunch hour. She walked toward the door, not needing to be led by Nate. I watched her go. Her head was down and I thought maybe more tears were coming.

Nate opened the steel door and then she was gone.

PART SEVEN

CASE KILLER

31

HALLER WAS BUOYANT as he and Arslanian climbed into the Navigator by the Spring Street exit from the federal courthouse.

"Harry, you should have seen it," he said. "Shami nailed it. The judge couldn't take her eyes off the screen the whole damn time."

Bosch didn't like hearing such talk. He knew anything could happen in a courtroom and didn't want Haller to jinx what sounded like a good morning for the team.

"Where are we going?" Bosch asked.

"Someplace good," Haller said. "We earned it. This woman is a giant slayer."

"I'm not sure," Arslanian said, "that we should celebrate until the judge rules on the petition."

"I agree, but I think she's going to walk," Haller said. "You nailed it, and after lunch, Harry will deliver the knockout punch."

"Don't forget, Morris still gets to take his shot at me," Arslanian said.

"There's no way," Haller said. "He just asked for the lunch break because he knows he's fucked. And it's only gonna get worse for him when Harry gets up on the stand with the cell data."

"Don't get ahead of yourself," Bosch said.

"Oh, come on," Haller said. "Grumpy old Harry. Let's go over to Water Grill. We'll get some good food for lunch and hold off on the celebration till this thing is over."

"I'll take you over there," Bosch said. "But I'm going to wait in the car. I need to go over everything again before I testify. Maybe you should think about going through it with me, get our ducks in a row."

"I'm not worried about it," Haller said. "Your testimony will be the frosting on the cake that Shami baked for us. I'm telling you, Harry, she clearly demonstrated that Lucinda could not have fired those shots."

"You give me too much credit," Arslanian said. "And you still have to finish presenting your case. You need to be ready for anything. You told me that a long time ago."

A few minutes later Bosch dropped them off in front of the restaurant on Grand Avenue. He then drove down the block until he found a parking space and pulled in. He reached back to the floor behind his seat and grabbed the file containing the printouts from AT&T that Haller would offer as exhibits to the court.

He started reviewing the printouts and checking the numbers against the map he'd unfolded on the passenger seat. He was rehearsing because he was nervous. He had taken new digital technology and reduced it to a distinctly analog presentation. He hoped it would be defining evidence in the case for Lucinda Sanz's innocence.

32

BOSCH SAT IN the last row of the gallery, waiting to see whether Hayden Morris was going to cross-examine Shami Arslanian or if it would be his turn on the witness stand. When the assistant AG called Arslanian back, no one seemed to notice that Bosch was in the courtroom, so he stayed put. Haller had been so enamored with Arslanian's direct examination that Bosch wanted to see how well she did under cross. As it turned out, he witnessed the case for Lucinda Sanz's innocence begin to crumble like a sandcastle.

And it took Morris no more than five minutes to do it.

It began when Morris asked Arslanian to put her re-creation program's table of contents back up on the big screen. She quickly complied with a few taps on her keyboard.

"Now, I want to draw your attention to the bottom right corner of the screen," Morris said. "That's a copyright protection notice, correct?"

"Yes," she said. "Technically, it's been applied for, but we are confident we will get it."

"Project AImy is the name of the re-creation software?"

"Yes."

"Am I saying that right? Like the woman's name Amy?"

"Yes."

"So that is *A*, capital *I*, not *A*, lowercase *l*?"

"Correct."

"Why is it spelled that way?"

"The program is built on a machine-learning platform I developed with my partner Professor Edward Taaffe at MIT."

"By *machine learning*, you mean artificial intelligence, don't you?"

"Yes."

"Thank you. No further questions."

Coelho excused Arslanian. Bosch looked at Haller and saw the lawyer drop his head. Something was going wrong. Before Arslanian was even through the gate to the gallery, Morris addressed the judge.

"Your Honor," he said, "the State moves to have the testimony and presentation of the witness struck from the record under Federal Rules of Evidence section seven-oh-two C."

Haller stood up to be heard. Arslanian quickly slipped into the bench where most of the members of the media were sitting.

"Your Honor?" he said.

"Not yet, Mr. Haller," the judge said. "You'll get your turn. Mr. Morris, do you wish to elaborate?"

"Thank you, Judge," Morris said. "In regard to expert testimony, section seven-oh-two C states that the testimony and presentation of an expert witness must be the product of reliable principles and methods. The use of artificial intelligence has not been approved in the U.S. District Court for the Southern District of California. Therefore, the witness's presentation as well as any testimony derived from her presentation must be rejected."

The judge was silent for a long moment and then turned her attention to Haller.

"Mr. Haller, I'm afraid he's right," she said. "This district is looking for a test case for the use of artificial intelligence...but it has not yet come to pass."

"May I be heard?" Haller said.

"You may," Coelho said.

"This is flat-out wrong," Haller said, pointing at the screen. "That program proves that Lucinda Sanz did not shoot her ex-husband and now you're going to take it away from her on a technicality? She has been incarcer—"

"It's not a technicality," Morris said. "It's the law."

"Mr. Morris, do not interrupt," the judge said. "Continue, Mr. Haller."

"She's been in prison for five years for something she didn't do," Haller said. "That program proves her innocence and everybody in this courtroom knows it. If it's not approved, then make *this* the test case. Your Honor, overrule the objection and we move forward and the AG can appeal."

"Or I could sustain the objection and you could file the appeal," Coelho said. "Different means to the same end. A higher court would decide this and you would have your test case."

"And how long is that going to take?" Haller said. "Another three years in prison for my client while we wait to be heard on the matter? The court is behind the times, Judge. AI is here—it's used in surgery, it's driving cars, it's buying stocks, it's choosing the music we listen to. Your Honor, the applications are endless. Don't send this woman back to prison because the courts are archaic and lagging behind the technology of the day."

"Mr. Haller, I understand your concern," Coelho said. "I truly do. But I am sworn to uphold the laws we currently have and I cannot anticipate the laws of the future."

"Judge, this hearing is supposed to be about finding the truth,"

Haller said. "What does it say about us if we know the truth and throw it away?"

"I'm sorry, Mr. Haller, it doesn't work that way," Coelho said. "It pains me, but the objection is sustained. The witness's presentation and testimony is stricken and will have no bearing on the court's eventual ruling on this matter."

"Shame on us," Haller said. "That we can't bring ourselves to do the right thing when it's there in front of us."

"Mr. Haller, you are now on thin ice with this court," Coelho said.

Haller put his hands down on the table and bowed his head. Bosch felt a deep hollow open up in his chest. Haller turned and looked at Morris, who was staring straight ahead.

"And you, Morris," Haller said. "How do *you* sleep at night? You're supposed to be a guardian, you're supposed to look for the truth, but you hide behind —"

"Mr. Haller!" the judge barked. "You are out of order. Sit down. *Now!"*

Haller threw up his hands in a gesture of giving up and sat down. He turned to Lucinda and whispered to her. Bosch could not remember ever seeing an attorney seem so upset by a judge's ruling. He wondered how much was performance and how much was true anger.

Coelho poured water from a pitcher into a glass. She took her time with it, perhaps believing that moving slowly would restore calm to the courtroom.

"Now," she finally said, "would you like to call another witness, Mr. Haller?"

Haller did not acknowledge the question. He kept whispering to Lucinda, apparently trying to explain what had just happened to her hopes of freedom.

"Mr. Haller?" the judge prompted. "Do you have another witness?"

Haller broke away from the huddle with Lucinda and stood up. When he spoke, his voice sounded strangled.

"Yes, I do," he said. "The petitioner calls Harry Bosch."

With the tension in the room still as thick as the marine layer on the Santa Monica bight, Bosch got up and moved forward through the gate. He was sworn in by the clerk and took the seat on the witness stand. He watched Haller move slowly to the lectern, still reeling from the loss of Arslanian's testimony. He started with basic questions about Bosch's pedigree.

"Mr. Bosch, how are you currently employed?" he asked.

"I work part-time as an investigator for you," Bosch said.

"And what is your experience in investigating criminal matters?"

"I was a detective with the Los Angeles Police Department for forty years, most of them working homicides. After I retired, I worked for a few years as a volunteer cold-case investigator with the town of San Fernando and later back with the LAPD."

"You know your way around a murder, I guess you could say."

"You could say that, yes. I've worked on more than three hundred homicides as either lead or backup investigator."

"Is it safe to say you have put a lot of bad people—killers—in prison?"

"Yes."

"Yet here you are, working to free a person who the State says is a killer. Why is that?"

This was the only question Haller and Bosch had rehearsed. After this, they would be winging it.

"Because I don't think she did it," Bosch said. "In reviewing the case, I found inconsistencies in the investigation, contradictions. That's why I brought it to you."

"I remember that," Haller said. "Now, as part of your investigation, did there come a time when you served a subpoena on a company called AT and T?"

"Yes, I did that last week."

"And what—"

Before Haller could get the question out, Morris interrupted with an objection.

"Your Honor," he said. "If Mr. Haller is going to ask about cellular data collection, then, again, we are going to have a discovery issue."

"How so, Mr. Morris?" the judge asked. "I seem to recall this was reported on the most recent discovery inventory Mr. Haller filed with the court."

"Yes, Your Honor," Morris said. "He turned over a printout of more than nineteen hundred pages of data from six different cell towers, and now, just four days later, he plans to introduce his specific findings in court."

"Are you asking for a continuance of the hearing so you have additional time to study the material?" Coelho asked.

"No, Your Honor," Morris said. "The State asks that the petitioner be disqualified from using this material because of bad faith in meeting even basic discovery standards."

"Well, that is certainly an extreme remedy," Coelho said. "I am sure the petitioner has something to say about that. Mr. Haller?"

"Your Honor, there is no bad faith here," Haller said. "And I'm tired of having to defend myself in regard to these matters that Morris brings up like a broken record. The rules of discovery are clear. I was under no obligation to turn this material over to him and his team until I decided that I intended to use it in court. I made that decision when briefed Friday morning by my investigator Mr. Bosch after he reviewed the materials. Please keep in mind, Judge, that I am a solo practitioner with one associate attorney and one full-time and one part-time investigator. Mr. Bosch received the data from AT and T last Tuesday afternoon and reported his findings to me on Friday morning. He is just one man. Morris, on the other hand, has the power and might as well as the personnel of the entire attorney general's office at his disposal. He is also representing the L.A. County DA's office in this matter, and last I checked, there are eight hundred prosecutors and two hundred investigators across the street in that office. And he couldn't get someone to help him look through this material over the weekend?

"Your Honor, that's where the bad faith is. What happened was that Morris guessed that I was dumping this material on him because it was worthless and he'd be spinning his wheels reviewing it. So he ignored it all weekend and now he finds out that maybe it is not so worthless, that there is actually exculpatory material here, and he wants to cry foul. I'll say it again, Judge: This is supposed to be a search for truth, but Mr. Morris is not interested in that. He's only interested in putting up roadblocks to the truth, and that to me is bad faith in its ugliest form."

Morris spread his arms like they were wings.

"Your Honor, really?" he said. "Mr. Haller, up there on his high horse, is conveniently forgetting the facts. The court approved the subpoena for records from AT and T more than three weeks ago. He waited until the eve of trial to execute it and gather the data. That was a planned delay, Judge, and he isn't fooling me or you. The People stand by the complaint and the suggested remedy."

"Your Honor, may I respond?" Haller said.

"No, I don't think I need you to, Mr. Haller," Coelho said. "I have a good idea of what you would say. I am not going to disqualify this material from introduction in the hearing. We are going to proceed with Mr. Bosch's testimony. And when direct examination is completed, I will give Mr. Morris time to prepare his cross if time is indeed needed. Now, let's take a ten-minute break, go back to our corners, and cool off, and then we will continue the hearing."

33

BOSCH SPENT MOST of the ten-minute break keeping Haller separated from Morris in the hall outside the courtroom. Haller was no doubt crestfallen by the Arslanian setback, as was Arslanian. She'd been scheduled to fly out on a red-eye that night but she insisted on delaying her return home so she could watch Bosch's testimony and be part of a brainstorming session afterward.

No name-calling or physical scuffles broke out in the hallway and soon Bosch was back on the stand awaiting the arrival of the judge and the prisoner. Lucinda came first, and after she was placed next to Haller, he immediately leaned toward her and started whispering. Bosch could tell by his gestures that he was trying to console her and tell her that losing Arslanian's testimony and presentation did not constitute the end of the world. The trouble was, Bosch wasn't sure Haller believed that himself.

The judge came through the door, took her position at the bench, and went back on the record, telling Haller to proceed. Haller took his legal pad to the lectern.

"When we were interrupted," he said to Bosch, "you were about to tell us about a collection of cell-tower data obtained with a subpoena. Why don't you walk us through the steps you took in getting that data."

"Well, we were interested in knowing Roberto Sanz's movements on the day he was murdered," Bosch said. "We knew he carried a cell phone and we got the number from Lucinda Sanz's phone records. She had called him several times on the evening he was killed. So from there, I went to a website where you plug in a cell number and it tells you which company is the carrier."

"For the record, what website was that?" Haller asked.

"It's called FreeCarrierLookup-dot-com. I put in Roberto's number and it determined that his carrier was AT and T. From there you prepared a subpoena for all data on all of AT and T's cell towers in the Antelope Valley for the day of the murder."

Haller whistled.

"That must have been a lot of data," he said.

"It was," Bosch said. "The printout was almost two thousand pages, single-spaced."

"In layman's terms, can you tell us what kind of data it was?"

"Well, every company has its own cell towers. Some geographic areas have more than others and that's why you see in the TV ads for these companies how they talk about the best coverage and so forth. If you have a cell phone, it is constantly in contact with all the towers in your area, and as you move, the connections move."

"Sort of like Tarzan swinging on vines from tree to tree, your connection moves from tower to tower?"

"Uh, I never thought about it that way, but yes, I guess it's like that."

"So you were able to find Roberto Sanz's number in these two thousand pages."

"I was. And I got a map of AT and T's cell-tower locations throughout the AV and—"

"'AV'?"

"Sorry, Antelope Valley."

"And how did that help you?"

"Like I said, a cell phone is connected to many of its carrier's towers at once, but the connection is strongest to the tower nearest the phone. And the data transmitted from the phone to the tower includes decibel strength based on proximity and GPS coordinates. That's why when you use a mapping app like Waze or Google Maps, you see your exact location on the screen."

"Are you saying that this data you collected with the subpoena showed exactly where Roberto Sanz was located throughout the day of his death?"

"Correct. And I was able to chart it on a map."

"Do you have that map with you?"

"Yes."

Haller turned his attention to the judge and asked if Bosch could step off the witness stand and display the map on a courtroom easel so that he could better explain his findings. With no objection from Morris, Coelho allowed it and the court clerk retrieved the easel from an equipment closet. Five minutes later, Bosch's unfolded map was clipped to the easel. There were three lines—red, blue, and green—charted on the map. Bosch had carefully drawn the lines with the map spread across his dining room table. He hoped his conclusions would be clear and understandable to the judge.

"Okay, so what do we have here, Detective Bosch?" Haller asked.

Before Bosch could answer, Morris objected.

"He is no longer a police officer or a detective," he said. "He should not be referred to as 'Detective.'"

"Sustained," Coelho said.

Haller threw a look at Morris that clearly said that was a chick-enshit objection, then moved back to his direct examination of Bosch.

"I see three lines on your map," he said. "Which is Roberto Sanz?"

"This one," Bosch said. "The green."

"I'm sure we will get to the others soon enough, but let's stick with the green. What did you find that was significant about Roberto Sanz's movements in the hours before his death?"

Bosch pointed to a spot on the green track.

"This place right here in Lancaster," he said. "The data showed that he was here for nearly two hours."

"And what is significant about that?" Haller asked.

"Well, two things. One is that this location is a hamburger place called Flip's and this was where Roberto Sanz had gotten into a shoot-out with four gang members the year before. The second is that it was established in the original investigation that Roberto was two hours late bringing his son home to Lucinda, and he told her he had had a work meeting. But it was determined that there had been no meeting involving his sheriff's unit. So this is new information plac-ing him at this business during those two hours — the place where he had been in a shoot-out the year before."

"And now, looking at your map, I see the red line inter-sects Roberto Sanz's green line at that location. Am I reading that correctly?"

"Yes. Those two phones were there almost the same amount of time. The red phone was actually there first, arriving six minutes before the green. Then they both left an hour and forty-one minutes later."

"And what did you take from that?"

Morris objected, stating that Bosch's answer would be speculation and not fact. The judge sustained the objection and Haller started another path toward the answer he wanted.

"How did you come up with the red line?" he asked.

"I thought that the length of time that Sanz was at Flip's seemed excessive," Bosch said. "It's a fast-food place and he's there an hour and forty-one minutes. Besides that, it was where he had gotten into a shoot-out, so why would he go there unless the location was important to what was happening that day? So I concluded that he was meeting someone there. This led me to search the data for another cell phone exhibiting the same GPS coordinates at the same time."

Bosch looked at the judge as he answered, hoping to get a read on whether he was explaining himself clearly. The judge's eyes were focused on the map and she gave no indication that she was confused. Bosch's attention was drawn back to Haller with the next question.

"But couldn't it have been a phone with a different carrier that wouldn't show up in the data?" Haller asked.

"That was the risk," Bosch said. "But I knew that AT and T gave discounts to military and law enforcement personnel, so I thought if he was meeting someone, there was a good chance it was a fellow LEO."

"'Leo'?"

"Law enforcement officer."

"Got it. So what did you find when you searched for another phone that was at Flip's?"

"I found the red phone and I concluded that Sanz was meeting with the holder of that phone. I assumed it was a car-to-car meeting in the parking lot."

Morris made the same objection, calling Bosch's conclusions speculation and not fact. Before Haller could counter, the judge overruled the objection, stating that Bosch's decades of experience as an investigator made his assumptions more valid than blind speculation. She told Haller to continue with his examination.

"Were you able to identify the owner of the red phone?" Haller asked.

"Yes," Bosch said.

"How?"

"I called it and a man answered with his name: MacIsaac. He basically hung up on me when I asked a question, but I already knew that name from my investigation of Roberto Sanz's activity on the day of his death. I had learned that Sanz had a meeting with an Agent MacIsaac an hour or so before he was killed. From there it was not hard to confirm that there was an Agent Tom MacIsaac on the roster of the Los Angeles field office."

"You're talking about the Federal Bureau of Investigation?"

"Yes."

"You said he hung up on you when you asked a question?"

"Yes. I identified myself, told him what I was doing, and asked if he'd had a meeting with Roberto Sanz on the day of Sanz's death. At that point he ended the call. I called back but he didn't answer. I then texted him but he didn't respond. He still hasn't."

Haller looked down at his notes, letting that last answer float in the room.

"Okay," Haller said. "Let's talk about the blue line. Your chart shows that the holder of the blue phone was tracking along with the green phone, correct?"

"Yes and no," Bosch said. "The data includes time stamps. It shows that while the blue phone followed the same path as the green phone, it lagged behind each geographic marker by twenty to forty seconds until the green phone stopped at Flip's."

"Does that indicate that the blue phone was following the green phone?"

"It does."

Bosch got the answer out as Morris was standing to make the same objection, that it was speculation. But once more the judge overruled the objection, saying that Bosch's conclusion was acceptable based on his experience and his expertise with the tower data.

"What happened when Roberto Sanz—the green phone—pulled into Flip's to meet with Agent MacIsaac?" Haller asked.

This time Morris was quick with the objection.

"Assumes facts not in evidence," Morris claimed.

"Again, I am allowing the answer," the judge said. "Mr. Morris, I think you know where this is headed and I find your constant interruption of the flow of testimony to be disruptive to the court's understanding of the case. Wait until you have a real objection, please. Objection overruled. Continue, Mr. Haller."

Haller waited for Bosch to answer. But he didn't.

"Do you need me to ask the question again?" Haller asked.

"If you don't mind," Bosch said.

"Not a problem. According to the data and your charting, what were the movements of the blue phone when Roberto Sanz pulled into Flip's to meet with Agent MacIsaac?"

Bosch used his finger to trace the blue phone's path as he answered.

"The blue phone drove by and stopped at the next corner at the ARCO gas station. It remained there for at least an hour."

"What do you mean by 'at least an hour'? Isn't the data complete?"

"It is. But the blue phone stopped transmitting GPS coordinates to the cell tower at that point."

"Just disappeared?"

"Correct."

"Does that mean the phone was turned off?"

"Yes, or put on airplane mode so it no longer sent signals to the towers in the area."

"Okay, let's go back. How did you come upon this blue phone?"

"Yesterday at the end of the court session, the clerk gave you the cell phone number of Sergeant Sanger, which you asked for when she was testifying. I took that number and looked for it in the tower data received from AT and T. I found it and tracked it."

Haller pointed to the map on the easel and spoke with exaggerated astonishment.

"That was Sanger's phone?" he said. "She was following Sanz?"

"It appears so," Bosch said.

"But at the ARCO, the phone suddenly went dark."

"Correct."

"And when did it come back online, according to the data?"

"That number, which is carried by AT and T, does not come up on any cell tower in the Antelope Valley from that point at the ARCO station until twenty-two minutes after Lucinda Sanz's 911 call reporting gunshots. That indicates that during that time, the phone was either turned off, on airplane mode, or out of reach of the area's towers."

"And where is the phone located when it does come back up after the shooting?"

"It reappears in Palmdale at a restaurant called Brandy's Café."

"Did you track it from there?"

Bosch pointed again at the map.

"Yes, the second blue line on the map. It goes from the café to the scene of the shooting at Lucinda Sanz's house."

"All told, how many minutes was the blue phone offline?"

"Eighty-four minutes."

"And Roberto Sanz was shot during those eighty-four minutes, correct?"

Morris leaped to his feet, shouting, "Objection! Your Honor, this is fantasy. I beg the court to stop this sheer speculation and innuendo when there is not an ounce of evidence that supports any conclusion other than Lucinda Sanz being the shooter of her ex-husband."

"Your Honor," Haller said, "the witness has worked three hundred murder cases. He knows what he is doing and knows what he's saying. Mr. Morris, with his barrage of objections, is just trying to—"

"Enough!" Coelho cried. "The objection is overruled for reasons previously stated. Continue, Mr. Haller."

"Thank you, Your Honor," Haller said. "Mr. Bosch, other than Sergeant Sanger turning off her phone, putting it on airplane mode, or being out of reach of the towers, is there any other explanation as to why her phone dropped its connection to the cell towers in the Antelope Valley?"

"No, nothing that I can think of."

Haller looked up at the judge from the lectern.

"Your Honor," he said, "I have no further questions."

PART EIGHT

SUBPOENA DUCES TECUM

34

THE ROOFTOP LOUNGE at the Conrad gave us a great view across down-town. It was the kind of view that made you love this city because it reminded you that anything was possible down there on the street.

But we were having none of that — Bosch, Arslanian, Cisco, and me. We sat there silently mourning the losses of the day. Bosch's testimony had been the lone shining moment for Lucinda Sanz's cause, but even that, it turned out, was too good to be true. Judge Coelho granted the AG's request for more time to study the cell-tower data we had presented. She recessed the hearing until the following Monday morning, giving Morris and his minions three days — five if they kicked into overtime and worked through the weekend — to find ways to undermine the impact of Bosch's testimony and evidence.

But that ruling was minor compared to the loss of Arslanian's testimony and crime re-creation. That ruling was a case killer and I found myself not only angry at Morris but also deeply disappointed in the judge for not making law and approving the AI-based re-creation. So we sat there with a stunning view of the city in all directions, but none of us could see the beauty in it. The sky was growing dim and so were Lucinda Sanz's chances of freedom.

"I'm so sorry, Mickey," Arslanian said. "If only I —"

"No, Shami," I said. "This is on me. I should have seen it coming. I should have asked you about the platform."

"You're going to appeal the judge's ruling, right?" Bosch asked.

"Of course," I said. "But like I said in court, in the meantime Lucinda goes back to Chino and waits it out. We're talking about years and years. Even if we win in the Ninth, it will go up to the Supreme Court. That's a five- to six-year ride. We may get lucky and make new law, but Lucinda will have served her sentence and be out by then."

"What about what you always say about not being able to unring the bell?" Cisco said. "The judge saw the whole thing, didn't she? She might have kicked it out, but she knows it was good stuff."

I shook my head.

"There's that, but the judge knows she's got the eyes of the AG on her," I said. "She'll bend over backward not to let it be part of her ruling."

"This is my fault," Arslanian said.

"Come on, give that a rest," I said. "I'm the captain of this sinking ship. It's all on me and I go down with it."

"Not if you put Sanger back on the stand and prove the lie," Bosch said. "The judge owes you one and she knows it. Prove Sanger a liar and she might give you MacIsaac. If we get him on the stand, we get the true story and it points to Sanger, not Lucinda."

I took a long pull on my cranberry and soda and shook my head again.

"I don't think Coelho thinks she owes me anything," I said. "Fed judges are appointed for life. They don't look back unless the Ninth Circuit tells them to."

That drew another long silence. I drained my glass and looked for the waitress.

"Another round?" I asked.

"I'm good," Bosch said.

"Another beer," Cisco said.

"I'm good," Arslanian said.

There was no waitress in sight. I stood up with my glass and grabbed Cisco's empty. I turned to go to the bar.

"I wish we had those GSR pads," Arslanian said.

I turned back around.

"Wouldn't matter," I said. "These people weren't stupid. They would have replaced the pads they used on Lucinda with pads loaded with GSR."

"I know that," Arslanian said. "And I know the evidence was destroyed after the case was adjudicated. But I'm not talking about testing them for GSR. If those pads were wiped over Lucinda's hands, they would have picked up skin cells along with any GSR. Most people, including defense lawyers, weren't really thinking about touch DNA back then. But testing is so sophisticated now that we'd be able to prove whether those pads were actually used on her."

I almost dropped the two glasses from my hands. I quickly put them back down on the table.

"Wait a minute," I said. "You may have just—"

I stopped speaking. My mind was racing through the documents I had seen from the original case against Lucinda.

"What?" Arslanian prompted.

"The DA's file from the original prosecution," I said. "We got a copy in discovery. There was an evidence transfer order in there. Frank Silver was going through the usual moves. He asked for an evidence split so he could have a private lab test the GSR. There were two pads and the judge had one of them transferred to Silver's lab. But then he pleaded Lucinda out and it didn't matter."

"You're saying that the pad might still be at the lab?" Cisco asked.

"Stranger things have happened," I said. "The file's in the back of the Lincoln."

"Be back in five minutes," Bosch said.

He got up and headed toward the elevator. I looked at Cisco.

"Cisco, give me your phone," I said. "Silver probably won't take a call from mine."

Cisco pulled out his phone, punched in the passcode, and handed it over. I took out my wallet and dug through it until I found the business card I had taken months ago from the slot next to Silver's office door. I had kept it in case I needed to reach him.

I called the cell number listed and Silver answered cheerfully.

"Frank Silver, how can I help you?"

"Don't hang up."

"Who is this?"

"It's Haller. I need your help."

"You need my help? Bullshit. You need my help hanging a five-oh-four around my neck. Have a nice night."

"Silver, don't hang up. I mean it, I need your help. And you know I never filed the five-oh-four. It was a prop."

There was a beat of silence.

"This better not be a trick," Silver finally said.

"It's not," I said. "I need you to think back to when you were working the case. You got an evidence split order so you could have a private lab test one of the GSR pads supposedly taken from Lucinda. You remember?"

"If it's in the file, then I did it."

"You don't remember?"

"I've had a few cases since then, believe it or not. I can't remember every detail about every case."

"Okay, okay. I get it. Neither can I. But do you know what lab you used and whether you or the court ever got the evidence back after testing? I don't remember seeing any lab report in the file."

Again there was silence and it was almost as if I could hear Silver's mind grinding on how to play this.

"You want the name of my lab," he said.

"Come on, Silver, don't blow your chance at this," I said. "Does the lab still have the GSR evidence?"

"As a matter of fact, I think it does. But they won't give it to anybody but me."

"That's fine. We need to confirm it still exists. If it does, then you might come out the hero in all of this."

"I'll call you in the morning."

"That—"

He disconnected. I gave the phone back to Cisco.

"What lab did he use?" Arslanian asked.

"He's being coy," I said. "Won't give that up or pull the evidence— if it still exists—unless he's sure he gets to be the hero."

"Guy's a loser," Cisco said.

"Yeah," I said. "But we need to play along or we may not get our evidence."

Bosch returned with the file from the Lincoln. I quickly brought him up to date.

"So we wait until tomorrow?" he asked.

"Let's see what's in the file first," I said.

I opened the file and flipped through the early motions of the case until I found Silver's request for an independent analysis of evidence. The request was approved with an order from superior court judge

Adam Castle to transfer one of the collected GSR pads to an independent lab called Applied Forensics in Van Nuys.

"We might have just gotten lucky," I said. "One of the GSR pads was transferred to Applied Forensics. Silver got a court order for the transfer, so it's likely that Applied Forensics would not have been allowed to destroy or transfer the evidence without a court order. And if such an order existed, it would be in this file. It means the evidence should still be there, even after five years."

"Then how do we get it?" Cisco asked.

"We don't," I said. "I've never used Applied Forensics, but they've pitched me for my business. They have a full DNA lab. All we need to do is get Silver to tell them to test the evidence for touch DNA."

"Not just that," Arslanian said. "There will likely be touch DNA from whoever wiped the pads *and* whoever was wiped. We need to get Lucinda's DNA to the lab for a comparison."

"Do we have her DNA?" Cisco asked.

"Not yet," I said. "But I have a plan for getting it. The question is, can we get a comparison done by Monday, when we're back in court?"

"If I stay on top of Applied Forensics we can," Arslanian said. "I'll camp out there and walk them through it."

"No, Shami, you need to get back home," I said.

"Please let me do this," she said. "I need to."

I nodded.

"Okay," I said. "So you three go to Applied Forensics in the morning. Silver will likely go there too, so be there as soon as they're open. I'll go see the judge. I'll wait to hear from you before I knock on her door."

"How do we know Silver won't try to run a game on us?" Bosch asked.

"I'll call him in the morning," I said. "If he becomes a problem, Cisco will make him see the light."

Everyone looked at Cisco. He gave us a nod.

35

ON WEDNESDAY MORNING at ten I was posted on the hallway bench outside Judge Coelho's courtroom. I knew the courtroom would be dark now that the habeas hearing was continued. While I was checking my phone for messages, the courtroom door opened and out stepped one of the journalists who had attended the hearing Monday and Tuesday. She was young, dark-haired, and attractive and had a serious air about her. I had not recognized her among the other journalists I knew from previous trials and cases.

"Mr. Haller, I'm surprised to see you here," she said. "I mean, with the case put over till Monday."

"I need to see the clerk about something," I said. "You're a journalist, right? You were here both days of the hearing."

"Yes, Britta Shoot," she said as she held out her hand.

I shook it.

"Shoot?" I asked. "Really?"

"Yes," she said. "I know, it's a little coincidental since this case is about a shooting."

"Who do you work for?"

"For myself mostly—I'm a freelancer. But I've had my stories published in the *New York Times, The Guardian, The New Yorker,* a lot of publications. I often write about technology and I'm working on a book about geofencing, how it's increasingly being used by law enforcement—and some defense attorneys like yourself—and the Fourth Amendment privacy issues and all of that."

"Interesting. How did you hear about this case?"

"Uh, a source told me that geofencing was going to come up. And, boy, it sure did yesterday with your witness Bosch. I'd like to interview him—and you—if you have time."

"It will have to wait until this is over. Federal judges aren't too keen on attorneys and witnesses from their ongoing cases talking to the media."

"It's a long-term project. The judge would not see anything until the book comes out, but I can wait. I know you have your hands full, especially after the ruling on the re-creation. AI in the courts is another story I'd like to write about."

She put her computer bag down on the bench next to me, unzipped it, and gave me a business card. It just had her name and phone number on it.

"That's my cell," she said.

"Four-one-five—you're down from San Francisco?" I asked.

"Yes. I'm going back up later today but I'll be sure to be here Monday."

"Yeah, don't miss Monday."

"Why? Got a surprise?"

"Maybe. We'll see. What were you in the courtroom for?"

"I wanted to get a copy of your subpoena for the tower data and a copy of what you entered as an exhibit. I got the subpoena but the cost of the data printout is a little over my budget."

"Yeah, they charge something like a buck a page for copying costs. Here."

I pulled out my wallet, dug out a card, and handed it to her.

"If you come back Monday, I'll give you a copy," I said.

"Thank you very much," she said. "You sure?"

"Yeah, not a problem."

"That's really nice. You're saving me money and time. I would have had to wait till the end of the day for them to copy everything. I can get back on an earlier flight now."

I held up her card.

"Cool," I said. "Maybe someday you can do me a favor. Interview me for your book or maybe a profile in *The New Yorker,* huh?"

She smiled.

"Maybe," she said. "See you Monday."

"Monday," I said. "I'll be here."

I watched her head down the hall to the elevator. I wondered who her source was and guessed it was probably someone in the AG's office who knew about the subpoena I had gotten for the cell-tower data.

I pulled my phone out and googled *geofencing* because I had never heard the term before. I was halfway through a *Harvard Law Review* article on the Fourth Amendment issues surrounding the use of cell data to track individuals when my phone buzzed. It was Bosch.

"Give me good news," I said.

"Good and bad," he said. "The evidence is still here and when they did their testing, they only used half of the piece they got. So there is a pristine half in cold storage."

"Okay, what's the bad news?"

"Second-Place Silver stiffed them back then. After Lucinda went to prison, he didn't need a report on the GSR and decided not to pay for it. So they don't like him too much for that. They're not giving up the evidence till somebody pays."

"How much is the tab?"

"Fifteen hundred."

"You have a credit card, Harry? Put it on that and expense it. You'll get it back."

"That's what I thought. There's one other thing. Silver is making noise about getting paid himself."

"Fucking weasel. Nobody's getting paid on this. Where is he? Let me talk to him."

"Hold on. He's with Cisco and Shami. I think Cisco wants to put him in a headlock and squeeze."

"Yeah, not yet. Put Silver on and then see if they'll take a credit card on the past invoice."

"Hold on."

I heard a door open and close and knew Harry had called me from his car. There was the sound of another door as he entered Applied Forensics. I heard some muffled voices and then Frank Silver was on the phone.

"Mick, you heard the good news?"

"I did. I also heard you're making noise about wanting money."

"This is only coming together because of me, and my time is money. I want a couple grand, that's all."

"First of all, we don't know what we have there yet. Second, I'm going to have to pay the bill you skipped out on five years ago. And last and most important, you're a witness in this case. If I pay you a dime before you testify and the AG finds out, you aren't a witness anymore."

"I told you, I'm not testifying. I'm not letting you throw me under the bus on an ineffective rap."

"That ship has sailed, Frank. You don't have to worry. That's not why you're a witness. If this pans out with Applied Forensics, I'm going to need you to get on the stand and set it up. Tell how the evidence got there and why it's still there five years later. It'll be your moment to be the hero."

"I like that. But then I get paid."

"Listen, there may be some CJA money when this is all said and done, but you don't get paid until we all get paid."

"'CJA'? What's that?"

"It's federal money for defense lawyers — the Criminal Justice Act. It won't be a lot but it will be something, and whatever we get, you'll get it all. I'm about to talk to Judge Coelho and I'll bring it up. Now put Harry back on the phone."

"Okay, Mick. By the way, I like Harry. But I don't like that big guy you got."

"You're not supposed to. Put Harry on."

I stood up and paced in the hall while I waited. I was trying to contain my excitement over what this could mean. Bosch's voice came back on the call.

"Mick?"

"Yeah. They taking your credit card?"

"Yeah, I gave it to them."

"Okay, what's Shami doing?"

"She's on a tour of the lab now. They love her. I guess she's sort of famous in her field."

"That she is. When she's finished with the tour, tell her to prep them for a court order directing them to test the evidence for DNA and then compare it to a sample that should be coming in by the end of the day."

"Will do. And we want a rush on it, right?"

"We will pay for expedited testing. Need this back by Monday."

"Okay. What about you?"

"I'm about to go see the judge to try to get this rolling."

"Good luck with that."

"Thanks, I'll need it."

I disconnected and headed to the courtroom door.

36

THE LIGHTS IN the courtroom were out except for the bulb positioned above the clerk's corral to the right of the judge's bench. Coelho's clerk was a young man fresh from USC Law named Gian Brown. He was more than used to me coming in over the past six months to drop off motions and subpoena requests for the judge. Brown told me each time that this task would be much easier on me if I just emailed the documents and requests, but I never did that. I wanted him to know me, to get used to me. I wanted him to like me. I learned he enjoyed a caramel macchiato on occasion and brought them to him from the building's cafeteria, even though each time he protested that the gesture would earn me no favors with him or the judge. I always said that I wasn't trying to procure favors because I didn't need any.

But now I did.

"Mr. Haller, you do know that we're dark today, right?" Brown asked.

"Must've forgotten," I said.

He smiled and I smiled.

"Then, let me guess, you have a motion for us," Brown said.

"I have an ask," I said. "A big ask. I need to see the judge about an SDT that is very time-sensitive. Is she here?"

"Uh, she is," Brown said. "But she's got her Do Not Disturb on."

He pointed to a small red light on a panel on the corral's half wall. Next to it was the button he pushed when all parties were present and ready for the judge to enter the courtroom.

"Well, Gian, I need you to call her or buzz her because she'll want to hear what I've got to say," I said.

"Um..."

"Please, Gian. It's important to the case. It's important that it be brought to her attention as soon as possible. In fact, I think she will be upset with you if she learns there was a delay because of a little red light."

"Okay, well, let me just go back and see if her door is open."

"Do that. Thank you. If it's closed, knock on it."

"We'll see. Just stay here and I'll be back."

He got up and went through the door at the rear of the corral into the hall that led to the judge's chambers.

I waited three minutes and then the door finally opened. Brown came through without the judge. He was shaking his head.

"Her door is closed," he said.

"Well, did you knock?" I asked.

"No. It's clear she doesn't want to be disturbed."

Without a second thought, I stood on my toes and leaned over the half wall of the corral. I reached my hand toward the judge's call button. My feet were in the air and I was balanced on the six-inch-wide wall cap.

"Hey!" Brown exclaimed.

I pushed the button and held my finger on it until my weight pulled me back and my feet were on the floor.

"What the hell do you think you're doing?" Brown yelled.

"I need to see her, Gian," I said. "It's an emergency."

"Doesn't matter. You had no right to do that. You need to leave the courtroom now."

I raised my hands and started backing away from the corral.

"I'm going to be in the hall," I said. "I'll be there all day or until she—"

I heard buzzing from the corral. Brown walked to his desk and picked up the phone.

"Yes, Judge," he said.

As he listened, I started returning to the corral.

"It's Mr. Haller," Brown said. "He pushed the button because I wouldn't disturb you."

I got to the corral and leaned over the half wall.

"Judge, I need to see you," I said loudly.

Brown put his hand over the phone and turned his back to me. "He said it's an SDT and there's a time issue," he said. "Yes, that was him. He's still here."

Brown listened for a few seconds and then hung up. He spoke with his back still to me.

"She said she'd see you," he said. "You can go in."

"Thank you, Gian," I said. "I owe you a macchiato."

"Don't bother."

"Extra caramel."

I went through the corral to the hall. Judge Coelho was standing in the open door to her chambers. Instead of a black robe, she wore blue jeans and a button-down corduroy shirt.

"This better be good, Mr. Haller," she said.

She turned and led the way into her chambers.

"Please excuse my casual dress," she said as she walked behind her desk. "Because of the continuance we are dark all day, and my plan was to catch up on my writing."

I knew that meant she was writing decisions and court orders. She took the seat behind her desk and pointed to one of the chairs across from her.

"Subpoena duces tecum," she said. "You are up to something you don't want Mr. Morris to know about. Yet."

"Yes, Your Honor," I said.

"Sit down, please. Talk to me."

"Thank you. Time is of the essence, Judge. We learned this morning that evidence from the original case was not disposed of after it was adjudicated five years ago. Lucinda Sanz's original attorney had received a split of evidence for independent testing—one of the gunshot-residue pads allegedly wiped over Sanz's hands and clothing."

"And you're saying it's still available?"

"It's at the independent lab that her attorney Frank Silver took it to. Applied Forensics in Van Nuys. We also learned that they did not use all of the material when they conducted a gunshot-residue test back then. They are still holding a piece of a GSR pad that was untested."

"And just what do you want to do with it?"

"Judge, I need a subpoena from you for a DNA swab from my client in the federal detention center. Then I need you to issue a sealed order directing Applied Forensics to compare her DNA to that of the untested evidence held at the lab there."

She stared at me for a long moment, trying to connect the dots.

"Okay, walk me through it," she finally said.

"Our contention has always been that the GSR evidence in the original case against Sanz was planted," I said. "It had to have been planted, because she did not shoot a gun. So, she was wiped by Deputy Sanger with GSR pads, but then somewhere along the line the pads were switched with contaminated pads that then tested positive for GSR. The DNA test we are asking for should find Sanz's touch DNA—skin cells—on the pad at Applied Forensics if it was actually swiped on her skin."

"Then the test you are asking for will cut both ways. If her DNA is found on that pad, your contention is proven wrong. Are you sure you want to take that chance, Mr. Haller?"

"Absolutely, Judge. We are all in."

"We? You've discussed the risks with your client? If her DNA is on that GSR pad, you know where this will go."

"She knows what's going on and she's all in too. She's innocent. She knows her DNA won't be on that pad."

It wasn't a lie. Lucinda had called collect from the detention center the night before and I had told her that there might be a remaining GSR pad from the original investigation. I walked her through what a DNA test could prove. She told me what I had just told the judge: that she was innocent and, if given the chance, would do the test.

"Your Honor," I added, "the cell-tower data plus the crime re-creation, though it was disallowed by the court, show my client's innocence. This test will as well."

"I admire your confidence in your client and what you believe the evidence will show," Coelho said. "But then why do you need the subpoena and court order to be under seal?"

"Because until we have a result, my fear is that there could be an obstruction of justice."

"Oh, come now, Mr. Haller. Do you really think so? Someone is going to break in at Applied Forensics and steal the evidence?"

"It's a possibility, Judge. Since taking on this case, both my investigator and I have had break-ins at our homes, although seemingly nothing was taken. My home office was ransacked and my computer destroyed—maple syrup poured onto the keyboard. These were acts of intimidation and I would ask the court to seal this until we have a test result. Once we have that, the court can share it with the world if it so wishes."

"Are there police reports on these break-ins?"

"Yes, we both made reports and I can request copies from the LAPD if the court needs them. But as I said, time is of the essence here. I also filed an insurance claim to cover a new computer and pay for the cleanup. In fact, they wouldn't take a claim without a police report. Anyway, in the old days when people wanted to intimidate you, they'd urinate or defecate on your stuff. But with DNA tracing, they got smarter. They used a bottle of my own maple syrup—a gift from my daughter."

"Lovely."

She paused for a moment, as if considering whether to believe me about the break-ins without seeing the official documentation.

"How fast can this testing be done?" she finally said.

"If we get Lucinda Sanz's DNA to them by the end of the day, we'll have results by Monday," I said.

"That will be a task, getting the marshals at detention to act that quickly."

"You could give me the subpoena and an order from you allowing me immediate access to my client."

Coelho shook her head. She started writing on a legal pad.

"No, we're not going to do that," she said. "I want the U.S. Marshals Service to handle the collection of DNA and its delivery to the lab. That way, there will be no issues later with chain of custody should this work out the way you think and hope it will."

"Yes, Your Honor," I said. "Very smart."

"Don't be obsequious, Mr. Haller. It doesn't look good on you."

"Yes, Your Honor."

"I'll prepare these now and have copies for you within the hour. It will probably take me the same amount of time it will take you to go to the cafeteria and get my clerk an apology macchiato."

I was silent. She looked up from her writing.

"Yes, he told me about those," she said. "Each time he told me. He didn't want there to be any question of favoritism."

"Understood," I said.

"You can go. Wait in the courtroom. Gian will bring you copies when they're ready."

"Yes, Your Honor. Thank you."

I got up and headed to the door. I was elated but trying not to show it. I put my hand on the knob but then looked back at the judge. She had already turned her seat to face the computer on a side table, but somehow she knew I had not left the room.

"Something else, Mr. Haller?" she asked.

"You said you were using the day for writing," I said. "Because of the continuance."

"Yes, I am."

"Would you reconsider the ruling on Dr. Arslanian's crime re-creation? Judge, I think you have a chance to make a sig—"

"Don't push it, Mr. Haller. If I were you, I'd leave while I was ahead."

"Yes, Your Honor."

I opened the door and stepped out.

37

ON SUNDAY, THE Lucinda Sanz team, now grudgingly including Frank
Silver, gathered without our client in the mock courtroom at South-
western Law School. As an alumnus who was a minor donor but had
a mostly positive public profile — especially after the Ochoa case — I
was afforded access to the school's facilities when they were not in
use. And so we set up shop in the small courtroom that featured a
judge's bench, a witness stand, and a small gallery. Monday would be
the day we won or lost our habeas motion and I wanted those who
could rehearse to rehearse.

The DNA results from Applied Forensics, which we'd expected
on Friday, were late, and I'd spent the past two days working on my
witness lineup the way a baseball manager works on a batting lineup
for the first game of the World Series. I had to figure out who was up
there to bunt, who might be able to steal a base, and who could bat
cleanup. I had to figure out what the opposing team would be pitch-
ing to my hitters and how best to prepare them.

The marshals hadn't delivered the DNA swab from Lucinda

Sanz to the lab until Thursday afternoon, and that was only after I had gone back to the courthouse, talked my way past a still-angry Gian Brown, and asked the judge to light a fire under the marshals.

With the delay, the earliest Applied Forensics could guarantee we'd have the results was noon on Monday. I had to schedule witnesses and rehearse on the assumption that I would have those results and they would be exculpatory for my client.

First at bat would be Harry Bosch. I had no choice there, unless Hayden Morris had taken his five days to analyze the cell-tower results and decided not to cross-examine him. But I thought this unlikely. At a minimum, Morris would assail Bosch's credibility. Bosch was old and largely out of the game. He had decades of experience working homicide investigations, but he had never before used geofencing—the term I learned from Britta Shoot—in an investigation. This made Bosch ripe for attack and I had to admit that this was what I would do if I were a prosecutor on this case. So I needed to make sure that Bosch was well armored and ready for Monday morning.

My hope was that Bosch's cross-examination would run through the morning and that I would have the Applied Forensics results in hand when it was time to call new witnesses to the stand. If Morris finished his cross early, I would need to wade in with a redirect examination of Bosch that would take us to the lunch break and possibly even further into the day.

Once Bosch was dismissed from the witness stand, Frank Silver was up. He would tell the judge how a piece of a GSR pad allegedly swiped over Lucinda Sanz's hands had been found in pristine condition in a Van Nuys lab five years after it was transferred there. Frank would be followed by a recall of Shami Arslanian and then the lab tech who'd conducted the DNA comparison. Though Stephanie Sanger was certainly not a member of my team, the main event would be her return to the witness stand. No rehearsal could prepare me for that. It would be up to me, and all I knew was that my questions to Sanger had to carry the information I needed to get to the judge. My feeling was that Sanger would not break on the stand and would confine herself to as few words as possible when answering questions under oath.

That was the lineup as I knew it so far. But there were always contingencies. The plan was to use the DNA evidence and Sanger's denials to force the judge to take action and compel FBI agent MacIsaac to appear for questioning. That was the ultimate goal: an FBI agent confirming under oath that Roberto Sanz was cooperating in an investigation of his own unit. If I got it there, I had no doubt that Lucinda Sanz would walk free.

Overall, the rehearsal went well. I put Cisco Wojciechowski up on the judge's bench so that there was an intimidating presence looking over the shoulder of the witnesses as they testified. Bosch was good on the stand — he'd spent hundreds of hours testifying in his career. Shami Arslanian was her usual charming and professional self. Jennifer Aronson, sitting in for Stephanie Sanger, gave one-word and sarcastic answers, but I was able to hone my questions in response and deliver the goods. The one fly in the ointment was Silver, who steadfastly inflated his own worth and legal acumen in answer to my initial questions. It forced me to reshape how I would question him when the testimony was for real.

I felt that it had been a successful day. We broke at five p.m. and I took everybody, even Silver, to an early dinner in the private wine room at Musso and Frank's. There was solid camaraderie on the team, and we all held up our glasses, whether they contained alcohol or not, toasted Lucinda, and promised to do our very best for her the next day.

It was after eight when I parked in the garage beneath my house.

My intention was to go directly to sleep so I would be rested and ready in the morning. I closed the garage and slowly climbed the stairs. Three steps from the top, I saw a man sitting in one of the bar chairs at the far end of the deck. His back was to me and his feet were propped up on the rail. It looked like he was relaxing and staring out at the lights of the city. The only thing missing was a bottle of beer.

He spoke without turning to look at me.

"I've been waiting for you for a couple hours," he said. "I figured on a Sunday night you'd be home."

The key to the house was in my hand. The door was at the top of the stairs. I knew I could get to the knob and get it open before he got to me. But something told me that if this had been a plan to intimidate or hurt me, it wouldn't be one man sitting leisurely at the end of the front deck. I moved the keys in my hand so one was jutting between my fingers and would do some damage if I had to throw a punch. I cautiously walked over. As I got close, a jolt went through me—the man was wearing a black ballistic mask that covered his whole face.

"Relax," he said. "If I'd wanted to put you down, you'd already be down."

I steadied myself, tightened my fists, and moved closer. But not close enough for him to reach out to me.

"Then what's with the mask?" I said. "And who the fuck are you?"

He lowered his feet to the foot rail of the bar chair and turned away from the view.

"I thought you were smarter than that, Haller," he said. "I obviously don't want you to see my face."

I suddenly realized who he was.

"The elusive Agent MacIsaac," I said.

"Bravo," he said.

"Something tells me you're not here to tell me you'll testify."

"I'm here to tell you I will not and that you need to stand down on that."

"I've got an innocent client and I think you can help me prove it. I can't stand down."

"Helping you prove it doesn't necessarily mean me testifying."

I thought about those words for a long moment as I stared at the eyes behind the oval cutouts in the mask. Before I could come up with my next question, he asked one.

"Why do you think I can't testify? Why is the U.S. attorney willing to defy a federal judge if it comes to that?"

"Because the Bureau will be embarrassed by what is revealed in court: that the FBI was willing to let Lucinda Sanz go to prison as long as it didn't come out that its agent's actions got her ex-husband killed."

MacIsaac laughed. It was muffled behind the mask, but I heard it and it made me angry.

"You're going to deny it even here?" I said. "Sanger watched you and Sanz meet. An hour later he was dead, and Lucinda goes down as the fall guy. Meanwhile, the Bureau — and you — look the other way."

"I want to help you but you don't know shit about what went down," MacIsaac said.

"So school me, Agent MacIsaac. Why won't you testify and what's with the fucking mask?"

"Can we just go inside? I don't like talking out here in the open."

"No, we're not going inside. Not until you tell me why you're really here."

"If we're staying out here because you want to keep me on camera, that's not happening."

I turned and looked up at the Ring camera I'd had installed under the roof eave after the break-in six months earlier. There was a Dodgers baseball cap hung over the lens.

"What the fuck?" I said.

"I'm not even supposed to be here, okay?" MacIsaac said. "I came because I understand what you're doing. But your case is more than five years old. We've moved on and I'm working on something else, something that cuts across lines of national security. I can't appear in court because I can't take any risks with that case. People could die. Do you understand?"

"You're telling me you can't show your face because you're working undercover."

"That's part of it, yes."

"There are no cameras in the courtroom. We could even arrange for you to testify in the judge's chambers. You could wear your mask, for all I care."

He shook his head.

"I can't go anywhere near that courthouse. It's watched."

"By who?"

"I'm not getting into that. It's got nothing to do with your case. The point is, I need you to stand down. We can't have this blow up in the media. There might be photos out there they could use. If that happens, I'm dead and the case I'm working is dead."

"So I'm supposed to just let my client rot in prison while you go on about your national-security business."

"Look, I thought she did it, okay? All these years I was mad at her because killing him ended the investigation. But then you come along and I'm following the case and I start seeing what you're seeing. I think you might have something, but I can't help you in court."

"Then what can you do for me? For her?"

"I can tell you that Roberto Sanz was no hero, but in a way, he was trying to be."

"The shoot-out at Flip's was no ambush. He was ripping those guys off. Tell me something I don't know."

"He agreed to wear a wire. That day we met, he said he would do it. We were going to take down the whole unit. And then an hour later, it was over."

"Because Sanger saw you two."

"I didn't know."

"Obviously. Let me ask you something: Did he come to you or did you go to him?"

"He came to us. He wanted to clear his conscience, try to make things right. The clique he was in was taking things too far."

"Just tell me this. He got killed right after you met with him, so how could you think it was his ex-wife?"

MacIsaac seemed to consider the question for the first time.

"Arrogance," he finally said. "We're the FBI. We don't make mistakes like that. I thought the meeting was clean. I had a backup and they didn't see anybody shadowing him. And then when I read about the evidence against your client, the GSR and all of that, I guess I believed what I wanted to believe. We shut down the investigation and moved on to the next one."

"And an innocent woman has been sitting in a cell for five years. Great story. Our tax dollars at work. But you need to give me something, MacIsaac, or this is all going to come out. With or without you on the stand, I'll get it out there. I've already started. And if I get the judge to compel your testimony and it blows your cover, I don't really care. Lucinda Sanz is not going back to that cell. You understand that?"

"I understand. And I have something for you. That's why I'm here. I want to trade. Sanz told me things in that meeting. The clique was just a ground team. They were working for something bigger."

"Who?"

"More like *what*. But we go inside to talk about it."

"What is the obsession with going inside my house?"

"We're exposed out here."

I knew not to trust this man inside or outside my house. But I had to know what he knew.

I realized that my left hand was still balled into a fist, with the teeth of my house key protruding between my fingers. I released my grip and the key fell into my palm.

"Okay," I said. "Let's go in.

PART NINE

TRUE BELIEVER

38

BOSCH WAS WORRIED. The rehearsal the day before had gone well. Posing as assistant attorney general Hayden Morris, Mickey Haller had cross-examined him intensely, hitting him most harshly on his lack of experience in using cellular data in homicide investigations. Bosch had held up well, by his own and Haller's estimation, and he'd thought he was ready for whatever Morris threw at him on Monday morning. But now, sitting on the witness stand and waiting for the judge to convene court, Bosch was worried because Morris was not alone at the AG's table. Next to him was a woman Bosch recognized as a former county prosecutor. She was good and tough and had been known in those days as Maggie McFierce. She was also Mickey Haller's ex-wife and the mother of his only child.

Maggie McPherson had taken a leave of absence from the Ventura County District Attorney's Office to aid her ex-husband when he was wrongly accused of murder. Haller was eventually cleared, and McPherson had gone back to Ventura, where she was in charge of the Major Crimes Unit at the DA's office. But that intel was obviously old, as it was now clear to Bosch that she worked for the AG. She was huddled with Morris at the opposing counsel's table in a whispered conversation. On the table in front of her was the thick stack of printouts of cell-tower data Haller had turned over in discovery. Morris had pulled in a ringer. Bosch knew that McPherson would handle his cross-examination.

Bosch looked over at the petitioner's table to see if Haller was exhibiting any concern or giving any indication of how he was going to play this. But Haller was preoccupied with the arrival of Lucinda Sanz from the courtroom holding cell. When she was finally seated and shackled to the table ring by the marshals, Haller looked around the courtroom. He noticed the journalist he had told Bosch about, gave her a nod, and continued his scan. Bosch caught his eye. Haller made a hand gesture—a flat palm down—that told Bosch to stay calm.

Bosch assumed that Haller was as surprised about Maggie McPherson's appearance as he was, but the Lincoln Lawyer looked cool, calm, and collected. Bosch took his cue from that.

Testifying in criminal cases was nothing new to Bosch. He had been in the witness box hundreds of times. When he had thought about it over the weekend, he realized that the first time he'd been called to testify was in a drug case in 1973. He had been in patrol then, a P-1 stripe on the sleeve of his uniform. He had found an ounce of marijuana during the pat-down of a man loitering near Dorsey High School. All these years later, Bosch clearly remembered the suspect he had arrested. His legal name was Junior Teodoro. He was twenty years old and a dropout from Dorsey. The alert had gone out in that morning's roll call about a dealer setting up near the school. Bosch and his partner at the time had spotted Teodoro, did a stop-and-hop so fast he couldn't run away, and caught him with the goods during the pat-down.

Bosch's testimony came at a preliminary hearing on the case. After Teodoro was bound over for trial, he and his attorney negotiated a plea agreement. Bosch remembered it so well because Junior Teodoro pleaded guilty and got a term of five to seven years in prison for something that fifty years later was no longer a crime. Bosch had often considered how time changed something that was righteous back in the day into something far from it today. He thought about how that bust and the harsh sentence that followed had changed the course of Teodoro's life. When Bosch was still with the LAPD, he kept tabs on him through the California law enforcement tracking system, running his name from time to time. The prison gate became a revolving door for Teodoro. Whenever Bosch looked him up, he was either back in prison or recently released and on parole. Fifty years later, Bosch was still haunted by his part in setting Junior Teodoro on that path. And that was his worry now — that his testimony under cross-examination might somehow contribute to Lucinda Sanz losing her bid for freedom and that it would haunt him for the rest of his days.

McPherson and Morris finished their whispered conference and McPherson reached down to a slim briefcase on the floor and withdrew a legal pad. She wrote a few notes on it and then placed it on top of the printouts, ready to take it all with her to the lectern. She glanced over at Bosch and caught him staring at her. Possibly sensing his alarm, she smiled. Of all his cases over the years, none had landed on her desk for prosecution, yet he knew she was a courtroom killer. So Bosch understood that her smile carried no warmth for him. It was the kind of smile a cat might offer a cornered mouse.

There was finally a call to rise from the courtroom marshal, and Judge Coelho took the bench. She noticed Bosch on the witness stand.

"Please be seated," she said. "I see Detective Bosch is already in place, but before we begin cross-examination, we have some business to attend to."

Rather than sitting down, Bosch turned to step out of the witness stand.

"That's all right, Detective Bosch," Coelho said. "This shouldn't take long. You may sit."

Bosch sat down, noting that she had called him Detective Bosch.

"Mr. Morris, I see you have expanded your team today," Coelho continued.

Morris stood to address the court.

"Yes, Your Honor," he said. "Assistant attorney general Margaret McPherson will handle the cross-examination of Mr. Bosch. She has expertise in the matters he testified to last week."

"Well, that answers the question of whether there will be a cross-examination," the judge said. "Mr. Haller, do you have anything you would like to bring to the attention of the court?"

Haller stood.

"Good morning, Your Honor," Haller said. "As a matter of fact, I do. The petitioner objects to the addition of Ms. McPherson to the State's team as a conflict of interest."

Morris stood back up.

"Just hold it right there, Mr. Morris," Coelho said. "What conflict is that, Mr. Haller?"

"Ms. McPherson and I were married at one time," Haller said.

Bosch turned to check the judge's reaction. It was clear she had not known of the marital history of the two lawyers before her.

"Interesting," Coelho said. "I was not aware of that. When were you two married?"

"It was quite a while ago, Your Honor," Haller said. "But there is an adult daughter and ongoing connections as well as ongoing upset over the dissolution of the marriage and its consequences."

"How so, Mr. Haller?" the judge said.

"Your Honor, I believe Ms. McPherson harbors resentment over her career as a prosecutor for Los Angeles County being...thwarted by her relationship with me. I would not want that to interfere with my client's ability to get a fair and impartial hearing on the facts of this petition."

The judge turned her attention to Morris.

"Mr. Morris, are you attempting to inject outside conflict into this proceeding?"

"Not at all, Your Honor," Morris said. "As I already stated on the record, Ms. McPherson is the expert on cellular data in the California Attorney General's Office. Last year, in fact, she was hired away from the Ventura County prosecutor's office because of her expertise in this field. This is an area of the law that is fairly new and that comes up frequently as alleged 'new evidence' in appellate and habeas briefs. This material was sprung on us last week, and with the continuance the court granted, I took it to our expert, Ms. McPherson, who has been analyzing the material in preparing for this witness's cross-examination. There is no conflict, Your Honor. My understanding is that the marriage has been over for more years than it existed. There are no custody disputes because their one child is an adult and lives independently of her parents. There are no disputes at all, Judge. In fact, two years ago Ms. McPherson took a leave from the Ventura prosecutor's office to provide legal help to Mr. Haller when he was charged with a crime."

"Is all that true, Mr. Haller?" Coelho asked.

"It is true there are no custody or other legal disputes, Judge," Haller said. "But on more than one occasion, I was blamed for setbacks, demotions, and changes in Ms. McPherson's career, and, as I said earlier, I don't want any possible grudge to hinder Lucinda Sanz's right to a fair and impartial hearing on the petition."

The judge frowned and even Bosch knew why. It was the judge who needed to be fair and impartial. Haller's argument was misdirected. But before the judge could speak, Maggie McFierce did.

"Your Honor, may I be heard?" she said. "Everyone is talking about me. I think I should be allowed to respond."

"Go ahead, Ms. McPherson," Coelho said. "But be brief. This is not family court and I don't want to turn it into an examination of a broken marriage and what grievances may exist therein."

"I'm happy to be brief," McPherson said. "The fact is, I hold no grudge against my ex-husband. It was indeed a complicated union between a prosecutor and a defense attorney, but it ended a long time ago. I have moved on, he has moved on, and our daughter is a grown woman making her way in the world. Mr. Morris did not even know of my marital history when he came to me last week and asked me to take a look at the material turned over in discovery. It wasn't until I started working on it that I noticed that it was my ex-husband's case and that the witness was Mr. Bosch, whom I have met on occasion. I immediately informed Mr. Morris but told him, as I am telling the court, that Mr. Haller and I have no conflict of interest. Our relationship as the parents of a young woman is not conflicted in any way and I hold no grudge against him, his client, or his witness."

"I am not sure that was brief, but the court appreciates counsel's honesty," Coelho said. "Anything else, Mr. Haller?"

"Submitted," Haller said.

Haller said it in a tone that dripped with defeat. He knew how this was going to go.

"Very well," the judge said. "It is this court's responsibility to remain fair and impartial in hearing evidence and determining the truth of things. I intend to do that. The objection is overruled. Now, Mr. Haller, is there anything else you would like to bring up with the court before we proceed with the witness?"

"Not at this time, Judge," Haller said.

Coelho paused and looked at Haller. Bosch knew she was expecting him to announce that he had new discovery material to give to the

AG. But there were no results yet from the DNA analysis begun the week before. This meant that Haller wouldn't know until he heard from Shami Arslanian, who was stationed at Applied Forensics monitoring the work, whether or not he had new evidence to help Lucinda Sanz's case.

"Very well," the judge said again. "Then let's proceed. Ms. McPherson, your witness."

39

FOR BOSCH, IT was a reminder of how far he had gone off mission. Maggie McFierce was a true believer, a career prosecutor who had never been lured away from the pursuit of justice to join the high-paid private sector. She had stayed on mission, and though jobs and agencies changed, she'd never wavered from the cause. And here was Bosch, heretofore a true believer, about to be pounded on the witness stand the way he had seen so many witnesses for criminal defendants get pounded in the past.

McPherson would be out to prove that Bosch was a gun for hire who would also lie for hire, who would cut corners and look only for the thing that would obscure the truth or hide it completely. She had no doubt done her homework on Bosch and knew his vulnerabilities. She attempted to exploit them right out of the gate.

"Mr. Bosch, how long have you worked as a defense investigator?" she asked.

"Uh, actually, I never have," Bosch said.

"You are working for Mr. Haller, are you not?"

"I am working on a specific project for him that doesn't involve defense work."

"Did you not work for Mr. Haller's own defense when he was accused of a crime?"

"I was more of an adviser. Like you were. Do you believe you have never worked for the defense?"

"I'm not the one answering questions here."

"Sorry."

"So what you're telling the court is that you don't consider working for Lucinda Sanz, an admitted and convicted killer, defense work?"

"Mr. Haller hired me to go through cases involving convicted people who claimed they were innocent. He wanted me to review them to see if any seemed plausible or worth another look. Lucinda Sanz's case was one of them and—"

"Thank you, Mr. Bosch, I didn't ask for the whole history of the case. But you would say that working on the Lucinda Sanz case is not defense work."

"Correct. It's not defense work. It's truth work."

"That's clever, Mr. Bosch. What happens in your so-called truth work if you come across evidence that someone is guilty of the crime they were convicted of?"

"I tell Mr. Haller that's it's a no-go and we move on. I look into the next case."

"And has that scenario ever occurred as you just outlined?"

"Uh, yes. Happened just a couple months ago."

"Tell the court about that."

"Well, it was this guy named Coldwell who was convicted of hiring a killer to murder his partner in a business investment. He was convicted largely on the testimony of the contract killer, who was also charged but was cooperating with the prosecution. He testified that he was paid twenty-five thousand dollars in cash to do the hit. The other evidence included Coldwell's bank records. The prosecution was able to show that exactly twenty-five thousand had been accumulated through ATM withdrawals and personal checks Coldwell wrote to friends who cashed them and gave him the money."

"What made you think he was innocent?"

"I didn't. I thought that his case might be worth another look. I interviewed him and he said that he could account for the twenty-five thousand and give information he picked up in prison that would impeach the contract killer. I'll spare you the full history on it, but I determined that Coldwell was guilty and we dropped it."

"No, please, don't spare us the details. What made him guilty — in your eyes?"

"He told me he had given the money to a mistress and that he couldn't bring that up at his trial because he was still married then and his wife's money was paying his trial lawyer. If they'd brought forth the mistress, Coldwell's wife would have cut him off financially. As it turned out, his wife divorced him a couple years after he was convicted, so now he was ready to use the mistress. He also told me that an inmate who had been transferred from the prison where the hit man ended up — Soledad — said the hit man was bragging up there about setting up Coldwell for the murder."

"Okay, let's stop there. I think we need to move to the case at hand."

Haller stood up and objected.

"Your Honor, she opened this door," he said. "And now all of a sudden she wants to slam it closed because she knows that finishing the story might show that the witness has integrity, and that doesn't fit with the State's plan to attack his credibility."

The judge didn't hesitate in sustaining the objection.

"Counsel is right," Coelho said. "This door was flung open by the

State. I'd like to hear the end of the story. The witness will continue his answer if he has more to say."

Haller nodded toward Bosch, thanked the judge, and sat down.

"I called the Department of Corrections," Bosch said. "With the help of an intel officer at Soledad, I was able to determine that the hit man and the transferred inmate Coldwell mentioned had never been in the same cell block and would not have crossed paths while they were both housed there. So that knocked that part of his story out. Then I talked to the mistress and she wasn't a good liar. Took me about twenty minutes to break her story. She admitted that Coldwell hadn't given her twenty-five thousand dollars, that she had lied about it because he'd promised her money when he got out and sued the State for wrongful conviction and imprisonment. So that was it. We dropped the case — Mickey and I."

"So, Mr. Bosch," McPherson said, "what you want the court to know is that you call them like you see them."

"I don't know if that was a question, but yes, I call them like I see them."

"Okay, well, then, let's talk about the Sanz case and how you saw it. Okay, Mr. Bosch?"

"It's what I'm here for."

"Do you know what geofencing is, Mr. Bosch?"

"Yes, it's kind of a fancy word for tracking the locations of cell phones through cellular data."

"It has become a useful tool for law enforcement, hasn't it?"

"Yes."

"In your direct testimony you said you have worked on hundreds of homicide cases, correct?"

"Yes, correct."

"In how many of those cases did you use geofencing?"

"None. It was a technology that really didn't come out until after I retired."

"Okay, then how many times have you used it as a private investigator?"

"None."

"What about as a nondefense investigator working for Mr. Haller?"

"This case was the first time."

"One case. Would you say that makes you an expert on geofencing?"

"An expert? I don't know what would make one an expert. I know how to read and map the data, if that's what you mean."

"How did you learn to read and map the data?"

"I had some help from Mr. Haller, who was familiar with geofencing from prior cases. But I learned the most when I studied the FBI's internal field resource guide for agents in this area of investigation. It was put together by the Bureau's Cellular Analysis Survey Team and is basically a how-to-do-it for agents. It's very detailed — over a hundred pages — and I read it twice before I started work on the data we received in this case."

McPherson had not expected an answer that complete and quickly went to sarcasm to cover her error in asking the question.

"Simple as that," she said. "Take an online course and you're an expert."

"It's not up to me to say whether I'm an expert," Bosch said. "But it was the FBI's online course, if you want to call it that. It was designed so that any agent could trace and map the movement of cellular devices. If you're suggesting that I did it wrong or got it wrong, I would disagree. I think I got it right and it raises a lot of questions about Lucinda Sanz's culp — "

"Move to strike the witness's answer as nonresponsive."

McPherson looked up at the bench, but before the judge could respond, Haller stood.

"Nonresponsive?" he said. "He didn't get the chance to finish his response."

The judge wasn't interested in parrying with the lawyers.

"Let's just move on to the next question," Coelho said. "Continue, Ms. McPherson."

Haller sat down. Bosch looked over at him for the first time during the cross. Haller nodded and did a small fist shake with his hand close to his chest. Bosch took it as a not-so-secret *Stay strong* gesture.

"Mr. Bosch," McPherson said, pulling Bosch's attention back. "Are you ill?"

Haller jumped up from his seat.

"Your Honor, what is this?" he said indignantly. "Counsel has no business asking about the witness's health. What does it have to do with any question before this court?"

The judge cast a stern eye on McPherson.

"Ms. McPherson, what are you doing here?" she asked.

"Your Honor," McPherson said, "if the court will indulge me, it will become quite clear what I'm doing, and Mr. Haller is well aware of what I'm doing. The witness's health is an issue if it affects his work."

"You may proceed," the judge said. "Cautiously."

"Thank you, Your Honor," McPherson said. Focusing again on the witness stand, she asked, "Mr. Bosch, are you presently being treated for a medical condition?"

"No," Bosch said.

McPherson looked surprised but quickly covered it.

"Then have you recently been treated for a medical condition?" she asked.

Bosch hesitated as he thought about how to phrase his answer.

"I was being treated earlier this year," he finally said.

"Treated for what?" McPherson said.

Haller, apparently sensing where this could go, stood again to object.

"Your Honor, last week my asking a witness for her cell number had Mr. Morris jumping out of his shoes," he said. "But now it's okay to drag a witness's personal medical history into the case? Aren't there limits to invasion of privacy in this court?"

"Mr. Haller makes a good point, Ms. McPherson," Coelho said.

"Your Honor, the witness's medical status is important to this case, and I can demonstrate why if I am allowed to continue," McPherson said. "Mr. Haller knows this and that is why he is jumping out of *his* shoes."

"Make it fast, Ms. McPherson," the judge said. "My patience is wearing thin."

Haller sat down and the judge told Bosch he must answer the question.

"I was being treated for cancer," Bosch said. "I was part of a clinical trial that ended almost six months ago."

"And was the treatment successful?" McPherson asked.

"The doctors seemed to think so. They said I'm in partial remission."

"And this clinical trial, was it to test a drug therapy?"

"Yes."

"Using what drug?"

"It was an isotope, actually. I believe it is called lutetium one-seventy-seven."

"You were being treated with this isotope while you worked on this case?"

"Yes. It was just one morning a week for twelve weeks."

"And what are the possible side effects associated with lutetium one-seventy-seven?"

"Uh, well, there's nausea, tinnitus, exhaustion. There's a whole list, but other than those I just mentioned, I didn't really have any side effects."

"What about confusion and memory loss?"

"Uh, I think those were on the list but I haven't experienced them."

"Have you experienced any cognitive impairment while working on this case?"

Haller stood, arms out in an imploring gesture.

"Your Honor...really?"

The judge pointed to his empty chair.

"Your objection has been overruled," she said. "Sit down, Mr. Haller."

Haller slowly sat down.

"Do you need me to repeat the question?" McPherson asked.

"No," Bosch said. "I can remember, thank you. The answer is no, I have not experienced any cognitive impairment."

"Have you asked a doctor about it or taken a cognitive test in the past six months?"

"No, I have not."

McPherson looked down at a document she had carried with her to the lectern.

"Earlier this year, did you report a break-in at your home?" she asked.

"Uh, yes, I did," Bosch said.

"And was this while you were being treated with the isotope lutetium one-seventy-seven?"

"Yes."

McPherson asked the judge to allow her to approach the witness with a document she called State's exhibit one. First McPherson dropped off copies to Haller and the judge. Bosch watched Haller read it and noticed alarm come into his eyes. He stood and objected, stating the document had not been submitted to him through discovery.

"Offered as impeachment, Your Honor," McPherson said. "The witness just testified to having no cognitive issues."

"Yes, I'll allow it," Coelho said.

Bosch braced himself as McPherson came to him with a copy of the document, and then returned to the lectern.

"Mr. Bosch, is that the police report from the alleged break-in at your home on Woodrow Wilson Drive?" she asked.

"Uh, looks like it," Bosch said. "That's my address. But I have not seen this before."

"Well, you were a police officer. Does it look official to you?"

"Yes."

"Then could you read the paragraph in the responding officer's summary that I have highlighted in yellow?"

"Uh, yes. It says, 'Upon questioning, victim seemed confused ... and unsure if a break-in had occurred. Victim is ill and being treated. Possible ... dementia. Walk-through of residence conducted. No evidence of burglary. No further follow-up is required.'"

Bosch felt his neck and back start to burn. He was stunned by what the responding officer had written.

"I wasn't confused," he said. "Because nothing was taken, I wasn't sure there had been a break-in. That's all. And *dementia* was his word, not—"

"Your Honor, move to strike the witness's last comment as nonresponsive," McPherson said.

"So moved," Coelho said. "Do you have any other questions, Ms. McPherson?"

"No, Your Honor."

She moved from the lectern and sat down next to Morris.

A silence engulfed the courtroom and Bosch noticed that no one was looking at him, not even Haller. It was like everyone was embarrassed for him. He wanted to shout, *I have not lost my mind!* but he knew that would support Maggie McFierce's implication.

"Mr. Haller," the judge finally said. "Redirect?"

Haller stood and slowly moved to the lectern.

"Thank you, Judge," he said. "Mr. Bosch, during the course of this investigation, how many times have you gone out to the state prison in Chino to visit our client, Lucinda Sanz?"

Bosch looked up from the police report that was still in front of him.

"Four times," he said. "Once with you, three times by myself."

"That's about an hour out, correct?"

"Yes."

"Do you use one of the GPS apps to find your way out there?"

"Uh, no. I know where it is."

"So you've never gotten lost or taken the freeway too far and gone past your exit?"

"No."

"You drive me often while we are working, correct?"

"Yes."

"I don't think I've ever seen you use a GPS app — why is that?"

"I don't use them. I know where I'm going."

"Thank you. I have nothing further."

PART TEN

THE GRAND MASTER OF SMOKE

40

I ASKED FOR the morning break as soon as Bosch was excused from the witness stand. The judge gave us fifteen minutes. Maggie McFierce grabbed her thin leather briefcase and was out of the courtroom and gone before I could get to her. It didn't matter, because I was more concerned about Bosch. I met him at the railing.

"Don't say anything here," I said. "Let's go out and grab a conference room."

We exited the courtroom. The hall was empty. No sign of Maggie. We walked to an attorney meeting room that was one courtroom down, a small space with a table and chairs and four windowless walls. I felt claustrophobic as soon as we walked in.

"Sit down," I said. "Harry, I don't know what you're thinking, but let it go. The cop who wrote that report was full of shit and so are Maggie and Morris. Fuck them."

"How did she know about UCLA?" Bosch said. "That could not possibly be discovery stuff. She —"

"I'm sorry, man. That's on me. Last time we had dinner together with Hayley, I mentioned that you were working for me and that I'd gotten you into that trial. It was before she even took the job with the AG. I can't believe she used it. I'm sorry, Harry."

Bosch shook his head.

"Well," he said. "How bad does it hurt us?"

"I don't know," I said. "I think the judge could see that you don't have any kind of problem. The whole thing is bullshit. And what it shows is that their so-called geofencing expert had to resort to character assassination because she could find nothing wrong with your direct testimony about geofencing. That's not going to be lost on the judge."

I took out my phone, turned it on, and waited for it to boot up.

"It's always been the defense lawyers who pulled that kill-the-messenger sort of shit," Bosch said. "Not the DA, not the AG."

"It was low," I said. "And I'm going to make sure she knows it."

"Don't bother. It's over. Have we heard anything from Applied Forensics?"

"Shami's over there. Last I heard they're still working on it."

I opened up a text to Maggie and started typing.

> *Now I know why you didn't invite Hayley to watch us in court. That was low, Mags. How could you do that?*

I reread what I had typed and then sent it. I checked my watch. We needed to get back into the courtroom in five minutes.

"Okay, are you good?" I asked.

"I'm fine," Bosch said. "But I don't think my saying I don't get lost while driving is going to be enough to fix the damage."

"It's the best I could come up with on the spot. But it's not just about that. You testified thoroughly and professionally last week. You were in complete command of the cell-tower data and the judge saw and heard that. She won't make any decision based on what just happened. I think we're fine. What I need now is for you to go find Frank Silver and bring him in. We're going to need him to testify if and when we get the results from Shami."

"What about Sanger?"

"She's last—after we have the DNA."

"And MacIsaac?"

"No MacIsaac. I'm not going that route."

"What? I thought this whole thing was to get the judge to—"

"All of that's changed. We'll never get MacIsaac on the stand, so we go without him."

"How do you know she won't order him to testify?"

"Because he paid me a visit last night."

"What?"

"After dinner, when I got home, he was sitting on my porch. He's working undercover on a national-security thing and they're not going to let him near the courthouse."

"Bullshit. They use that national-security crap anytime they don't want to—"

"I believed him."

"Why?"

"Because he gave me something. Something I can use against Sanger."

"What?"

"I can't say at the moment. I have to figure a few things out and then I'll tell you."

Bosch looked at me as though I had just said I didn't trust him.

"Look, I'll bring you into the loop as soon as I can. I need to get back to court now, and you need to find Second-Place Silver."

Bosch nodded.

"Okay," he said.

He got up and turned to the door.

"And I'm sorry, Harry," I said. "About what Maggie pulled in there."

"It's not on you, Mick," he said. "I'll let you know when I have Silver ready to go."

In the hall, he went one way and I went the other, toward the courtroom. Before I got there, Maggie hit me back with a text.

A lawyer once said that all was fair on the proving ground of the courtroom. Oh, yeah, I think that lawyer was you.

I decided not to respond. Instead, I called Shami Arslanian.

"Where are we?" I asked.

"We just got results," she said. "I'm looking at them now."

I braced myself. This was the case.

"And?" I prompted.

"There was DNA on the swab," she said. "It's not Lucinda's."

I suddenly, almost involuntarily, moved to one of the marble benches lining the hall and sat down, the phone pressed against my ear. In that moment, I felt that we would win, that Lucinda Sanz would walk free.

"Mickey, are you there?" Arslanian said.

"Uh, yeah," I said. "I'm just...this is incredible."

"There is a complication."

"What's that?"

"The DNA that's there comes from two other people. One is unknown. But we already matched the other because it belongs to a former lab tech at Applied Forensics. They always run matching to their own personnel to guard against contamination."

"What does this mean, Shami?"

"The lab tech it matches has not worked here in four years. It means that at some point when the evidence was brought here, it got mishandled and contaminated with his DNA. Again, we're talking about touch DNA, which at the time they didn't have a protocol for."

I closed my eyes.

"Jesus Christ. Every time I think we've grabbed the brass ring, something goes wrong and we've got shit."

"I'm sorry, Mickey. But the important thing is that Lucinda's DNA is not on the GSR pad. This proves your theory of the crime. Are you saying you won't be able to use this in court?"

"I don't know. I really don't know. But I need you to get back to the courthouse as soon as you can with whatever reports you have there. Get the name of the tech from before and whatever documentation there is about the contamination. You'll probably have to explain everything in an evidentiary hearing before the judge. I'm going to go ask for that now."

"Okay, Mickey, I'll grab an Uber."

I disconnected and tried to compose myself, channeling the ghost of Legal Siegel. *Breathe it in. This is your moment. This is your stage. Want it. Own it. Take it.*

I got up off the bench and reentered the courtroom.

41

OVER MY OBJECTION, Judge Coelho held the evidentiary hearing behind closed doors. The Latin term for it was *in camera,* which sounded like the opposite of a private meeting. I had opposed it because if the judge ruled against the introduction of the DNA findings, I wanted the world to know it and share in my outrage. But my argument for an open hearing fell on deaf ears, and I found myself sitting next to Hayden Morris in front of Coelho and her massive desk in chambers. My client was deemed unnecessary to the hearing and was waiting in the courtside lockup for me to tell her how things shook out.

"Before we begin, we need to inform Mr. Morris of what has transpired over the past five days," Coelho said. "Last Wednesday, Mr. Haller came to me and informed me that evidence from the earlier adjudicated case had been located. He asked for sealed orders that would allow him to pursue the testing of this evidence."

"What was the evidence?" Morris asked. "And what tests are we talking about?"

"It gets complicated, Mr. Morris," the judge said. "I'll let Mr. Haller explain the details."

She nodded to me and I took up the story.

"Yes, Your Honor," I said. "During the initial prosecution of the case five years ago, defense counsel—a lawyer named Frank Silver—asked for a split of evidence so he could conduct independent testing. There were two gunshot-residue pads presumably used to swipe Lucinda Sanz's hands, arms, and clothing. As you know, GSR was a key piece of the prosecution's case. The court gave him one of the two pads to have independently tested for gunshot residue."

"This was before the plea agreement?" Morris asked.

"Exactly," I said. "The pad was transferred to Applied Forensics, an independent lab out in Van Nuys that still operates today. While that was happening, plea negotiations began, and as we all know, Lucinda Sanz took the plea deal. She went off to prison after pleading nolo, and Silver never bothered going back to Applied Forensics to retrieve the evidence. We learned of this Wednesday, checked it out, and the evidence was still in storage at the lab—largely because Silver never paid the lab's bill."

"You've got to be kidding me," Morris said, shaking his head. "This sounds like a setup if I've ever heard one. Your Honor, why are we even considering this?"

"Let Mr. Haller continue," Coelho said.

"Think what you want," I said. "But I came to the judge Wednesday and asked for orders to have the remaining pad tested for DNA, because if the pad was actually swiped over my client's hands and clothes, we would find her DNA—her touch DNA—on the pad. I have a forensics expert who backs me up on this. The judge then ordered the U.S. Marshals to swab Sanz and take her DNA sample to Applied Forensics."

"I don't care who backs you up," Morris said. "This is incredibly unusual and the wrong protocol. This should have been handled by either the sheriff's lab or the state DOJ's crime lab, not some fly-by-night lab in the Valley."

He said it in a tone that suggested all of the San Fernando Valley was a haven for fly-by-night businesses and people.

"Mr. Haller asked me to seal the orders," the judge said. "He wanted the evidence analyzed privately because of his concerns over obstruction from within the government agencies. I agreed. The orders were sealed until there were results. If this goes any further, you will have the opportunity to test the evidence at the lab of your choice, Mr. Morris. Now, Mr. Haller, I assume you called for this session because you have results?"

"Yes, Your Honor," I said. "The lab results are in. The GSR pad did contain gunshot residue. Two unique DNA profiles were also identified and compared to my client's profile. There was no match. That pad was never swiped over my client's body, and this is proof that she was framed for her ex-husband's murder."

"It's proof of nothing," Morris said. "This is incredible. The court has been manipulated by this...this grand master of smoke. Your Honor, this evidence, if you want to call it that, is clearly not admissible."

"I believe that is a decision for the court to make, Mr. Morris," the judge said. "And perhaps you would like to explain how the court has been manipulated. I'm sure Mr. Haller has witnesses and documentation of every step of this process over the past five days. I'm sure his forensics expert, whom we have already heard testimony from, is standing by to render her expert opinion that a pad wiped over a person's body and clothing would have to pick up that person's DNA. Where is the manipulation of the court?"

"Your Honor, I'm sorry if I impugned the integrity of the court,"

Morris said quickly. "That was not my intention. But this story is too far-fetched. It's eleventh-hour pyrotechnics by counsel designed to distract the court from the evidence of direct culpability that has always been there."

"If it is eleventh-hour pyrotechnics, I'm sure the state's lab will bring it to light," Coelho said, annoyance in her voice.

"There is also a bit of a complication," I said.

Coelho turned her annoyance in my direction.

"What complication?" she said.

"As I said, there were two unique DNA profiles found on the GSR pad," I said. "One remains unidentified. The other has been identified as a lab tech who previously worked at Applied Forensics."

Morris threw his hands up in exasperation.

"Then the whole thing's tainted," he said. "It's inadmissible. No question."

"Again, there *is* a question and it's for the court to decide," Coelho said.

"I would argue that it's not tainted," I said. "The evidence was submitted for GSR analysis and was handled by the lab tech according to that protocol, not DNA protocol. Not *touch*-DNA protocol. Five years ago, there were very few labs that even had protocols for touch DNA. But that was not the purpose of Frank Silver's original submission."

"Doesn't matter," Morris said. "It's tainted. It doesn't come in. Inadmissible, Your Honor."

I looked at the judge. My argument had been directed toward her, not Morris. But I didn't want her to make a ruling yet.

"Your Honor," I said, "I would like to make a motion to the court."

Morris rolled his eyes.

"Here we go," he said.

"Mr. Morris, I've grown weary of your sarcasm," Coelho said. "What is your motion, Mr. Haller?"

I leaned forward over the edge of her desk, shortening the distance between us and cutting Morris out of my peripheral vision. This was between me and the judge.

"Judge, if we want the truth, if this is truly a search for the truth, the court should issue an order to have the unidentified DNA found on the GSR pad compared to DNA swabbed from Sergeant Sanger."

"No way!" barked Morris. "That is not happening. And it would prove nothing anyway. So what if Sanger's DNA is on it? She's on record as having collected the evidence."

"It proves the setup," I said. "That she turned over dirty GSR pads that were never wiped over Sanz's hands. It's proof of Sanz's innocence and proof that Sanger is guilty as sin."

"Your Honor," Morris said, "you can't—"

"I'm going to stop you there, Mr. Morris," the judge said. "This is what we're going to do. I'll take Mr. Haller's motion as well as the question of admissibility under advisement and will issue my decisions after some research and deliberation."

I frowned. I wanted her to rule on everything right now. Judges and juries were the same. The longer they took to decide, the more likely the outcome would be adverse to the defense.

"We're going to take our lunch break now and will reconvene court at one o'clock," the judge continued. "Mr. Haller, have your next witness ready to go then."

"Your Honor, I can't put my next witness on," I said.

"And why is that?" Coelho asked.

"Because I won't know whom to put on until I know your rulings on these matters," I said. "They will dictate my next move."

Coelho nodded.

"Very well," she said. "Let's push the afternoon session until two o'clock, and you will have my rulings on these matters then."

"Thank you, Judge," I said.

"Thank you, Your Honor," Morris said.

"You can leave now, gentlemen," the judge said. "I have work to do. Would you ask Gian to come back here to get my lunch order? I won't have time to leave chambers."

"Yes, Judge," I said.

Morris and I stood up in unison and I followed him out. Once in the hall, I spoke to his back.

"I don't know how this is going to shake out," I said. "But just so I'm ready for anything, have Sergeant Sanger back at the courthouse at two."

"Not my job, man," he said. "She's your witness."

"And she works for you and takes calls from you. Have her there or I tell the judge I told you I was recalling her and you refused to cooperate. You can explain it to her then."

"Fine."

When we got to the door to the courtroom, he looked cautiously over his shoulder at me. But I made no move to pin him against the wall as I had done before. And he made no comment that spurred me to do so. But the moment made me realize something. I reached forward and put my hand on the door, preventing him from opening it.

"What are you doing?" he said. "Are you going to attack me again?"

"You knew, didn't you?" I said.

"Knew what?"

"About my ex-wife. You brought her in here to stir things up, knock me off my game, because you knew about us."

"I don't know what you're talking about. I had no idea you two had been married."

"Yes, you did. You knew. Who's the grand master of smoke now, Morris?"

I took my hand off the door and he opened it and went through without another word to me.

42

TEAM SANZ HAD a long working lunch at Drago Centro during which I reported on the in camera hearing and we planned the endgame of the case, which would depend on how the judge ruled. If the lab results were admitted, the strategy was obvious: I'd use Silver and Arslanian to introduce the timeline and evidence and then I'd bring it all home by calling Sanger back to the stand and confronting her with solid evidence that the GSR pads she had turned in had not been wiped over Lucinda Sanz's hands. But if Coelho ruled the lab results inadmissible, I was left with only Sanger and not a lot to back up any sort of confrontational examination. Agent MacIsaac had given me a tip, but it was nothing more than innuendo. Sanger might be able to bat it away like it was a fly buzzing around her face.

"If you were betting, which way do you think she'll go?" Bosch asked at one point.

"First of all, I wouldn't bet," I said. "It's too close to call. It's going to come down to whether she makes the legal call or the moral call.

What does the law tell her to do? What does her gut tell her is the right thing to do?"

"Shit," Cisco said. "Then you'll have nothing to go after Sanger with. Game over."

"Maybe not," I said. "I had a visitor to my house last night, Agent MacIsaac. He was there to let me know that he would never testify in this case and the U.S. attorney was ready to back him on that and even defy a subpoena from a federal judge. But he didn't come empty-handed. He told me why Roberto Sanz had gone to the Bureau and volunteered to wear a wire. It was about Sanger..."

I gave the intel that MacIsaac had given me and we spent the rest of the meal brainstorming ways of getting it into court. It was clear it would come down to my questioning of Sanger and finding the opportunity to confront her — easier said than done.

After our pasta, we bundled into the Navigator, and Bosch took us back to the courthouse. As we came out of the elevator and approached Coelho's courtroom, I saw Sergeant Sanger waiting on a bench in the hall. She stared unflinchingly at me as we passed by, as if daring me to challenge her. I knew then that, one way or the other, I would do everything I could to take her down after the judge made her rulings.

I sat at the petitioner's table and waited for Lucinda to be brought to the courtroom and for the judge to follow. I didn't unpack my brief-case. I wanted to know which way I was going first. I looked up at the angry eagle, composed myself, and waited.

The questions came fast and furious from Lucinda once she was brought from lockup to the table.

"Mickey, what's going on?" she asked. "I didn't know what was happening and I was waiting so long in there."

"I'm sorry about that, Cindi," I said. "We're going to get answers very soon. We went into the judge's office and I presented evidence that showed that the gunshot-residue test was wrong. Was a setup, actually."

"Who set me up?"

"Somebody in your ex-husband's unit. Probably Sanger, since she's the one who did the test on you."

"Does that mean she killed Robbie?"

"I don't know that, Cindi, but put it this way: If I need to convince the judge that it was somebody other than you, I'm going to point at her. She's smack-dab in the middle of this, and if it wasn't her, then she knows who it was."

Lucinda's face grew dark with anger. She had served five years for somebody else's crime, and now she might have a name and face to focus that anger and blame on. I understood her.

"But listen," I said. "There are complications with the evidence we uncovered, and we have to see if the judge is going to let it be part of what she considers. That's why everything's been delayed. The judge has been back there in chambers working on it."

"Okay," Lucinda said. "I hope she does the right thing."

"Me too."

I went quiet and thought about how I would react to each of the judge's possible rulings. This led me to a plan I thought might help me salvage the case should the ruling not go my way. I quickly fired off a series of texts with instructions to Harry Bosch and Shami Arslanian. Bosch was in the hall watching Frank Silver in case he decided to hightail it before testifying. Arslanian was out there too, waiting to see if she would be called back to the witness stand.

Before Bosch responded to confirm that he understood my plan, the judge emerged from chambers and I had to turn off the phone. Coelho got right down to business.

"All right, back on the record with *Sanz versus the State of California,*" she said. "Continuing the habeas hearing. Gentlemen, is there any new business to discuss before I make rulings on the motions before the court?"

I half expected Morris to try to continue the arguments he'd made in chambers, though it was pretty clear the judge was past all that and ready to rule. But Morris declined to add anything to the record, and I had nothing to add either. I looked at Lucinda and gave her an encouraging smile, but she didn't know how important the next few minutes would be.

"Very well," the judge said. "In regard to the motions brought before the court this morning, let's start with the State's contention that the evidence is inadmissible because of contamination and mishandling by the lab that conducted analysis of the gunshot-residue pad submitted by the defense. The fact pattern shows that the contamination by a lab tech occurred several years ago when the evidence was submitted under different circumstances and protocols. The contamination did not occur during the most recent analysis conducted. It also should be noted that the tech's DNA exemplar was available for comparison, as it is standard practice in certified DNA labs to check findings for contamination by lab personnel."

I could tell that Morris's contamination argument was not going to carry the day. The judge was going to shoot it down. I began to get the stirrings of hope and excitement.

"I believe that what is most important here is not whose DNA was found on the evidence but whose wasn't," Coelho said. "The petitioner's DNA was not found on the evidence and that is as troubling to the court as it is exculpatory to the petitioner."

I looked at Lucinda. It was clear she could not follow the legalese threaded through the judge's words, but I gave her a half smile of reassurance. So far, this was going our way.

"Something was wrong about this case and the investigation from the very start," the judge continued. "And it is the court's hope that a proper investigation of the investigation will follow these proceedings. However, the court is also troubled by the petitioner's defense in regard to the original charges against her."

And now I felt it. The other shoe was going to drop. The judge was not going to allow the evidence into her ultimate decision on the petition.

"The foundation of the habeas corpus motion is to bring forth new evidence that proves the unlawful detention of the petitioner," Coelho said. "I'm sorry to say, this evidence is not new. It has been sitting undisturbed in a lab for five years, and it clearly could have been accessed and tested for the petitioner's DNA from the very beginning of the prosecution of the case. The claim by the petitioner that touch DNA was unavailable at that time is not correct. There are notable criminal cases involving the use of touch DNA much earlier than this, including the Casey Anthony case in Florida and the Jon-Benét Ramsey investigation in Colorado. So the court must decide whether this evidence is new or if it was available to be pursued and analyzed five years ago, before the petitioner's plea of nolo contendere to the crime."

I couldn't believe this. I lowered my head, I could not even turn to look at my client.

"The court finds the latter," Coelho said. "This evidence could have, possibly should have, been pursued by the defense five years ago and is therefore excluded from these proceedings. The petitioner may very well be left with a valid claim of ineffective assistance of counsel regarding the initial pleading of this case, but that is not part of this motion and hearing."

I shot up out of my seat.

"Your Honor, those cases you mentioned are outliers," I said. "They were massive investigations that took time and money. This science wasn't used in more ordinary cases. The original attorney on this was ineffective, yes, but not in this regard. No one was using it then."

"But someone could have, Mr. Haller," Coelho said. "And that's the point."

"No! You're not doing this."

The judge looked at me for a moment, stunned by my outburst.

"Excuse me, Mr. Haller?" she finally said.

"You can't do this," I said.

"I just did, Mr. Haller. And you need to—"

"It's wrong. I object. It is proof of innocence, Judge. You can't just throw it away because it doesn't fit with the rule of law."

The judge paused, then continued in an even tone.

"Mr. Haller, be careful," she warned. "The ruling has been made. If you think it is in error, then there are remedies you can pursue. But don't you dare challenge me here. If you have another witness, then call that person to the stand and we will proceed."

"No, I won't," I said. "This is a sham. You killed the re-creation, and now you kill this. My client is innocent and at every turn you have disallowed the evidence that proves it."

The judge paused for a moment, but her anger toward me did not abate. It seemed to boil up into her eyes. She stared daggers at me.

"Are you quite finished, Mr. Haller?"

"No," I said. "I object. The evidence is new. It's not five years old. It was determined in a lab this morning. How can you claim it's not new and send this woman, the mother of a young boy, back to prison for a crime she didn't commit?"

"Mr. Haller, I will give you one chance to sit down and close your mouth," Coelho said. "You are dangerously close to being in contempt of this court."

"I'm sorry, Your Honor, but I won't be muzzled," I said. "I must speak the truth because this court will not. You kicked out the crime re-creation, and that's okay, I can live with that. But the DNA...the DNA proves that my client was set up for this murder. How can you sit there and say it's inadmissible? In any other court in this country, it would be proof of—"

"Mr. Haller!" the judge yelled. "I warned you. I find you in contempt of this court. Marshal, take Mr. Haller into custody. This is a federal court, Mr. Haller. Talking back to the court and insulting its rulings might work for you in state court, but not here."

"You can't shut me up!" I yelled. "This is wrong and everyone in this place knows it."

I was pushed forward by Marshal Nate and bent over the table. My arms were roughly pulled behind my back and my wrists cuffed tightly. A hand gripped the back of my collar and I was pulled into a standing position. The marshal then turned me and shoved me toward the door to courtside lockup.

"Perhaps a night in jail will teach you to respect the court," Coelho called after me.

"Lucinda Sanz is innocent!" I yelled as I was pushed through the door. "You know it, I know it, everybody in the courtroom knows it!"

The last thing I heard before the door was shut was Coelho adjourning court for the day.

It was just what I'd hoped would happen.

PART ELEVEN

A CHORUS OF HORNS

43

BOSCH WAS DRIVING the Navigator, Arslanian in the passenger seat next to him. They were moving in slow traffic on the northbound 101 freeway.

"Do you think she'll hold him overnight?" Arslanian asked.

"Sounds like it," Bosch said. "Sounds like he really made her blow a gasket. Sort of wish I'd been in the courtroom for it."

"Do you think he'll be in danger in there?"

"They'll likely isolate him. The last thing the judge wants is for a lawyer she stuck in there to get hurt."

"Well, will he be kept in the court holding cell all night?"

"No, they'll take him to MDC."

"What's MDC?"

"Metropolitan Detention Center — it's the federal jail. They don't keep any overnighters in the courthouse jail. Everybody is bused back to MDC at the end of the day. He's probably on a bus now, or the marshals might move him solo because of his VIP status."

"I hope so."

"He'll be all right. I'm sure he factored it all in before he went nuts with the judge. When he got accused of murder a few years ago, he spent three months in county and managed to stay safe. You heard about that, right?"

"Oh, yes. I was ready to come out if needed but then you and the others on the team got it done."

"Yeah, including Maggie McFierce, who tore me up pretty good on the stand today."

"You know, I considered becoming a lawyer, maybe adding a law degree to the others. But then I thought, *Nah, too many gray areas and shifting loyalties. I'll stick with the science side of things.*"

"Good plan."

"Anyway, I just can't believe the judge's ruling on the science."

Bosch didn't reply. It had been as Haller had said at lunch. The judge chose to go by the book, not by what was right. No gray area there.

"She's exiting," he said.

Arslanian looked through the windshield. Bosch switched lanes so he could follow the car they were tailing.

"Where do you think she's going?" Arslanian asked.

"No idea," Bosch said. "I don't think she lives this far from the AV."

Sanger was driving a Rivian pickup truck. There were so few of these on the road that it was an easy follow, allowing Bosch to fall far back and not be noticed. But as he went down the Ventura Boulevard exit he realized he was going to end up only two cars behind her at the traffic light. If Sanger checked her mirrors, she might recognize the Navigator and the two people in it.

It was a two-lane turn. The Rivian was in the inside lane with another pickup truck behind it. Bosch stopped behind the second pickup and lowered his sun visor. The bed of the truck in front of him had a pipe rack and other air-conditioning maintenance equipment that worked well as a blind.

A homeless man stood on the shoulder with a sign asking for help in any form. When nothing came from the Rivian, he started walking down the shoulder, holding up his hand-lettered cardboard sign.

The light stayed red.

From his vantage point, Bosch could see the side of the truck in front of him as well as Sanger's truck. He saw the driver's-side window of the Rivian go down. He saw cigarette smoke escape as Sanger extended her hand and arm out the window and threw something onto the shoulder by the homeless man's backpack and plastic milk crate.

"She just threw something out the window," he said. "I think it was a cigarette butt. That'll work, right?"

"Yes!" Arslanian said. "Definitely. Do you see it?"

"I think so."

"Let's get it."

"We'll probably lose her if we stop."

"It's okay. The cigarette is all we need. We go straight to the lab with it."

The light turned green and the Rivian took off, went left across the overpass, and down to Ventura. Bosch checked his rearview and saw that he now had two cars behind him. He hit the emergency blinkers and pulled the Navigator onto the shoulder as far as he could, but there wasn't enough room for him to get completely out of the traffic lane and still have space to open his door and get out.

A chorus of horns followed this move. Undaunted, Bosch put the vehicle in park, got out, and found the homeless man standing in the thin channel between the Navigator and the concrete retaining wall that lined the exit ramp.

"Hey, what the fuck?" the man said. "You almost hit me."

"Sorry about that," Bosch said.

He closed the car door and walked to the spot by the milk crate, pulling out his phone as he approached. He crouched at the spot, his knees sending stress signals to his brain. He surveyed the area and saw the cigarette butt on the loose gravel. He opened his camera app and took a photo of the cigarette butt in situ — as it had been found — just in case the evidence collection was challenged in any way. He put the phone away and pulled a ziplock bag out of his coat pocket. Using the bag as a glove, he picked up the discarded butt and sealed it inside.

He got up, turned, and headed back to the Navigator. The homeless man was still standing there, a puzzled look on his face.

"Hey, man, that cigarette is mine," he said. "This is my spot. I own it."

"It's just a butt," Bosch said. "She smoked it down to the filter."

"Doesn't matter. It's mine. You want to buy it?"

"How much?"

"Ten dollars."

"For a cigarette butt?"

"Ten dollars, man. That's the price."

Bosch reached into his pocket and pulled out his money. He had a twenty and a ten. He held the ten out to the man.

"Do you mind stepping back so I can get back in the car?" Bosch said.

"Sure thing, boss."

He grabbed the ten and backed away.

Bosch got in the Navigator and closed the door. He handed the ziplock to Arslanian as he checked the rearview to see if it was clear to enter the traffic lane. She examined the contents of the bag without opening it.

"This is going to be perfect," she said. "We got lucky."

"About time," Bosch said.

"I thought we'd be following her all the way to the Antelope Valley and then some. Then have to look through her trash."

"Me too. So, Applied Forensics?"

"Absolutely. I'll call ahead so they're ready for us. If we get this in now, we could have what we need by tomorrow."

The light turned green and Bosch muscled the Navigator into the traffic lane in front of a car, garnering another angry horn rebuke from the driver. Bosch held his hand up, waved his thanks, and drove on.

As they headed toward Van Nuys, Bosch put things together.

"She broke into my house," he said.

"Who did?" Arslanian asked.

"Sanger."

"When was this?"

"Like seven months ago. I wasn't sure till now. I smelled cigarette smoke when I came home and found the place open."

"Did she take anything?"

"No. She just wanted me to know. It was an intimidation tactic."

Bosch smiled and shook his head.

"But it didn't work, because I wasn't sure if I had left the door open and was just losing my mind," he said. "You know, like dementia or something. I thought the cigarette smell might have been a side effect from the isotope they were putting in me."

"Then I guess it must be nice to know there really was a break-in, which sounds weird said out loud."

"Yeah, I guess you're right."

Bosch thought about the police report that Maggie McFierce had used to embarrass him in court and suggest he was losing his mind. He now felt vindicated.

PART TWELVE

THE PROVING GROUND

44

IN THE MORNING the marshals moved me back to the federal court-house on the seven o'clock jail bus. I then spent the next two hours in the main courthouse jail with other detainees awaiting transfer to specific courtrooms and their holding cells. I was wearing federal blues and was unsure what had happened to my clothes, wallet, and phone. I was eventually moved to the cell off Judge Coelho's court-room. Lucinda Sanz was already in the cell next to mine. We couldn't see each other but we could hear each other.

"Mickey, are you okay?" she whispered.

"I'm fine," I said. "How are you feeling, Cindi?"

"I'm good. I can't believe they made you stay the whole night."

"The judge wanted to make a point."

Marshal Nate came into the holding area, unlocked my cell, and handed me a brown paper bag.

"Your clothes," he said. "Get dressed. The judge wants to see you."

I dug through the bag. My suit was crumpled into a ball on top of my shoes.

"Where's my phone?" I said. "And my wallet and keys?"

"Locked in my desk," Nate said. "You get it back when the judge tells me to give it back. You've got five minutes. Get dressed."

"No, I'm not getting dressed in this stuff. The suit's wrinkled. If you're going to take me to see the judge, I'll go like this."

"Suit yourself — no pun intended."

"Good one, Nate."

"Do I need to put the belly chain and cuffs back on or are you going to behave?"

"No need."

He walked me out of the cell and past Lucinda's on the way to the courtroom door.

"Hang in there, Lucinda," I said.

I was walked through the courtroom, which was dark except for the single light over Gian Brown's corral.

"All right to take him back?" Nate asked.

"She's waiting for him," Brown said.

He gave me and my attire the once-over.

"Are you sure you don't want to change into your clothes?" Brown asked.

"I'm sure," I said.

The marshal opened the half door to the corral and we walked through to the hall that led to the judge's chambers. Nate knocked on the judge's door and we heard her call to enter.

Nate walked me in and sat me down in one of the chairs in front of the desk. Judge Coelho sat on the other side of it.

"I gave instructions to put you back in your suit, Mr. Haller," she said.

"The suit's toast," I said. "It's a Canali. Italian silk that's been balled up in a paper bag overnight. I need my phone so I can get a fresh suit delivered."

"We'll get you your phone. Nate, please have that ready for Mr. Haller when we're through here. You can go back to the courtroom now."

Marshal Nate looked hesitant.

"Are you sure I shouldn't stay, Judge?" he asked.

"I'm sure I will be fine," Coelho said. "I'll call when it's time to retrieve Mr. Haller. You can go now."

Marshal Nate left the room and closed the door behind him. The judge looked at me for a moment, assessing me and determining what to say.

"I'm sorry it came to this, Mr. Haller," she said. "But the disrespect you showed the court yesterday could not be allowed to stand. It is my hope that you used the night to reflect on how you handled yourself in my courtroom and that you can assure me it won't happen again."

I nodded.

"I reflected on a lot of things, Judge," I said. "I apologize for my words and actions. I am contrite. It won't happen again, I promise you."

The only thing I had resolved during my overnight in a cold solo cell was never to address Coelho as *Your Honor* again.

"Very well," Coelho said. "Apology accepted. You are released from contempt, and perhaps we can get a rush on your suit so that we don't lose the entire morning. I will tell all parties to be in court by eleven to proceed."

"Thank you," I said. "I'd like to get out of this outfit as soon as possible."

"I just buzzed Gian, and Nate will have your property out there."

"When you put out the word about resuming the hearing, can you make sure that Sergeant Sanger is on notice to return to court? She'll most likely be my next witness."

"I will order her return."

Five minutes later I was sitting in the courtroom taking my phone out of a plastic property bag. The first call I made was to Bosch.

"Mick, you're sprung?"

"Yeah, just now. What's happening? Where are you?"

"We're at Applied Forensics. We brought in a cigarette butt from Sanger, and fifteen minutes ago Shami said they need two more hours."

"Okay. I can deal with that. As soon as you know something, text me."

"You got it."

I disconnected and then called Lorna Taylor.

"Oh my God, Mickey, are you all right?"

"I am now."

"Where are you?"

"In the courtroom. I need you to get me a suit, shirt, and tie and bring them to me here."

"Not a problem. Which suit?"

"I think the Hugo Boss. The gray with the light pinstripes. A light blue oxford, and just pick any tie. You know where the key is, right?"

"Same place?"

"Same place."

My next words were spoken in a low whisper so Gian and Nate could not overhear.

"Lorna, listen, don't hurry. Don't get here with the suit until at least twelve thirty. Harry and Shami need the time."

"Got it."

I raised my voice to its normal pitch and said, "Okay, I'll probably be back in holding, so just bring it to the courtroom marshal. His name is Nate."

"Got it. I'm leaving now to go to your place."

"Thanks."

I disconnected and got up. I presented myself to Marshal Nate and said I'd like to wait in holding so I could visit with my client and then change when my fresh suit arrived.

I realized as I was taken back into holding that I had not eaten anything and should have asked Lorna to bring me a PowerBar. The emptiness in my stomach was accentuated by the anxiety I was feeling about what was happening at Applied Forensics. I knew I was taking my last shot with the gambit I had played over the last two days. It was going to be do-or-die time very soon.

45

THE HEARING ON the habeas motion did not get back under way until almost two o'clock, thanks to Lorna's delay in bringing my suit. The judge wasn't too happy about the late start but I was pleased because I now had everything I needed to face Stephanie Sanger one more time on the witness stand. Bosch and Arslanian had come through. Arslanian was outside in the hallway and ready to testify, and Bosch sat in the first row of the gallery next to the Channel 5 courtroom sketch artist.

After Judge Coelho convened court and told me to proceed, I recalled Sergeant Stephanie Sanger to the witness stand. The judge reminded her that she was still under oath.

"Good to see you again, Sergeant Sanger," I began. "I want to start today by asking you about some testimony and evidence that came in last week. Specifically, the cell phone data that was examined by my investigator."

"Is there a question in there?" Sanger asked.

"Not yet, Sergeant Sanger. But let's start with this one. On the day

Deputy Roberto Sanz was murdered on the front lawn of his ex-wife's house, were you following him?"

Sanger stared at me with her dagger eyes before answering.

"Yes, I was," she said.

I nodded and jotted a note down on my legal pad. No matter what Maggie McFierce had done to Bosch's credibility on the stand, the data contained irrefutable facts, and Sanger was in no position to deny them. But I still was surprised by her straightforward answer to my first question. It knocked me off my game because I was expecting to have to ask several questions before I finally got her to admit that she had followed Roberto Sanz. My legal pad was covered with follow-up questions that I no longer needed. It made me jump to an improvised set of questions I should never have asked.

"You admit that you were following Roberto Sanz on the day of his death?"

"Yes, I just did."

"Why were you following him?"

"Because he asked me to."

There it was. With one ill-advised and improvised question, we were off in uncharted territory, and I had no doubt that what would come out would be a concocted story that explained the incontrovertible cell data. I knew that if I didn't bring it out and attempt to control it, Hayden Morris would do that on his re-cross. I had to handle this right now and then get back to my intended path.

"Why did Roberto Sanz ask you to follow him?" I asked.

"Because he was meeting with an FBI agent and he was worried that he was being set up," Sanger said. "He wanted me to watch in case something went wrong and he needed me to come to the rescue."

Sanger and the AG were doing exactly what I had been doing throughout the hearing: taking the negatives and owning them. If it looks bad that you were following the murder victim, then say the murder victim asked you to — there was nobody alive to refute it.

"He would need you to rescue him from an FBI agent?" I asked.

"Not necessarily in that moment," Sanger said. "More like later, if someone had to vouch for his story that he had met with the FBI and turned down whatever it was the Bureau wanted."

"He never told you what the Bureau wanted?"

"He never got the chance."

"Then how do you know he used the meeting to turn down the FBI?"

"He told me ahead of time that that's what he planned to do."

It was a story that didn't make a lot of sense on close inspection. But I knew if I waded into the bog any further, there might be all manner of hidden traps below the murk for me to stumble into. I had already done enough damage by giving Sanger the chance to explain the cell data. I improvised as best I could in the moment.

"And you never filed a report on this or told the investigators of Sanz's murder about it?" I asked.

"No, I didn't," Sanger said.

"Sanz gets murdered after a clandestine meeting with an FBI agent and you didn't think the homicide investigators would want to know that?"

"I didn't."

"And why is that?"

"I thought it would taint Robbie Sanz's reputation. He was dead, his ex-wife had killed him, and I didn't think it had to be brought up."

Once again I had opened an exit for her. I had to find my way out of this bog.

"All right, let's move on, Sergeant Sanger," I said. "Please describe for the court the protocol you followed when you conducted the gunshot-residue test on Lucinda Sanz on the night of her ex-husband's murder."

"It's pretty simple, really," she said. "The stubs come in a package of two and—"

"Let me interrupt you there. Can you explain what you mean by 'stubs'?"

"They are round foam disks with a carbon adhesive that picks up the gunshot residue when wiped over a person's hands and arms."

"So you opened a package containing two stubs when you tested Lucinda Sanz?"

"Correct."

"Did you wear gloves when you did this?"

"Yes, I did."

"Why is that, Sergeant Sanger?"

"So I would not possibly contaminate the stubs. I carry and handle a weapon, so my hands could have GSR on them. It is standard protocol in the department and all other agencies to wear gloves while conducting a GSR test on a suspect."

"You are saying that at the time, Lucinda Sanz was already a suspect?"

"No, I was talking about general protocol. In the case you are specifically referring to, Ms. Sanz was not considered a suspect at that time. We viewed her as a witness, primarily, until we gathered all the facts."

"Why were you so quick to test her for GSR if she was just a witness?"

"Because, first of all, gunshot residue sheds from the skin. It is best to take a GSR test within two hours of a gun incident. After four hours it is useless because of shedding. And second, we didn't know what we had out there, so we wanted to cover all the bases. I conducted the test and it turned out later to be positive. I think I already testified to all of this."

"That's okay, Sergeant Sanger. We want to make sure we get it right. How did you find out that the test was positive?"

"The lead investigator called me to tell me and to thank me for running the test so early. It was a very solid positive response for GSR, he said."

I asked the judge to strike the second half of Sanger's answer as nonresponsive to my question, but Coelho overruled me and told me to move on.

"So you did everything by the book — isn't that correct, Sergeant Sanger?"

"Correct."

"You gloved up, opened the testing package, conducted the test, then resealed the stubs in a lab bag."

"Correct."

"No contamination."

"Correct."

"And you gave that lab bag to Deputy Keith Mitchell to turn over to the homicide investigators, yes?"

"Yes."

Morris stood up and objected.

"Your Honor, counsel has already been over this in his direct examination," he said. "Why are we wasting the court's time with this?"

"I was wondering the same thing, Mr. Haller," Coelho said.

"Judge, my next questions should pretty much get us into new territory," I said.

"Very well," she said. "But I'm putting you on a short leash. Proceed."

I looked at my legal pad and composed myself and the next question.

"Sergeant Sanger, are you familiar with touch DNA?"

Morris was quickly up on his feet again.

"Your Honor, sidebar?" he said.

Coelho signaled us forward with her hand.

"Come up," she said.

Morris and I went to the bench, and the judge leaned forward to hear his objection.

"Your Honor, counsel is straying into an area of questioning the court ruled inadmissible yesterday," Morris said. "I don't know if he is trying to set up another outburst followed by a rebuke from the court, but he is obviously heading toward the forbidden zone."

"Not true, Judge," I said quickly. "I don't intend to ask this witness anything about the lack of Lucinda Sanz's DNA on the GSR pad. The court's ruling was crystal clear to me yesterday."

"I would think that a night in jail would keep you far away from what was ruled out yesterday, Mr. Haller," Coelho said.

"It has, Judge," I said. "And you can put me back in the cell if I bring up my client's DNA or lack thereof."

"Very well, proceed," Coelho said. "Carefully. Objection overruled."

We went back to our places and I checked my notes.

"Again, Sergeant Sanger, are you familiar with touch DNA?" I asked.

"I know what it is," Sanger said. "But I'm not an expert on it. We have a lab for that."

"Well, you don't need to be an expert to answer this. How is it, with the protocol you say you followed in collecting GSR from Lucinda Sanz, that your own DNA ended up on at least one of the GSR stubs you allegedly swiped on Lucinda Sanz's hands and arms?"

Morris bolted up from his chair as if he had received an electric shock. He spread his arms wide.

"Your Honor, counsel has done exactly what he just said he would not do," he said.

"No, I did not," I said quickly. "I asked the witness if—"

"Let me stop you there," Coelho said. "I'll see both of you in chambers right now. Everyone else can take a fifteen-minute break."

She left the bench in a swirl of black robe. Morris and I followed.

46

STILL IN HER robe, the judge looked at us from behind her desk.

"Sit," she commanded. "Mr. Haller, I find myself losing patience with you once again. I can't believe it's because you find the accommodations at the Metropolitan Detention Center to your liking."

"No, Judge," I said. "Not at all."

"Then I don't understand what you're doing," she said. "As Mr. Morris has already pointed out, you are walking dangerously close to fire. I ruled the lab results proffered yesterday inadmissible, and here you are, asking the witness about lab results."

I nodded in agreement as she said it.

"Judge, you ruled that the GSR pads could have been tested for Lucinda Sanz's DNA by the defense at the time of the initial prosecution of this case," I said. "You ruled that it wasn't new evidence brought to light under the requirements of habeas but rather a misstep by the defense attorney back then and therefore inadmissible. As I said during the sidebar, I am not going there."

"Then where are you going?" Coelho asked.

"The witness just testified to the protocols she allegedly followed when she tested Lucinda Sanz for gunshot residue. She gloved up, opened the testing package, swiped the stubs over Sanz, and resealed them in the package. I am prepared to provide the court with evidence that Sergeant Sanger's DNA is on the stub turned over to the defense five years ago and held secure at Applied Forensics ever since."

"You did a comparison with her DNA?"

"Yes, Judge."

"And where did you get her DNA, since this was not a court-ordered analysis?"

"Sanger is a smoker. Her DNA was taken from a cigarette butt she discarded yesterday after court. My investigator and forensics expert collected it and took it to Applied Forensics for comparison to the unidentified DNA found on the stub from the Sanz case. Just so you know, this analysis did not require examination of the GSR pad, which is evidence and would have required an order from you. This was a comparison of DNA from the collected cigarette butt to the unknown DNA profile found during the earlier analysis of the evidence. We got the results just before court convened today. It's Sanger's DNA and I am entitled to ask her how it got there."

Morris made a groaning sound that he rolled into an objection.

"It's just as inadmissible as yesterday," he said. "Plus, it's impossible to get a DNA analysis done in less than twenty-four hours."

"Not if you're willing to pay," I said. "And if your forensics expert is nationally recognized and overseeing the work."

"Mr. Haller, where do you think you're going with this?" the judge asked.

"Where we have always been going with this case," I said. "Lucinda Sanz was set up for her ex-husband's murder. The key piece of evidence in this setup was the GSR found on her hands. Not only did it indicate that she had fired a gun, but it appeared to catch her in a lie, and from there the investigators never looked at anybody else. It is the petitioner's theory and belief that at some point after Sanger swabbed Sanz and before Mitchell handed the evidence to the homicide investigators, the pads—or stubs—were replaced with pads dirty with GSR. So, Judge, you want to know where I'm going? I'm going right at Sanger. I want to know how her DNA ended up on that pad."

Coelho was silent as she tracked my argument. I took the time to pile on before Morris could.

"This is new evidence, Judge," I said. "It's not something the original defense could have come up with because Sanger's name is not even in the police reports. Now, you kicked out the crime re-creation and the DNA from yesterday, but together these things make clear what happened. Stephanie Sanger now even admits to seeing Roberto Sanz meeting with an FBI agent but not reporting it to the investigation. Why? Because she's the one who killed Sanz and set up his ex-wife to take the fall."

The judge continued to stare at me without really seeing me. She was going through the steps, checking the logic of my theory. Morris had apparently already dismissed it, probably because it had come from a defense attorney and he was trained never to agree with one.

"This is fantasy," he said. "Your Honor, you can't possibly be considering this as valid. It's smoke and mirrors—exactly what Mr. Haller is known for."

Coelho stopped analyzing and looked at me.

"Is that what you are known for, Mr. Haller?" she asked. "Smoke and mirrors?"

"Uh, I hope it's for more than that, Judge," I said.

She nodded, her expression unreadable. But then she said the magic words I'd been waiting for.

"I'm going to allow it," she said. "Mr. Haller, you can ask your questions and we'll see where it goes."

"Your Honor, I have to object," Morris said. "This is pure —"

"Mr. Morris, you already objected and I just overruled the objection," Coelho said. "Is that not clear to you?"

"Yes, Judge," he said weakly.

"Thank you, Your Honor," I said.

With her ruling, she was now redeemed in my eyes.

The judge stayed behind when we left her chambers. I followed Morris back to the courtroom. He was silent the whole way, walking fast, as if to get away from me.

"Cat got your tongue, Morris?" I said. "Or is it the weight of knowing you're on the wrong side of this one?"

He didn't respond other than to hold up a fist, the middle finger extended. He went through the door to the courtroom and didn't bother to hold it open for me.

"Nice guy," I said.

In the courtroom I saw that the spot where Bosch had been sitting was empty. I headed out to the hall, hoping to find him and Arslanian before the judge took the bench and convened the hearing again.

I found Shami on a bench next to the courtroom door but there was no sign of Bosch.

"The judge is going to allow Sanger's DNA," I said. "You will have to testify about the cigarette butt — the collection of it and everything else."

"Mickey, that's great," Arslanian said. "I'm ready."

"Where's Harry? We may need him if the judge wants to see his photos of the cigarette."

"When Sanger left the courtroom, he followed her out. He told me he wanted to keep an eye on her in case she made a run for it."

"Seriously?"

"Cop instincts, I guess."

I had never doubted Bosch's cop instincts. Arslanian's answer gave me pause as I thought about how I would continue the case if Sanger was in the wind.

PART THIRTEEN

THE MAN IN BLACK

47

BOSCH WANTED TO get closer so he could hear their conversation but he couldn't risk it. He was obviously known to Sanger and he had seen the man in the back row of the courtroom. If either saw Bosch they would more than likely shut down what looked like a heated conversation. So Bosch watched from afar, using a bus-stop shelter in front of the courthouse on Spring Street as a blind.

Sanger and the man she was talking to were in the designated smoking area on the north side of the courthouse. She stood next to a concrete urn that served as a trash-can-size ashtray. Sanger was smoking but the man she was talking to was not. He appeared to Bosch to be Latino. He was short with brown skin, jet-black hair, and a mustache that extended beyond the corners of his mouth. Their conversation seemed confrontational. The man was dressed completely in black, like a priest, and he leaned slightly toward Sanger as he spoke. And Sanger leaned toward him, shaking her head emphatically as if she disagreed with whatever the man was saying.

Bosch checked his watch. The courtroom break was almost over and he needed at least five minutes to go back in through security and take an elevator. When he looked back at the smoking section, he saw the man lean in even closer to Sanger and grab the front of her uniform with one hand. It happened so quickly that there was almost no struggle from Sanger. With his free hand the man pulled Sanger's weapon from her holster, pressed the muzzle to her side, and fired three quick shots, using her body to muffle the reports. He then pushed her into the urn and she toppled over it to the ground. A woman passing on the sidewalk screamed and started running away from the courthouse.

The man with the gun didn't even look up. He stepped around the urn, extended his arm, and fired one more time, finishing Sanger with a head shot. He turned and walked calmly out of the smoking area. He crossed the front steps of the courthouse, moved quickly out to the sidewalk, and headed south on Spring Street. He carried the gun down at his side.

Bosch stepped out of the bus shelter and ran up the steps and into the smoking area. Sanger was dead, her eyes open and staring blankly at the sky. The final bullet had hit her in the exact center of her forehead. Blood soaked her uniform and the concrete next to her body.

Bosch turned. The killer was now a block away on Spring. A uniformed marshal had stepped through the heavy glass doors of the courthouse after hearing the shots and the pedestrian's scream. Bosch moved toward him.

"A deputy's been shot," he said. "That guy walking down Spring is the shooter."

Bosch pointed toward the man in black.

"Where's the deputy?" the marshal asked.

"In the smoking area," Bosch said. "She's dead."

The marshal ran off toward the smoking area as he pulled a radio from a holster on his belt and yelled in the call.

"Shots fired, officer down! North side smoking area! Repeat, shots fired, officer down."

Bosch looked down Spring Street. The killer had passed City Hall and was almost to First Street. He was getting away.

Bosch started down Spring Street in pursuit. He pulled his phone and called 911. An operator answered immediately.

"This is 911, what is your emergency?"

"There's been a shooting outside the federal courthouse. A man killed a sheriff's deputy with her own gun. I'm following him south on Spring Street. I'm unarmed."

"Okay, sir, slow down. Who got shot? You said a deputy?"

"Yes, a sheriff's deputy. Sergeant Stephanie Sanger. The federal marshals are there and I'm following the shooter. I need backup to Spring and First Street. He's literally walking by the PAB right now."

The Police Administration Building was on the east side of Spring. As Bosch followed, he saw the killer cross over to the west side of the street and continue walking beside the old Los Angeles Times Building toward Second Street. As he'd crossed the street, he had glanced back up Spring as if looking for cars, but Bosch knew he was checking to see if he was being followed. Bosch was more than a block away and did not attract the gunman's attention.

"I think he's going to turn west on Second," he said.

"Sir, are you law enforcement?" the operator asked.

"Retired LAPD."

"Then you need to stop and wait for the police officers to arrive. They have been dispatched."

"I can't. He's getting away."

"Sir, you need —"

"I was wrong. He didn't turn on Second. He's still on Spring, heading south toward Third."

"Sir, listen to me, you need to stop what you're doing and —"

Bosch disconnected and put the phone in his pocket. He knew he needed to pick up speed if he was going to keep the gunman in sight. He got to the corner of Spring and Second just as the gunman reached Third Street and turned the corner out of sight. Bosch started to run and crossed to the west side when there was an opening in traffic.

At Third, Bosch turned right and saw the gunman halfway up the block to Broadway. He had crossed over to the south side of the street. Bosch stayed on the sidewalk on the north side, slowed his pace, and tried to regulate his breathing. Third Street ran slightly uphill and Bosch started huffing. The adrenaline flood that had hit his bloodstream when he saw Sanger murdered in broad daylight was starting to ebb.

The gunman crossed Broadway against the traffic light and turned left on the other side. By the time Bosch got to the corner, the light had changed and the walk signal was flashing. Bosch crossed and watched as the gunman ducked into the Grand Central Market.

Bosch could hear sirens now, but they weren't close. His guess was that the officers he had asked for had responded to the shooting scene rather than to the location he had given the 911 operator.

The market was crowded with people buying groceries or in line to order from the many different food stalls. Bosch entered and at first did not see the man in black. Then he appeared on the stairs at the midway point of the split-level market. At the top of the stairs he looked back but did not focus on Bosch in the sea of shoppers. Bosch guessed that he was looking for uniforms, not an old man in a suit.

Bosch noted that the man was no longer carrying the gun in his hand but his shirt was now out of his pants. That told Bosch he had not ditched the gun. It was tucked into his pants under his shirt.

The gunman went through the block-long market, emerged on Hill Street, and without hesitation waded out into traffic and crossed the road. Bosch came out of the market in time to see the man go through the turnstile at Angels Flight and climb into the waiting train car.

Bosch knew he had to hold back. He could not get into the train car without exposing himself to the killer. He stayed across the street and watched as the door closed and the car started to move slowly up the tracks toward the terminus at the top of Bunker Hill.

Angels Flight was a funicular that was billed as the shortest train route in the world. It had twin antique railcars that went up and down 150 feet of elevated track. They were counterbalanced, with one going up while the other came down, passing each other at the mid-point of the tracks. Bosch crossed Hill Street as the second car arrived at the lower turnstile. He got on along with a handful of other passengers and sat on one of the wooden bench seats. He waited anxiously as the train car rumbled up the tracks.

At the top of the tracks was a plaza surrounded by the towering glass buildings of the financial district. Bosch had moved to the upper door of the train car so he could be the first one off when it reached its terminus. The Angels Flight ticket booth was there and he had to pay a dollar before he could get through the upper turnstile. He pulled his money out and saw that the smallest bill he had was a twenty. He pushed it through the opening in the booth's glass.

"Keep the change," he said. "Just let me through."

He went through the turnstile and once out in the open plaza did a 360-degree sweep with his eyes but did not spot the man in black.

Bosch saw an opening between one of the towers and the contemporary art museum to his right. He headed that way, breaking into a trot. When he reached Grand Avenue he did another 360 but there was still no sign of the man in black. He was gone.

"Shit," he said.

He was panting. He bent over and put his hands on his knees so he could catch his breath. He was sweating badly.

"You okay, sir?"

Bosch looked up. It was a woman carrying a bag from the museum store.

"Yes, I'm fine," he said. "Just a little winded. But thanks."

She moved on and Bosch straightened up and scanned the street a final time in both directions, once more looking for the man in black. Nothing caught his attention. No pedestrian, no car. The gunman could have gone a dozen different ways after getting off Angels Flight.

Bosch's phone buzzed and he saw that it was Haller calling.

"Mick."

"Harry, where the fuck are you? I need you back here. Something's going on. The clerk got a call and—"

"Sanger's dead."

"What?"

"She's dead. Somebody shot her with her own gun when she was on the smoking patio outside."

"Oh, shit."

"I followed him but I lost him on Bunker Hill."

"You saw it happen?"

"From a distance. I'll need to talk to the police and give them what I know."

"Absolutely."

"What happens now? With the case."

"I have no clue. I assume the judge will adjourn for the day. This is unbelievable."

"Did she kick out the DNA again?"

"No, it's in. She ruled for us. But I don't know what will happen without Sanger."

Bosch realized that Haller would not have been allowed to use his phone in the courtroom.

"Where are you?" he asked.

"The hall outside the courtroom," Haller said. "The judge sent me out to find you and Sanger. Who was the shooter?"

"I don't know but he was in the courtroom today. Back row. I saw him."

"A Latino guy?"

"Yeah."

"I saw him too. I don't remember him from previous days."

"I don't either. I'm heading back but I'll probably be tied up with the police for a while."

"Got it. I'll go see what the judge wants to do."

Bosch disconnected and walked north on Grand, turned right on First, and headed to the Civic Center. He was thankful it was downhill most of the way. By the time he got back to the federal courthouse, the entire Spring Street side of the building was cordoned off with crime scene tape, and the area was overrun with officers from the LAPD, the sheriff's department, and the U.S. Marshals Service.

Bosch walked up to an LAPD officer standing at the yellow tape. His name tag said FRENCH.

"The courthouse is closed, sir," French said.

"I'm a witness," Bosch said. "Who do I talk to?"

"A witness to what?"

"To the deputy getting shot. I followed the shooter but lost him."

The officer suddenly looked alert.

"All right, you need to stay here."

"Fine."

Officer French took a step back and started talking into his radio.

As Bosch waited, he saw a van from Channel 5 pull to the curb. A woman with perfectly coiffed hair jumped out of the passenger side with a microphone already in her hand.

PART FOURTEEN

EL CAPITAN

48

LATE FRIDAY MORNING I was summoned to Judge Coelho's courtroom. It had been three days since she had adjourned the habeas hearing in the wake of Stephanie Sanger's murder. I had spent most of that time watching and reading news reports on the killing, waiting for the media to connect the dots. Finally, there was a story this morning in the *Times* by their veteran crime reporter James Queally that delved deeply into Sanger's background and activities, and most likely that had prompted the summons from the judge.

Queally reported that Sanger was a member of a sheriff's clique called Los Cucos and that investigators of her murder had found connections between her and a Mexican cartel that had compromised her and forced her to do its bidding, which may have included a series of contract killings of cartel rivals in California. The story also detailed the Roberto Sanz case from his murder to his ex-wife's current bid to be exonerated. The *Times* report was the first to reveal that Sanger had been testifying in that habeas case just minutes before she was killed outside the courthouse.

Unnamed sources told the newspaper that the working theory of the investigation was that Sanger had been killed to prevent her from testifying further and being pushed to cooperate with authorities.

I had talked to Queally off the record, telling him both what I knew as fact and what I believed. Without naming Agent MacIsaac, I reported what MacIsaac had told me at my house earlier in the week: that on the day of his murder, Roberto Sanz had informed the FBI agent that Sanger and other deputies in the Cucos were controlled by members of the Sinaloa cartel operating in Los Angeles. I also told Queally my own working theory, based on the fact that she had followed Roberto Sanz and had seen him with the FBI, that Sanger had killed him. The reporter had taken it from there, confirming the facts and ferreting out new ones, and the story was on the front page above the fold of the print edition and was the lead in the newspaper's digital edition.

When I got to Coelho's courtroom, Morris was already there waiting. He did not acknowledge me. He sat stone silent at the State's table, not even responding when I casually said hello to him as well as to the court's clerk and the stenographer, Milly.

Gian Brown called the judge in chambers to say all parties were present and she told him to send us back to her along with the stenographer. We went silently. Morris looked like he'd experienced a couple of sleepless nights.

The judge's robe was on a hanger on the back of the door to her chambers. She was dressed in black pants and a white blouse.

"Gentlemen, thank you for coming," she said. "Let Milly get set up and then I'd like to go on the record in the Sanz matter."

"Should Lucinda be here?" I asked.

"I don't think it's necessary for this meeting," Coelho said. "But I did tell the marshals to bring her over from MDC for the afternoon session."

That told me that the case wasn't over — yet.

We sat silently as the stenographer moved into the corner behind the judge's desk, sat on a padded stool already there, and poised her fingers over her steno machine.

"Okay, on the record again with *Sanz versus the State of California*," Coelho said. "Mr. Haller, where are you with the presentation of your case?"

I'd known she would ask this question and was prepared for it.

"Your Honor, in light of what has transpired and the fact that I can't continue with Sergeant Sanger as a witness, I'm prepared to rest my case and proceed with final arguments. If final arguments are even necessary."

Coelho nodded, having expected that answer.

"Mr. Morris?" she said.

The prosecutor seemed to sense that the case was on the line. His tone was defensive from the start.

"The State is ready to proceed, Your Honor," Morris said. "We have witnesses, including a witness who will testify that Lucinda Sanz confessed to her that she killed her husband."

I smiled and shook my head.

"You can't be serious," I said. "Your witness is a little leaky, Hayden. She's a convicted killer who concocted this confession from newspaper stories she had her brother pull from the library downtown and read to her over the phone."

I could tell that the brother was new information to Morris and that he was realizing that his team had failed to properly vet the witness.

"One day," I went on. "That's all it took to find the brother. I was going to destroy your witness on the stand. But it doesn't matter now. Have you read the paper today? Sanger was a killer and she killed Roberto Sanz. There is no doubt about that. And my investigator witnessed her murder. She was arguing with a guy she obviously knew—she let him get close enough to grab her gun. Bosch spent an entire night with the cops, the DEA, and everybody else, looking at mug shots. The guy he identified as the shooter is a *sicario* for the Sinaloa cartel. A hit man!"

Morris shook his head as if to ward off the truth.

"She pleaded no contest," he said.

He'd gone back to his case mantra: Lucinda pleaded no contest to killing her ex-husband. Innocent people didn't do that.

"She had no choice," I said. "That's what this is about. She got railroaded. She had a bad lawyer, and the key piece of evidence against her was manufactured by Sanger. We were in the middle of proving that when Sanger was put down."

Morris looked at the judge, ignoring me.

"Judge, we are entitled to present our case," he said. "He got to present his. Now we present ours."

"You're not entitled to anything, Mr. Morris," Coelho said. "Not in my courtroom. Not until I tell you what you are entitled to."

"Apologies, Your Honor," Morris said. "I misspoke. What I meant was—"

"I don't need to hear it," the judge said, cutting Morris off. "I'm prepared to rule on the petition. I just wanted to give you gentlemen a heads-up. At two o'clock we will convene in the courtroom and I will announce my decision. That will be all for now. You may go."

"You can't do this," Morris said. "The State strenuously objects to the court's rendering of a decision before the State has presented its case."

"Mr. Morris, if the State disagrees with my ruling it can take the matter up on appeal," Coelho said. "But I think your appellate branch will look at the case closely and decide not to embarrass itself. We are adjourned and off the record now. I will see you both in the courtroom at two. In the meantime, go have a nice lunch."

"Thank you, Your Honor," I said.

I stood up. Morris looked paralyzed. He seemed unable to get up from his chair.

"Mr. Morris, are you leaving?" Coelho asked.

"Uh, yes, I'm leaving," Morris said.

He rocked back, then forward, using the momentum to launch himself out of the chair.

This time I led the way back to the courtroom, and when I got to the door, I opened it wide for Morris to go through first.

"After you," I said.

"Fuck you," he said.

I nodded. I had seen that coming.

In the courtroom I checked the time and saw that I had a solid two hours before the hearing resumed and Coelho gave the ruling that I believed would end the case. Still, I didn't think there was enough time for me to get over to MDC to prep Lucinda before they started procedures to move her to the courthouse. I texted Bosch and told him to pick me up out front.

I took the elevator down and saw Bosch in the Navigator when I stepped through the heavy lobby doors. I glanced along the front of the building to the designated smoking section on the north side. It was still taped off and I wondered whether the tape had just been forgotten or if there was still an on-scene investigation at the spot where Sanger was killed.

I opened the front door of the Navigator and jumped in.

"Harry, we just climbed El Cap," I said. "Let's go eat."

"Where?" Bosch said. "And what's that mean?"

"I told you about climbing El Cap. The judge is going to rule on the habeas this afternoon and she's going to rule for us. Let's go over to Nick and Stef's and get steak for lunch. I always eat steak when I win."

"How are you sure it's a win? The judge told you this?"

"Not in so many words. But I feel it. My courtroom barometer tells me this is over."

"And Lucinda is going to walk?"

"Depends. The judge could vacate the conviction and set her free. But she could also send the case back to the district attorney's office and let them decide whether or not to take her to trial. If that happens, she could keep Lucinda incarcerated until the choice is made or until the AG's office decides if they're going to appeal. We'll know for sure at two."

Bosch whistled as he pulled the Navigator away from the curb.

"And all because you pulled a needle out of a haystack," I said. "Amazing. We make a good team, Harry."

"Yeah, well..."

"Come on, man. Don't rain on the parade."

"No rain. But I'll wait till it's official. I don't have a courtroom barometer."

"I gotta call Shami. She'll want to be in court for this."

"What about Silver?"

"Second-Place Silver can read about it in the news. I'm not doing him any favors. He cost Lucinda five years of her life."

Bosch nodded in agreement.

"Fuck him," he said.

"Fuck him," I repeated.

"What about her kid?" Bosch asked. "Should we get him to court?"

"Yes, good idea," I said. "I'll call Muriel at lunch, see if they can come down. I'll need her to bring some clothes for Lucinda. Just in case."

As Bosch drove to the restaurant, I worked my phone, texting news about the two o'clock hearing to James Queally, Britta Shoot, and all the other reporters I knew. I wanted everybody there.

49

THE COURTROOM WAS packed by two o'clock. In the first two rows of the gallery, members of the media were sitting shoulder to shoulder. The Sanger killing and the mysteries surrounding it was the biggest story going at the moment, and thanks to the *Times* article it was clear that the nexus of the case was courtroom 3 in the U.S. District Courthouse.

The two rows behind the media contained several members of Lucinda Sanz's family, including her mother, son, and brother, as well as a variety of citizen observers, defense attorneys, and prosecutors who knew this courtroom was the place to be. In the last row, all the way in the back corner, sat Maggie McPherson with our daughter, Hayley. I was happy to see my daughter but puzzled by my ex-wife's decision to be there, especially after her efforts against my client's cause.

There was a palpable sense of momentousness in the air. The feeling that something unusual, maybe even extraordinary, was going to happen ramped up another notch when Lucinda was brought through the door from holding — for the first time not in MDC blues. Her mother had brought clothes for her and I got them to her in holding in time for her to change before the hearing. She wore a light blue Mexican housedress with short sleeves and flowers embroidered along the hem. Her hair was not in a tight ponytail but down and framing her face. A hush fell over the gallery as Marshal Nate escorted her to our table and cuffed her to the ring — hopefully for the last time.

"You look great," I whispered. "I think it's going to be a good day. Your son and mother and other family members are here to see it."

"Is it okay for me to turn and look?" she asked.

"Of course it is. They're here for you."

"Okay."

She turned and looked back into the gallery and tears immediately came to her eyes. She clasped her free hand into a fist and held it to her chest. I don't know if I had ever been more moved by something I saw in a courtroom. When Lucinda turned to the front to hide her tears from her family, I put my arm around her shoulders and leaned in close to whisper.

"You've got a lot of love behind you."

"I know that. They never gave up on me."

"They knew the truth. And they're going to hear it said today."

"I hope so."

"I know so."

The silence from the gallery seemed to increase the tension in the room, and it doubled when two o'clock came and went without the judge emerging from chambers. The minutes ticked by like hours. Finally, at 2:25, Marshal Nate gave the order to rise as the judge took the bench. Coelho carried a thin file and seemed to be all business from the start.

"Please be seated," she said. "We are back on the record with *Sanz versus the State of California*. It looks like we have a full house today. I want it known that the court will not tolerate any outbursts or demonstrations of any sort from those in the gallery as we proceed. This is a court of law and I expect decorum and respect from all those who come through these doors."

She paused and scanned the gallery as if looking for dissenters. I saw her eyes hold for a moment when she reached the area where Maggie McPherson was sitting. Her focus then moved on, and with no challenges to her authority, Coelho finally brought her eyes down to me and then over to Morris. She asked if there was any new business before she proceeded to issue her ruling on the habeas petition.

Morris stood up.

"Yes, Your Honor," he said. "The State of California, representing the people of California, renew our objection to the court's decision to leapfrog the State's case in this matter."

I stood up and was ready to argue the point if needed.

"'Leapfrog,'" the judge said. "An interesting choice of words, Mr. Morris. But as I said earlier in chambers, the State's remedy here is to appeal the rulings of this court."

"Then the State asks that this hearing be continued until there is an appellate ruling," Morris said.

"Not happening, Mr. Morris," Coelho said. "You file your appeal, but I am ready and I am going to rule today. Anything else?"

"No, Your Honor," Morris said.

"No, Your Honor," I said.

"Very well," Coelho said.

She opened the file she had brought with her, put on a pair of glasses, and began to read her decision aloud. I looked over at Lucinda sitting next to me and nodded.

"The writ of habeas corpus is a fundamental pillar of our justice system," Coelho said. "Chief Justice John Marshall wrote nearly two hundred years ago that habeas corpus is the sacred means of allowing for the liberation of those who may be imprisoned without sufficient cause. It safeguards our freedom, protects us from the arbitrary and lawless actions of the State.

"It is my job today to decide if the State made a lawless action in imprisoning Lucinda Sanz for the murder of Roberto Sanz. The question is complicated by the fact that the petitioner, Ms. Sanz, pleaded no contest to a charge of manslaughter. After carefully reviewing the evidence and testimony presented during this hearing and considering what happened outside court this week, the court holds that the petitioner saw the plea agreement she was offered as the only light at the end of a dark tunnel. Whether she was coerced by her attorney at the time — not you, Mr. Haller — or concluded on her own that she had no choice but to accept a plea agreement does not matter to this court. What does matter is the clear mandate of the Constitution and Bill of Rights that habeas relief be granted when the state court's determination of a case is an unreasonable application of the law. This court finds that the petitioner has established that by producing clear and new evidence of the manufacturing of evidence against the petitioner."

I made a fist and turned and whispered to Lucinda.

"You're going home."

"What about a trial?"

"Not when there's manufactured evidence. This is over."

Because I was turned toward Lucinda, I didn't see Morris stand to object.

"Your Honor?" he said.

Coelho looked up from the document she was reading.

"Mr. Morris, you know better than to interrupt me," she said. "You will sit down. I know what your objection is and you are over-ruled. Sit down. Now!"

Morris dropped down into his seat like a bag of dirty laundry.

"Continuing," Coelho said, "as I expect no further interruptions."

She looked down and it took her a moment to find the spot where she had left off.

"The actions of the sheriff's department, particularly those taken by the late Sergeant Sanger, so damaged the integrity of the investigation and subsequent prosecution as to permanently embed it with reasonable doubt. Therefore, the ruling of this court is to grant habeas relief to the petitioner. The conviction of Lucinda Sanz is vacated."

The judge closed the file and took off her glasses. The courtroom remained silent. She looked directly at Lucinda.

"Ms. Sanz, you are no longer convicted of this crime. Your freedom and civil rights are restored. I can only offer you the apology of this court for the five years you have lost. Godspeed to you. You are free to go, and this court is now adjourned."

It seemed that it wasn't until the judge had gone through the door and left the courtroom that everybody remaining took a breath. But then the sound of excited voices exploded in the room. Lucinda turned and hugged me, throwing her free arm around my neck.

"Mickey, I thank you so much," she said, her tears smearing my freshly dry-cleaned Canali suit. "I can't believe this. I really can't."

While she held me, Marshal Nate came to the table and unlocked her wrist. He started to remove the cuff.

"Can she leave from here?" I asked. "Or does she have to go through the MDC?"

"No, the judge set her free, man," Marshal Nate said. "She's free to go. Unless she left property behind at the jail and wants to get it."

Lucinda turned from my chest to look up at Marshal Nate.

"No, nothing," she said. "And thank you for being kind to me."

"Not a problem," Marshal Nate said. "Good luck to you."

He turned and walked back to his desk by the holding cell's door.

"Lucinda, you heard him," I said. "You're free. Why don't you go see your family now."

She looked over my shoulder at her family waiting in the gallery—her son with her mother, brother, and several cousins. To a person, they had tears running down their faces, even those whose clothing couldn't hide the tattoos affirming their allegiance to White Fence.

"I can just go?" she asked.

"You can just go," I said. "If you want to talk to the media after you see your son and everybody, I'll tell them they can find you outside the courthouse where they can set up cameras."

"You think I should?"

"Yes, I think you should. Tell them what you've been through these last five and a half years."

"Okay, Mickey. But first, my family."

I nodded. She got up, walked through the gate into the gallery, and was soon being hugged by her son and all her family members at once.

I took it all in for a long moment and then I heard my name called from the front row. It was Queally. I walked over to the rail, and the reporters squeezed together to hear me.

"For those of you who need film, my client and I will hold a press conference outside the courthouse on the Spring Street side. Bring your cameras and questions and I'll see you there."

I turned to look at the AG's table and saw that Morris was already gone. He had probably slipped out while Lucinda and I hugged and celebrated our victory and his loss. When I looked at the back of the courtroom, I saw my daughter and ex-wife still seated in the last row. I walked through the gate, went down the center aisle, and slipped into the now-empty row in front of them.

"Congratulations, Dad," Hayley said. "That was amazing."

"I call it the resurrection walk," I said. "You don't get too many of them. Thanks for coming, Hay."

"I would have missed it if Mom hadn't called me," she said.

I looked at Maggie, unsure how to proceed. Luckily, she took the lead.

"Congratulations," she said. "I obviously was on the wrong side of this one. Please apologize to Harry for me."

"Well, he's around here somewhere," I said. "Maybe you could say that to his face."

"Apologize for what?" Hayley asked.

"I'll tell you in the car," Maggie said.

I nodded that that was okay with me.

"Now what?" Maggie asked. "Are you going to sue the county for millions?"

"If my client wants me to. I'll have to talk to her."

"Come on, you know you're going to sue and you're going to win."

There was an edge to her voice. She still had to bust on me even though I had won the day. I let it go. Maggie didn't have the same hold over me she'd once had. I had reached the point where her disappointments in me no longer mattered.

"We'll see," I said. "It helps when the other side has manufactured evidence."

Hayley pointed behind me and I turned to see Gian Brown standing at the railing.

"The judge would like to see you in chambers," he said.

"Right now?" I asked.

He nodded and I realized it had been a dumb question.

"I'll be right there."

I turned back to my daughter.

"Can you come out tonight and celebrate with me?" I asked.

"Sure," she said. "Where are you going to go?"

"I don't know. Dan Tana's, Musso's, Mozza? You pick."

"No, you pick. Just text me where and when."

I looked at Maggie.

"You can come too, you know," I said.

"I think you should celebrate with your daughter," she said. "Have a great time. You earned it."

I nodded.

"Well, I guess I should go see what the judge wants," I said.

"Don't keep her waiting," Maggie said.

I walked down the row to the center aisle and got there just as Bosch came through the door from the hall.

"Were you here?" I asked. "We won. Lucinda is free."

"I saw," he said. "I was standing in the back."

"Where's Shami? Did she see it?"

"She was here but she went back to the hotel. She's going to try to get a red-eye back to New York tonight. I'll take her to the airport."

A sudden involuntary need took over and I reached out and hugged him. He stiffened but didn't pull away.

"We did it, Harry," I said. "We did it."

"You did it," he said.

"No, it takes a team," I said. "And an innocent client."

We awkwardly disengaged and both looked at Lucinda, still surrounded by family, her once-manacled hand grasping her son's.

"That's a beautiful thing," Bosch said.

"It is," I said.

We watched silently for a moment and then I saw Gian standing and staring at me from his corral. I nodded to him. I was coming.

"I gotta go see the judge, but two things, Harry," I said. "As soon as I'm finished with her, we're going to have a press conference outside on the Spring Street side. I know it's not your thing, but I would like you there if you want to be there."

"And the second?" he asked.

"Dinner tonight. To celebrate. Hayley's coming. Bring Maddie if you want."

"That's something I'm up for. I'll check with Maddie. Where? When?"

"I'll text you."

I started walking toward the railing.

"Hope to see you downstairs," I said. "You deserve to be there. Call Shami and see if she'll come back for the press conference. And for dinner. We'll get her to the airport afterward."

"I'll call her."

I left him there, went through the gate, and crossed the proving ground to go see the judge.

The door to her chambers was open but I reached in and knocked anyway. She was behind the desk, no longer wearing the black robe.

"Come in, Mr. Haller," she said. "Have a seat."

I did as she instructed. She was writing on a legal pad and I said nothing to interrupt. She finally put her pen into the holder of an ornate desk set with her name engraved on a brass plaque and looked up at me.

"Congratulations," she said. "I believe the petitioner in this case had a formidable advocate at her side."

I smiled.

"Thank you, Your Honor," I said. "And thank you for cutting through all the distractions and smoke screens to get to an incisive and just ruling. You know, I rarely venture into federal court, because, well, it's kind of David versus a bunch of Goliaths most of the time, but after this ex—"

"I know what you did, Mr. Haller," she said.

I paused. Her tone had grown too serious for a post-hearing meeting between a judge and attorney.

"What I did, Your Honor?" I tried.

"I took the long lunch to review everything that was presented before I made my determination," she said. "That included my prior rulings and actions. And I realized what you'd done in my courtroom."

I shook my head.

"Well, Judge," I said. "I think you're going to have to share it with me because I don't really —"

"You intentionally drew me into holding you in contempt," Coelho said.

"Judge, I don't know what —"

"You needed time to conduct your DNA test before continuing the case. Don't sit there and deny it."

I looked down at my hands and spoke without looking at her.

"Uh, Judge, I think I'm going to take the Fifth on that."

She said nothing. I looked back up at her.

"I should file a complaint with the California Bar for conduct unbecoming an attorney," she said. "But that could significantly damage both your record and your reputation. As I said, you are a formidable advocate and we need more of them in the justice system."

I started to breathe easier. She wanted to scare me, not destroy me.

"But your actions cannot go by without any consequences," she continued. "I'm holding you in contempt, Mr. Haller. Again. I hope you have a toothbrush in your briefcase. You're going to spend another night at MDC."

She picked up the desk phone and pushed one number. I knew Gian was on the other end of that call.

"Please send Marshal Nate back," she said.

She hung up the phone.

"Judge, isn't there a fine I could pay?" I said. "A donation to the court's favorite charity or —"

"No, there's not," she said.

Marshal Nate entered the room.

"Nate, please take Mr. Haller to holding," Coelho said. "He'll be spending the night at MDC."

Nate looked puzzled and didn't move.

"He's being held in contempt," the judge explained.

Nate moved forward and grabbed me by the arm.

"Let's go," he said.

50

IT WAS A long night marked by a fellow inmate's incessant howling. There was no rhyme or reason to it, just a repeated announcement of mental illness. Since sleep was not an option, I spent the time in the dark of my solo cell sitting on its thin mattress, my back to the concrete wall, toilet paper stuffed in my ears, thinking about prior moves and next moves in my life and work.

The Lucinda Sanz case felt like some sort of pivot to me, as though it might be time to move in a new direction. Chasing cases to feed the machine, grab headlines, and pay for billboards and bus benches — I could not see it being my final destination. I could no longer see it as even valid.

But a pivot to what?

My long night of discontent ended an hour before dawn when my breakfast was delivered — an apple and a bologna-on-white-bread sandwich. I hadn't eaten since lunch with Bosch the day before, and the jail breakfast tasted as good as anything I'd ever had at Du-par's or the Four Seasons.

The cell had a three-inch-wide escape-proof window. Soon after morning light started to filter in through the glass, a detention officer opened the door of my cell, dropped a bag containing my suit on the floor, and told me to get dressed. I was being released.

There were men and women in this place who had been held for weeks or months, but my sixteen hours of sleep deprivation and isolation were enough for me. This time they changed me. Something had started with Jorge Ochoa and reached a crescendo with Lucinda Sanz. It was a need to change.

At the release unit I was handed a ziplock bag containing my wallet, watch, and phone. I looked at these things and wondered if I needed them anymore.

A few moments later I stepped out through a steel door into the sun and began my own resurrection walk.

ACKNOWLEDGMENTS

I usually use this space to thank those who helped me with the research, writing, and editing of the book. Like Mickey Haller says at the end of the Sanz case, it takes a team. Those who helped know they helped, and I thank them for their efforts and for being part of the team. But this time I want to acknowledge the readers of my work and the booksellers around the world who have stuck with me for thirty-plus years: Thank you. I have lived an amazing life as a storyteller. I cherish it, respect what it means, and know that none of it would have been possible without you.

ABOUT THE AUTHOR

Michael Connelly is the author of thirty-seven previous novels, including the *Sunday Times* bestsellers *Desert Star*, *The Dark Hours* and *The Law of Innocence*. His books, which include the Harry Bosch series, the Lincoln Lawyer series, and the Reneé Ballard series, have sold more than eighty-five million copies worldwide. Connelly is a former newspaper reporter who has won numerous awards for his journalism and his novels. He is the executive producer of three television series: *Bosch*, *Bosch: Legacy*, and *The Lincoln Lawyer*. He spends his time in California and Florida.

To find out more, visit Michael's website, or follow him on Facebook or Twitter.

www.michaelconnelly.com
🅵 /MichaelConnellyBooks
🆈 @ConnellyBooks